THE LOST DRAGONRIDER OF LAMAR

THE LOST DRAGONRIDER OF LAMAR

THE DRAGONRIDERS OF LAMAR
BOOK 1

A J WALKER

An A J Walker Novel.

First published in the United States in 2025 by Mystic Lake Publishing

Paberback first published in 2025 by Mystic Lake Publishing

Copyright © Mystic Lake Publishing 2025

Formatting by Mystic Lake Publishing

The moral right of A J Walker to be identified as the author of this work has been asserted by him in accordance with the Copyright, Designs and Patents Act 1988.

This is a work of fiction. All the characters in this book are fictitious, and any resemblance to actual persons living or dead is purely coincidental.

All rights reserved. No part of this publication may be reproduced, stored in a retrieval system or transmitted in any form or by any means, without the prior permission in writing of the publisher, nor to be otherwise circulated in any form of binding or cover other than that in which it is published without a similar condition, including this condition, being imposed on the subsequent purchaser.

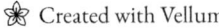 Created with Vellum

For my Friends and Family,
Thank you for inspiring me to keep writing and chasing my dreams. You're the best.
Motivate to Dominate!

PROLOGUE

The bitter stench of burning sap filled Tel Roan's nostrils as he crested the rise, each step crunching on charred bark. Through his bond with Ingamar, he tasted a metallic tang of energy on the air. A telltale signature of a Hyalite preparing to pierce the veil. His dragon's consciousness brushed against his own, a wordless warning thrumming through their shared connection.

Tel raised his gauntleted hand, golden eyes narrowing to predatory slits as he signaled his Honor Guard to hold their position. The firestorm raged ahead, its flames dancing among the trees with unnaturally vibrant colors as supernatural power leaked through from the god's realm. Lightning burst through the thunderhead above in impossible patterns, a promise from the eight gods that one of them was attempting to influence events in their world. Hyalites, the very essence of a god's power, would be forced through the veil into Sataran, manifesting as a mystic orb. The power it contained would bring rise to a new dragonrider. For his King and country, Tel Roan and his dragon were here to ensure that next rider would be bound to the Kingdom of Lamar. Only...

Where is the Nordraven Army?

"There should be someone here to challenge us," he whispered, the thought echoing simultaneously through to Ingamar. The great golden dragon rotated overhead, his scales reflecting the strange light of the divine storm.

Just then, Gavon's voice carried up from below the rise, "Sir?" The Knight of the Vermillion Keep stood ready for his orders, his ceremonial armor gleaming despite the ash that now filled the air.

Tel stood head and shoulders taller than the average-sized Knight. Having risen to rank of Paragon to the Vermillion Keep, Tel's physical prowess was what every soldier expected from their leadership, a thick chest, broad shoulders, proud chin, and a regal air about him that made his every move seem practiced and thought through. Since becoming a dragonrider, he looked more elf than human. His golden eyes were flecked with green, his features slightly more angular, like the gods that produced them in their likeness. With his supernatural brismil plate armor and matching sword, he gained added strength, protection, and speed. Tel Roan's reputation was legendary even beyond the Keeps of Lamar.

"What news of the scouting report? Where is the enemy army?" Gavon asked.

Tel's fingers brushed the pommel of Stormbreaker in its scabbard, feeling the sword's eagerness to be drawn. Even sheathed, the brismil blade radiated a cold that cut through the nearby firestorm's heat. "They're not here."

"Sir? This is the right firestorm, is it not?"

Tel reached through his bond again, letting Ingamar's keen senses wash over him. The dragon's vision pierced the smoke to locate the ribbons of divine energy rippling through the flames. The veil between the god's realm and their world was thinning, an indicator that this storm was no ordinary firestorm. "Yes," Tel said, certainty hardening his voice. "This is the storm that will produce the Hyalite I foresaw. It will contain one of the three most powerful god's abilities. The rider it produces could swing the balance in Lamar's favor."

"Then we are the first here..." Gavon said. "We could end this war once and for all. Lamar could finally control the Everburning Forest. Nordraven would never create another enemy rider again." Gavon's enthusiasm couldn't mask the tremor of awe in his voice.

Tel's jaw tightened, "Something isn't right. At least one of Nordraven's Kings should be here with an army and a dragonrider." His hand clenched Stormbreaker's hilt. "Hyalites don't go uncontested. Especially not an orb containing the strongest essence of the gods we've seen in a century."

Tel felt Ingamar's muscles bunch as the dragon banked through a column of smoke. The veil between worlds was growing thinner. Tel could feel it in his bones, in the way his brismil armor hummed against his skin. The ancient dragon scale that formed his brismil armor sang with remembered power.

"Send for Venrick," Tel commanded, already moving toward the heart of the storm.

Gavon's voice carried a note of distaste. "Not your Honor Guard? Are you sure you want the half-breed?"

Tel turned, his eyes flashing with a dangerous light. "Question another of my orders and you'll be holding a spear in the front line, taking orders from a squad leader well beneath your rank."

"Summoning the half-breed, Sir." Gavon answered through tight lips.

"And Gavon," Tel's voice stopped the Knight before he could retreat. "Take the Honor Guard with you when you return to the troops. Disperse yourselves among the flanks and rear. Be ready for an ambush. Nordraven could be planning to block us from returning to Astral City."

As Gavon's armored footsteps faded, Tel strode into the firestorm. His brismil armor was forged from dragon magic, naturally turning aside any effects of the fire's heat. Lightning flashed overhead as the veil stretched paper-thin, ready to tear. At any moment, one of the gods would send down their gift: the Hyalite orb containing the essence of divine power.

The air crackled as a bolt of lightning tore through the firestorm, striking the ground with a thunderous impact that Tel felt deep within his bones. Ingamar recognized it and shared in the moment when the boundary between mortal and divine realms grew gossamer-thin.

In the smoking crater, a blue light pulsed like a newly formed star. The Hyalite lay nestled in a bed of white-hot coals, its rough-hewn surface catching the storm's light in ways that hurt Tel's eyes to look at. Celestial power radiated from it in waves that made his teeth ache and set the scales of his brismil armor humming in a harmonic response he had no control over.

"The Hyalite," Tel breathed, disbelief coloring his words. No challenger had appeared to contest this prize.

The snapping of a branch split through the inferno, sharpening Tel's senses to a razor's edge. "Venrick," he called, expecting his Squire's familiar presence.

Instead, he found himself facing a mountain of blue-skinned muscle and primal rage. The Morsythian towered fifteen feet tall, its elongated ivory tusks gleaming in the light of the flame. Red eyes blazed with unnatural intellect, and black tribal tattoos writhed across its arms like living shadows.

"Morsythian," Tel named it, his tactical mind already cataloguing the wrongness of its presence. These northern orcs weren't known for their interest in magical artifacts. They were not agents of Nordraven, merely an independent tribe that remained neutral in the war. "What are you doing here?" he asked, more to himself than the foreign creature. Their kind couldn't even channel magic. Yet something about this one made Ingamar's consciousness recoil.

Tel extended his arm, calling Stormbreaker into being. The brismil blade materialized in a cascade of smoke and shadows, its dark blue surface drinking in the surrounding light. Power radiated through the weapon, a residual effect drawn from its origin as a dragon claw. The sword was massive, four hands thick and six feet long. Despite the size, it felt perfectly balanced in Tel's grip, like an extension of his body.

The Morsythian charged with a roar that shook dead limbs from burning trees. Tel leapt aside, his brismil-enhanced muscles carrying him an impossible distance. His fingers brushed the Hyalite's surface. A divine energy exploded through him. The world spun; Stormbreaker vanished in a trail of vapor. Though the sword was not gone. He knew it would reappear in that instant, sheathed in the scabbard attached to Ingamar's saddle. As long as he wore the brismil scale armor, all he needed to summon Stormbreaker was to will it to appear in his hand.

Tel's eyes narrowed as he rolled to his feet and studied his opponent. The amulet around the Morsythian's neck was out of place. It held no sigil or crest from any Kingdom in Sataran. It glowed with an eerie crimson light that felt wrong in ways Tel's magical senses couldn't quite define. No ordinary trinket could grant a savage the power to challenge a Paragon of the Vermillion Keep, let alone a dragonrider.

The orc moved with impossible speed, snatching the Hyalite in one massive hand. Tel pursued, drawing on his bond with Ingamar to push his enhanced abilities to their limit. Trees shattered around him as he vaulted through the burning canopy, twisting in mid-air to land between the Morsythian and escape.

Stormbreaker sang as Tel struck, expecting to taste flesh, but deflected by that impossible crimson light. The amulet flared brighter, and Tel felt his magical senses twist sideways, his perfect control over the brismil blade suddenly uncertain.

Their battle escalated, each exchange revealing more impossibilities. The Morsythian's strength matched Tel's. The crimson amulet continuing to warp the orc's natural flow of magical energy. Only when Tel employed his centuries of tactical training, feinting with one hand while manifesting Stormbreaker in the other, did he finally gain advantage.

The blade materialized through the orc's arm at the elbow, severing it in a spray of dark blood. The Hyalite tumbled free, and Tel snatched it from the air, feeling divine power pulse against his palms even through his armor.

The crimson light flickered and died. The orc's remaining hand drew a crude blade, but now his movements were predictable, mortal. Tel deflected each wild swing with practiced ease, his mind racing. "What are you doing here, chasing after a Hyalite in Lamar?"

The monster's only response was a pain-filled roar as he pressed his assault. The amulet's light sputtered back to life, and Tel struck with precision, severing its chain. "Who sent you?"

The change in the Morsythian was immediate and disturbing. His blue skin paled, his movements grew unsteady. Red eyes lifted to track Ingamar's circling form overhead with an intelligence that shouldn't exist in such a creature. His mouth opened as if to speak, then his massive form toppled forward into the ash.

Tel recoiled as angry red welts began to appear beneath the creature's skin, spreading like poison through its veins. He kicked the amulet away, its dying light fading to a hollow yellow husk.

Tel felt Ingamar's desperate need to flee this corrupted place. He launched himself skyward, brismil power carrying him above the burning canopy. His dragon swept beneath him with perfect timing, their movements synchronized through years of partnership.

"Venrick," Tel commanded as he settled into the saddle, "take me to him." The words were unnecessary, their bond would have been enough, but something about this encounter made him need the comfort of spoken orders.

A shadow fell across their connection like storm clouds blotting out the sun. Ingamar's mighty form trembled beneath him, instinctual terror flooding through both of them. Tel had never felt such fear from his dragon, not in all their years of battle together.

"What is it?" Tel asked, though the answer was already darkening the horizon. Two dragons emerged from the storm clouds, their riders' cloaks snapping in the gale. The larger beast's scales were darker than a moonless night, its milky eyes rimmed with gold, unmistakable even at this distance.

"Into the spires," Tel commanded, his thoughts and voice merging into a single imperative that sang through their bond. Ingamar banked hard, relief flooding their connection as they raced toward the Floating Islands of the Everburning Forest. Ancient magic kept these fragments of earth suspended; their surfaces crowned with twisted trees whose roots dangled like golden curtains in the wind.

Ingamar's terror drove them deeper into the maze of floating stone, each beat of his wings carrying them through gaps barely wide enough for his wingspan. Tel felt every twist and dive as if they shared one body, their movements flowing together with the precision of decades spent as one being.

The golden dragon latched onto a limestone cliff face, talons scoring deep grooves into rock stained amber by centuries of leaching roots. Tel's hands tightened on the saddle's worn leather, the Hyalite's divine energy pulsing against his side where he'd secured it. He could taste Ingamar's desperate need to flee, to take wing and not stop until they reached the safety of the Vermillion Keep.

But fleeing would mean death. Tel had seen Marcel Heartfell's work too many times; the blackened ruins of villages, the twisted remains of dragons and riders who'd tried to escape rather than stand and fight. He pressed his consciousness against Ingamar's, offering centuries of shared courage against primal fear.

The larger black dragon emerged around a neighboring spire like a nightmare taking form. Where Ingamar's smooth golden muzzle transitioned into a spiked mane of scaley spines, White Eye's spiked muzzle led to curling horns. Where Ingamar's eyes were a deeper gold than his scales, White Eye's were an unsettling milky color rimmed with thin a golden line. Marcel Heartfell sat astride the muscular dragon, protected with black brismil plate armor trimmed with white and wearing a copper cape. They were the colors of death in the Northern Kingdoms.

Stone shards suddenly formed in the air like spiked daggers being ripped from the cliffs of the Floating Islands. They tore through the air, narrowly missing Marcel and his mount. The Nordraven rider wheeled away, revealing Tel's unexpected ally. It was a dragonrider in Vermillion red, its dragon's scales gleaming an unfamiliar emerald in the storm light.

Tel seized the moment, spurring Ingamar into a backward dive off the cliff. They twisted in free-fall, dragon and rider moving as one, before descending toward the distant canopy. The forest below offered cover, but more importantly, it offered closer quarters where White Eye's superior size would work against him.

They burst through the unburnt canopy, Ingamar's instincts guiding them through a maze of trees. Tel relinquished control entirely, trusting in Ingamar as branches whipped past close enough to brush his armor. They emerged into a clearing where Venrick waited with the supply wagon. The two draft horses danced nervously at their sudden appearance.

"Venrick!" Tel called, leaping from the saddle with the Hyalite tucked against his chest. "The chest, now!"

His Squire's green eyes widened at the sight of the orb, but he moved without hesitation, tossing the enchanted chest designed to transport the Hyalite. Tel caught it one-handed, his fingers already tracing the protective runes that would secure the Hyalite within.

"Ready yourself with the brismil bow," Tel commanded, his voice tight with urgency. "We'll have unwelcome company soon."

"You've always been a better shot," Venrick countered, reaching for the dragon horn bow. "Lend me your blade instead."

"I'm afraid I can't this time, friend." Tel's gaze lifted to the horizon. "Marcel Heartfell is coming."

The name fell between them like a death sentence. Venrick's face drained the color from his half-elven features. An instant later, iron discipline reasserted itself. He stood tall, his muscular shoulders pulled back and his square jaw raised. "I thought Marcel was serving in Skol to the east, outside your range."

"Apparently not." Tel pressed the locked Hyalite into Venrick's hands. "Secure this in the wagon and arm yourself as I asked."

The black dragon's massive form blotted out the sun as Marcel Heartfell descended, trailing ribbons of darkness that seemed to drink the very light from the air. Power gathered around his blade. Tel felt the magical pressure building in his bones, in the vibrating plates of his brismil armor, in the very air between worlds.

"Now!" Tel commanded, and Venrick's arrow sang

through the air with impossible speed. The brismil-forged shaft pierced White Eye's protective wards as if they were mist, finding its mark in the soft flesh where wing met breast. The great beast's roar of pain shattered the air, its fire-breath dying in its throat as it spiraled down toward the edge of the clearing.

Tel vaulted into Ingamar's saddle, their minds sliding together like pieces of a puzzle finally made whole. But before they could take flight, a red flash sparked near the fallen rider. Tel's senses screamed in warning. The explosion that followed wasn't fire or lightning, but something older, something that he hadn't faced before.

The blast shattered Marcel's wards like glass, and in their wake came something Tel had never seen in all his decades of magical combat. Ghostly tendrils of pure force materialized from the forest's shadows, hundreds of dark spectral arms writhing with impossible purpose. They wrapped around Marcel like living chains, crystallizing into ice that should have held any normal rider immobile.

But Marcel Heartfell was far from normal. His black armor flared with energy, and the frosty bonds that were forming a cocoon of ice around him shattered. A dozen more shadow-arms lashed out from the treeline, but Marcel moved with horrifying speed, his blade leaving trails of smoke and flame in the air as he spun.

The power flowing through Marcel's sword wasn't just magic, it was something from another realm. He launched himself from White Eye's back, trailing celestial blue fire as he arced toward the forest edge. Tel caught another glimpse of their mysterious ally, a figure wearing a red cloak matching other Paragons in the Vermillion Keep.

Impossible, Tel thought, then Marcel struck.

The resulting explosion stole both sound and sight. Tel felt Ingamar tumble beneath him, their bond fluctuating wildly as the dragon fought to maintain control. The impact when Tel hit the ground drove the air from his lungs and sent fractures through his perfect connection with his dragon. He rolled through dirt and debris, his enhanced senses struggling to pierce the supernatural fog that now blanketed the clearing.

Through the haze, Tel saw White Eye's massive form, jaws locked around the throat of a green dragon that thankfully wasn't Ingamar. Marcel emerged from the fog like a demon, his blade still glowing with flame. Tel called Stormbreaker to hand, reaching through Ingamar to summon the heavenly strength that had served them for so many years.

The first rule of magical combat was simple: strike first, strike hard. Tel sent his power coursing through the earth, turning solid ground to hungry quicksand beneath Marcel's feet. But the Northern rider countered with horrifying precision, transmuting Tel's trap into a sheet of black ice that reflected the strange light of their battle.

They clashed in a fury of steel and sorcery, every strike carrying enough power to level a fortress. Marcel's blade threw impossible shadows as they fought, and something dark and hungry pulled at Tel from behind, but his armor's added strength let him press through.

Yet something was wrong. The bond with Ingamar felt increasingly distant, like a voice calling from the bottom of a deep well. Tel fought to find an opening in Marcel's defense, but his focus was now divided between this immediate threat and the weakening of his connection to Ingamar. When a fraction of his attention slipped, something from behind him whispered past his guard.

Tel barely felt the cut. It was a ghost's touch, a winter breeze across his neck. But suddenly Ingamar's presence in his mind wavered. Desperate, Tel reached for his power, casting the spell for the earth itself to swallow his opponent. The magic responded, but it felt wrong, hollow, draining away his very essence as the ground cracked beneath them.

His head titled sideways, no, fell completely away, and Tel found himself looking up at his own body from the blood-stained grass. His last sensation was the feeling of his magic pouring out uncontrolled, taking with it everything he was or would ever be. The spell he'd begun exploded in a final burst of golden light, and Tel Roan, Paragon of the Vermillion Keep, felt his bond with Ingamar snap like a heart breaking before the eternal darkness claimed him.

1

LARK

The lark-shaped pendant warmed against her chest like a captured star, its pulses matching the heartbeat of the firestorm blazing within the Everburning Forest. Flames danced between the towering evergreens, not with the mindless hunger of natural fire, but with terrible purpose. Ribbons of orange and gold painted the late afternoon sky with something hauntingly familiar. The blaze moved like a living thing, drawing patterns that tugged at the empty spaces of Lark's missing memories.

A force deep within the firestorm called to her, an energy pulling at her core with primal intensity. Every fiber of her being resonated with the storm's wild power, humming like a plucked string. Her body vibrated not with fear but with recognition, as if the blaze spoke a language she nearly understood. The pendant's heat spread through her chest with an unnatural warmth, urging her forward.

A small hand gripped her wrist, its human warmth breaking through the fire's hypnotic song. Reality crashed back in waves: the crisp scent of pine boughs, their needles brushing gently in the wind, the hint of a metallic tang fading from her tongue.

"Lark, what are you doing?" Paq's voice carried equal measures of fear and concern. "You have to stay here. If a god's power is coming through the storm, armies will be fighting for it."

Lark looked down through overhanging strands of her own wavy brown hair. Her green eyes cleared, the haze in her vision receding to see the boy standing there.

Fear had carved lines into his young face that shouldn't be there, his angled jaw clenched tight as his eyes darted between her and the villagers who had gathered nearby. The crowd pressed together like cattle before a storm, all watching the firestorm's advance with a mixture of awe and terror.

"Did I hear someone say there was a dragon?" The question rose unbidden from some deep well of certainty within her.

Paq nodded, his grip tightening as if he could anchor her to earth when the primal need pulled at her soul.

Despite her best intentions, she let her feet take another step toward the storm raging in the distance. The pendant pulsed against her collarbone, each beat sending ripples of warmth through her body, matching the rhythm of the flames. Every step toward the forest felt like walking through a dream. It was all wrong, yet somehow right at the same time, dangerous and inevitable.

"I'm serious, Lark, you can't go out there. Not yet," Paq whispered, his voice cracking with urgency.

"There's something out there." Her hand rose to the necklace of its own accord, fingers curling around metal that should have burned but instead felt cool and familiar. It was the only thing she had from her past, a representation of who she was from before; the version of herself she could not remember. "I can feel it," she said.

"You can't go alone. Wait for the harvest," Paq urged. "The forest isn't a controlled area of the kingdom. The Nordraven Kings and Lamar are constantly battling for control of its resources. It's not a friendly place for a lone wanderer. Besides the armies, orcs, goblins, and shades roam the trees. That's just to name a few of the terrors, and that's not including the unbonded dragons. Firestorms attract all manner of nasty attention."

The warning should have chilled her blood, but instead it sparked another flash of that inexplicable certainty. "Not all dragons are inherently evil. It's their riders who can turn them to darkness."

Paq's dark eyes narrowed, suspicion replacing fear. "How can you know that, but not your own name?"

The question struck like a bolt of lightning, illuminating the unending emptiness where her memories should be. "I don't know," she admitted. The details of how she came to be here in the village with Paq swirled like smoke in her mind, visible but impossible to grasp. "Maybe I heard it from those talking about the dragon," she added, gesturing to the murmuring crowd.

But the excuse rang hollow even as she said it aloud. This knowledge felt older, deeper, as real as the pendant's heat against her pale skin. She'd heard Paq speak of the Everburning Forest's dangers before. Of how something out there claimed at least one of the wheat harvesters with every run. Yet an urge to go into the forest pulled at her, a compulsion that made her muscles tremble with the effort to stay still.

Smoke spiraled skyward, evening's darkness pooling around the thunderhead that loomed over the forest like a god's anvil. Lightning flashed through the clouds, each bolt igniting new flames that fed the inferno's persistent growth. Thunder rolled across the land like the voice of a dragon, each growl felt through the strange sensations coming from her necklace.

Lark tugged at the pendant, its swelling of warmth a distraction, but the chain held firm. She felt for a clasp or a weakness so she could remove it, but none existed on the seamless golden links. Somehow, the necklace was bound to the storm. That tingling thrill of recognition danced strongest where the lark-shaped pendant rested against her clavicle, as if trying to remind her heart of something her mind had forgotten.

"Lark, you're doing it again," Paq warned. "It looks like you're about to go running off into the forest at any moment, and I'm not the only one taking notice."

The villagers whispered; their scowls heavy with suspicion directed at her. She felt their eyes like physical things, pressing against her with the weight of judgment.

"I won't go," she forced herself to say. "I won't, I promise."

"Good because the harvesters need you," Paq said. "Delger says it's been a struggle since Cleft and Boyd disappeared three storms ago. I've heard the storms get more violent as the Flashover approaches. Can you believe it's going to happen this year?"

"The Flashover?" The word echoed strangely in Lark's mind, like a bell rung in an empty temple. A shadow of meaning flickered at the edges of her consciousness, there and gone like smoke on the wind.

"Don't tell me you've never heard of the Flashover?" Paq said, propping his gangly hands on his narrow hips. Where his hand-me-down rags hung loose on his slight frame, Lark's muscular physique filled the borrowed clothing: brown pants and a stained long-sleeved shirt Paq had come up with for her. her. She was taller than other women in the village. Under the smudges of dirt, her skin had a lively glow, her features more prominently defined, like the busts of the goddesses at the village shine. Lark often caught the young men staring at her with intrigue, much different than the judging glares they directed at her when others were around.

Lark shook her head, and a lock of red umber hair came free, curving around her flawless face. She tucked it back into her bun, the simple motion carrying an odd sense of habit. The word "Flashover" sat heavy on her tongue. She savored it, hoping to spark some recognition from her past. But like everything before a few days ago, only fog remained. A haze thicker than the smoke that clung to the thunderhead, obscuring seventeen or possibly twenty years of memories. She had no way of knowing exactly how much time she'd lost to the amnesia.

"No," she admitted. "I don't know what the Flashover is."

Paq's face lit up with the fierce joy of sharing secrets. He peered up at her, his gap-toothed smile showing where adult teeth were just beginning to emerge through pink gums. "You're pulling my leg. Honest, how can a lady as old as you never have heard of the Flashover before?"

"I'm not an old lady," Lark protested, the words carrying an edge of uncertainty. She viewed herself as young for a woman, stronger than everyone else in the village, and more capable, despite her lack of knowledge. But how could she know her true age when the past was nothing but shadow?

"To me, pretty much everyone here in the village is old, except the other kids," Paq said. "You're no old hag though. You're much better looking than any other lady in this village. But you still should've heard of the Flashover. Especially because it's happening this year and it's so rare."

"Paq, don't be rude." Ellowin's arrival carried the grace of a summer breeze, her thick brown curls bobbing above pointed shoulders. "You can't insult a woman and then follow it up with a backhanded compliment. She said she can't remember what the Flashover is, so leave it at that."

Despite their supposed dozen-year age gap, Ellowin's smaller frame and youthful glow made her seem younger than Lark, though that assessment, like everything else about Lark's past, rested on shifting sands. Giggles sounded from somewhere nearby.

The snickers of watching children died on Lark's piercing look, their retreat instant and telling. It wasn't just the young ones who reacted this way. Throughout the village, eyes slid away from hers like water off glass, everyone keeping their distance. Everyone except the harvesters, who met her gaze with judgment. She understood their wariness. She was the stranger, the one without roots or remembrance, found wandering the road with not even a name to call her own.

"The Flashover happens once every five hundred years," Paq said, his voice deepening slightly. "All four realms align, creating an overlap between the worlds."

"There's more than one world?" Lark asked.

"Where do you think the elves, dwarves, magi, and everything magical come from?"

She shrugged. "I haven't thought about it."

"First, there's our world, Sataran," Paq counted on dirt-stained fingers. "Then there's Aetherion, the realm of the gods. That's where magical energy comes from. It shows up here in the form of Hyalite orbs and Yogo Sapphires, which contain the energy magi, elves, dwarves, and so on wield."

"And dragonriders?" Lightning split the sky and Lark tasted something strange on the air, a faint metallic tang that quickly faded from her lips.

"Yes, I don't know exactly how it works; they use a Hyalite to do it, but that's a whole other talk we can have later," he said. "Next, there's the fae realm. Not much is known about them, but it's where magical creatures like dragons and rimeshade came from."

"Rimeshades don't exist," Ellowin cut in, but her voice carried an edge of uncertainty, as if speaking of them suddenly made it possible.

"Yes, they do," Paq insisted. "Barson told me about an orc village in the North that was completely turned to ice because a frost wielding shade took hold there. There were no survivors."

"If there weren't survivors, how did they know it was a rimeshade? Some dragonriders can wield ice. Barson is spreading rumors. You shouldn't look up to him just because he's a harvester," Ellowin said.

Their argument about Barson's tale faded into the background as Lark's attention fixed on the thunderhead over the forest. It moved unlike any rainstorm that had come through the village recently. It wasn't driven by earthly winds, but by currents of power that made the old-growth forest shiver in its wake.

"What's the fourth realm?" she asked, the words rising over the siblings' bickering.

"Thalindor. It was the world where the children of the gods were sent to live."

"Children of the gods?"

"He means elves, dwarves, magi, orcs. They're the races that can wield power without having to bond with a dragon," Ellowin clarified.

"Why would they come here to this world if they have one of their own?" Lark asked.

"Nobody around here seems to know. Maybe because of the dragons, but then why did the dragons come if they had a world of their own, too?" he replied.

"The dragons came because of the Hyalites," Lark found herself saying, the knowledge flowing like water from a weeping dam, "but stayed because of the bonds they formed with those who can hone their powers."

"That's an idea," Ellowin scoffed.

"She could be right," Paq argued. "There's a prophecy that sounds similar. It's about the Flashover though."

"What is it?"

"Paq, don't. He's going to tell it wrong," Ellowin said.

"I'm telling the story," he spit.

Ellowin huffed, spinning on her heels and leaving them to join the stirring crowd.

"When all four realms align, a dragon and rider will bond with Aether's power..."

As he spoke of the prophecy, Lark barely heard him. In her mind's eye, she saw a rider emerging triumphant from storm clouds, a Hyalite blazing with divine light and held firmly in the rider's grip. The image carried the weight of truth. Not imagination but memory. Not prophecy but promise. The pendant's heat spread through her chest like liquid fire, and somewhere in the storm's heart, something ancient stirred in response.

"The ending is kind of bleak," Paq's voice drew her back. "If they fall to the darkness, death and destruction will spread in their wake." After the last word left his lips, they stood in chilling silence.

As darkness gathered, Lark found her attention drawn to the approaching wall of water, the Giving Rain. It advanced like a curtain of liquid night, its leading edge shimmering with life.

Around them, the villagers moved with practiced urgency, preparing the harvesters for their deadly task. Their tools caught the storm's light in ways that made the etched runes seem to writhe, symbols bound to serve the time-honored tradition they were about to commence.

A final strand of lightning forked through the dissipating

storm anvil. With shocking clarity, her first true memory surged to the front of her mind's eye. It included a man's face appearing with crystal clarity. His jaw was sharp as winter wind, those forest-green eyes holding secrets deeper than the realms themselves. Brown hair fell in rough waves around ears that carried the slight point of man's mixed with elven bloodlines. In his hands, he cradled a box embossed with unfamiliar symbols. They seemed to beat in time with her pendant's heat. The memory felt so real she could almost touch him, almost grasp what secret he held...

Then it was gone, scattered like a shattered pane of glass, and with it the warmth from her pendant. Questions hounded her, yet the emptiness where the answers should be yawned wider than ever, a chasm darker than the night sky.

Why can't I remember?

2

HARVEST RUN

The harvest call rang through the twilight air.

"Harvesters, gear up! We head north in ten," Delger announced. His broad shoulders, dark hair and weathered face marked him as one who had survived countless runs into the Everburning Forest. His voice carried the weight of authority earned through decades of experience.

They were the village elite, though not by choice or for glory. Necessity had forged them into warriors who toiled between the Kingdoms of Nordraven to the north of the Everburning Forest and the Kingdom of Lamar to the south. The villagers settled here along the southern edge of the forest for one reason: to harvest fire wheat. The village was located in the region of some of the most active fire behavior. Lamar's major hub, Astral City, lay several days' trek to the southeast. Storms near this tiny village drove wildfire with recurring frequency into the depths of the vast forest. Delger and the others earned a living for the entire village by frequenting the contested forest, chasing after a prize that dragons also coveted. They weren't after the magic that the gods produced in these storms; Delger's team was after the wheat that grew in the wake of a firestorm.

Each harvester wore leather armor that bore the scars of previous runs, the material worked to a suppleness that whispered rather than creaked. They positioned daggers strategically across their chests, waists, and legs. But it was their scythes that marked them as truly different. They bore six-foot shafts of seasoned wood crowned with curved blades that engulfed the fragile traces of light; tools that could serve as both a harvesting implement, or an instrument of death.

Lark stood apart, painfully aware of her outsider status. Her borrowed clothes were tight, stitched with a patchwork of mended holes as though they'd been discarded by a soldier. The brown pants and green wool long-sleeved shirt blended in with the forest, but the outfit was a far cry from the protection she'd need against anything other than the men's prying eyes and the chilling bite of the storm's wind. The hole in her boot seemed to mock her with every wiggle of her exposed toe.

"Don't just stand there," Paq's voice cut through her self-doubt, his boney elbow finding her ribs with familiar comfort. "Do as Delger says. Get your scythe and basket. The wheat will be sprouting and full grown by mid-day tomorrow."

"You think this is a good idea?" Lark gestured to her makeshift armor, feeling the weight of unspoken judgment from the assembled harvesters. "Everyone here has held me at arm's length, steering clear ever since I arrived. Why are they so willing to send me into the firestorm?"

Paq's eyes sparked as he explained, "First of all, you're not going into the firestorm. That's what the kings contract the Paragons to do. Only the most experienced soldiers and Knights will dare to enter the flames if a god has pushed its power through the veil." He paused, letting the weight of those words settle. "No, you're going to the burn. Before the Giving Rain hits, anything seeking power will be fighting to escape. Once the fire's out, it's a mad dash to get back to the protection of their army. They'll be long gone from the area by the time you all arrive. Most likely, the deadliest thing you'll run into is other harvesters."

The mention of the Giving Rain sent a subtle vibration through Lark's necklace, though she tried to ignore it. "Those among this group?" she asked, watching as shadows lengthened across their gathering faces.

"Only the strongest of us can run in the harvest," Paq said, his voice dropping to match the gravity of his words. "Those who are tested and have proven that they can hold their own should the group come under attack."

"I haven't proven myself."

"But look at you, you're built for this with those long legs. And that's exactly why you need to go with them. What better way to gain the favor of from the rest of the village than by contributing to a successful harvest."

"Don't people die during these harvests?" she asked reluctantly.

"Not every time, although the average works out to be about one each, but you can beat the odds," Paq said with a smile that didn't quite reach his eyes. "You'll do great! I know you will."

Lark's curiosity overcame her apprehension. "What happens if we run into another group of harvesters?"

"If it's on the way in, and they're from Lamar too, some will work with us. But usually it turns cutthroat by the time everyone reaches the fire wheat, especially if you encounter harvesters from Nordraven. But don't worry, there's loads and loads of the wheat after a burn like this. How else do you think dragons get to grow so big without devouring entire towns every other day?"

"Dragons eat fire wheat?"

"They love the stuff," Paq said, giving her a sidelong glance that suggested she should have known this essential truth. "One seed is enough to feed a person for a whole day. Imagine how long a whole field would last for a dragon."

"How big is this wheat?" she asked, her mind painting pictures of strange and magical crops.

Paq's hands formed a circle the size of Lark's defined quadricep. "That big around and the stalks are way taller than me. The seeds are what we want."

Lark's hand drifted to her thigh, measuring, calculating, wondering how many seeds she could carry in the large wicker pack. The practical concern grounded her, even as her mind wandered to thoughts of dragons and magical harvests.

"Now get your scythe and go before you miss the harvest." Paq's urgency broke through her reverie.

She took the scythe in hand, its weight unfamiliar yet somehow right, and made to join the group of harvesters. The absence at her side was immediately noticeable. "Aren't you coming with me?"

"No," he said, scuffing the ground with his foot, suddenly looking very young. "Pa says I'm not old enough yet. That it's too dangerous."

"What if I cut down the wrong wheat? I don't know what fire wheat looks like."

Paq's confidence returned in full force. "You won't mistake it for anything else. You can do this, Lark. You're stronger and faster than anyone here. Well, maybe not so much as Mr. Delger there, but as long as you make it to the wheat, you'll do great."

"How do you know that? You've only known me for a few days." The question carried more weight than she intended, touching on deeper uncertainties about her own identity.

"You're different. Like me," he smiled. "Just keep your eyes on Delger and his son, Tharon. Do what they do. Trust me, they'll wish they had ten more of you by the next firestorm."

Lark shouldered the scythe, its weight a constant reminder of the dangers ahead. Paq's exaggerated farewell waves followed her as she merged with the harvesters, like a tributary joining the growing river. Delger moved through their ranks with the practiced eye of a veteran, his inspection methodical and unforgiving. Each harvester's equipment received his scrutiny: straps tested, blades examined, preparedness assessed with touches that spoke of years of experience. When he reached Lark, he scoffed, his reaction carrying the weight of unspoken judgment, but he moved on without comment.

"Harvesters, with me," he commanded. The group surged forward into the forested hilly terrain.

Lark found herself caught in the current of bodies, her senses heightened with both excitement and apprehension. Through the press of moving forms, she searched for Tharon, letting conversations wash over her like waves. When his name drifted through the air, she caught sight of him. She noted his dark hair, stern brown eyes, and strong jawline. The sight triggered something deep within her memory, overlaying his features with those of another, the mysterious figure from her vision, his pointed ears and striking green eyes haunting the edges of her consciousness.

Following Paq's advice, she became Tharon's shadow, even as her mind wandered to places beyond the forest floor. The cool evening air chilled the sweat that had beaded on her brow. She imagined what it would be like to be a rider flying over the forest, instead of running through it toward the firestorm. She generated the thought with ease. What it would be like to fly on the back of a dragon. The bond that connected a rider with a dragon. Feeling the web of magic that tied them together, connecting their minds into one. How it would feel feeding off each other's emotions, knowing the other's every instinct and reacting in kind. In her mind's eye, it was becoming a reality, almost like a memory, but closer to a dream.

"Do you think there's any chance that this storm produced a Hyalite?" The question came from a young man running alongside Tharon; blonde-haired and blue-eyed, his voice carried an edge of restrained excitement.

"Why are you excited about Hyalites? Barson, we're harvesters. You know we can't collect them, even if we somehow stumbled upon one," Tharon's response sounded a warning that brought Lark back to the moment at hand.

Barson, Lark's mind cataloged the name, remembering Paq's earlier caution about threats from within the squad.

"Ashes, Bar, even trying to collect a Yogo is against the law. Every subject of Lamar knows that."

"I understand why Hyalites are such a big deal. Their power can give rise to world-changing magicians. I mean, dragons can wield massive amounts of magical energy and even they need to share the power contained in a Hyalite with a bonded partner. But what about Yogos? Why does the King need his Knights and Paragons to collect all of them? Why can't we keep what we find?" Barson complained.

"Hyalites contain a sliver of a god's power in their glass orbs. Once the orb is tapped, that power finds a host. If the host isn't strong enough to control the released power, the power kills them. But if they can control the power, if they've been trained in how to receive it and survive, that wielder can do whatever they want with their power, good or bad. Not even a contract with a King can really control what they do with the magic. That's why they try to foster the allegiance of their Paragons and Knights," Tharon tried to explain, though many of the details were beyond his knowledge. "Clearly something the King of Lamar and Kings of Nordraven are doing is these dragonriders and magi loyal to their cause, otherwise the effort to collect these powers would be a free-for-all."

"Paragons and Knights make exuberant amounts of money on their contracts with the King, and the Dukes of the Keeps. At least that's how they do it in Lamar," Barson said.

"I think it's something else that's keeping them in check," Tharon mused.

Could Tharon be right? Surly there isn't enough money to stop dragonriders and magi from competing among themselves... or are they that superficial?

"Yogos are pure magical energy," Tharon continued. "Elves, dwarves, magi, they can all tap the energy in Yogos to craft spells. Each offers a one-time use. The Kingdoms want all of the Yogos they can get because the more energy they collect, the easier it is to control their people and offer them safety in their daily lives. Without these laws, random people could use these powers to create chaos. Understand? I admit that it's a bit confusing," Tharon added.

"Yes, I understand. But we're out here in the forest where they most often occur. I don't see why can't we keep some to sell to those who would pay big money for it? It would sure help out the small villages out here," Barson said.

"Well, we're not Nobles. We don't have any rights to magical property that comes through the veil in Lamar. My father says there's a whole global economy based on Yogos that I don't pretend to understand. We, as common folk, have the right to go and collect fire wheat, that's it."

"I understand the value of the magical energy that breaks through these storms, but I still don't get why can't we sell a few small Yogos without the King or any other Nobles knowing?" Barson insisted.

"It's been tried, and proven too risky. This is exactly why Nordraven and Lamar remain at war. It's why the dragonriders aren't fully committed to fighting in the battles in the eastern part of the Everburning Forest. You control the region of the forest that produces the power, and you control money and magic."

That's why Nordraven and Lamar are at war, for control over the creation of new magical energy, Lark thought.

"Besides, if you did manage to collect a Yogo and tried to sell it, you'd be risking more than just your fate. You'd be risking the safety of our entire village. Do you want the King of Lamar's magi to come looking for you?" Tharon said.

"How would the Magi Order ever know? They can't keep track of every sliver of power that comes through the veil in a storm, can they?" Barson asked.

Tharon's voice dropped lower. "Somehow, they know. Collecting a relic of power without a contract from the King would not only be breaking the law, but you would become a target. Out here in the forest, if those allowed to collect the relics found out you'd collected one, they could kill you, and nobody would ask questions. Best to leave the powers to the Paragons, the Knights, and their troops to fight over."

"I heard that some of the people watching this storm saw a dragon. That means this was one of the storms the gods used to send some power through the veil. I wonder which god it was? Aether's obviously the preferred, as he's the most powerful god, but any of them would be unbelievable," Barson said with a bit of awe in his voice.

"I saw them. It wasn't just a dragon, but a dragon *and* a rider. They passed the storm by, which means no Yogos, no Hyalites," Tharon said.

"No?" Barson asked. "But why were they flying near the firestorm?"

"It could've been Tel Roan out scouting for Nordraven forces. I've seen him before, you know," Tharon said.

"How did you know it was him?"

"There's only one Paragon of the Vermillion Keep who rides a golden dragon."

"I wish I'd seen a dragonrider," Barson pouted.

"You go out on these harvests often enough and you'll start seeing things you wish you hadn't," Tharon warned.

"Like a battle or two. Wouldn't that be something to tell the lads about," Barson said. "You know, I heard a rumor that an army marched from the Vermillion Keep not more than a week ago. That means one of these storms recently could've produced a Hyalite."

"Or they're going to stop a Nordraven attack. It's reason enough why we won't ever see a Hyalite. They're rare, even for the Paragons to find."

"Two Hyalites in a month would be unusual," Barson said.

"Two a month? From the same region of the forest? Try two in a year from the same region," Tharon corrected.

"My father says it depends on the year. There's the Flashover coming up, which means the Hyalites that make it through the veil will be from the more powerful gods, giving riders the power to control elements of the earth like water, rock, and air. Aether might send one through and that rider would have the ability to control celestial elements. They would have the power of the stars at their fingertips... Who knows what's possible?"

"Hyalites and the powers they can give a dragonrider aren't something you need to be thinking about," Tharon warned.

"But Yogo Sapphires are something we could find. They can form in clusters and sometimes get overlooked, so my uncle says."

"Not once has my father, or any of the other fire wheat harvesters from our village found a Yogo Sapphire forgotten on the ground after the Giving Rain."

"That's only true until I find one," Barson said.

"Only bad things come to those who carry objects of power, mark my words, Barson. If you ever find a Yogo, you best leave it where it lies."

"I could pay to feed the whole village for years with just one Yogo. Imagine how much you could get for discovering a Hyalite."

"Put that notion right out from your mind. If you don't, I'll pound it out of your head for you. Don't entertain going out looking for objects of power again," Tharon said.

"The King wouldn't know. We could start going a little earlier to the burn after the storm, while the wheat is still sprouting and not yet blanketing the ground. Then we could see if there's anything that someone forgot to pick up. What's the harm in that?"

"I warned you," Tharon said, drawing a dagger.

Lark's heart raced.

"I'll put it from my mind, promise," Barson said, backing off with arms spread wide.

Tharon sheathed his dagger.

"What if we were attacked, like you were on your last harvest run, and we found one on them?"

"We'd leave them with the dead."

"Pa told me what happened when those Nordraven orcs surrounded you and Delger. The two of you had to—"

"We did what needed doing, so we could keep harvesting. The fire wheat is valuable enough on its own. Anyone who gets greedier than that deals with the most powerful people hunting them down. There's a reason why my father's been in charge of the harvest for so many years. We don't go off chasing storms to fight orcs and other Northern monsters. That's what the Paragons and their Knights are contracted to do. If you want to do that, then head south to Astral City. Getting accepted into Vermillion Keep's

Training Academy is the only way to become a Paragon in Lamar."

Tharon glanced over his shoulder in frustration and noticed Lark there for the first time. He made awkward eye contact with her as they ran. She averted her gaze, pretending that she hadn't just heard everything they'd said.

Barson followed Tharon's eyes, then slipped a dagger from his sheath. Before it was out, Tharon stilled his hand. With a single shake from his head, the blonde harvester sheathed his weapon.

"Has anyone other than a Paragon won a Hyalite before?" Barson asked.

"If they have, the dragonriders make sure they don't last long," Tharon replied.

"Aren't the Paragons supposed to be heroes? They fight to gain control over these powers, so the armies can keep us safe from Nordraven attacks. That's why they make so much money, they're the most honorable soldiers there are."

"The Paragons may be called heroes, but they will do anything to gain control of a Hyalite. Honoring their contracts comes with more than money: it's power, status, and fame. Getting those Hyalites is more important to them than fighting for their country. It doesn't matter who has it," Tharon said.

"They wouldn't kill someone who found it by happenstance, would they?"

"You get between anyone trained in magic and something as valuable as a Hyalite, there's no telling what they would do," Tharon said.

When they finally halted for the night, the forest had transformed into a realm of shadows. Delger's orders rang through the clearing, sending harvesters scattering to claim patches of moon-lit earth for rest.

While others attended to water and bedding, Tharon

ventured into the darkness in search of firewood. Lark followed, drawn by both Paq's advice and some deeper instinct she couldn't name. The midnight forest was a different world entirely. Ferns unfurled between weathered trunks, their fronds catching what little moonlight filtered down from above. The diamond-plated bark of blackened trees marked scars of past fires.

As she braced against one such tree to snap off a dead limb, an orange flash sent her stumbling backward. The necklace came alive with warmth, a gentle tingling that seemed to resonate on the air. Quick as thought came a shower of sparks. From it something alive was produced, not a simple ember, but a creature with purpose, dancing through the air like a playful spirit. It came to hover on a branch opposite her position.

The sparks coalesced, transforming into an image that stole Lark's breath. There, hovering near the tree, was a small woman of living flame. She was beautiful, more goddess-like than lark in her tiny form. No larger than Lark's hand, the woman's long flame-red hair flowed down past her shoulders. She wore a dress of red flames, the fire around her skin a light blue before transforming into orange and yellow. She flew without wings, passing through the air with a playful demeanor. Each movement left trails of light in the deepening dusk. But Lark had no time to marvel at the fae creature's beauty.

From the shadows beyond the flaming woman came movement. Figures in light armor materialized like spirits from the darkness.

"There she is," one voice growled, deep as ancient stones.

"The one that needs to be culled from the herd," another added, his words rasping like steel on stone.

The third figure moved with deadly grace, drawing twin daggers in a motion smooth as flowing water. The others followed suit, their metal gleaming in the moonlight. One harvester's fingers danced across his blade, adjusting its balance before sending it spinning through the air with deadly precision.

Instinct took over, not learned but remembered, as if awakening from a long slumber. Lark dropped the wood she'd gathered save for one substantial piece. Her body moved with fluid certainty as she spun behind the tree. The thrown dagger passed through the space where she had stood. It clattered an instant later against a fallen log.

"Get her!" the raspy-voiced harvester commanded.

The night erupted into chaos. For the first time she could remember, Lark was in a fight for her life.

3

HYALITE

Survival instinct crashed over Lark like a tidal wave, her muscles coiling instantly. Three harvesters stalked toward her through the old-growth forest. Their daggers' sharp steel whispering quiet menace. The promise of death sent her pale skin prickling. She had no blade of her own, only a hefty branch salvaged from the scattered firewood. Yet as her fingers closed around its rough bark, the wood seemed to come alive, as if awakening to her touch.

A hint of movement to her left caught her eye. She pivoted, the branch becoming an extension of her arm as she ducked beneath a whistling dagger. Though it missed, the weapon left a trail of disturbed air that tingled against her skin. In one fluid motion, she brought the branch around, connecting with her attacker's skull. She felt the impact through the wood. A dull thud echoed through the darkening forest. The attacker crumpled against the wide tree trunk; his body gone slack.

Another dagger spiraled through the air, its polished edge passing unseen through the shadows. Pain flared across her shoulder as the blade kissed her flesh, but Lark barely registered the sting. Her world had narrowed to survival, every sense heightened to an almost supernatural degree. She rolled forward, bringing the fight to her attackers with a fluid grace, both foreign and achingly familiar. The branch became a staff in her practiced hands, striking with precision. Three of her strikes landed in rapid succession: stomach, chest, throat. Her opponent stumbled backward, his feet tangling with a fallen log. The crack of his skull against stone rang through the clearing with terrible finality.

The third harvester moved like a deadly shadow. Her fingers splayed to reveal two more daggers held with lethal expertise. They flew from her grip, cutting the air with a sharp hiss. Time seemed to slow down as Lark's body responded without a thought. The branch swept upward, catching one blade mid-flight. Its tip buried deep into the wood with a solid, THUNK, sending vibrations into her palms. She deflected the second dagger with a movement pulled from muscle memory.

As Lark wrenched the embedded dagger free, the forest seemed to hold its breath. The woman lunged, but her attack was cut brutally short. She staggered, hands flying to her throat where a dagger hilt now protruded. In the ethereal moonlight, Barson and Tharon stood like sentinels among the trees, their weapons still at the ready.

Barson approached the fallen harvester with practiced calm, cleaning his blade on her padded armor with methodical precision. The metal made a soft singing sound as it slid against the leather.

Tharon's voice cut through the heavy silence. "Harvest law says only the Squad Leader can approve the death of another harvester. Any attack on a harvester's life without express permission is considered an attack on the Squad Leader and answered in equal retribution."

Lark lowered the captured dagger. "What about them?"

She gestured to the fallen figures, exasperated, trying to ignore the way their shadows seemed to stretch unnaturally in the fading light.

"Take their blades if you want. You defended yourself fairly. Those kills are yours," Tharon said, his voice holding no judgment.

"I didn't kill..." The words caught in her throat as her eyes fell on the wrong angle of one man's neck, the dark stain spreading beneath the other's skull. "I didn't," she repeated, but the denial felt hollow against the evidence before her. Something stirred in her mind—a flash of violence, of necessity and survival, but it slipped away again.

"We both saw what happened. You might not have meant to end their lives, but they definitely meant to end yours," Tharon said, his gaze lifting to the triple moons hanging like watchful eyes in the darkening sky. "The moons will be setting soon, and it will be pitch black out here. You should come with us. We don't know what kind of creatures could be lurking nearby."

Lark's oval eyes narrowed to emerald slits as she searched the canopy for the mystical flaming woman, but she had vanished. The warmth of her necklace had receded with the fire fae, a reminder that not all of the forest's secrets were meant to be understood.

Heeding their warning, Lark gathered her scattered firewood, keeping with her the single dagger. Back at the camp, she added her wood to Tharon and Barson's pile, watching the shadows dance as others coaxed flames from the darkness.

In the dim light, Lark discovered a small pouch on her basket. Within, Paq had tucked away a simple meal of bread and cheese. She ate alone, the distance between herself and the others around the fire felt both physical and metaphysical, the chasm likely carved by violence and uncertainty. The dagger never left her grip as she lay back to look through a gap in the canopy where stars shone overhead like silent guardians.

Her thoughts drifted to the firestorms, to the power that made dragonriders wage war across the burning skies. Sleep washed over her like a heavy fog.

Her dream was startlingly clear. She was soaring above the forest, but this was no ordinary flight. Every sensation was deliberate. The wind bit her face as powerful muscles of the dragon moved beneath her. The dark timber below passed like a sea, rolling through the forested mountains like waves beneath the dragon's powerful wings. Suddenly great islands of stone appeared, hanging hundreds of feet above the Everburning Forest, somehow defying gravity.

A firestorm raged in the near distance. Its massive thunderheads hummed with a magical power. Lightning arced between clouds in patterns too precise to be natural, each strike carrying the potential to herald the power of a god. She watched with the patience of a hunter, waiting for the strike that would birth a Hyalite into her world.

The dragon's muscles bunched beneath her, eager to pierce the curtain of Giving Rain trailing the storm. Lark redirected a primal urge, heeding a whispered warning.

When it finally came, the strike split reality. The bolt carved through smoke-choked clouds, lancing into the inferno below. For a breathless moment, the world held still. Then came the explosion, a devastating burst of power tearing through the realms, creating a gateway to the gods.

Lark's chest swelled with a wild mix of emotions. She surrendered to the dragon's instincts, their consciousnesses merging until she couldn't tell where her desires ended and the dragon's began. They shot across the skies as one, the wind's scream becoming their battle cry.

Below, at the fire's edge chaos erupted in terrible splendor.

The Lost Dragonrider of Lamar 39

Northern giants, their massive forms dwarfing the burning trees, swung clubs that could shatter stone. Beast-folk charged, their fur-clad forms crowned with sprawling horns, their war hammers carving devastating arcs through the smoky air. Hulking orcs clashed with human legions, their thick swords sounding in tune with the firestorm.

In this vivid dream, Lark and her dragon pierced the storm's watery veil, steam erupting from her plate armor as they plunged into the smoke-filled forest. The heat pressed against them like a living thing, hungry and insistent, but the plate of her dragon-scale armor shed it like water. Lark felt her dragon's senses lock onto their prize—the source of magic that called to them both like a siren song. In the heart of a blackened crater, cradled by the ashy debris of a runed tree, a rough-hewn orb glowed bright. It pulsed with an otherworldly blue light, each beat sending waves of raw power rippling through the air.

A shadow materialized through the flames, resolving into a dark figure that landed before them. The enemy rider's black plate armor seemed to drink in the firelight, giving nothing back. His brismil spear trailed smoke like a banner, its tip vibrating with supernatural power. Clasped around his shoulders, the rider wore a copper cloak, its hood drawn up to mask his identity. The dragon beneath him fixed on Lark with murky white eyes that seemed to see through to the depths of her soul, promising violence with every breath.

The spear leveled at her drew Lark's full attention. The brismil blade at her side called to her. She held out her hand. Smoke traced the weapon's form as it materialized in her grip, the afterimage burning itself into the air.

Dragon and rider moved as one, their battle cry shaking the air around them. Then the dream shattered like glass—

"Lark!" A voice cut through her dream like a knife. "Get

up! It's time to go." Hands gripped her shoulders, shaking her with urgency.

The transition from dream to reality was jarring, but her body responded before she was fully awake. She still held the dagger she'd claimed the night before. Without thinking, she struck upward with deadly precision, the blade finding padded leather.

"Ah!" Tharon recoiled, his hand going to the tear in his armor where Lark's blade had found its mark. Relief flooded through her when no blood seeped from the wound, but the horror in his deep brown eyes struck a chord in her psyche.

That look, raw and visceral, she'd seen it before. An elf with piercing green eyes had worn the same expression, his frozen features twisted in anguish. Slowly, Tharon's face replaced the elf's, the similarity so stark it made her head swim with half-remembered pain.

Tharon left her, joining the rest of the group as they ventured out toward the burn. When the sun reached its zenith, they found themselves at the edge of the previous day's burn. The landscape transformed from forested hills to timbered mountains.

In the valley the firestorm had changed the dense pine forest to an ocean of wheat. The flowing stalks were a testament to the profound magic that had coursed through the storm. This crop reflected the immense power it required to so dramatically change the landscape and yield a crop so quickly. From the edge of the treeline, purple and yellow seed heads swayed in repeating patterns as the wheat blanketed the narrow valley. The stalks had already grown to a height nearly as tall as Lark's six feet. The seed heads were as thick as her muscular thigh, supported by stalks as wide as her arm, just as Paq had described.

"Set scythes to work," Delger commanded. "Only cut

what you can carry back. The far end of the field speaks of other harvesters. Stalks don't dance that way on their own."

Lark took up her scythe. Each swing became a meditation she'd felt before. The *shick-shick* of the blade through sturdy stalks merged with her breathing in a comfortable rhythm. Each arc of the blade quieted the chaos in her mind. The motion felt purposeful. Time lost meaning.

"Lark!" Delger shouted. She straightened, suddenly aware of her solitude in the vast field. The path behind her stretched like a scar through the wheat, leading back to where the others prepared to depart. Their wicker packs bulging as they filed back into a line.

Delger's suntanned face shone with sweat and concern. She gathered her cut wheat, the weight of it grounding her in the present. The rope at her basket's base became an anchor as she lashed an additional armful to its crown.

She looked back at the unharvested wheat. "There's still more," she began, but Delger's expression stopped her.

"It will not go to waste," he said, gesturing toward movement in the distance. Other harvesters emerged like spirits through the wheat, not human like Lark and Delger. Some had ears that tapered to elegant points; others had skin unlike human tones, their colors closer to moss and darkening storm clouds. "We're not the only ones who hear the fire wheat's call. Take more than we can carry, and they'll remind us why Southerners shouldn't harvest in *their* forest."

"They're Nordraven orcs," Lark breathed.

"Their harvesters carry ancient grudges, but they're not as ruthless as their soldiers," Delger said. "Be grateful we've beaten the wild dragons to this feast." His eyes swept the crystal-blue expanse overhead.

"Wild dragons will come?" Lark asked.

"Wild dragons answer to no rider's will. They're creatures

of pure instinct and ancient hunger," he said. "Come. We move without rest until we reach the village. The forest has its own appetite for what we've claimed."

The return journey became a lesson in endurance, each step a battle against exhaustion and the weight of their harvest. They slogged on through the day and into the night, guided by the light of the three moons. Every flash of light in her peripheral vision made Lark's heart leap. She hoped to again glimpse the mysterious fire woman—that impossible fae being of flame that had appeared like a broken reflection of her own past.

Dawn colored the world in shades of violet, orange, and yellow as they reached the log homes at the edge of the village. Lark added her harvest to the communal pile. Her bundle stood out for its size and also her effort. Delger's approving touch on her shoulder felt like acceptance, like belonging.

A crowd gathered on the dirt-packed road. Paq's familiar form bobbed at the edge, as he tried to peer over the press of bodies.

Lark came to his side, and asked, "What's happening?"

"A messenger from Astral City," Paq said. "I can't see him or hear what he's saying though."

Lark lifted him by the armpits and hoisted him onto her shoulders.

The messenger stood out among the dull crowd, his patchwork cloak of varying shades of the vermillion red known to represent the Keep throughout history. His silver, braided hair and waxed mustache were refined and clean. His brown eyes lingered on Lark with an intensity that made the hairs on the back of her neck stand up.

"That's right, it happened less than a week ago," the messenger was saying to an older woman in the group. "The Nordraven Kings are outraged. They've sent troops to comb the area. I'm only here to give you all fair warning. You would be wise to clear out of here now. By this time tomorrow, they'll be rampaging through here, leaving no survivors."

"Northern troops," Paq said, his legs reflexively tightening on Lark's shoulders. "They haven't come this far south in my lifetime."

"They haven't?" Lark asked.

"Not here, they go farther to the east where the forest burns less frequently and the armies battle for control of the territory, but here, the Paragons have always held them at bay."

"Tel Roan was killed," the messenger said now.

"No!" the crowd argued.

"It's true. He was beheaded," the man said. An astonished hush fell over the crowd, many of the villagers whispering in disbelief. "His dragon fled into the forest. No Knight has been able to find Ingamar."

"Who killed him?" Delger asked, joining the crowd with Tharon and Barson.

"It was none other than Marcel Heartfell," the messenger said. "The King of Skol has recovered Marcel's dragon, White Eye. The dragon was wounded before Tel was killed, but the rider, he's still out there. Marcel is likely wounded and extremely dangerous. Northern troops are coming this way uncontested as the Astral City Army was sent to support other Paragons from the Vermillion Keep northeast of here.

"Because of the Vermillion Keep's delay in reaching the scene, The Nordraven troops taking advantage and moving through the area quickly so they'll be gone when reinforcements arrive from Astral City. They're turning over every rock and leaf in search of the purportedly wounded Marcel, their most valuable rider. They will stop at nothing to destroy the mysterious dragonrider who was working with Tel Roan at the time of his death."

"Tel Roan was working with another rider?" Tharon asked, others in the crowd shaking their heads.

"Why do the people shake their heads at that?" Lark asked Paq.

"Tel Roan always worked alone. He never worked with anyone. Everyone around here knows that," Paq stated firmly, sounding older than his seven years.

"This mystery rider was wearing a uniform of the Vermillion Keep, though the Keep denies contracting any new Paragon dragonrider. This new rider's dragon was killed in the fight. They found the beast dead not far from where Tel Roan was slain, near the Floating Islands. Between the Vermillion Keep's anger over such a great loss and the North's outrage that Marcel is missing, you all are not safe here. Skirmishes in this area along the southern edge of the forest will surely escalate; your village will be caught in the crossfire."

"They haven't found Tel's dragon?" Delger asked.

"No, Ingamar is most likely missing or dead. If Marcel had taken him back to the North, the Vermillion Keep would know by now. Marcel and the unknown rider are still at large. Don't accept any newcomers into your community. These outlaws are dangerous. You must leave here at once and do not plan to return."

"But this is our home," Tharon said in protest.

"Yeah, we should defend it," Barson added.

"Any resistance and the Nordraven troops will burn your simple log homes to the ground. I offer you fair warning. That is the best I can do for you."

The townsfolk stirred as the man departed, off to warn others in the area. Lark lowered Paq from her shoulders. He started pacing, rubbing his hands together fiercely, so much so that they started turning red with irritation. Paq wouldn't look Lark in the eye.

"Paq, what's wrong?" Lark asked, though something deep within her whispered that she already knew the answer.

"I, um..." His grimace spoke volumes. "How much of the day I brought you into our village do you remember?"

The question tore open empty space as she struggled to recall. "You found me. I was walking..." The words felt hollow, rehearsed. "You led me here, showed me the village. Then to your farm, food, shelter..." Each memory seemed to sit like an ill-fitting mask over something darker, deeper.

Paq groaned, hands twisting together. "That's not everything."

"It isn't? What do you mean?"

"I need to show you," he said quietly, taking her by the hand and pulling her up the main road while trying to avoid attracting unwanted attention.

Paq led her west, away from the cluster of homes comprising their village. They walked along the edge of the fields, out to where the road abutted the forest before turning out into the river valley to the south and the rest of Lamar proper. At the second bend where the road curved back into the forest, Paq stopped. He steered Lark off the main path and several hundred feet into the forest. There, he pointed to a pile of leaves and woody debris at the base of a wide oak tree.

The pile looked natural at first glance, but suddenly she remembered. Urgently, she cleared away the camouflage to reveal a leather pack made of a quality far beyond their village's means. The ivory toggle felt cool against her fingers.

Each item she withdrew told its own story of elegance and purpose. Finely made boots, clothing stitched with expensive wool, armor designed for both protection and ease of movement. The blue travel cloak's autumn leaf filigree caught the morning light.

The weight that remained at the bottom of the bag pulled at her with gravitational force. As her fingers brushed the rough surface of the stone, something electric shot through her body. The orb emerged into daylight like a star, its blue light pulsing with a rhythm to match her heartbeat. The pendant at her throat flared in response, hot enough to brand; a fragment recognizing its whole.

"Is that…" she said, holding her breath.

"I think it's…" Paq paused as the truth finally broke free. "It's a Hyalite."

4

ASHIN' KID

The orb pulsed like a living heart in Lark's hands, each beat sending ripples of ethereal blue light across her skin. The air around it seemed to bend and twist, as if reality was warping from its presence.

"No, it can't be," Lark said, her voice barely above a whisper. She extended the roughly shaped sphere toward Paq. It glowed in her palms with crystalline twilight. The warmth emanating from it and her pendant combined reminded her of the firestorm, wild, untamed, and vibrating with energy.

"I don't want it. Do you know what would happen if they found out?" Paq asked, gesturing toward the village.

"Maybe it's not what it looks like," she suggested, tracing her fingers along orb's uneven surface, feeling each knobby ridge and smooth valley.

Paq's expression soured, his young face carried shadows far too old for his years.

"It could be something else," she said, lifting it skyward. "Yeah, I don't know, it could be a gemstone with a bluish essence, not a Hyalite."

Sunlight filtered through the sphere giving it an ocean-like color. The blue radiance expanded and contracted with a hypnotic rhythm, each surge sending luminescent tendrils racing across its surface like creeping frost. The lines of light etched themselves into the uneven exterior before retreating, drawing back into depths that seemed to stretch far beyond the orb's physical dimensions. The colors shifted between shades of sapphire and midnight, each swell growing stronger, more insistent, as if responding to her touch.

"How would you know what it is? You can't remember anything from before," Paq challenged.

The heat of the lark pendant surged, suddenly becoming so warm that she thought it might brand her. The sensation triggered a memory from her past. Lark's breath caught as the vision seized her. The orb slipped from her grip.

In the memory she stood over the elf, his green eyes fixed eternally on the endless sky above. They reflected nothing. An ornate box lay beside him. The surface was carved with runes that were written in a language she had understood then but couldn't understand seeing them now. The sound of retreating hooves thundered in her ears as a wagon disappeared into the distance, its passage violent across rough terrain. In her hands, she held two impossible things: a massive sword that trailed wisps of smoke and a pulsing orb. The orb's light was somehow both beautiful and terrible. Dread filled her like lead as she thought, *What have I done?*

"Careful with that," Paq's voice cut through the vision.

The warmth from her pendant subsided to a tolerable reminder against her chest.

As if handling a serpent, Paq used a stick to nudge the orb back into the leather pack. "We don't know what it can do," he said.

"How do you know it's a Hyalite? Have you ever seen one?" Lark asked, still searching for a way to deny the orb's supernatural presence.

"No, but I've heard the stories about them. It's the reason why Nordraven and Lamar are at war, to gain control over the Everburning Forest because Hyalites appear here. Paragons and Knights are contracted to seek them out and retrieve them for their Kings. Magi, elves, dwarves, orcs, and dragonriders all use their magic to win these glowing balls. They'll kill anyone who gets in their way. Imagine what Nordraven will do if they find it here, with us." His eyes darted to the shadows between the trees, as if expecting armored figures to materialize at any moment.

"You're overreacting. You haven't seen one before, so how can we know this is what it looks like?" Even as she spoke, Lark tasted the bitter lie.

"I've never seen a rock or gemstone glow like that. This is different. I can feel energy coming off it." Paq's voice dropped to a whisper, as if speaking too loudly might wake whatever power slumbered within the orb.

"You don't know what you're talking about," Lark snapped. The words escaped before she could catch them, sharp with an anger she didn't fully understand.

Paq flinched, curling inward. Lark felt ashamed.

"I'm not going to hurt you. I'm— I'm just... I'm worried. I'm not mad at you. Give me a minute to think this through." Her hands shook as she stuffed the clothing back into the pack and started toward the road.

What the ash is happening? she wondered. The weight of the pack seemed to increase with each step, as if the orb was drawing strength from her uncertainty. She tried to focus on one question at a time. How had she acquired something that pulsed with such raw power? The energy it radiated felt familiar.

She couldn't shake the clarity of her memory of the fallen elf. Had she been his executioner? She saw no blood in the vision and those striking eyes held accusations she couldn't answer. The orb had been in her hands then, just as it was now. The connection slowly tightened, like a noose around her neck.

Was it a memory or a dream? The question burned in her thoughts as she emerged onto the road, her feet carrying her in restless circles. *If that was a memory and not a dream, and I did take this orb, who was I?*

"Lark, are you okay?" Paq's voice carried the tremor of genuine concern as he cautiously approached.

"I don't know, Paq. I have no idea who I am. I don't know where I came from. Then you show me this bag with that in it..." her voice trailed off, so the only sound was the crunch of gravel beneath their feet.

Paq shied away again, and the gesture sent a spike of pain through her heart. Even now, after bonding to the point that she felt more his sister than Ellowin in a few short days, her presence inspired fear.

"It's not your fault. I'll be okay. We just need to figure this out," she murmured.

"How? You can't remember."

"Let's start with what we know." She gestured to the road, "You said I was walking here, just outside the village, which is along Lamar's northern border."

"That's right, we're at the south edge of the Everburning Forest, northwest of Astral City," Paq responded. "When I found you, you had this far-off look in your eyes. Your face wasn't full of color like it is now. It was white, like those Lords and Ladies from the paintings in Astral City. Except, you weren't wearing any powder or whig. Your hair wasn't fixed up like you have it now in that bun, it was all kinky and frazzled, a real wild mess. You looked lost."

"Okay, good. I was disheveled and lost."

"Disheveled?" Paq's brow furrowed in confusion.

"It means I was how you described me. Something traumatic had happened. But my clothes were clean," she added, peering into the bag.

"No, you were wearing those dirty torn-up clothes you have on now. The brown pants, some poorly fitted boots, and that long sleeved shirt, all stained and patchy."

"I thought you gave these to me. Didn't these belong to one of your siblings?"

"I only got Ellowin as a sister. It's tight on you, but that get-up is much too big for her. I don't know what all those brown stains are, but you weren't wearing what was in the bag," Paq said.

Lark tried to remember their first meeting. "Was I wearing this necklace?" Her fingers traced the familiar contours of the lark pendant.

"That's why I named you Lark," he said with a nod, a ghost of a smile crossing his face.

"What happened when you found me?"

"Let's see. What's the first thing you remember?" Paq's voice held an edge of hesitation.

"Being at your family's farm." The memory the only solid ground she could find. The warmth of hay in the barn, the steady sound of horses breathing in their stalls, the feeling of finally being *somewhere*. These sensations were real, weren't they?

Paq ran his hand through his dirty brown hair and whistled through the gap in his teeth. "Lots happened before then."

"You took my things, but I didn't resist?" If she had known what the Hyalite was, why hadn't she fought to keep it hidden?

"You didn't put up any fuss. You were like a mind-numb person. When I opened the pack and saw what it held, I tried to give it back to you. You didn't seem to know what it was.

That's why I hid it out here in the forest. Didn't want anyone back home to think you were strange."

"They did anyway," Lark frowned.

"That's because you are strange." His simple honesty somehow hurt worse than any judgment.

Lark narrowed her eyes, feeling the familiar surge of otherness that had haunted her since awakening to this false, unsteady reality.

"After that, I asked you a slew of questions, but you just moaned at me like a cow, or no. It was more like a mongodo grunt. You know?"

"Mongodo?" She saw a flash of massive beasts, steam rising from their armored hides, the ground trembling beneath their hooves. The image felt real, yet how could she know such things?

"Yeah, they're similar to wild cattle, but bigger, tougher hides. Dragons love to eat them, too," Paq said, seeming to enjoy knowing more than she did about something.

The mention of dragons sent another ripple through her consciousness; massive wings blocking out the sun, the smell of smoke and sulfur, a roar that shook the very foundations of the world.

"Anyway, I took you to town. You followed without any fuss," he explained. "There was a broke down wagon some folks were fixing. They asked for a hand; you just picked the thing up. Never seen anyone pick up a loaded wagon by themselves before. The folks put the wheel back on, thanked you, but you never said a word. Just continued staring off in that disk-el-viled way."

"Disheveled," she corrected automatically, the scholarly word feeling strange against the rustic backdrop of their conversation. Another piece of herself that didn't quite fit.

Through the haze of their discussion, Lark's heightened senses suddenly caught something else. Her ears perked up.

She could hear a faint thundering rolling toward them across the landscape. She turned to look northward, scanning the horizon where the forest met the sky. No firestorm built there, yet the thundering grew louder, more insistent. Something approached on iron-shod hooves.

"Do you hear that?" she asked.

"Hear what?" Paq replied, his young face scrunched in concentration.

Lark's gaze swept westward, following the rolling hills that carved a valley between the Astral Mountains and the Everburning Forest. The landscape seemed to hold its breath as figures materialized in the distance. Riders on horseback flashed sunlight off their armor. Copper-colored cloaks billowed behind them like war banners. The warning of Nordraven troops came to mind.

"Armored men are riding this way," she announced.

"What!?" Paq's voice cracked with fear, rising to a squeak. He stretched upward, straining to see what her keener eyes had already identified. "That little puff of dust?"

"Yes," Lark answered with certainty. "There's a half dozen or so. They must be a scouting party riding ahead of Northern troops."

"What are they?"

Lark's scowl deepened. Her necklace warmed, as if trying to tell her something.

"Are they human, orc, elf, what?"

"They're armored. I can't tell, but they are riding hard and look as though they're prepared to fight."

"Those are Nordraven soldiers. They have to be. We need to warn the others."

"You won't make it in time," she said, already calculating distance, their speed against the riders'. The space between the village and the approaching riders seemed to contract with each thundering hoofbeat. "You should hide somewhere safe while they pass."

"I can't let them go into the village looking for that orb. What if they feel the energy from it, too, and know it's nearby? You heard what that messenger said. They'll burn everything to the ground. No survivors."

The words hung heavy in the air between them. "If you go now, they'll see you on the road," Lark said.

"Unless..." Paq trailed off, his tone carrying a desperate hope that made Lark's heart ache.

"What?"

"You could try to stop them." The suggestion landed like a stone in still water, ripples of possibility spreading outward.

"How? I'm not a soldier; I don't have a sword." Even as she spoke, she remembered the feel of the massive blade she held in her vision.

"You got that Hyalite somehow. You won a dagger on your harvest, and you already had that fancy one in your bag," Paq said. "Lark, you are stronger and faster than anyone in the village. There's some in our village who could fight, but most won't. We owe it to them to give them time to flee. You are the best chance we have at giving them time enough."

Her instincts urged her to flee to seek self-preservation. She groaned at the recklessness of standing against mounted warriors. She had no ties here save for one, the boy before her. He stared with his wide brown eyes glistening with desperation and trust. "I'll be risking my life for the lives of the village. Most of whom don't accept me."

"You'll be saving mine, too. That has to be something." The simple truth cut through her defenses.

Lark ground her teeth and flexed her hands. The riders drew closer. Paq's soft eyes drove her to ignore her instinct to run. With a voice that carried the weight of her choice, she said, "Alright, fine. Run and warn the villagers to leave immediately. But you'd better stick to the forest or they'll see you. If they do see you running for town, I can't promise that I'll attract all their attention."

"I'll never forget this, Lark. You're a good person." The words struck her as something she wasn't sure she deserved. "Don't let them get what you've got in that bag. They'll kill you if they find out. The Hyalite is what led them here. The Northerners won't stop looking for it until they find it. You're not safe as long as it's in your possession."

"Then I'll get rid of it as soon as they're gone," she said in a rush.

"No, they could find it. With Tel Roan gone, there isn't a Paragon in the Vermillion Keep who can take on the toughest Nordraven riders. You have to take the Hyalite to Astral City and deliver it to the General in charge at the Vermillion Keep. They'll make sure the Hyalite stays out of the hands of the Northern Kingdoms."

"I can't do that. I need to stay here with you," she said almost whining, the words of a child trying to hold back the tide.

"Lark, you don't understand," Paq insisted. "I thought if we hid the Hyalite, they wouldn't be able to find it all the way out here in our little village. But they have. Those soldiers know something is here. I'm sure of it. Why else would they be riding so hard? Nordraven and Lamar won't stop coming for the Hyalite until one of them has it." His words tumbled out, each one closer to goodbye. "You can't come with me. I need to stay with my family and move somewhere safe. That means away from you and that Hyalite for now."

"But I don't want to lose you, Paq." The raw vulnerability in her voice surprised her. "You're the only friend I have."

"I'll always be your friend, Lark." His eyes shone with tears he refused to let fall. "And when you're done bringing the Hyalite to the Vermillion Keep, come find me. But right now, we don't have a choice. Goodbye, Lark, and good luck. I did what I could to help you for as long as I could."

"I won't abandon..." she started, but Paq was already melting into the trees. Lark wiped away a single tear. The bag containing the Hyalite vibrated, answering the rhythm of the approaching hooves.

Anger boiled up inside her. She wanted to hurl the cursed orb into the depths of the forest and run after Paq; she longed to cling to the simple life she'd found here. But that wouldn't save him or his family from the Nordravens' wrath.

Lark inhaled deeply, drawing herself up to her full height. She rolled her shoulders back, and stood ready to face down the approaching storm of riders. *I won't let them take Paq away. It might lead me away from him for a time, but I won't let them hurt my friend.*

The daggers felt right in her hands as she belted them on, their weight an extension of her will. She slung the bag over her shoulder, securing the precious cargo. Her fingers flexed around the hilts with the certainty of muscle memory.

Lark's heart thundered, but her hands held steady. As she searched for a spot to launch her ambush, she questioned if she was really about to do this for Paq. The answer came not in words but in the absolute conviction that flooded her being, anchoring her to the place where everything would change.

"Ashin' kid," she swore.

5

DEATH FROM ABOVE

Lark crouched in the undergrowth, coaxing herself to breathe in slow even pulls like the easy swaying of the trees. The sharp needles pressing against her skin kept her alert. She positioned herself at the threshold where the trees gave way to open ground, feeling the boundary between safety and exposure as keenly as a blade's edge. A dust cloud billowed through the canopy, marking the riders' path. They thundered toward her along the edge of the Everburning Forest.

Six riders emerged from the treeline, moving three abreast with the practiced ease of veteran soldiers. Their copper cloaks flowed off their shoulders. The clinking symphony of their armor, chain mail whispering beneath padded leather, steel plates gleaming, all marked them as prepared for battle. Weapons hung from their belts. Their swords had surely tasted blood, axes had split bone, daggers had found spaces between armor. These men weren't like the people in the village, raising families, harvesting wheat, and living a relatively simple life. These brutes walked a different path, making violence their craft.

For an instant Lark wondered which side of that line she fell on. Her thoughts often drifted to who her family was, if she still had one? Whether she'd been raised in a human settlement like Paq's, or something different? The weight of the Hyalite in her pack forced those questions from her mind, Lark fearing the answers.

I can't believe I'm about to do this for that little squirt, Lark thought. Before doubt could take root, she stepped into the road.

She planted her feet with deliberate care, feeling the earth beneath her boots. The Hyalite's weight pressed against her back, while her unsheathed dagger lay bare, thirsty with anticipation. The riders reined in their mounts, the sudden silence hanging thick as smoke. Those in the rear rose in their stirrups. Their armor creaked as they strained to assess the lone figure that dared to block their path.

Why aren't they committing? she wondered. A moment later she understood. Only a fool would charge blindly into such a scene without measuring their opponent.

"Who goes there?" The lead rider's deep voice rang out.

Lark remained silent, letting her presence speak for her. *Ashes, what if they don't come after me and go straight for the village? Maybe Paq was wrong, and they don't know the Hyalite is here.*

"Be you friend of Nordraven or do you bow to the sole monarch of Lamar?" The man's voice carried the edge of a command now, authoritative and threatening.

I'm not either, for all I know, she thought.

When she offered no answer, the leader drew his broadsword. The massive blade, nearly as tall as a man, rang out with deadly promise. Yet his arm held steady, the weapon becoming an extension of his will rather than mere steel. His mount answered to invisible signals, advancing as he requested. The others followed in his wake, their formation tight as a coiled spring.

I have their attention, now what? The thought barely formed before she moved. In a single motion, she shrugged off the pack and held it aloft, letting it become a target. The lead rider's advance faltered, his sword dipped slightly, and uncertainty crept into his posture.

"What is that?"

"It's what you're looking for," she said with a touch of challenge. "But you'll have to take it from me to find out."

The leader responded by issuing sharp commands to his troops. "Gordon, flank left. Melrose, hook left. The rest of you, with me."

Lark moved into the natural fortress created by the dense thicket of saplings. The young trees grabbed at her clothing. Their branches caught the folds of her shirt as she threaded through gaps that seemed to close behind her. The spaces between trees grew ever tighter until she had to break stems to force her way through.

The hoofbeats sounded a frustrated staccato as the riders encountered this natural barrier. Lark's movements slowed to a predator's careful stalk. She positioned herself behind a fallen giant. The tree's massive trunk offered both concealment and advantage. Again, she stilled her breathing to let her senses expand. She would use them to track her pursuers.

Motion to her left drew her attention. Someone was finding a path through the trees. The sound of his approach awakened something in her. Her body tightened with coiled energy.

The aggressor's massive form emerged into view, his presence commanding even atop his dapple-gray mount. His physique was one of brutal efficiency: shoulders broad as an ox's yoke tapering to a thick waist, all encased in steel that caught the filtered forest light. But it was his face that drew her attention. One eye dead and milky as morning fog, the other sharp and predatory, both bisected by a scar that told its own story of violence and survival. The short-handled axe in his grip seemed almost delicate against his bulk, yet Lark read the deadly expertise in how he held it.

"Gordon, do you see where she went?" The leader's tense voice carried through the thicket.

"No." he replied in a raspy voice. "She must be pinned down in this grove somewhere."

"Remember what General Barrik said." The name sent an involuntary shiver down Lark's spine. "Follow through on anything that doesn't seem right."

"We'll find 'er, Hoss. No stone unturned," Gordon said, his words carrying the weight of grim promise.

He turned his mount toward her. Lark's hand tightened on her dagger. Their eyes met across the space between the trees. His single good eye widened in recognition. Uncoiling with the potential energy she'd stored, Lark struck.

Her world narrowed to pure instinct. Her body moved with liquid grace, each motion precise and deadly. Gordon's delayed cry of warning died in his throat as his horse reared. The animal recognized the threat before its rider could react. Lark was ready as he fell toward the forest floor. She stabbed, her dagger finding the vulnerable gap between armor plates before he could raise an arm in defense. The light faded from his eye and his massive form crumpled.

"Gordon? What's happening over there?" Hoss's voice sounded panicked.

The horse bolted, which was enough to let the others know of Gordon's demise. Lark claimed the brute's axe, the weight familiar in her grip.

"Melrose, status?" Hoss's voice cracked.

The Lost Dragonrider of Lamar 61

The sound of breaking branches heralded the approach of another threat for Lark.

"Gordon's dead but I got the devil in my sights!" Melrose shouted as he charged, sword bared.

The dance began anew. Lark moved like flame warping around steel, her body responding to threats before her mind could process them. The warmth from her necklace seemed to guide her movements as she spun away from Melrose's blade, bringing Gordon's axe around in a devastating arc. The weapon bit through the gap in his chainmail and leather padding on his thy with terrible efficiency, drawing a cry of pain that echoed through the trees.

"I don't care how thick it is, cut your way through!" Hoss commanded from beyond the thicket, desperation coloring his words.

Melrose wheeled his mount around, preparing for another charge. Something deeper than instinct took hold of Lark. A fragment of whoever she had been before. She launched herself forward. Using a fallen branch as a springboard, she soared through the air. Melrose's sword swept up to meet her, but her axe was already there, catching his blade with impossible accuracy. The impact sang through her bones as she twisted past his guard, colliding with his armored form and dragging him from his saddle.

They hit the ground in a chaos of steel and leather. The impact drove the breath from her lungs. Moving with the efficiency of a trained soldier, Melrose attempted to pin her with grappling holds that should have been effective. But her body knew the corresponding counter moves, how to twist and turn to slip free.

When his legs locked around her ribs, she felt the pressure points instinctively. Her knee found his groin as she broke his arm hold, the crack of bone accompanied his cry of pain.

Weapons scattered in their struggle, but Lark's eyes found

Melrose's sword. His boot caught her as she lunged for it, sending her sprawling just short of the hilt. She twisted, catching his follow-up kick and using his own momentum to shatter his knee. As he fell, she saw his hand moving to his belt, caught the glint of steel sailing past her head. The throwing knife cut through her shirt like a whisper of death, but her body was already moving, already knowing. Before he could draw another blade, his own sword found his heart.

The pendant's heat began to fade as she stood over him, her breath slowing to controlled gasps. The forest seemed to hold its breath as she listened to the three remaining soldiers hacking their way through the thicket with Hoss stationed at the opposite edge in wait. Their desperation was palpable, fear had begun to override their training. She retrieved Gordon's axe, its heft a grim comfort as she melted into the shadows between the trees.

Like a ghost, she stalked through the saplings until she was mere inches from her remaining prey. They moved with frantic energy, their blades hacking at the vegetation that seemed to resist every stroke. She waited, patient as death itself, as the first two passed her hidden position. When the third came within reach, her hand shot out with terrible purpose, yanking him backward onto her waiting blade. Her other hand clamped over his mouth, muffling his final breath.

"What was that?" One of the remaining soldiers spun around, eyes widening at the empty space where their companion had stood. "Where did Cedric go?"

"Melrose, report?" Hoss's voice trembled with barely contained terror.

The silence that followed was heavy with understanding. Lark snuck toward them, her movements silent as falling snow.

"Did you hear that?" The dark-haired woman's whisper wavered, her scarred face taut with tension.

The Lost Dragonrider of Lamar 63

"It's a Southern magus, isn't it? She's taking us down one at a time. Coming out of nowhere like a rimeshade," her companion replied, fear lacing his voice.

"Shh," the woman hissed. "It's no rimeshade or magus. Just a woman. A highly trained soldier."

Just a woman, Lark thought, the words echoing through the hollow spaces where her memories should be. Slowly, she drew Gordon's axe, raising it with infinite care.

"Did you see something move?" the woman asked, her sword probing the spaces between trees.

"No."

"Just there," she breathed, the tip of her blade parting the branches near Lark's position.

The gap she created was all Lark needed. Her dagger and axe moved in perfect harmony, guided by the same mysterious force reawakened within her. Both weapons found their marks with surgical precision, and two more bodies crumpled to the forest floor, their final breaths lost among the whispering pines.

"Crass, Hopa, report?" Hoss called.

Lark emerged from the thicket like an avenging spirit. Hoss's eyes widened with a recognition, his sword arm falling limp at his side.

"You? Death from above—" His words ended in a gurgle as her dagger found his throat.

Lark wished time would slow as she caught him, lowering his massive frame to the forest floor. "Wait, what were you saying?" Urgency colored her voice as she recognized something in his fading gaze.

His eyes blinked rapidly, his tongue working as if trying to free trapped words. Finding them, he whispered through blood-stained lips, "Oh, is that what it feels like?"

"Do you know me?"

"I..."

"Who am I?" The question tore from her throat. In futile desperation, she shook his shoulders. But Hoss's head only lolled lifelessly. His secrets died with him as his eyes grew distant, then empty.

Lark dropped to her knees, exhausted. Six Northern soldiers lay dead by her hand. Not once had she hesitated, not once had she questioned the lethal dance her body seemed to know by heart. Just as with the harvesters, she had let instinct guide her hand, and death had followed.

Her link to the past, to who she was and why she could move like death itself, felt as fragile as spring frost before the sun. The pendant's warmth faded. And darkness engulfed her.

In sleep's embrace, she found herself soaring through endless skies. The dream felt more real than memory. She sat astride a massive dragon, its scales dark as midnight, while wind whipped through her umber hair. The landscape below was a tapestry of brown grass and jagged mountains, but her attention was fixed on another dragon and rider fleeing before her.

She felt an ocean of energy held back by the flimsiest of dams, begging to be released, to be shaped by her will. A spell formed on her lips. Light erupted from her outstretched hand to illuminate the space between her and her victim. But as the magic cascaded forth, dread bloomed in her chest. A chilling certainty that something had gone terribly wrong.

She awoke with a gasp, heart thundering against her ribs. The ground was solid beneath her. The whispering pines offered a stark contrast to the endless sky of her dream. Nearby in the woods lay the six bodies.

Who am I?

The question echoed through the hollow spaces in her mind. Her time with Paq remained clear: helping out around his family's farm, the harvesting of fire wheat, the simple peace of having a purpose. But everything before remained shrouded, save for that one clear moment with the striking elf, his emerald eyes wide as she held the orb. The uncomfortable weight of the Hyalite pressed against her hip.

"Paq," she whispered his name like a prayer, fear for his safety driving her to her feet.

She dropped Gordon's axe, leaving it in the dirt near its owner. With the Hyalite and her few belongings secure, she ran for the road. Moonlight illuminated the path in shades of silver, exposing fresh scars in the earth where a large cavalry force had passed. Her heart clenched, realizing the extent of her exhaustion allowed her to sleep through the rumbling of galloping horses nearby. In a panic she sprinted back toward the village, each step carrying her closer to a truth she already feared.

As she rounded the final bend, the sight drove her to her knees.

"No." The word fell from her lips in disbelief.

The wooded hollow that had cradled Paq's village was now a graveyard of shattered dreams. Smoke rose from the ruins. Tears carved clean paths through the soot on her cheeks as she searched desperately for any sign of life.

"Paq!" Her voice rang through the village remains, each repetition more desperate than the last. But try as she might, she discovered no signs of death, just destruction. The livestock had vanished, too, as if the entire community had been spirited away before the torch was put to their homes.

Paq was able to warn them in time, she hoped.

"Paq!" she called into the surrounding forest, to no avail. The cavalry's passing had obliterated any tracks that might have told her where they fled.

Lark looked into her pack and stared at the Hyalite. Its blue glow thudding in time with her racing heart. This mystic orb had shattered the fragile peace she'd briefly enjoyed and had destroyed in moments what a few days of patient work had created. She had wistfully hoped to forge a new life without the burden of her past.

The pendant seemed to scream with heat now, protesting her actions as she removed the Hyalite from her pack. The orb's inner glow surged as if feeding off her rage. This supposed gift from the gods was nothing but a curse, a poison that destroyed everything it touched.

"If they want this ashing thing, then they can have it!" The words tore from her throat as she hurled the Hyalite down the road with all her strength.

Lark turned her back, choosing a direction that felt right and started out. But each step away from the village and the abandoned orb felt wrong. A chilling regret tugged at her, urging her to return. The Hyalite called to her. She glanced back, its light no longer pulsing, but instead the orb burned dull against the dirt road.

Without warning, her necklace sent a sensation through her chest, warming in the same way it had when she was in the forest. Sparks materialized beside her to coalesce into a small woman of living flame. The fire fae danced through the air, singing a sweet song, completely captivating Lark's attention. It flew circles around her head, showering her with harmless sparks as the warm tones of her song lulled Lark into a trance. Soon, she found herself walking back toward the village.

"What are you doing?" Lark said, shaking herself free of the fae's siren song. "I'm not going back there."

The fire fae responded by singing louder, gesturing toward the Hyalite. She flew in spirals around her, showering Lark with sparks and a warmth that blurred her focus. The soothing, coordinated sensation the fae and the necklace had over her pulled her back into the trance. Her limbs grew heavy with artificial peace as the creature's spell took hold. She started following the fae again, drawn by her hypnotic song and dance. A section of the village that continued to burn caught her eye, shocking her back to the here and now. Lark was almost through the village now, heading toward the Hyalite.

"No!" she said, stopping herself and trying to shoo the flaming woman away.

But the fire fae was relentless in its purpose. Again and again, it led her back with its hypnotic song. Each attempt to abandon the orb ended in failure. After what felt like hours of futile resistance, Lark finally surrendered to the inevitable.

"Fine, I'll take the Hyalite," she said, bending to retrieve the orb. Its surface was warm against her palms, almost alive.

The fire fae celebrated her decision with an aerial dance of pure joy. Her flames burned brighter with approval.

"You really want me to have this?"

"Yes," she hummed, smiling as she twirled, flaring her red dress of flame.

"You can sing, and you can talk?" Lark asked.

"To those who can see me," she replied.

"If I'm going to be saddled with this burden... what's your name?" Lark addressed the fae while carefully returning the Hyalite to her pack.

"Nix."

"Like a phoenix?" Lark asked, startling herself with how she was able to remember the creature who could be reborn by fire.

Nix nodded.

"Well, if I'm going to do this, I won't be keeping the Hyalite forever. I'll do what Paq insisted and take it to the Vermillion Keep."

"Yes," Nix said, as she flew in excited patterns, each circle growing more elaborate than the last.

"I'm not doing this for you," Lark snapped at the flame-wrought being. "I'm doing this for Paq."

"Come," Nix said, humming as she flitted off, leading Lark away from the village.

"Is this the way to Astral City?" Lark asked.

"This is the way," the fae said, humming her song again. The tones were warm and inviting like the heat she emitted. She flew through the air, leading Lark on.

"Show me the way, little fae," Lark said as she reluctantly followed.

6

JUDGEMENT

Venrick slowed the cart before the bridge spanning the chasm to the Vermillion Keep. Red turrets erupted over the outer wall like the thorns of some great beast looking down on him and the rest of Astral City with unblinking judgment. The beating wings of a dragon coming in to roost pulsed overhead. Its emerald scales caught the late afternoon sun before its serpentine tail disappeared behind the massive anvil-shaped landing area atop the Keep's central tower. This was the moment Venrick had been dreading since he first drew breath in Tel's service.

How did it come to this? he wondered.

Tel Roan, the pride of Astral City, was dead. His dragon was missing, their prize Hyalite gone, and worst of all, his Squire had survived. There was an unspoken rule at the Vermillion Keep, one etched in blood and honor rather than stone. No Squire succeeded where their superior had failed. Those who did were branded as cowards, exiled, or worse, condemned as traitors to King and Country. The weight of that tradition pressed down on Venrick's shoulders, threatening to crush him beneath centuries of precedent.

In all his years serving at Tel Roan's side, through countless hours of training and heroic acts performed in the Keep's name, Venrick had never imagined joining the ranks of the few Squires throughout history who'd made this trek back to Astral City without their Paragon. An icy shiver ran through him as he grappled with that harsh reality, each breath feeling like a betrayal. He had survived, while Tel Roan had fallen.

Venrick's pulse quickened as he clicked his tongue, signaling Thunder and Giant into motion. The two draft horses moved forward, their hooves clacking over the stone bridge. As he neared the entrance, his gaze remained fixed on the Vermillion Keep. Crimson turrets crowned the thick battlements guarding the main portcullis, their surfaces etched with runes that shimmered and shifted in the corners of his vision. Slotted windows dotted the ramparts like watchful eyes, each one holding shadows that seemed to move with purpose.

A dozen auxiliary buildings on either side of the main entry lined the rising slope, their red slate roofs peaking over the rampart like the scales of some great dragon, echoing the Keep's majestic design. Towering over it all stood the Vermillion Keep proper, its thick walls adorned with dwarven runes hosting great power. The spells here weren't mere decorations. They were living things, ancient magics that rendered the Keep nearly impenetrable to outsiders. Every stone hummed with protective spells, creating a barrier that even the most powerful mages approached with caution.

This fortress was home to the dragonriders of Lamar, the beating heart of the kingdom's northern defenses. Venrick had dreamed of ascending through these gates on his own his whole life, but never under these grim circumstances.

At the gatehouse, Venrick submitted his weapons. His nerves betrayed the storm of emotions raging beneath his carefully maintained composure. Each blade, each tool represented years of training with Tel, memories that cut deeper than any steel ever could. A guard, broader and more imposing than Venrick's athletic frame, scrutinized the tattooed insignia on his forearm with predatory intensity. The emblem of his rank as a Squire smoldered beneath the man's gaze, each intricate line a testament to promises now broken by death's intervention.

Venrick could feel the magic in the air as though it were a living thing. His half-elven senses detected subtle currents of power flowing through the stone beneath his feet. Wards wove patterns that his mind could almost grasp but never quite hold. The sensation was both familiar and foreign.

"If you're a Squire, where's your Knight?" the guard asked, his words carrying the weight of centuries-old prejudice toward mixed-race ethnicities.

"I wasn't squiring for a Knight," Venrick replied, pulling his arm away and replacing his vambrace. The metal felt cold against his skin, a stark reminder of the armor he'd worn that fateful day.

"You, a half-elf, squiring for a Paragon?" The man's laugh held no warmth.

"I was," Venrick said, clenching his jaw against the tide of grief and anger that threatened to overwhelm him.

"A dragonrider?" another guard asked, cocking his brow with theatrical skepticism that barely masked his contempt.

"That's right," Venrick said, raising his chin.

"Why did you say, I was? Once a Squire, you are a Squire until you get accepted into the Keep's training academy or somehow skip right over to becoming a Knight yourself. I don't recall seeing you in this year's new recruits, and you're no Knight."

"My Paragon died." The words fell from Venrick's lips, each syllable echoing with finality.

The silence that followed was filled with unspoken accusations, broken only by the distant roar of a dragon. The guards exchanged glances.

"A Squire outlived his Paragon?" The guard's face hardened, narrowing his eyes at Venrick. "How'd he die?"

A vein in Venrick's neck began pulsing, each beat a reminder of life that should have been forfeited in service to his Paragon. He considered, not for the first time, why he'd bothered to return at all. He could have disappeared into the shadows between worlds, been declared dead, found a fresh start in Gambria, Lamar's neighboring kingdom to the east, where the weight of the Keep's tradition didn't press quite so heavily on his shoulders.

But the truth was, the elves of Gambria, like those of Lamar, didn't accept him. The elves viewed his human heritage as a stain that could never be cleansed. And humans? They never gave him a fair chance, their judging gazes always catching on the slight point of his ears, the otherworldly grace that marked him as different. The Keep was more than Venrick's only option; it was the only place he'd ever felt like he belonged.

"Go on, tell us. How did you survive when your Paragon died?" The guard probed, testing Venrick's resolve.

"I don't need to explain anything to you," he replied.

"I reckon that's why he's here," the other guard said. "He's here to be judged. Usually, when a Paragon is killed, the Squire has either died bravely trying to prevent a superior's demise or is quickly slaughtered in the aftermath."

Like a shadow taking form from nothing, someone appeared. He was a lean man, head-and-shoulders taller than Venrick's six-feet-two-inches. The stranger's head was a mat of slicked black hair shining with oils. His dark eyes held depths hinting at a wealth of power and knowledge better left unexplored. His large, gauged ears marked him as someone who had walked the boundaries between conventional magic, being the verbal spell work magi used to shape the energy stored from a Yogo Sapphire or Hyalite, and something more sinister, like the wild powers born from the realm of the fae.

His middle-aged face was clean-shaven, features gaunt and angular to the point of being bird-like. The stranger moved with a fluid grace that defied natural law. He fell in alongside the guards, his sudden appearance startling them with its impossible certainty. Without word or warning, he gripped the brawny guard's shoulder and pulled him aside with an ease beyond physical strength; a reminder that in this realm of dragons and magi, muscle meant little against the weight of true authority.

The guard's face twisted into a knot of protest, ready to challenge this intrusion until recognition dawned in his eyes. The change was profound, cold and absolute. Whatever question had lived on his tongue died.

"You're Tel Roan's Squire." The pale-faced stranger's dark eyes demanded more than Venrick's attention. He wore black clothes adorned with ornate patterns of silver leaf and vine filigree. A high-collared red cloak rested on his angular shoulders, clasped together with a ruby amulet whose surface crawled with runes.

Around his narrow waist, he wore a black leather belt studded with dozens of Yogo Sapphires, each one pulsing with its own rhythm of blue radiance. The stones hummed with stored energy, each gem a reservoir of power that could fuel the mage's spells.

"Yes, I'm Venrick, Tel Roan's Squire," Venrick announced.

"I've been waiting for your arrival," the stranger said. His dark eyes flickered to the side of Venrick's head where slightly elongated ears held back his thick brown hair. The glance lasted less than a heartbeat, but in it, Venrick felt the weight of judgment that had haunted him since birth. He was too elven for humans, too human for elves, and now perhaps too alive for a dead Paragon's Squire.

"Nobody told me you were of elven origin," the stranger continued.

"I wasn't aware the interrogation would start at the gatehouse, with a mage. I understand my rights. I will speak on record with a Captain of the Keep," Venrick said, his words emerging with a strength that surprised even him. He heard the echoes of Tel's training: *stand tall, speak true, never let them see the doubt that plagues your heart.*

"I am no common mage," the man responded, his lip quivering slightly. "I am Archmagus Hierro De Vonte, or Lord De Vonte to you. Anything you say to me is held in the confidence of both the Order of Paragons and the Order of Magi."

The revelation hung in the air like storm clouds heavy with lightning, threatening to break open the sky itself. "The Order of Magi?" The question escaped before Venrick could contain it, carrying with it all the weight of childhood stories whispered in dark corners. The tales of wizards who walked the boundaries between realms, who held power over life and death, and often imposed their will over human rulers. "I wasn't aware wizards held any authority over Keeps."

"Who else could keep an organization with so many powerful heroes compliant with the Kingdom's best interests?" Hierro's smile was a thing of shadows and edges. "The Duke of Astral City and General Ashbrook of the Vermillion Keep do not have the resources to devote their undivided attention toward this task. With the war against the four kingdoms of Nordraven drawing most of King Agadorn's attention, he has tasked the Order of Magi to police the Paragons. So, when one of them dies unexpectedly, I, as High Authority in the region, take particular interest."

Venrick swallowed hard, feeling the noose of fate tightening around his neck with each passing heartbeat. He understood with crushing clarity that he stood not before any official, but before someone who had the authority to change or end his life.

"Come, young Venrick, or are you old? I can never tell with your kind," Hierro said.

Venrick lifted his smooth chin, leveling his stern expression at the Archmagus. "Half-elves age slower than humans, true, but don't let my youthful appearance lead you to judge me as an adolescent. When I came of age, I trained for years before I found my way to Tel Roan over ten years ago."

"You really are young then, not even twenty. Although, compared to someone as old as I, everyone from this century seems young," Hierro said with a wicked smirk. "Come, we have much to discuss." Hierro's long, boney arm wrapped around Venrick's shoulders like a serpent claiming its prey. He steered them through the gatehouse and toward the castle's inner compound. No guard uttered even a whisper of complaint. Their silence was more damning than any protest could have been.

"Wait, the cart," Venrick hesitated. The wagon represented his last tangible connection to Tel, to the life they'd shared, to everything that was now slipping away.

"The wagon and horses will be looked after. You have my word." Hierro promised.

Once past the battlements, they moved along paved stone streets. Workshops, forges, and stables bustled with activity; the rhythmic percussion of hammers pounded like heartbeats. Knights and soldiers drilled in formation on the armory grounds, their movements a dance of deadly precision forged from discipline, practice, and repetition.

But it was something else that caught Venrick's attention. A massive, chained creature thrashed within the courtyard. Its presence was a violation of natural law. Two curling horns wrapped its head like a crown of bone and darkness, its fur was matted and wild. Long claws sliced through the air at the surrounding Knights, each strike carrying enough force to shear through plate armor like parchment.

Venrick slowed his pace, allowing Hierro to pull ahead as he paused to study the beast. Its hulking, shaggy figure loomed just beyond the open doorway, partially obscured yet undeniably powerful. The creature's red eyes met his for a heartbeat that stretched into eternity. Within them, he saw something that resonated with his own existence, a being caught between worlds, neither one thing nor another, powerful and feared for that very reason.

"Venrick, keep up. The General despises tardiness," Hierro's voice cut through his thoughts. The Archmagus whispered a spell, his fingers flicking through the air with casual grace. The double-wide doors swung shut with an invisible force.

"That was a real kurr," Venrick breathed, the words emerging with a mix of awe and terror. "They train against real monsters?" The question carried all the weight of his denied dreams, of every time he'd been told he wasn't worthy of the Academy's hallowed halls.

"That information is between those training to fight for the Vermillion Keep and the instructors of the Astral City Paragon Academy," Hierro's words fell like ice shards, each one deliberately crafted to cut deep into old wounds. "Paragon's Squires who are under scrutiny for failing in their primary objective are not permitted such luxuries."

The comment pierced Venrick's armor of carefully maintained composure. Each rejection had carved another notch in his soul. The three Paragon training academies of Lamar stood as both beacon and barrier. The Keeps who sponsored the training of new Paragons acted as a promise of transformation designed to turn the best soldiers and Squires into Knights, setting them on the path to become Paragons of Lamar. Yet for Venrick, this remained an impossible dream.

The Keep's entrance hall unfolded before them. Towering columns rose toward the vaulted ceiling, each one bathed in streams of sunlight that poured through massive windows. Stained glass in the upper panes depicted intricate scenes of triumph and tragedy, their colored light casting ever-shifting patterns across the stone floor; heroes and monsters locked in eternal combat.

Majestic carvings of mythical beasts loomed above; their stone eyes followed Venrick. Dragons with wings spread wide enough to shadow armies, griffons poised in eternal vigilance, wolves caught mid-howl, and azgron crocs frozen in poses of terrible majesty. Each creature was a testament to the power the Keep commanded.

Venrick's boots scuffed lightly on the crimson carpet that stretched the length of the hall like a river of blood. Hierro angled toward one of the many alcoves that led to an adjoining room. Within it, magical torchlight flickered, bathing the space in a warm but eerie glow. Those gathered around a table at the room's center fell silent as Hierro and Venrick entered, their eyes locking on him like a predator watches its prey.

A glass-rattling THUD shook the window.

Venrick's hand flew to where his sword should have been. Around the table, several of the well-dressed individuals cursed, their composed facades cracking for just a moment.

"Blazing birds," a stout balding dwarf with a bushy salt-and-pepper beard muttered. His eyes held the sharp calculation of one who had seen too much to be truly startled. "Those winged creatures have been banging against that pane of glass all morning."

"Hierro, who is this young man?" The question emerged from a strong-chinned woman with silver hair and military bearing. "Another one of your warlock assistants brought into the Keep without Duke Ronan's approval?"

Wrinkles formed in the corners of her mouth and at the edges of her violet eyes, but they weren't the marks of age so much as the physical manifestation of power wielded over decades. Venrick recognized her then, General Ashbrook, Commander of the Vermillion Keep.

"Duke Ronan would be well served by allowing more of my assistants inside these walls. However, the King saves our members for the most important issues across Lamar. With a war looming at the southern border with Sojax, and the pressure to control the Everburning Forest before the Flashover begins, this competition over Hyalites and Yogos is more pressing than ever." His dark eyes flickered with something that might have been amusement, though it held no warmth. "The majority of our order is trying to secure alliances with the other neighboring kingdoms to the east and west, Gambria and Doran, so that if Sojax and Nordraven align, we here in Lamar will not be crushed. No, this half-breed," he continued, waving off-handedly in Venrick's direction, "is not a member of the Magi."

"Then who is he and why have you summoned us?" General Ashbrook asked. Her calm but authoritative voice betrayed deeper currents of concern that rippled through the chamber like invisible waves. "With Tel Roan gone, we're scrambling to find a replacement who will keep Nordraven dragonriders from dominating the firestorms in this region."

"This matter concerns your beloved Paragon's death," Hierro said. "Venrick, meet General Ashbrook."

His sharp green eyes met hers as he thought he saw a hint of recognition in the mentioning of his name.

"And this honorable dwarf is the General's right hand, a master of underground warfare, Commander Belfour," Hierro continued, each introduction another thread in the web of authority drawing tight around Venrick. "Commander Englestad is an expert in forested defense, and his Captain Limosuel is rapidly becoming the prodigy of overland attacks."

Hierro's gesture toward the final figure carried a different weight entirely. "And that is my apprentice, Joc." The man wore no military uniform or red cloak, though the pendant around his neck matched Hierro's. It was covered in runes that seemed to shift and change when directly viewed.

"This was Tel Roan's Squire?" Commander Englestad pointed with a gloved hand.

Hierro nodded.

"And he came here on his own?" Limosuel asked, crossing his arms as he leaned back in his chair.

"Correct. Young Venrick here did the right thing, he didn't flee to rebel forces hiding in the Everburning Forest. He has returned to the Vermillion Keep to face our judgement." Hierro said.

"We're proceeding without the Duke?" Ashbrook's question hung in the air like fog.

"Duke Ronan planned to be here but sends his apologies. Something came up that took precedence this morning," Joc said, his eyes never leaving Venrick's face as he studied him with calculating intensity.

The Duke was going to judge me personally? The thought exploded in Venrick's mind. He had expected a Captain, perhaps one of the Commanders or even a Knight, but this gathering of authority seemed unnecessary.

"This is the Squire who survived Marcel Heartfell?" Commander Belfour's question emerged with a strong dwarfish accent.

General Ashbrook cleared her throat, demanding their attention. "Squire, tell us how is it that you were not killed along with your Paragon? Those who are as skilled and highly trained as Tel Roan do not die an easy death."

"Did you not receive the letter I sent?" Venrick asked.

Ashbrook frowned.

"I wrote everything down in detail," he pressed. "It might be easier for you to read it first and then question me."

"You will explain yourself here or we will judge you a coward now and be done with this." Her words fell cold as northern ice.

"The letter captures—"

The General's voice rose over his, "If you don't explain it now, you'll no longer be associated with the Vermillion Keep. You'll be branded a traitor and exiled from Lamar. If that's what you want, continue insisting we read this non-existent letter. We've already heard the account from Tel Roan's Honor Guard who rushed back to save him, and your absence was the only notable mention of your name. Explain why you abandoned your Paragon in his hour of need?"

Venrick's gaze found Hierro's dark eyes, seeking something, sympathy, understanding, even the barest acknowledgment of the impossible position he found himself in. But the Archmagus offered nothing but that same calculating stare, cold and deep.

"Tel had led his forces with several Knights to the edge of a firestorm," Venrick began, the memory unfurling with devastating clarity. "They were expecting that an important Hyalite would be produced. He went ahead with his Honor Guard to scout for the Nordraven troops. When he located none nearby and realized that the firestorm had produced a Hyalite with no clear challengers, Tel sent his Honor Guard and the troops back. He requested I assist—"

"Tel Roan would not send for a Squire to assist with Hyalite retrieval," Englestad interrupted.

"Paragons do not trust such important matters to Squires over their Honor Guard," Limosuel added.

"The Honor Guard did mention Tel's request to have his weapons wagon brought forth," Ashbrook conceded.

Venrick drew a breath and continued, "On Tel's way back with the Hyalite, he was spotted by Marcel and another Vermillion Keep rider. Tel and Ingamar evaded them while the rider from the Keep fought with Marcel."

The silence that followed gripped at his throat, begging him to break it with a condemning statement, but he held firm, letting them marinate in his truth.

"You're lying," Ashbrook accused. "This is why rumors are spreading that the Keep lost two Vermillion Keep riders to Marcel."

"No, there was another rider there in a Vermillion Keep uniform. They wore the red, the same as Tel Roan's. Whoever it was, fought Marcel and White Eye with a high degree of competence. Tel broke away and met me near the edge of the burn. We secured the Hyalite. When White Eye emerged, I shot him with Tel's brismil arrow." The memory of the bow's tension, the whisper of fletching against his cheek, the moment when his life hung suspended between heartbeats, it all rushed back with devastating clarity.

"As if Tel would let you wield his bow," Joc scoffed, his voice carrying venom.

Captain Limosuel's long middle finger descended upon a document in his stack with the finality of an executioner's blade. "There are no orders from the King or any of the Dukes that issue another dragonrider to go beyond the confines of their current contracts. No rider in all of Lamar was ordered to fly into Tel Roan's territory, especially none from this Keep."

"Your papers don't reflect what really happened out there," Venrick said insistently. "Do you papers tell you how the magic Marcel used rendered me unconscious before I could put myself between Marcel and Tel?"

"These papers are verified reports. They are the facts, half-breed," Ashbrook warned. "Tel was the only dragonrider of Lamar authorized to be there."

Hierro leaned forward, his presence emerging like an unnatural shadow. "Let's say there was a third rider," he offered. "Where are they now? The Honor Guard reported no sightings of another dragonrider."

"They flew in from the North. The Honor Guard couldn't have seen them from their position in the forest," Venrick insisted.

"These rumors of a third dragonrider have been circling for few weeks now and no evidence has come forward," Ashbrook said.

"That's what happened," Venrick said flatly.

"It does beg the question," Hierro added, his dark eyes widening, "what caused Marcel to go missing in action?"

"Nordraven could be lying to us about having recovered only his dragon," Balfour entertained.

"Marcel hasn't reported back?" The question burst from Venrick's lips before he could contain it.

"We've confirmed that they recovered White Eye," Ashbrook said. "He was wounded in the right shoulder by a brismil arrow. Marcel, however, is still missing if we're to believe the Nordraven reports."

"Maybe he finally died," Balfour said. "We always said Tel Roan was the only one equally matched who could face him."

"White Eye remains in Skol," Ashbrook countered sharply. "Why would he still be there if Marcel were dead?"

"Did you see Tel's death?" Commander Englestad asked.

Venrick's response emerged as a living memory. "After I hit Marcel's dragon with a brismil arrow, he crashed into the clearing. The third rider attacked, sending a ripple of energy blasting off Marcel's wards. The last thing I remember seeing was Tel and Ingamar being overtaken by the blast and falling to the field." His voice caught and he cleared his throat. "I was launched off my feet, struck the side of the wagon and woke up there. Tel was dead and Ingamar was gone."

"And the Hyalite stolen," Ashbrook added.

"What kind of power did this third rider use to create a shockwave of energy?" Hierro's question emerged like a snake, coiling through the chamber with deliberate intent. His dark eyes reflected something deeper than curiosity, lusting for more power.

"I don't pretend to know the secrets of the gods that pass their powers on through the bonds of dragons and into their riders," Venrick replied.

"Riders with Paq, the god of air's power could generate that kind of effect, though Lamar hasn't had a rider with that gift since long before Tel Roan's time," Joc interjected. His smooth voice drew quizzical expressions as they all contemplated this possibility.

"What of the god of the celestial, Anther? His power could generate that kind of explosion," Venrick offered, breaking the silence.

"Paq, the god of air, yes, his gift is possible among Hyalites near the Flashover, but Anther. He is the god of the stars and has no interest in our small realm." Hierro chuckled. "He hasn't sent a Hyalite through the veil in my lifetime, and I've seen the last two flashovers."

"How can you know that? Lamar doesn't succeed in collecting every Hyalite produced in the Everburning Forest," Venrick challenged.

"You forget your place, Squire," Ashbrook snarled. "You are not a Paragon of Lamar. You are not a Knight of the Vermillion Keep. You are not qualified to speak about Hyalites. Tel Roan died on your watch, and you did nothing to save him. You lost his dragon and let Marcel escape with the Hyalite."

The accusations fell like hammer blows.

"I put everything into working with Tel," Venrick said, letting his emotions go unchained. "He trusted me, that should speak volumes to my character. I did everything I could to help."

"You were working for Tel, not with him," Ashbrook corrected, her voice threatening to end the hearing. "You were his Squire, not his Knight."

"Venrick has applied to the Paragon Academy here in Astral City, right?" Joc's question emerged smooth as poisoned honey.

"What does that have to do with this?" Venrick asked, trying to rein in his emotions.

"Joc's right," Hierro said, leaning on the table with his elbows, his fingers steepled before him. "I understand your application was denied for the third time at this location, not including the times you've applied and been rejected from the Stormwatch Paragon Academy and the Lamar City Paragon Academy."

Venrick nodded, unable to deny the truth.

"If you've failed to be accepted after ten years of serving under one of the best Paragons in Lamar's history, what makes you think you were capable of coming back here and convincing us to let you advance your career with the Vermillion Keep?" Hierro asked.

"I am more suited to the task than most Knights who are under contract with the Keep's employ today," Venrick said. He felt Tel's presence then, like a phantom warm against his shoulder, years of training and trust formed a shield against their doubt. "If I were human or full elf, I would've been accepted the first time. Tel knew that I was overlooked, which is why he trusted me to work with him once he trained me."

Hierro's dark eyes narrowed. "If that were true, surely one of the other more accepting academies would've recognized your talent. Elves, magi, and dwarves are all granted a fair chance."

"And what about mixed-bloods, how many are enrolled?" he asked.

"Currently, none in Astral City. And after considering your petition for special acceptance, I'm confident we've made the correct choice. You do not have what it takes to become a Paragon. Mixed-bloods have made it to Knighthood, but never has one become a leader the Keep has deemed worthy of advancing to Paragon," Ashbrook said flatly.

"Did he actually think that we would allow him to become a Knight in training after this tragedy?" Commander Englestad asked the group at the table as though Venrick wasn't present.

"Without the letter I sent, how did you know I petitioned for special acceptance to the Academies?" he surmised.

"You keep referencing this letter," Hierro said, pulling it from his breast pocket with deliberate grace.

Venrick stared in disbelief. It really was his letter, as he noticed the blood stain he'd left on the far corner.

"I considered sharing it when you brought it up, but with these kinds of things, it's always better to hear your account face-to-face."

The chamber seemed to darken, shadows growing from the corners.

"I thought you might change your lie and tell the truth about what happened to Tel." Hierro's words rang through the silence that took hold. "Pity for you that you chose to stick with your lie for the second time. I think I speak for all of us when I say your petition to be forgiven for losing a Hyalite and accepted into the training program is denied."

This manipulation tore at Venrick's heart. The weight of

what the Archmagus was saying settled down on him and seeped into his bones.

"It's a shame," Joc's voice emerged smooth as glass. "Though he was denied by the academies for all those years, it's apparent that his Paragon trusted him to defend a Hyalite." The words carried undertones of a poison that had yet to reveal itself.

"In his version of the story, yes, but how do we know if Tel truly trusted him?" Limosuel added.

"When I spoke to Tel's Honor Guard, they mentioned it wasn't the first time they'd been called back while his Squire was summoned for the retrieval of powerful objects," Commander Belfour argued.

"Maybe if you had successfully brought back the Hyalite, then we might've considered giving you a chance to prove yourself," Englestad said offhandedly.

"With your track record of failed Academy applications, and now this failure with Tel Roan," Ashbrook said, folding her arms and leaning back in her chair, clearly having made up her mind, "I don't see how we could give you another chance."

Venrick's chest tightened as she spoke.

"We can't allow Hyalites to go missing. There is no other recourse but to give Venrick the most severe punishment," Ashbrook announced.

Venrick's throat constricted, suddenly feeling as dry as the southern deserts. His tongue cleaved to the back of his throat as he attempted to voice an argument, but their authority was too powerful. These people were supposed to see how hard he'd worked over the years. How every sacrifice and every moment were devoted to proving himself against impossible odds. Every time he'd reached for something greater it seemed to slip through his fingers because of his heritage. Nothing about this meeting had gone the way Venrick had hoped. His only surprise was that he was still alive.

"If I may," Hierro's voice cut through the horrifying sentence closing in around Venrick. As the Archmagus raised a single boney finger, the rest of the leadership hung on his words. "Before you sentence this young man to exile or death, I would like to offer an alternative. Something that has proven successful lately."

"What kind of alternative?" Ashbrook asked, thin lips becoming a hard line.

"As long as Marcel and Tel Roan's dragon are missing, maybe we allow young Venrick the opportunity to prove himself worthy of retrieving the lost Hyalite."

"He can't possibly get a Hyalite back from Marcel," Ashbrook protested. "Nordraven's entire force of Paragons is out looking for their rider. He would pose a security risk once he was captured. He knows too much."

Hierro tapped his finger against the ruby clasping his cloak together, and said, "I have a way around that."

"You do?" Ashbrook asked.

"If given the ability to keep those secrets, where's the harm in letting a Paragon's helpless Squire attempt a mission that Tel Roan himself would likely have failed? If he proves himself by collecting the missing Hyalite and returning it here to the Vermillion Keep, Venrick will have proven himself worthy of acceptance into your trainee program."

Venrick's mind buzzed with possibilities, hope springing from him that he might leave this Keep alive.

"And in the more likely event that he fails," Hierro continued, his dark eyes settling on Venrick, "he'll be gone forever."

"Why wouldn't he just run away?" Belfour asked.

"Like I said, I have a way around that kind of behavior."

"How?" The question emerged from Ashbrook.

Hierro rose, his presence a source of gravity drawing the group's energy. "I can create a conjuring that will keep him on task and tight-lipped, under pain of death," he said.

"You can do that with Yogo energy?" Ashbrook asked.

"I can do it with a different kind of magic. Something the magi of the North have been able to do."

"You're talking about a curse?" Ashbrook said.

"Their dark roots can yield most auspicious fruit if done correctly. Even the King has authorized us to use it, sparingly of course."

Venrick's hope for a life beyond the chamber fell inward. The others eyed one another like wolves smelling a change in the wind.

"Curses are not legal in Lamar," Belfour announced.

"Nor are they ethical," Ashbrook agreed, but beneath her certainty a line of shadows darkened her brow.

"You were going to condemn him to death, were you not?" Hierro said, stating it as if it were fact.

Ashbrook nodded slowly…

"This is much more humane," Hierro reasoned, seeing Ashbrook's look of consideration. "Once cursed, Venrick will have no choice but to complete the task or die."

"How could you ensure this without assigning one from the Magi Order to follow him constantly?" Ashbrook asked.

"A touch of dark magic from the fae realm, the curse, is imbued into this," Hierro said, pulling forth a crimson ruby on a golden chain. The artifact emanated an unnatural pulse, much different from the hum his Yogo Sapphires emitted. "Once cursed, he'll be bound to this rune-cast amulet. Its power will keep his life tied to the conditions we set for him. If Venrick takes the amulet off, his blood will boil."

Venrick took a step back, feeling the magical presence of the mages in the room ready to take hold of him.

"That necklace can keep a curse active?" Limosuel asked.

"With Joc's help, he and I have created a form of power not thought possible before," Hierro replied.

"I don't know," Englestad said, his voice shaky with

doubt. "This kind of magic hasn't been seen in the Keep since the Dark Times."

"It offers us a larger net to track down the Hyalite without costing the Keep anything," Hierro insisted. The red amulet dangled from his fingers like a pendulum counting down the moments until it would grace Venrick's neck.

"How would it work?" Ashbrook asked, her violet eyes reflecting the desire to acquire the lost Hyalite.

"The curse binds Venrick to this amulet. Through the runes carved into its surface, Venrick will be held to the task of retrieving the lost Hyalite. If he were to tell anyone about the curse or if he were to take off the amulet, he would die."

"And if he abandons the task?" she prompted.

"If he runs away from it and fails to attempt the task, he'll die. But if he completes the mission and brings the Hyalite back," Hierro continued, "I will remove the curse, and he will be free to enroll here in the best of the Paragon training academies Lamar has to offer."

"How would you make it so he can't tell others about it?" Ashbrook asked.

"I can design the boundaries of the curse to limit any direct language that acknowledges his situation under a curse. He couldn't tell anyone."

"This object of his undoing will be his own salvation," Joc added with a wicked smile.

"To others it will seem as though he is after the Hyalite as revenge for Tel's death or for his own personal gain or what have you," Hierro finished.

General Ashbrook studied her companions' reactions with the intensity of one who has witnessed too many impossible things to discount even the most terrible possibilities. The silence grew between them like a void. "Getting the Hyalite back is the most important priority. We will dedicate our resources to finding it, including this Squire," she stated.

Venrick backed toward the door. This wasn't happening. It couldn't be happening. Every step he'd taken in Tel's service, every moment spent proving himself against impossible odds, had led not to acceptance but to this crucible of dark magic and desperate choices. He couldn't allow them to use him this way, not after everything he'd sacrificed in the Keep's name.

"Lord De Vonte, do it," General Ashbrook's command shattered Venrick's hope for some reasonable or favorable resolution.

Suddenly Joc was there. Venrick struggled, writhing to break free, but the mage held Venrick in place with a strength that belied his wiry appearance. From under his breath, Venrick heard the apprentice chanting in a strange language.

Hierro was there, his hand raised. Pale fingers stretched toward Venrick, splayed like the bones of a living ghost. Swirling energy formed around them, each curl and twist passing from the Yogos on his belt. The tang of magic tasted thick on the air, just as it had in that clearing where Tel fell.

Darkness crept into Venrick's vision. His body went limp. The light evaporated, leaving behind only a darkness as vast and complete as the space between stars.

7

IT'S A START

Venrick lay in the charred grass where wisps of fire still smoldered between the blackened blades. The final moments of Tel Roan's passing replayed themselves like a feverish dream. The rotten smell of acid and sulfur filled the air, blending into a tacky taste at the back of his throat. He watched himself as if through a gossamer veil, his own body sprawled unconscious with his eyes left eerily wide open in the wake of his Paragon's death.

A woman stood beside him, her presence commanding yet ethereal. Her eyes, the deep verdant green of a springtime forest, held an air of dread as she searched his face. The stern set of her full lips betrayed the goddess-like beauty of her appeal. Her umber hair danced like woven streamers in the wind. Her plate armor was masterfully crafted to her warrior's form, while complimenting the feminine curves of her body. The armor held the subtle sheen of brismil enchantment. She bore a matching brismil sword across her back, her hand held to the side, ready to summon it at a moment's notice. While the vision was threatening, Venrick couldn't take his eyes off this beautiful stranger for an entirely different reason than fear.

As he regained consciousness, Venrick's heart thundered in his chest, each beat sending fresh waves of pain through his skull. The boundary between dream and waking wavered. His mouth felt as though he'd been gargling sand, though he knew no wine or mead had passed his lips.

Who was that woman? The question echoed in his thoughts. Even at his most inspired, he couldn't have conjured someone who embodied such raw power and otherworldly beauty in equal measure.

Reality slowly came into focus around him. Tel's massive six-wheel weapons wagon stood sentinel nearby. Thunder and Giant were, miraculously, still hitched to its frame. The massive draft horses grazed in a meadow that seemed too vibrant, too alive, given the weight of what Venrick had just been through. In the distance, the old-growth pine of the Everburning Forest rose like pillars, their massive trunks disappearing into a canopy of green. A threatening storm gathered strength on the horizon. Thunder clouds merged with columns of smoke. Lightning scored through the building firestorm, bright white bolts crackling through like spears of godly power.

"What's happened to me?" he said, not seeing anyone familiar. His memory of the meeting in the Vermillion Keep returned in fragments, sharp-edged and burning. Archmagus Hierro De Vonte's face looked down on him with grim determination. The General's presence, heavy as an executioner's axe. The air in the room had actually twisted with dark fae magic. Then came the truth, more devastating than exile, more final than death.

He fingered the ice-cold chain permanently affixed to his neck. The crimson amulet hung like a drop of frozen blood; its weight far greater than the ore it was cast from. The truth could no longer be denied. Venrick bore a curse that made death seem merciful.

This can't be happening.

He got to his feet and assessed the situation. He stood alone now outside the city wall that had sheltered him since Tel Roan saw something other than a mixed-blood in him. The Vermillion Keep's rejection stung worse than the curse. Though he'd devoted his life thus far to its protection, the leadership no longer recognized him as one of their own. The missing Hyalite hung over him like a guillotine.

"Where do I start?" he said to no one, the words scattering on the wind.

What would Tel do? he wondered.

Tel would have donned his brismil armor and ridden north like an avenging storm. He would have faced down the four Kings themselves, dragon-fire and fury made manifest. But Venrick had no dragon's wings to carry him northward, no armies to command. No brismil armor to—

The thought struck him at once. *Tel's brismil scale would've materialized back in the chest.*

He vaulted toward the rear of the wagon that was built with ironwood and boxy like a mobile cabin. The door groaned open, the wards allowing Venrick to duck through and enter.

Inside, he silently inventoried Tel's mobile armory, each piece with its own story. Stories he knew first-hand. Spears that could pierce a northern wolf's hide leaned against swords that bore gouges from monstrous kurr claws. Flails whose heads had broken shades rested beside axes that could bite through a Northern orc with ease. Bows hung with their quivers, one of which Venrick had used to shoot down a dragon. Yet among this arsenal of legends, one item stood apart: Tel's brismil scale and sword pair.

Venrick moved a heavy trunk aside to reveal a false panel

craftily designed into the rear corner. Within it, three enchanted chests rested undisturbed, each vibrating with protective wards. Three repositories of power, each sealed with spells that could give even a god pause. He retrieved the smallest, its weight deceptive for its size.

"How could something so rare, so powerful, have been overlooked?" His whispered words stirred the magical currents in the air, resonating against the weapons around him. A chill crept up his spine, not from fear but from proximity to such concentrated power.

His hand brushed the raised runes on the lid, and the magic responded instantly. Light spiraled from the ancient symbols like liquid starlight, flowing across his skin until he glowed. The wards recognized him, or should have, their magic beat in time with his heart. A soft click echoed through the wagon, but when he tried to lift the lid, it remained sealed as if forged from a single piece of metal.

A memory rose, sharp and crystal clear. The elven fortress in Gambria materialized around him, its living walls of ancient heartwood held centuries of accumulated magic. Spiraling patterns of silverleaf decorated the wood beams with a warm, gentle luminescence.

Tel stood before him. The Paragon's presence filled the chamber like the summer storm clouds heavy with Giving Rain. "Venrick, place your hand on this chest," he commanded, his voice resonating with the quiet authority of one who had lived a full life as a dragonrider.

"What will it do?" Venrick asked, remembering how the magic emanating from the chest felt like heat from a hearth.

"These runes," Tel traced a finger over the symbols, making them flare with sapphire light, "will deny entry to all others. The magic woven here is both ancient and eternal, powerful enough to resist divine interference. Only the most formidable mages in recorded history could hope to breach these wards."

The elven enchantress beside them continued with her work. Her fingers danced through the air as she wove spells so complex they left afterimages in Venrick's vision. "When she finishes, only you and I will command these locks. Not even the King himself could extract a Hyalite without our consent."

The complexity of the magic still left Venrick in awe. No Yogo Sapphires gleamed from its surface; no Hyalites pulsed with stored power. The wards operated on principles older than the Kingdom itself, a testament to a magic that had outlived empires. That had outlived Tel.

The brass hinges gleamed mockingly as Venrick held the locked chest. Venrick blinked, watching his reflection fracture across the polished surface as his smile crumbled.

"Why?" The word escaped as barely a whisper. He tried to open it again, feeling the subtle ripple of protective enchantments beneath his fingertips.

His muscles strained against the unyielding magic. The veins in his forearms stood out like twisted rope. The lid remained immovable, radiating a quiet defiance in rhythm with his mounting frustration.

"But I was there when he cast the spells," Venrick protested, his voice echoing hollow against the wagon's thick wooden walls. The magic did not respond to him, a silent reminder of his oversight.

He pulled out the largest of the three small chests Tel had concealed in the wagon's false panel. The hidden compartment still carried the faint scent of sawdust and preservation spells. Only one chest yielded to his touch, the Hyalite container. Its empty interior reflected how he felt at the moment, devoid of hope.

Then, understanding crashed through him like a wave of

ice water. During the chests' creation, he'd only placed his hand on one. "I'm an ashing fool!" Venrick cursed.

The smallest chest slipped from his fingers and clattered against the floorboards. He looked around, searching for an answer. Then, with desperate hope, he had an idea. His gaze darted to the larger chest, the one that had housed the Hyalite. Though empty at present, it held something else, traces of the magical signature of the perpetrator who broke into the chest.

Could that work? The thought materialized slowly. *The chest is magical, and equally powerful magic would have been used to open it. If there's even a trace left from whoever cast it a tracking charm could work...*

The chest sat innocently before him, but Venrick's mind raced through the implications. Marcel would have needed immense magical power to break through the enchantments, and such force would have left scars in the very fabric of the spellwork. Invisible wounds that, with the right charm, could lead him straight to the thief.

Venrick ducked back out of the wagon and strode back to the horses. Their reins felt cool and familiar against his palms.

"Thunder, Giant, I think it's time we go and visit a certain goblin informant," he said with determination.

Giant's snort carried a distinctly skeptical note as Venrick coaxed his massive head away from the sweet mountain grass.

"I know how it sounds, but I don't have many options, and it's a start."

He guided the bulky wagon toward the mountains. Within days, Venrick had arrived in a mountain pass where few traveled. He unhitched Thunder and Giant, leaving them to amble into the sunlit clearing beneath a towering granite cliff. The entrance to the goblin's cave was a masterwork of natural camouflage, just another shadow among countless fissures scaling the thousand-foot wall of the unnamed peak in the Astral Range.

As he approached the cliff base, something rolled beneath his boot. Smooth and round, it triggered instinctive revulsion. He stumbled, sending loose stones skittering across the ground.

"What the?" The words died in his throat as he looked down. A sun-bleached skull grinned up at him. His eyes traced the grisly trail to its owner. A skeleton sprawled in eternal repose, its long-sleeved ring mail hung like tarnished scales around yellowed bones. The rusted sword belt served as both a grave marker and a warning. Goblins were magic creatures not to be trifled with.

The path up the scree field seemed to lengthen with each step. Loose stones shifted dangerously beneath his feet. The air grew thinner and carried whispers of old violence. Each breath tasted of long-spilled blood.

A narrow ledge jutted out from the mountainside, barely wide enough for someone to edge along. A hundred feet of empty air yawned beneath, hungry for the unwary. Venrick pressed his shoulder against the granite face, feeling the stone's natural cool against his body. Deep claw marks scored the ledge, their edges still sharp despite countless seasons of wind and rain. Dark stains mottled the rock face. The stains spoke silent testimonies of those who had died here. The mouth of the cave bore the lingering traces of Ingamar's fury. Black scorch marks were visible from where dragon-fire had taught this goblin the wisdom of cooperation with a dragon and his rider.

Should I be doing this? he wondered as the wind tugged at his clothes. *Is my life worth risking against a creature who'd gladly see our Kingdom fall?* But the curse around his neck acted as a chilling reminder. Choice was a luxury he no longer possessed. The Vermillion Keep's rejection had sealed his fate, forced his hand, and turned his perception of who he had been fighting for on its head. He wasn't acting in the interests of the Kingdom anymore. He was acting for self-preservation.

"I can do this," he whispered in an effort to convince himself.

The entrance to the cave gaped before him; darkness seemed to bleed outward into the daylight. He entered the hungry shadows. Dank air assaulted his nostrils as a mixture of cave filth and sweat underlaid with a foreign musk that could only be one thing, goblin-scent. Deep in the darkness, a sickly yellow light shone, but something was off about the glow.

Venrick focused on the dim light, taking a careful step forward. A loose stone beneath his foot betrayed him, skittering across the cave floor with a sound like rattling bones. The yellow glow vanished instantly, plunging him into absolute darkness. His heart hammered against his ribs. He held his breath and listened, only to hear the thunderous silence of his own blood rushing in his ears.

Then came the clicking.

It started softly, a gentle tap-tap-tap against stone that echoed wrongly in the darkness. The sound grew closer, each click accompanied by the scrape of claws on rock. Now a low, guttural groan reverberated through the cave. The sound carried centuries of malevolent cunning. When the goblin finally spoke, his words dripped with spite.

"Venrick," Zorjan's voice rasped, the name becoming something else entirely in the goblin's mouth. "What are you doing here?"

8

HARDIN

The salt-laden breeze blew across the bustling port of Stormwatch, where weathered wooden planks groaned beneath the weight of endless foot traffic. Hardin leaned against a shipping crate that bore the scars of countless voyages, its wooden surface smooth from years of handling. His shoulder brushed against Sasja's leg with deliberate gentleness, like a moth drawn to flame. When she allowed the contact to linger, his heart performed an intricate dance in his chest, a symphony of hope and disbelief intertwined.

Their voyage across the strait from Doran still felt dreamlike, as though the eight gods themselves had conspired to place her in his path. He had expected her to disappear into the labyrinth of streets within the city the moment they made port. Yet here she was, her presence as tangible as the ruby pendant that hung around her neck, catching in the light with an almost supernatural radiance.

Hardin cleared his throat, the news clipping tight in his calloused fingers as he held it out. "Tel Roan Killed. Dragon

Gone Missing. Astral City Shocked at Nordraven's Escalation."

Sasja's glacial blue eyes held his hazel gaze captive. Her hair was the opposite of his dark black shaggy mop. Her braids were blonde like spun gold, the tips danced against his shoulders with a teasing intimacy as she leaned over him. The warmth of her sent playful shivers down his spine.

"Tel Roan, isn't he the Paragon you were telling me about; the one you were traveling to Astral City to see? You wanted to hire him, right?" she asked, her voice sounding sweet like summer wine.

"Hire a Paragon like Tel Roan..." Hardin allowed his mind to wander through a path of an impossible dream. If he was built more like a soldier of Lamar instead of the wiry, tan-skinned singer he was currently, he might've entertained coming to Lamar with hopes of training to be a Knight.

What a wonderful fantasy that would be, he thought.

Yet, the weight of the coin given to him by respected members of his town pressed against his hip. The hidden purse acted as a constant reminder of their trust in him. A purse that might as well have been filled with wishes for all the good it would do in securing a true Paragon's services.

My best hope lay in finding a Knight whose ambitions have dulled to the point of accepting this modest sum.

He considered telling her the truth. But blonde-haired, blue-eyed, Lamarian beauties like Sasja didn't waste precious moments with penniless dreamers from a westerly kingdom.

"Isn't that what you told me when we boarded the ship at Dagger's Landing?" Sasja asked.

"That's right, I did say that. I'm on a quest to hire a hero from the Vermillion Keep," Hardin declared, his focus returning. Sasja's golden braids tickled his scalp, and he tilted back to meet her azure gaze.

"I've never met anyone as young as you who was rich enough to afford a Paragon," Sasja mused.

"That may be true," he said. His thought faded into nothing as her fingers trailed through his dark wavy hair with deliberate grace. He felt as though he were floating as she continued tracing the sharp angle of his jaw, ghosting across the stubble that marked his attempt at rugged masculinity

"You must have come from a Doranian Princedom to have that kind of money," Sasja murmured.

Truth writhed inside him, demanding release. The collected hopes of his people weighed heavier than any coin purse.

"It's a group of investors actually," Hardin said, the lie tasting of ash. Somehow, this young woman was able to make him say things he otherwise wouldn't.

"What will you do with all the money now that Tel Roan is dead?" Sasja's question cut through the spell her gentle touch had over him.

"I thought I'd still—"

The thundering of boots against wood shattered the moment. Hardin's senses snapped to attention. Through gaps in the stacked crates on the wharf, he caught sight of a newly familiar shop owner leading a contingent of city watchmen in matching armor.

"Ash," he cursed.

Sasja transformed beside him as she dropped from her perch with liquid grace. The playful girl vanished, replaced by something altogether more dangerous. She snatched the burlap sack from beside his lute with practiced efficiency, her earlier languorous touches now seemed like the careful assessment of a thief studying her mark.

Was she only staying with me for a chance at my money?

The question should have stung more as he realized the truth of it. Yet he couldn't quite extinguish the flutter in his chest when she moved close to peer around the edge of their hiding place.

"I told you, you shouldn't have taken that outfit from Monsanto's window display," Hardin accused, but the words lacked real conviction. In his mind's eye, he saw his journey crumbling.

His imagination created the scene with brutal clarity: Sasja's false tears, would flow freely before the guards. Her voice, so recently warm with affection, would turn to poison. *Honest, sir. He put me up to it. He's got a way with words, being a silver-tongued bard and all. He forced me to take the fine clothes. See, they aren't even for a woman.*

The male jailers would believe her, they always did. The beautiful young innocent woman would weave her spell of deception while Hardin's protests withered and died in his throat. Then it would be the mines in the southern Astral Range. Not the beautiful halls of dwarven mines under the Everburning Forest, no. He would be sent to a place where hopes go to die and dreams turn to dust. All because he couldn't resist the wiles of a girl with ocean-blue eyes and a smile that promised adventure.

"They're probably going to think I stole the coin I have on me as well," he muttered.

"Hush your mumbling," Sasja commanded in a surprisingly sharp tone. "I can see a way out of this before Monsanto gets here. Just keep your head down and follow me."

Hardin secured his lute with the shoulder strap and set out to follow her. Sasja approached the dock's edge. A rope tied to one of the posts anchoring the wharf was strung in a taut line from the wharf to the ship moored there. Starting from the post under the cargo crates, the line stretched fifty feet to the portside of the ship. Sasja was studying it.

Is she going to climb that rope? That's insane, they'll see us.

Sasja tied the burlap sack containing the stolen goods to

her belt before peering over the edge. Hardin's blood ran cold as he, too, peered into the churning waters below.

Beneath the surface, certain death swam in unpredictable patterns. The monstrous crocks flashed in streaks of purple and dark blue. Azgron crocks patrolled the waters, ever so patient to await their prey. Like dragons of the sea, their scaley bodies and powerful jaws, made them the nightmare of any creature careless enough to enter the water. These predatory creatures, were living legends. The azgron crock was the focal point of many a sailor's darkest tales. They haunted the space between dragon and demon in the hierarchy of terrors in Sataran.

Hardin's memory of his first azgron sighting rose unbidden. The creature was sprawled across the main pier back in Doran. Its massive form dwarfed the fishing nets that had somehow proved its undoing. At first, Hardin thought it was a fallen dragon; then, a noble beast brought down by mortal means and fished out of the water. But as Sense Kalu said the name, Hardin saw it. Something darker lurked in the creature's cold dead eyes. The way its scales glistened with an almost hypnotic beauty, their purple-blue iridescence masking armor that could turn aside a ship's ram. Primal fear had clutched him then as it did now. The azgrons below mocked his dreams of heroism.

"I saw one of them hiding in that stack," a thick southern accent cut through these thoughts, the footsteps of pursuit slowing to a deliberate stalking pace.

Hardin's gaze snapped away from the water for just a moment, catching a glimpse of Sasja as she made her choice. She leapt out away from the wharf's edge. His heart stopped in a moment that seemed infinite. Saja hung with her arms outstretched suspended between the ship's rope and certain death twenty feet below. An instant later, her grip caught the line. It flexed as she used her momentum to swing, horizontally, around the rope. Sasja thrust her hips just before letting go, giving herself the perfect arch to land back on the opposite side of the shipping crates. Landing safely on the other side of the cargo stack, she disappeared from view. A breath later and she'd stuck her head back out, leaning over the water. Her rich blue eyes caught his, extending both the invitation and challenge to follow.

"Check right there," Monsanto said, nearing the slot in the cargo where Hardin hid.

The mooring rope lay before him, a lifeline and a judge. *You can do this,* he told himself. Without looking down, he launched himself into empty space.

The world dissolved into pure sensation. The wooden planks vanished beneath his feet and were replaced by the vast nothingness that expanded between him and the water's surface. The air seemed to hold its breath as he stretched for the rope.

The coarse fiber met his grasp with a shock wave that rippled through his sinuous body. Reality arrived with brutal clarity. Momentum carried him in an arc. He pumped his hips like Sasja had, every taut muscle straining toward a landing that suddenly seemed as distant as his home's salvation.

The gap stretched before him like a cruel joke, the dock's edge retreating even as he flew toward it. Something in Sasja's expression shifted: hope crumbling into horror as she realized what he already knew; he wasn't going to make it.

He collided with the edge of the dock. As he folded, the air escaped his lungs in a soundless cry of protest. The edge of the dock had caught him across his diaphragm. His fingers scrabbled desperately against the smooth wooden planks, seeking purchase in a vertical world. Each attempt to find a grip sent splinters beneath his nails.

Just when he was certain that all was lost, Sasja's hands found his arms. Her firm grip and arm strength belied her delicate appearance. She pulled, muscles trembling with effort, while below them the water erupted in a spray of primal violence.

A snap clapped behind Hardin, followed by a splash that echoed across the dock. Sea spray painted his skin with tiny droplets.

"Careful, Monsanto," a voice drifted from the far side of the cargo as Hardin regained his footing. "The azgron are aggressive this close to the docks."

"I'm fine. That one missed," Monsanto responded, revealing a tremor.

"They have taken three lives already this year from those who come too close to the edge," the guard continued.

"I saw something move. They were just here," Monsanto protested.

"There's nobody here," the guard replied.

"I will have my compensation," Monsanto huffed, the threat sounding emptier than before.

"From the sound of that azgron, whoever might've been here may be gone for good. Taken from the edge of the dock like those ill-fated," the guard replied.

"Hardin," Sasja whispered his name, her hand finding his with a warmth that seemed to chase away the chill of their brush with death. The gesture carried none of her earlier calculated seduction. This was something raw and real, born in their shared survival.

They fled across the wooden floorboards of the wharf, bobbing in and out of stacks of crates and groups of sailors and fishermen crowding the docks. They didn't slow until their feet found solid ground. Hardin chanced a glance back to watch their pursuers continue a futile search among the piles of crates filled with everything from more common items like grains and clothing to more precious commodities like spices and metals.

The city of Stormwatch spread out before them. The Keep rose above it all, its golden peaked towers piercing the sky like the spears of giants, its stone-gray walls a monument to the heroes both magical and mundane who trained there. But despite the impressive castle and its protective surroundings, the absence of dragonriders here was an indicator of its reputation. Storm Keep was second when it came to Paragons and Knights of Lamar. The Vermillion Keep held on to the top of that roster in Lamar.

Hardin followed Sasja through row after row of multistory buildings offering a mixture of the established wealth in Stormwatch. Some were brick, built with lavish touches. Others were stone quarried from the Astral Mountains. Most buildings were wood, however, harvested from the forests at the foot of the Astral Range on its west side, not too far from Stormwatch.

Sasja's speed began to outpace Hardin's and he found himself struggling to keep up.

"Hey, wait up!" he called to her, but the young woman acted as though she didn't hear him.

They jogged past bodegas, taverns, and narrow doorways. Hardin kept a bead on her as she cut through crowds that reflected the city's living tapestry of cultures. Each face Hardin passed held its own story. Humans of all races and ethnicities. He passed between elves and half-elves, some with long hair covering their pointed ears, others displaying them proudly. Hardin's eyes widened when he spotted dwarves toiling in jewelers and smithies, their lives hardened by exile among humans. He nearly tripped when he saw orcs mingling with pedestrians, clearly people seeking refuge from battles fought too long in the North.

Sasja ducked into a tavern where patrons sat on wooden barrels around tables. "Here, put this on," she said, offering him the bag of stolen goods from Monsanto's.

"I... I don't know," he said, noticing the suspicious glances that followed them as they sought open seats. "It feels wrong. Shouldn't we return it?" he said, trying to sound less unsure than he felt.

"And risk being caught!?" Sasja said.

"Hey," a hulking orc said from behind the bar. "We don't serve Doran pacifists. This is a Veteran-only tavern."

"We're just passing through," Sasja said, attempting to diffuse the tension.

"You can stay, he needs to leave, now or I'll call the Watch," the orc bartender said.

"No need to raise the alarm," she said flicking a coin to him as she added, "We're leaving."

She led Hardin through to the back door and out into a shadowed alley.

"I won't give the clothes back to him face-to-face," Hardin said, glancing to either side to see if anyone had pursued them. "I was thinking it would be best to wait until nightfall. I can leave them on the back steps. No harm, no foul."

The wrinkle of Sasja's nose spoke volumes. "If you don't want to wear it, I'll keep it. Do you know what kind of money I could get for this?" she gestured with the bag. "It's well made. Monsanto's is quality leathercraft and the best fine stitching this side of the Astral Range."

City Guards in light armor rounded the corner heading toward them.

"Ash," Hardin cursed.

Sasja forced herself onto him, pushing him up against the brick wall at his back. She put her hands in his hair, moving her face dangerously close to his and whispered, "Put your arms around me."

Hardin hesitated, caught off guard by her sudden forward action.

"Quickly, so they don't recognize us if Monsanto has already spread the word."

Hardin did as she asked, taking her into his arms and holding her tight. She kissed down his neck, stirring a slew of emotions within him. As the guards passed, they murmured to one another, chuckling and egging the young couple on. They continued out into the next street without recognizing either of them.

Sasja abruptly pulled away from Hardin's neck, grabbing his hand that had drifted down below the small of her back and pulled it away with force.

"What?" he said as she narrowed her blue eyes at him. "I was trying to sell it."

"And it worked," she said. For an instant he thought he saw a flash of a smile on her face, before she forced a flat expression. "You're really not going to take the clothes I grabbed for you?"

"Why did you take them? I told you I couldn't afford them," he asked.

Sasja measured him with a lingering stare. "Why don't you spend your money?" She tilted her head with deliberate grace, the ruby pendant at her throat drawing his attention. "You have plenty, as you say. Enough to buy a Paragon. So why not spend some on yourself?"

"This isn't my money. I can't spend it like that," he said, his hand instinctively moving to cover the pouch.

"The investors who gave it to you are expecting you to spend it all on the hero's service?"

He nodded.

"Just go to Storm Keep and get a Paragon there. They are half the cost. Then you can spend some of that coin on things you can enjoy, like these clothes."

Hardin's fingers found the clasp of his worn brown vest, the metal cool against his skin as he covered the telling stains on his once-white shirt. Each mark was a reminder of the path that had led him here. "For one, Storm Keep doesn't have dragonriders," he countered.

"They have Magi, which are just as clever at using magic, sometimes they are better at knowing how to use it against people."

"I need to go to Astral City."

"Why go all that way when there's a host of Paragons and Knights here at Storm Keep, all of whom would work for a much better price?" her voice cracked slightly, betraying a hint of desperation. Hardin almost thought she sounded like she was trying to plead with him to change his plans.

"I'm aware, but they aren't what I need. I need a specialist. Someone who's faced threats from the North that aren't the everyday, run-of-the-mill monster." His voice dropped to a whisper. "I need a dragonrider or someone who's worked alongside a dragonrider and has a specific set of skills."

"You'd save a lot of time, money, and heartache by going to Storm Keep right now." Sasja's tone softened, taking on the honeyed quality that first ensnared him on the ship. "It's what a girl like me would want you to do. You want to impress someone like me, don't you Hardin?"

The air between them thickened, the lust he felt while she distracted the City Guard returned, but Hardin's response was steady. "I'm not going to settle for less."

Something shifted in Sasja's eyes then: respect warring with frustration, calculation dancing with what might have been genuine concern. "You're never going to convince a Paragon from the Vermillion Keep to help you, or a Knight for that matter. Not a single one of them will take you seriously with that little pouch of coins you have." Despite her honest intentions with the warning, her words cut into him. "I don't care if you told me it was full of Yogo Sapphires, they would still turn you away. Those kinds of people are signing contracts with High Nobles, Dukes, Duchesses, and the King. What are you to them?"

"That's why I brought my lute," Hardin said. He tried to summon back the flirtatious Northern girl from the ship, but that version of Sasja seemed to have evaporated.

"You've got the right smile to be a successful bard, I'll give you that," she said, her words carrying an almost maternal sadness now, "but I'd wager you can't sing a tune. You should go back home to Doran before you get chewed up and spit out. Lamar isn't a place for a Doranian pacifist. This is a kingdom that runs on wealth won in battles and has violent contests for control over the territory where Hyalites are won and lost, and not by negotiations and peace treaties."

The challenge in her words ignited something in him. "I *can* hold a tune. Listen," he declared, swinging the lute around on its strap with practiced grace. His fingers found the strings as naturally as breathing, and when he strummed the first chord.

"In the Frost Fang Mountains where no warrior dares tread,
Through the biting wind that turns hope to dread.
I passed through storms and mountains old,
To seek a treasure of untold gold."

A shadow fell across them, ending Hardin's smooth voice with the summons of worn leather and sharpened steel.

An orc more threatening than the others in Stormwatch materialized from the intersection. He was like a spirit of violence given flesh. His copper cloak clung tightly around thick shoulders. The massive sword across his back a clear warning. His mossy weathered green skin, his grim face broader than any man's, with tusks that gleamed like ivory daggers above his thick bottom lip. Leather armor creaked across his shoulders, vambraces guarded forearms thick as tree branches.

Each heartbeat stretched as the orc moved with impossible speed. One moment Hardin was singing, the next he was stumbling aside, his song cut short as Sasja was swept up in a single powerful arm. Her scream shattered the afternoon like breaking glass, her kicks futile against her captor's iron grip. The street erupted in gasps and cries as others froze in shock.

"Sasja!" Hardin cried out, his fingers clawing at the orc's copper cloak.

With strength that seemed to defy nature, the orc launched them both over the intersection. Fifteen feet of space vanished beneath his leap as though it were nothing more than a crack in the road. He landed on the far side as graceful as a cat. In the space of a breath, the orc and Sasja vanished into the shadows of the opposing alley, leaving behind nothing but echoes and the lingering notes of their unfinished song.

9

THE POUR HOUSE

"Hey, stop that orc!" Hardin shouted, but the street swallowed his words. Not a single soul moved to help. Humans, elves, dwarves, and orcs alike shied away from his alarm. There was an unspoken rule here, one that he thought he'd escape by coming to Lamar. When it came to confrontations with anyone wearing Nordraven's copper colors, common folk weren't willing to fight. But Hardin had stood by watching Nordraven imposing its will on his people for too long. He wouldn't let them push him around anymore.

He took off at a sprint, crossing the intersection, and angling into the alley where the orc had stolen off with Sasja. Bystanders parted before him like subjects before their king. Ahead, the bulky Northern orc moved with surprising grace, each footfall purposeful as he headed toward the port district.

Is this Monsanto's doing? The possibility that Monsanto held contracts with the four allied kingdoms of Nordraven sent a chill down Hardin's spine. He'd heard that merchants near the border maintained such ties. But an orc of this caliber, this was an expense for protection far beyond what a simple clothing and mercantile merchant could possibly afford.

He said Sasja had stolen from him before, Hardin remembered. His thoughts went to the blood-red pendant suspended from a golden chain around her neck. Something about that jewel seemed off; perhaps it had been stolen and the underlying reason for this hostile encounter.

The orc ducked into a covered entryway, his copper cloak trailing through the darkened alcove. Hardin slowed as he approached. Two more massive forms materialized from the shadows. More orcs with mottled green skin. All wore the same copper cloaks, the mark of loyalty to Nordraven's army.

This definitely isn't just about the stolen clothes, Hardin thought. *But what do they want with Sasja?* he considered, knowing soldiers like these were usually fighting wars against Lamar's Army east of the Everburning Forest where firestorms were smaller and less frequent. Hardin didn't notice any Nordraven Paragon or Knight heading the group either.

"Where did you take her?" Hardin demanded, attempting to push past the living wall of muscle before him. The sharp scent of orc pierced his nose, made all the more offensive by the mixture of leather, steel, and animal fur.

With a snort, one of the orcs brushed him aside as if the gesture was as casual as shewing a fly. In reality, Hardin felt like he was being struck by a tree branch.

"Where did he come from?" the taller soldier rumbled, his twin ivory tusks making his Northern accent sound even harsher.

The shorter one shrugged, muscles rippling beneath his cloak. "He shouldn't have been able to pass the wards. Maybe they weren't done right."

Hardin rushed forward again, his body colliding with immovable flesh. The orcs stood like stone pillars, unmoved by his desperate attempt to breach their defense. The larger one, with a rounded gut as hard as iron, seized Hardin and hurled him backward. The rough stone wall caught him, reminding him of his training.

The large-bellied orc leveled his gaze at Hardin. His eyes held an unsettling emptiness, like two pools of midnight black water, stagnant in the quiet depths of the earth. The orc advanced on him.

Remember what Sense Kalu taught you. Don't let your emotions take control. Defend yourself only. The instruction was clear as temple bells. This wasn't just his first fight outside the training dojo. It would also be his first time fighting orcs.

His knee found the orc's belly; the impact sent ripples through solid muscle. Hardin slipped through the orc's attempted headlock. Hardin reset his stance. His feet found purchase. He knew his next move. When the orc reached for him again, Hardin ducked beneath the massive arms, spotting the universal weakness all beings share. His boot crashed down on the orc's foot, and the resulting roar echoed off the alley walls.

The orc's transformation was mesmerizing. His somewhat lax features suddenly came alive with anger, green skin folding into sharp lines of rage. Hardin's slight smile tasted of triumph as he settled back into his defensive stance, his body humming with adrenaline.

The roundhouse kick came as naturally as breathing. His heel connected with the orc's temple. The impact sent the massive figure stumbling, and something electric coursed through Hardin's veins. Why had his people forsaken such formidable arts as Dor Bishdo? The defensive philosophy of Doran suddenly felt like a chain rather than a shield, and for one dangerous moment, the thrill of offensive control tempted him.

But before he could savor his revelation, the shorter orc moved with surprising fluidity. Through the gap, behind the orcs, appeared a sight that stopped Hardin's heart, Sasja's face. Her eyes were wide with an emotion he couldn't quite name. Was it concern? Fear? Or something darker? Then she vanished behind a wall of green flesh as half a dozen more orcs poured into the alley.

Hardin's world dissolved into a chaos of fists and boots. His knuckles found one orc's jaw, a hollow victory before hands like iron lifted him from the ground. The cobblestones rose to meet him with bruising force. Something massive crashed into his back, driving the air from his lungs in a rush that carried with it all his dreams of being a hero. Each kick that followed was a lesson in humility, every stolen breath a reminder of his own mortality. Darkness crept in from the edges of his vision, carrying with it the bitter taste of failure.

"Stop!" Sasja's voice cut through the haze. "Stop it. He isn't a threat to you."

The words hung in the air, weighted with layers of meaning that Hardin's pain-addled mind struggled to grasp. When she spoke, it wasn't with the terror of being a captive, but with authority.

"What's this Doranian worth to you?" she demanded.

"One less Southerner is no bad thing." Another voice joined in. "We should kill him and be done with this."

"He is not why you are here." Sasja's voice changed, her soothing tones giving him some sense of hope.

"We must honor the pact. We're bound by powers that will not let us leave until we are paid a debt. This human will pay with his blood. We'll need a soul for the magus to grant us passage. The human's will do just fine."

"Not with his blood. He will pay with coin. That will satisfy your pact, will it not?" Her interruption cut through their advances, stopping them with the prospect of wealth. The ruby at her throat seemed to be glowing with its own light now. The crimson eye watched Hardin's undoing.

The orc bobbed his massive head. "It will, but this man is nothing, a nobody. Who is offering this payment? You?"

"He has money. Check his belt. You'll find there's a substantial sum of coin there." The practical brutality in her voice was worse than any physical blow he'd endured.

A hand like stone rolled him onto his back. The simple movement sent cascades of pain through his body. The coin purse tore free from his side.

The orc weighed it in his palm, the coins within singing a mournful song. "Lady Sasja spoke true. He's paid his debt. We'll find another soul for the magus' dark magic. Let the welp go. Maybe this Southerner will learn some humility. He can spread the word that it doesn't pay to interfere with Northern business."

This warning passed him by. Hardin focused on something else entirely. *Lady* Sasja. The title echoed in his head, each repetition revealing another layer of deception.

"I will speak to him before we go," Sasja said. Several orcs looked at her quizzically. "To instill the sentiment so others like him know to fear Nordraven," she added.

When she knelt beside him, her familiar scent of sweet herbs and summer winds cut through the metallic tang of his own blood with cruel clarity. The orc who remained to watch loomed like a mountain over them.

Hardin stirred against the cobblestones, pain striking with each movement.

"Don't move. Stay down until we're gone," she murmured. She touched his shoulder, the softness of her presence seeming impossible to her betrayal. The burlap sack of stolen clothes settled beside him with a gentle wrinkle. "Here, take this as a peace offering. Do not return it to Monsanto's shop or pay him any compensation. Monsanto is a Northern swine. He is in deep with the King of Wintermire. Everything he earns goes toward funding syndicates that cause unrest in this region of Lamar."

Her tone sounded honest, her words felt genuine, yet how could he trust anything she said now? "You, Nordraven, a magus, why?" he managed through the pain, each breath a reminder of how far he'd fallen.

"If you knew anything about Nordraven magi, you would know that I can't tell you. You shouldn't have tried to intervene. You're lucky they didn't kill you to use your life energy for his evil magic."

Then she bent down, and time seemed to freeze. Her lips met his. The pain of his cracked lips became a counterpoint to the intoxicating softness of her mouth, creating a moment suspended between agony and bliss. When she pulled away, the loss felt like a small death.

"Know that our time together from Dagger's Landing to Stormwatch was real," she whispered, her words like a confession. The ruby at her throat pulsed once in warning and the significance of it made sense. "I'm truly sorry I had to do this to you. You should've gone when I told you to. Lamar is no place for a man like you."

Hardin's mind cleared enough to see the truth that had been there all along. Her capture hadn't been a capture at all; it was a homecoming. These Northern brutes weren't her captors but her escort, and the beautiful, vulnerable girl he'd met on the ship was merely a role she'd played to perfection. A role she'd been forced into, bound by a curse, fueled by the illegal use of magic contained in her pendant. Just like the curse that held his hometown captive.

"I... I don't—"

The words died in his throat as reality splintered around him.

"Don't speak. Stay down until I'm gone." Her voice held genuine urgency now. "Trust me, if you try to rescue me again, they will kill you. Please don't follow me." Something defiant stirred in her eyes. "Go to the Pour House at the crossroads near the northeast edge of Stormwatch. Ask after Cheyanne. She can get you home safely and keep Monsanto's thugs from finding you." The ruby around her neck flared. "I'm sorry, Hardin. I hope you find what you're looking for."

Then she was gone, leaving behind only the ghost of her warmth. Hardin lay there, each breath a reminder of his shattered illusions.

"Wait," he called into the void. But the word fell into silence, as meaningless as his attempts to save her.

Hardin lay there, questioning how she had played him. *But she genuinely seemed surprised when the orc came for her.* Something about her task had changed. Was the Northern wizard, the magus, who held power over her able to sense Sasja's actions the whole time?

A cry rang out from somewhere in the street near the alley and Hardin's mind cleared.

"My money!" he nearly shouted as he re-focused on why he'd been sent to Lamar. This was the very reason, to free his people of a curse keeping his family and loved ones trapped there, toiling in the caves in search for something these Northern magi wanted.

The lute against his back was undamaged, miraculously, a small mercy in a world that had revealed itself to be far more complex and crueler than he'd prepared for. The other two-thirds of his fortune was secure within the wooden instrument, but that wouldn't be enough to afford the help he needed. With teeth gritted against both physical and emotional pain, Hardin forced himself to stand. Each movement was a negotiation with his battered body.

Stubborn as the mountains of Doran, Hardin couldn't let the orcs simply vanish with everything. He pushed open the door through which the orcs had disappeared, determined to recover any of the things he'd lost.

"Give me back my mon—"

He blinked in confusion. The storage room before him was barely larger than a ship's cabin. The space could scarcely hold two orcs, let alone eight and the woman who had rewritten his understanding of truth with a single kiss.

"What?" The question addressing the empty room escaped his lips despite the fact that there was no one present to answer him.

Beyond the room's far wall, no more than ten feet distant, a yellow light seeped through cracks in a wooden door. The latch moved with deliberate patience, and as it swung inward, Hardin found himself face-to-face with a dwarf whose appearance seemed both perfectly ordinary and utterly impossible in its timing.

The elderly dwarf's lantern illuminated a worn carpenter's hammer in the dwarf's other hand.

"Get outta here, ya hoodlum," the dwarf growled, his furry brows drawn together.

Hardin retreated through the doorway, his mind a battlefield of competing realities. The gang of orcs had vanished, leaving behind only dust-laden shelves and the lonely sentinels of half-burned candles.

"I said, get, or I'll raise cane, youngster," the dwarf threatened.

Stiffly, Hardin backed into the alley, keeping one eye on the hammer in the dwarf's hand. Each step sent waves of pain through his body, though the real torment went deeper.

"Where the ash did they go?" The question emerged as barely more than a whisper.

The answer came as the realization raised the hairs on his neck. Something was watching him, something that existed in the cracks between his known world and the reality Sasja had exposed.

An orange light flickered into existence behind him. "No," he said closing his eyes and fleeing into the street. His heel caught on a raised cobblestone and he found himself sprawling across a wooden cart.

"Hey, watch it," snapped a woman whose weathered face twisted into a scowl as she swatted at him with a leather-bound book. Her crooked nose, spotted and pitted from years of hard drinking, seemed to shift slightly when he wasn't looking directly at it.

"Sorry," Hardin mumbled. The vendor's face transformed as he examined her more closely.

"Are you okay, lad? Someone rob you?"

The spark showered to life above her head, swirling with terrible purpose as it began to form into a small flaming woman. "No," Hardin choked out, squeezing his eyes shut against the impending horror. He fled back into the alley where he'd been beaten, where at least the pain had been honest and straightforward.

Not the sign of the fire fae, he pleaded silently, pressing his eyes closed so tight that small white lights blossomed. He froze in place, willing the ambassador of the night court away, praying it wouldn't appear to herald his death. But some truths cannot be denied.

The scream he'd heard just after the Northern orcs' disappearance revealed itself with terrible understanding. They hadn't simply vanished through a hidden passage. The magus the orcs mentioned had used forbidden magic. Illegal, immoral, dark magic at the cost of an innocent life. One powerful enough to transport eight full-grown orcs and Sasja to another location.

From the street beyond, the first cries for help rose like a lit funeral pyre. Hardin's heart clenched, knowing with terrible certainty what those people were finding. Since Sasja had paid the orcs with a third of his community's savings, his life was spared. The spell that created the portal picked another at random, heralding the fire fae and death.

"Someone get help!" The shout echoed off the surrounding walls. Hardin knew with certainty that nothing could help them now. The evil magic had claimed the life of whoever had fallen victim to the magus' power.

Warning bells tolled from Storm Keep, a signal triggered no doubt by the wards protecting the city. Illegal magic had been used. Armored soldiers, Knights, and perhaps a Paragon would be investigating shortly.

Hardin stumbled through the alley. There the burlap sack rested, and something hit him. He wondered why Sasja, someone being forced into operating by a Northern magus' curse, would steal them for him? Perhaps it was a symbol of freedom, an attempt for her to do something for someone else without being commanded under pain of extreme retribution. In that moment, he decided to keep them and collected the stolen clothes. They were an anchor to a world that was revealing itself to be anything but ordinary.

He ventured out into the city, keeping his head low when he passed guards rushing toward the streets near the port as he continued toward the northeast edge of Stormwatch. The thick stone walls of Storm Keep rose in the near distance, imposing, yet somehow less substantial now that he had witnessed the careless act of dark magic.

Is there still enough to hire a hero from Storm Keep? he wondered.

The coin secured within his lute remained. A third of his fortune was now lost to Northern hands. The stolen clothes were poor compensation, but sentimental now that he was beginning to understand Sasja's position. Even if he sold them, they wouldn't come close to making up the difference.

Hardin decided his goal had not changed. When he left home, finding someone to lift a curse had seemed a straightforward quest. Now, he understood that straightforward paths existed only in children's tales.

The first moon crested over the horizon. Its light fell on Hardin as he neared the crossroads at the edge of the city. Astral City called to him, its promise of dragonriders and heroes still resonating despite the change in his funds.

When he finally reached the intersection, he read the sign on the building painted in white letters: The Pour House Inn and Caravan. Sasja's voice echoed in the chambers of his memory. "Ask after Cheyanne. She can help you more than I ever could."

He pulled open the door that led to a lobby. Upholstered leather chairs with sunken seats were arranged around a small table. They looked worn but to Hardin they appeared warm and inviting. Several books lay open on the table. Their pages ruffled slightly though no breeze stirred the air.

The stillness in the lobby was disrupted by a rustling from behind the desk.

A young woman materialized from behind the counter, rising with the silence of a ghost. Her skin was a few shades lighter than Hardin's own, her height two inches more than his. She was built like a weapon, strong, athletic, but with surprisingly feminine features and a beauty that rivaled Sasja's. The angles of her face were sharp, almost elf-like, though her ears were round like a human. Her oval green eyes burned with an intelligence that seemed to pierce the veil between ordinary and extraordinary. Their gaze fell on him from beneath a wild mane of umber hair that defied both gravity and convention.

Like her hair, the woman's clothes told a story opposite her beauty and composure. She wore rags that might have been borrowed from a destitute farmer, all stained and torn.

The Lost Dragonrider of Lamar 123

The pack on her back was of a quality to rival Monsanto's leatherwork, its fullness hinting at secrets. The weapons she wore, two daggers, were arranged with careful precision, and suggested she was more than ready to defend herself.

"Have any rooms available?" he ventured, leaning against the counter as much for support as casual affect. "Preferably single bed," he added.

"Sorry, can't help you," she replied, continuing her search through a drawer.

"What?"

"I said I can't help you with that," she repeated.

"Don't you have any vacancies?"

"I don't work here. I just arrived. I'm looking for a room key."

"Are you Cheyanne?"

"No, they call me Lark."

"Lark?"

"That's right, like this necklace," she said, revealing her clavicle where the golden pendant rested.

"I see," he managed, allowing his gaze to drift to the golden lark that clung there. "I'm Hardin Morningstar."

10

STORMWATCH

Lark emerged from the edge of the forest, her skin tingling as she crossed the threshold between shadow and light. The world unfurled before her, each detail sharp and vivid in the crisp afternoon air. Rolling hills swept down from the woods toward the distant coast. The slopes were adorned with widespread fields, each a different shade of harvest gold and fading green. The snowcapped mountains ran parallel to the coast, their peaks wreathed in clouds as if supporting the weight of the sky.

Farms dotted the valleys, their neat plots giving way to the organized chaos of civilization. Buildings crowded together in the distance. Structures pressed against one another like saplings racing to dominate an opening, all vying for the sunlight. Above it all, a castle of dark granite commanded the horizon. Its towers pierced the heavens with great golden spires and domes. Glittering windows caught the sun's rays, transforming the fortress into a beacon of cut gems. The city wall, weathered but proud, encircled it all. Paths wound through the urban sprawl like strokes in a painting, each one leading to new ground.

After days of traversing the fringe of the Everburning Forest, a wilderness spanning the continent between the four kingdoms of Nordraven to the north, and the Kingdom of Lamar to the south, Lark had grown used to being alone... Nearly alone. The small woman who defied gravity by flying wherever she wished, was rot with flames like a creature of the fire, and whose red dress accentuated her heavenly form like a reincarnation of a goddess, continued to guide her. However, the sight of such bustling civilization made Lark anxious.

I don't remember seeing this many people, she thought, her heart quickening at the prospect of entering the fray.

The golden pendant at her throat suddenly warmed, its heat familiar yet different. It was more intense than the gentle warmth that typically heralded the fire fae's presence. The sensation beat against her skin like a second heart, resonating with another source of energy nearby.

"Nix?" she called out. The forest seemed to hold its breath, waiting.

A flicker of golden light caught her eye from within the trees, but something about it felt... wrong. Different. Larger. Lark stepped into the forest once more, leaving behind the well-worn dirt road. The shadows between the trees deepened. Then she saw it. A figure darker than the surrounding forest emerged from among the large ferns in the undergrowth.

Lark caught her breath as her mind struggled to process its size. This was no small woman from the fae realm. This creature dominated the space between the trees. As it moved, light caught its scales, each one flashing with the same golden radiance that preceded Nix's appearances but manifesting a hundredfold. An inexplicable pull drew her forward, stronger than fear, stronger than reason. It was the same magnetic attraction she'd felt during the firestorm.

Her feet carried her closer. The creature before her stood at least ten feet tall, its body broader than two warriors standing shield-to-shield. Its scales clicked together with the precision of master-crafted armor, each plate catching and reflecting light like polished gold. It remained as still as a statue, a living monument to some arcane beast.

"Nix, did you transfor—"

The words died as the creature moved.

Its serpentine neck curved gracefully, bringing a horned head low enough that one massive golden eye caught a shaft of sunlight. That eye fixed upon her with an intelligence that felt older than the forest, its pupil contracting slightly as it studied her. Her necklace vibrated with increasing intensity, its heat building until it nearly burned, as if recognizing kin.

"Dragon," she breathed, the word carrying the weight of legend.

The peaceful moment shattered at the sound of approaching travelers: hooves striking earth, metal clicking against metal, wheels creaking their protests about the road's uneven surface. The dragon moved unimaginably smoothly, dropping below the cover of the undergrowth. Its retreat made less sound than a falling leaf, though Lark caught one final glimpse of its tail, thick as her torso, slipping above the ferns. The golden scales caught the light one final time before the magnificent creature vanished into the shadows of the forest.

As the dragon's presence faded, the vibration in her necklace subsided to a gentle hum. Then, with a familiar burst of flame that momentarily turned the air to summer, Nix materialized beside her, the woman's fiery glow a comfort after such an overwhelming encounter.

"Nix, did you see that?" she whispered.

"I didn't see it, but I could feel its presence," she said, twirling excitedly with her red dress of flames spitting out sparks. She twirled so fast and excitedly that her glow flared bright like a beacon.

The approaching wagon grew louder. Reality reasserted itself. Lark moved just off the road, her hand finding the reassuring grip of her dagger. Nix hovered above the ferns near her shoulder, her warmth spreading through Lark's chest.

"Nix, take cover. You'll give us away."

Nix swam through the air next to the road, curious about the approaching company.

"They're going to see you," Lark warned again, but Nix wasn't listening.

Lark scrambled to subdue her, waving to try and shoo her away before the approaching wagon came into view. In the effort, Lark lost her footing, catching her boot on an exposed root. She tumbled unceremoniously into the road, the mundane world rushing back to meet her with all its solid certainty.

"Whoa," a man's voice called from the wagon.

Lark found her footing at the edge of the road. Her dagger gleamed with a cold purpose in her hand, its familiar weight grounding her as her attention split between searching for Nix and studying the speaker. The dwarf who addressed her sat like a carved mountain in the driver's seat; his thick red beard masked his hardened jaw. His bald head bore tattoos of dwarven runes. Three parallel scars carved paths across his skull. His keen eyes glared through brows as dense as brambling brush, carrying the sharp assessment of one who had seen too much to trust easily.

The dwarf's wide-knuckled hands, marked with the calluses of both craft and combat, moved with swiftly as he wrapped his fingers around an ornate war hammer. The weapon itself was a masterwork of dwarven craft, its head etched with spiraling patterns, its handle wrapped in leather darkened by years of use and care.

"Name yourself and your allegiances," he demanded.

Lark held her tongue, weighing each detail of his appearance with the careful attention of one who had learned survival through observation. The dwarf wore studded leather armor that bore the marks of regular use and careful maintenance. Chainmail glinted beneath it like fish scales in deep water. A round shield hung on the wagon's exterior; its surface decorated with runes that matched those tattooed on his skull.

No copper cloak, she noted, feeling some tension ease from her shoulders.

"What are you doing out here, lurking at the edge of the forest?" he asked.

"I—" she began, but her words faltered as Nix darted through the wagon window like a stray ember. A warm glow, reminiscent of hearth-fire, briefly illuminated the wagon interior through the canvas covering.

"Answer me. Are you from Nordraven or are you a citizen of Lamar?" The question came sharp as struck flint.

Nix emerged from the opposite window, her flame-spun dress casting dancing shadows across the dwarf's weathered features as she hovered above him, though he showed no sign of seeing the ethereal display.

"Is there anyone in there?" Lark asked, watching Nix's movements.

The fae woman shook her head, her fiery hair rippling in its living flame.

"Do you understand what I said?" Lark pressed, mesmerized by Nix's emboldened nature.

"Are you calling me stupid?" the dwarf barked, his grip tightening on the war hammer until his knuckles went white. The weapon seemed to respond to his anger, a subtle warmth emanating from its runes.

"What? Er, no. I wasn't talking to you," Lark replied, suddenly aware of how crazed she must appear.

The dwarf's brow furrowed, his quick glances over each shoulder careful and practiced. "There's nobody there. Just us, like I thought," he declared, his gaze passing through Nix as though she were nothing more than warm air.

Nix floated to Lark's side, her voice carrying the gentle melody of summer wind. "He's right, it's just us out here."

"It's just us," she replied to Nix.

"What's wrong with you?" the dwarf asked, his words cutting through her wonder.

Lark's attention rebounded between the dwarf, the luminescent form of Nix, and the shadow-wrapped section of forest where the dragon had appeared. The magic of the moment clung to the air, making everything feel slightly unreal.

"Answer the question or so help me, I'll—"

"I have no allegiances that I'm aware of," Lark interjected, finally focusing fully on the dwarf. The words tasted of truth on her tongue.

"Not many people can say that honestly. You have no allies?"

"I may not have allies, but I've made an enemy of Nordraven. I warn you, dwarf, if you're loyal to the North and take hostilities against me you'll be putting yourself in grave danger."

The dwarf's grin split his beard exposing teeth stained by years of pipe-smoke and strong drink. "Any enemy of Nordraven is a friend of mine." He set down the war hammer, though it remained within easy reach, its runes still pulsing with latent power. "What are you doing out here all alone and without a horse?"

"I'm headed to the city."

"The city, ya say?"

She nodded.

"I'm headed there myself." He scratched his beard studying Lark with a stoney gaze. Finally, he broke like split granite, "Do you want a ride?"

"To the city?"

"No, to the Northern kings themselves," he said, sarcasm dripping from his words. "Of course, into the city, you wing-bat. It's a ways yet and I could use the company. Been on the road a few days without anyone to talk to. It can make an old dwarf like me a little loopy, although after running into you, I might not be so bad after all."

Nix spun excitedly, her flaming dress flaring out at the knees as she twirled. "Yes, yes, go with him," she said in her honey sweet voice.

"When did you learn to be so trusting of strangers?" Lark said to the fire fae.

"What was that girl? I didn't hear you; you're going to have to speak up. I have some hearing damage. Used to work in the mines," the dwarf said.

"I wasn't speaking to you," Lark clarified, this time loud enough for the hardened dwarf to hear.

"I can't explain it, but I think he can help with your task," Nix said.

Lark fixed her gaze on Nix, her embodiment of living flame casting ephemeral shadows that only Lark could see. The peculiar doubling of reality, having Nix hover mere inches from the dwarf while he stared unseeing through her radiant form, sent a disconcerting shiver down Lark's spine.

Lark nervously weighed her choices, the path ahead fragmented like light through crystal. The coastal city's gray Keep beckoned, but something felt wrong about following Nix's advice to go with the dwarf.

Nix's presence flickered with increasing urgency. The fae's trust in the dwarf reverberated through their strange bond, but Lark had deeper questions.

"You're not with the North?" Lark said, approaching the driver's bench.

"If I were, and you named yourself my enemy like you did, we'd already be fighting, and you'd be in a world of pain."

"No, I wouldn't," she said flatly.

He leaned away from her, his serious expression widening to a grin. "You're strange, and I like that. Not afraid to call yourself an enemy of the North. I think we'll get along just fine. My name is Ezra Steelbinder." He offered his iron grip to assist Lark into the cart.

"Thanks, but no thanks. I can get to Astral City on my own." She sheathed her dagger and turned toward the coast.

"If you're trying to get to Astral City, you're going the wrong way," Ezra said.

Lark stopped. "That right there," she pointed to the castle near the coast, "is the Vermillion Keep. The city there is Astral City."

"That's a Keep alright, but it's not the Vermillion Keep. You should've deciphered that by the castle's gray walls. They aren't red like they are in Astral City."

"That's not Astral City?"

"No. That's Stormwatch and Storm Keep," Ezra said. "Astral City is on the northeast side of those mountains, nestled in a valley just south of this forest," he pointed with his bearded chin toward the mountains off to their left.

"My mistake. I'd best be on my way," Lark said.

"If you take this road, it will be a few weeks on foot. Dangerous and hard weeks at that. There are firestorms that flare up from nowhere, there's all manner of fae creatures crawling through the forest, including wild dragons, and the Paragons are about to renegotiate their contracts with the King. That always increases tensions over whose troops are patrolling which regions of the forest. Needless to say, I wouldn't go that way if I were you," Ezra said.

Nix floated down before her like a flaming ember. "Go with him. He is friendly and knows a lot about the world."

Like you know anything about who to trust in this world, Lark thought.

"Yes, I do." Nix said.

Lark withheld the insult she'd prepared in response.

"That's right. When your guard is down, I can hear what you're thinking," Nix said. "You really should be better about keeping your thoughts to yourself."

"The fastest way to Astral City is by going back to the crossroads at Stormwatch," Ezra interrupted. "From there, you can take the road to the base of the Astral Range and follow it around through Fletcher's Passage. From there it's two days south. The next caravan leaves in the morning. You're welcome to join in if you can pay."

"The crossroads?" she asked.

"Aye. It's at the edge of the city. I'm going there if you want a ride," Ezra confirmed, making the offer again.

Lark looked back into the forest where the wild dragon had been.

"Go with him," Nix insisted.

"Alright," she said, giving in to Nix and Ezra both. "I'll ride into the crossroads, but that's as far I'm going with you."

Lark made for the wagon door.

"Can't ride in there. You'll have to sit up front with me," Ezra said.

"Is there someone in there?" Lark asked.

"No, but this wagon has rules. Paying customers only for the wagon. Seeing as you don't have much of anything on you, you can't afford to ride in the wagon. Besides, I like to keep an eye on strangers who ride with me. Sit up here and we can get to know each other."

Nix bobbed along happily. Lark reluctantly climbed up onto the driver's seat and sat down on the bench next to Ezra. The dwarf relaxed the reins and clicked his tongue to get the horses moving again.

"So," Ezra said, breaking the silence. "What's your name?"

"Lark," she answered.

"Like that bird on your necklace."

"That's right."

"Where are you from, Lark?"

"A village, few days back that way," she said, thumbing over her shoulder.

"Does the village have a name?"

She shrugged.

"You're not from around here, are you?"

"What gave it away, that I don't know where Astral City is or that I can't name the village I came from?"

"No need to get testy about it. I only ask because anyone who's seen a map of Lamar would know the difference between Stormwatch and Astral City. What's your reason for wanting to go there, if you don't mind me asking."

"I made a promise to someone that I would go."

"I think I understand," Ezra said.

"Do you think he knows about the Hyalite?" Nix asked from her shoulder.

How would he know about the Hyalite? Lark thought.

"I think he is a warlock," Nix said.

Does that mean he can sense it?

"I've had my run-ins with your type before," Ezra was saying. "Seen a lot since my days as an instructor at the Astral City Paragon Academy. You were part of that village that was burned down a ways back east, weren't you? Since most of the soldiers are off fighting in the eastern region of the forest, you thought you could go to the city and try to get a Knight of the Vermillion Keep to come and help. Am I right?"

"How do you figure that?"

"I'll enlighten you, only because I know I'm right. You were a fire wheat harvester, one of the best in your village based on your age, your athletic build, and those daggers you wear. Your village didn't venture very far away from their settlement, other than when you and your townsfolk would go harvesting in the forest. If they had, you would know where the Vermillion Keep was. With the recent chaos caused by Nordraven, I'd guess you are the last surviving member of your home. You're angry at the North and want justice. You're going to Astral City to get help from either a Knight or a Paragon. Either that or you're going to join one of their troops and likely get sent across the kingdom to wage war in the northeast where the firestorms aren't as destructive. Whichever it is, revenge won't bring them back. What's in the past is behind us."

Lark held her tongue, letting his words melt over her like warm honey. He wasn't completely right, but the dwarf had guessed many of the aspects of her experience that she could remember.

"If you don't mind my observations, it seems like you don't have much money to your name. Looks to me like it's what you got on, your pack there, and that fancy dagger, all of which you'll most likely be needing. You might have better luck finding help from Storm Keep. The heroes for hire in Astral City are costly," Ezra said.

"Could the Paragons of Storm Keep defeat a Nordraven dragonrider?" she asked.

"They have many talented Knights, a few elves and dwarves, others from the Magi Order, but I doubt you could afford the Paragon who would be able to compete with a Northern rider, regardless of the Keep," Ezra said.

"Can any in Stormwatch win a Hyalite or a set of Yogos from an enemy of the North, yes or no?" she asked.

"Tel Roan was one of the few who always could. Now that he is gone. I can't confidently say if any of the Paragons left in Northern Lamar could go up and consistently win against the best of the Northern riders. It will skew the Hyalite and Yogo collection to their favor and I don't know how that will affect Lamar in the long run. For the war effort. It would mean a shift. Dragonriders would be able to fully invest their efforts to deciding the fate of the war. Since I've been alive, they've always focused on finding and collecting Hyalites."

"If money weren't an object, I'd contract a dragonrider Paragon to wipe out the Nordraven kings for what they did to me. They took everything I knew," Lark said.

"Revenge is a dish that is best served cold, but no matter how it's served, it can never undo what's already come to pass," Ezra said.

What if it's the only thing on the menu.

As twilight approached, the sun bled golden light across the horizon. The dwindling rays illuminated the clouds in swaths of flame reminiscent of Nix's transformations. The city awakened with flickering lanterns. Soon, an inn with a dimly lit sign in front announced the Pour House, its L-shape forming a shadow that stretched across the intersection, backlit by the purple-stained sky. The wooden sign creaked gently in the evening breeze.

"Thanks for the ride," Lark said, disembarking toward the packed gravel intersection.

"Hang on. Where are you staying?" Ezra stopped her.

"Don't know yet. I'll find some place."

"You can stay here, at the Inn."

"You don't have to buy me a room."

"I wasn't planning on it," he replied.

Lark's breath caught as her gaze fixed upon the war hammer held firm in his calloused hands, its leather grip worn smooth by years of use. A primal instinct rippled across her skin, raising the hairs on the back of her neck as she met his cold stare. The moment teetered like a scale balanced on a knife's edge, her decision to strike or dodge vanishing as Ezra's deep voice rumbled forth.

"I'm partners with the elf who owns this establishment," he replied in a harmless tone.

Lark's shoulders sagged with relief, the taut coil of angst within her releasing.

"You don't need to pay. Just go into the main office there, the door should unlock for you. Grab a room key from behind the front desk." As she turned away, he brought his great hammer to rest over his shoulder. "I'm leading the caravan to Astral City in the morning. We meet at sunrise."

"I can't afford the caravan," Lark said.

"We'll discuss it in the morning," he grinned, the creases at the corners of his eyes as his beard turned up in a smile hinted at hidden intensions.

"Let's go," Lark said to Nix, her feelings toward Ezra's kindness as murky as the void of her past.

Nix flew toward the paneled wooden door. Lark heard a click as the fire fae opened it.

"You can unlock doors?" she asked.

"Not regular doors, only these kinds," Nix replied with an innocent giggle.

"What does that mean?"

"That I'm special and you can thank me later," Nix winked.

Lark passed through the empty lobby, only looking long enough to ensure no threats would assail her from darkened corners. "We need to talk," she said, attention shifting to the drawers behind the front desk.

"About what?" Nix came to rest in a seated position, hovering several inches over the drawer Lark opened.

"You have some explaining to do," Lark said.

"I do?"

"Yes. You had decided I needed to follow Ezra without me properly considering it."

"I can't explain it. It just felt right," she said.

Lark sighed, "What about the dragon I saw in the forest. You didn't give us a chance to see if it was trying to show me something."

"Oh, I forgot about the dragon," Nix said, twisting her fingers through her flaming red hair. "I don't know why he was so interested in you."

The sound of someone's throat-clearing shattered the moment like a stone through glass. Behind the desk, Nix disappeared in a spectacular display of elemental chaos. Her flame-spun figure collapsing inward as she winked out in a cascade of golden sparks. The sudden absence of Nix's warmth left the air and Lark's pendant feeling unnaturally cold.

She rose from behind the counter, the movement carrying the startled energy of a disturbed animal, only to find herself facing a young man. His lute hung across his back, its polished wood glistening in the lanternlight. Evidence of violence told of his misfortune in vivid detail. Dried blood traced a dark constellation down from his nose. The taint of a recent altercation in a back alley shone all over his worn clothing. A crimson stain had bloomed across his once-white shirt. One eye had swollen shut, the yellow swelling around it deepened in shades of purple that faded to a black arch contouring his high cheekbone. He held a simple burlap sack that sagged to the ground.

"Have any rooms available? Preferably single bed," he said, his voice cracking as though he was forcing himself to be bold.

"Sorry, can't help you," Lark replied, dropping below the counter to hunt out the room keys.

"What?" he said in surprise.

"I said I can't help you with that," Lark reported, not bothering to meet his gaze again. She didn't work there.

"Don't you have any vacancies?"

"I don't work here. I just arrived. I'm looking for a room key."

"Are you Cheyanne?"

"No, they call me Lark."

"Lark?"

"That's right, like this necklace," she said, annoyed and in disbelief of how clueless this young man seemed to be.

"I see," he said.

Lark found a key in the drawer, took it, and looked up. She noticed his gaze lifting sharply from the necklace.

He straightened, a touch of rose coloring his cheeks. "I'm Hardin Morningstar."

11

THE CARAVAN

For an instant, when Lark took him in a second time, she was reminded of her recurring memory. For a blip, she wondered if this could be the striking half-elf from that vision. Though handsome, Hardin's presence felt quite different from the man she repeatedly saw in that snippet of memory. That stranger was green-eyed like her, dark-haired, muscular and armored. His ears came to short points that protruded from his shaggy hair. He was lying flat on his back, staring up from the ground, unmoving as Lark stood over him with a Hyalite in one hand and a brismil sword in the other. But Hardin was not that man. For one thing, he was not half elf.

As he stated his name, Lark's fingers brushed unconsciously against her pendant. She assessed this Hardin Morningstar. He'd been in a fight, clearly, but why? All he had was a lute and burlap sack full of clothing. He didn't even have a knife on his belt. He was lean, tan-skinned, dark-eyed, and had a wispy mustache over his upper lip. He was shorter than Lark by two inches and had the look of a young man who wasn't looking for trouble, but trouble found him anyway.

The empty lobby grew awkwardly silent. Hardin cleared his throat.

"Is someone after you? It was, Hardin, right?" Lark asked.

"That's right, and not anymore. It was just a bit of bad luck. I'll be fine. Lark, right?"

"Like the bird," she nodded. "You said you wanted a room?" Her fingers found the iron keys in the drawer.

"Yep. I'll settle up with the owner in the morning."

"At sunrise," she said, gesturing toward the wagon outside. "His name's Ezra."

"I thought it was Cheyanne?" Hardin said.

"They're partners. Ezra's taking a caravan to Astral City in the morning," Lark said.

"To the Vermillion Keep?" he asked, his eyes growing wider, reflecting an inner light.

"You're heading there, too?" she asked.

Without answering, Hardin's gaze fell to the key she'd placed on the wooden counter. As his fingers closed around it, something surged through Lark like a struck bell, bringing with it the ghost-image of another man, another lute, another time. The memory burned bright as a falling star before fading to dust.

"Thanks," he said, turning toward the hallway door.

"Have we met before?" Lark called after him, trying to grasp the memory that danced just beyond her reach.

Hardin paused in the doorway and glanced over his shoulder. The lanternlight caught his profile, casting half his face in shadow. "Not unless you've ever been west of Dagger's Landing."

As he disappeared down the hall, warmth bloomed in her necklace. Lark looked down to find Nix had materialized, her presence a comfort against the growing mysteries of her past. Lark took a key and climbed the creaking stairs to her own room.

The Lost Dragonrider of Lamar 141

The chamber was small but sufficient, with a sturdy bed and a window that faced the darkened rural sprawl. She closed the wooden shutters against the night and placed her bag on the bed with reverent care. Her fingers found the Hyalite within. Touching it sent shivers of recognition through her bones. In the darkness of her satchel, it glowed with a blue light that seemed to breathe, each gentle wave of illumination matching the rhythm of her heartbeat. She stared into its depths, hoping for answers.

"Did you feel that something was off about that man?" Nix's voice chimed like crystals in the wind.

"He seemed vaguely familiar. I could've sworn that I knew him from somewhere, but I can't be sure. He didn't recognize me, though," Lark said.

"He wasn't like the others," Nix said, her form flickering slightly.

"What do you mean?"

"There was something about his aura that didn't feel like the people from the village. He was human right?"

"People's auras feel different to you?" Lark asked, gaining the sense that Nix had picked up on this when first assessing Hardin. The reason why she disappeared as soon as she heard him speak.

"They're different for each race. Humans' auras usually feel very passionate . Dwarves are grounded and firm. Elves are faint, and hard to sense. But his was, like something from before, but I'm having difficulty remembering," the fae trailed off as though her memories were shrouded in mist as well.

"He seemed human enough to me."

"Yes, I think he is, but his aura.... It was different," Nix said.

"You're confusing me; how was his aura different?"

"It's hard to explain. It's like looking at a painting where someone used all the wrong colors. The shapes were familiar, but they didn't look quite right," she responded.

The necklace trickled with warmth against Lark's throat as she asked, "He avoided answering when I asked him about the Vermillion Keep. Do you think he knows about the Hyalite?"

Nix's form dimmed. "Anyone who knows you have a Hyalite will try to take it from you or kill you. Especially the people you took it from."

"Do you know who I took it from?" Lark asked, feeling foolish for not having thought to ask the fae earlier.

"Yes, I think so... or. No, that's not right," she said struggling, her form weaving like a candle about to blow out. With an effort, she gasped, and said, "I can't remember. I'm sorry Lark."

"You can't remember either? You knew me from before, didn't you?"

Nix's contemplative silence filled the room before she nodded, her movement leaving trails of firelight. "Yes. I have known you a long time, I think."

"Can you remember who I am?" The question hung suspended between them for a moment.

Nix twisted in uncomfortable patters as she fought with the answer. "You are Lark, I am Nix."

"Those aren't our real names, are they?" Lark stated.

Her headshake sent orange light reflecting across the bed sheets.

"Do you know why you led me here instead of to Astral City like you led me to believe?" Lark said, her anger starting to rise.

Instead of answering, Nix drifted across the bed's surface. She was fixated on the Hyalite, its inner light seemed to reach out to her like tendrils of blue flame. Lark found a grip on her emotions, realizing if Nix had been with her from before, perhaps whatever had caused Lark's amnesia may have somehow influenced Nix, too.

"What about the dragon?" Lark asked.

"I don't know him," the fae answered dreamily, still staring at the Hyalite.

"Do you know why the dragon showed itself to me?"

"It wanted to get a better look at you, of course," Nix giggled.

"But it ran away."

"It was spooked by the dwarf."

"What was it doing out there alone?" Lark asked, now considering the dragon she'd heard had gone missing several weeks ago.

"Dragons live in the wild. They're more common where there aren't a lot of people. At least that's how it is in my realm," Nix said, shifting to face Lark again.

"There are dragons where you come from, too?"

"Of course. Where do you think your dragons migrated from, silly? Only, our dragons don't seek out Hyalites and expand their power by bonding with riders," Nix clarified.

"Is that what the dragon was doing, trying to bond with me because of the Hyalite?" Lark asked.

Nix shrugged, sending ripples through her flaming form.

"Ezra doesn't seem to see or hear you like I can. Is that normal?" Lark asked.

"He should be able to, I think. People like you see and hear me," she said.

"What does that mean, someone like me?"

"I can't remember," Nix said, flying within a hand's width from Lark's chest and staring at the gold necklace.

The pendant shared a connection to Nix, its warmth growing as Nix glared at the golden lark. The metal felt alive against Lark's skin, responding to the fae's proximity. Yet when Lark's fingers searched for its clasp to give her some relief, she found only seamless metal.

"What are you doing that for?" Nix asked.

"You can read my mind, can't you?" Lark quipped.

"Only when you're shouting your thoughts at me. When you keep them to yourself it's harder." Her eyes closed in concentration. A moment later, they snapped open with the sharp clarity of revelation. "You can't take the necklace off. It doesn't come off."

"What?" Panic fluttered in Lark's chest like trapped birds as she pulled at the chain, but it remained immovable. The metal thumped like something trapped inside, responding to her distress, and sending waves of warmth through her body that she knew she should recognize.

"Stop it. Why are you doing that?" Nix said, fear in her voice.

"I want to take it off," Lark said, with mounting anxiety.

"You can't," Nix said almost harshly.

"Why not?"

Nix's fiery face wrinkled in her effort to remember.

"If you know what happened to me, why I can't remember anything from before the village, you must tell me," Lark demanded.

"Stop asking or he will—"

Nix's form erupted into a shower of sparks. Her disappearance left the air feeling hollow, incomplete, as if a crucial thread had been pulled from the tapestry of Lark's understanding about the world.

"Nix? Where'd you go?" Lark's voice fell flat in the suddenly empty room.

Only the fading pulse of the necklace against her throat answered, its touch a reminder that she wasn't gone forever, just hiding in another plane of existence.

Exhausted, Lark fell back onto the bed, holding the Hyalite above her. Countless lights danced within its depths. The longer she gazed into it, the more the boundaries between herself and the orb seemed to blur, as if they shared the same pulse, the same breath, the same essence.

When she slept, a dream rose up to meet her like an old friend. The forest in her vision was alive with magic, each fern and tree held centuries of knowledge in its very fiber. The air tasted of pine sap and dew drops.

Tastes in a dream, she thought, *how interesting*.

This time the dragon's presence filled the clearing. Its golden scales caught the filtered sunlight. Each breath it took sent ripples through the magical currents that flowed invisible but tangible between them.

Still in her dream world, their hearts found the same rhythm, an unspoken trust building between them. The dragon's golden eyes held galaxies of wisdom. Lark reached out to touch him and in that suspended moment before contact, she felt a familiar brush against her mind. Consciousness pulled her back like a hand through water, leaving only the phantom warmth of almost-touched dragon scales tingling in her fingertips.

"Whoa," Lark breathed, new surroundings rushing into focus. The room was dark, broken only by the Hyalite's radiance.

With care, she tucked the Hyalite back into her pack. Cool predawn air seeped in through the window, carrying hints of pine smoke and morning frost into the room. The shutters creaked on iron hinges when she opened them to the new day.

"Nix, are you out there?" she whispered, casting out into the darkness. No reply.

Stormwatch sprawled before her, a tapestry of dying lantern-light and emerging dawn. The golden sun crept above the horizon. Lark shed the farmer's clothes and dressed in her stored garments. The tailored clothes fit her perfectly. She wasn't surprised but she still couldn't remember where they'd come from.

The lightweight shirt settled comfortably against her skin, its leaf-stitch patterns flowing from shoulders to elbows. The vest melded seamlessly over it. The fabrics were a masterwork of sea-blue and supple brown leather that moved with her like elven-forged armor. Its high collar embraced her throat where the mysterious necklace hung. Its V-shaped cut allowed for the fluid movement of a practiced fighter. Each button snap gleamed with the subtle sheen of well-worn brass.

Her hands glided over the vest's form-fitting contours, appreciating the craftsmanship that seemed appropriate for both beauty and functionality. The pants continued the theme. The fabric a forest green and soft as a summer breeze where flexibility was needed. They were reinforced with leather worn with a patina from adventures she couldn't recall. Perfectly contouring the full muscular curves of her lower body, they tapered perfectly into her well-worn mid-calf boots.

The leather cuffs clicked into place around her forearms with satisfying finality, securing sleeves that might otherwise betray a crucial moment's movement. The crowning piece, a deep blue cloak, settled across her shoulders with a comforting embrace. Its embroidered autumn leaves were a beautiful mixture of yellow, orange, and red.

Checking her reflection in the age-spotted mirror, Lark saw a warrior clothed in functionality and grace. The daggers she'd managed to collect nestled against her sides and spine like old friends. She twisted her thick umber locks up into a practical bun to complete her transformation from refugee to someone who commanded respect.

The morning air carried the scent of horse and leather as she emerged from the inn onto the front porch. Ezra's voice cut through the dawn. He spoke with authority. Five wagons stood at the ready, their sturdy construction well suited for a journey across Lamar. The large horses were bred for hauling; their muscular frames dwarfed the sleeker Northern warhorses she remembered from the attack.

Her attention was drawn to several fur-clad figures by the stables. Their bearded faces and foreign garb set them apart like wolves among sheep. Something about their presence made Lark's senses tingle. Their gazes lingered too long on her.

"Lark," Ezra announced his approach. "I almost didn't recognize you with those new duds. You look ready and suited for travel."

"About that. I'm not sure I can afford the room for last night. And this trip to Astral City..." she shook her head. "You said they were on the other side of the Astral Range, the northeast end, a few days from Fletcher's Passage," she said pointing to the pink and orange glow of the sunrise in the east, over the Astral Mountains. "I'll walk. I can handle myself if any danger arises."

"Like I said last night, don't worry about the room. It's on me. Cheyanne won't mind as she's not in Stormwatch at the moment. As for the trip, my security team backed out at the last minute. You say you can handle yourself and you've escaped Nordraven soldiers before. Do you think you can handle the work?"

"Work?"

"Yes, I'm asking if you will work for me. Provide security for the caravan. I've got wards set on the wagons. I'll just need to know in advance if there's someone charging up from behind to try to rob us or, fires forbid, we come across a rogue Nordraven troop."

Lark checked after the bearded men near the stables, only to see they had disappeared.

"You're not going to find another guide to Astral City

that's willing to let you go for free, I'll tell you that right now," he added. "But it's up to you. Go it alone, or ride in the rear with us." Ezra made like he was going to leave.

"Are meals included?" Lark stopped him.

He studied her again. "You'd better be worth your weight when it comes to fighting... Sure, the meals are included."

"I'll do it," she said.

"Excellent, you can take the bench seat on top of the rear wagon," he said.

Just then the doors to the inn burst open. Hardin barreled out like he'd been riding a storm front. "Hold the wagons!" he called. "I can pay for passage," he added, waving to gain their attention.

Ezra intercepted him, surprising Lark with his speed. "Hold up, lad. You want passage, you talk to me."

"I need to get to Astral City," he said.

"You're in the right place. We have one more spot if you can pay."

Hardin fished a handful of coins from his pocket and handed them to the dwarf.

Ezra sifted through them, shook his head, and said, "That's not enough."

"What?"

"You're two bronze short."

"That's not what I read on the bulletin while I was paying for my room this morning."

"I set the rates. There's a late fee, and it's two bronzes," Ezra said, crossing his powerful arms.

"Sasja said Cheyanne would help me," he said.

The dwarf drew his mouth to a hard line, tugging the thick cords of his beard. "I don't know no Sasja, but Cheyanne wouldn't appreciate her name being used to trick me."

"Can I pay the two bronzes with something other than

coin?" he asked, slipping the polished lute around and gripping it by the ornately carved neck, ready to play.

"Are you any good?"

"The best west of Dagger's Landing," he said.

"Prove it."

> "In the Frost Fang Mountains where warriors dare to tread,
> Where the biting wind screams with dread.
> I passed through storms and mountains old,
> To seek a treasure of untold gold.
>
> Through icy caves and shadows deep,
> In a place where ancients go to sleep.
> The path was harsh, the nights were long,
> But resolve forced me on."

Ezra's expression didn't change as the crowd leaned closer, eager to hear the next verse and clearly enjoying the production.

> Beyond the moons, where dragons roam,
> I found a place the fae call home.
> With sword in hand, I broke the fold,
> To claim a prize worth more than gold."

"That's good enough, lad," Ezra said, stopping him. "Seems like they approve of your singing. Do it for them after dinners and you can come with us."

"Meals included?" Hardin asked, hope dancing in his almond eyes.

Ezra caught Lark's smirk, then said, "Ah, what the heck, sure, meals included."

"Thank you. You won't regret this."

"You'll join the wagon in the rear," Ezra said. "That's everything and everyone. Find your stations and let's get moving. This caravan isn't going to make it to Astral City by hanging around here."

Each wagon stood as a testament to dwarven craftsmanship. Their wooden frames were carved from timbers undoubtably harvested from the Everburning Forest. They served as moveable cottages for the nomadic warlock. Above each driver's bench, canopies woven with weather-resistant canvas provided shelter from the elements, while doors carved with intricate joining techniques offered multiple escape routes and windows punctuated the wooden chaises.

Ezra's personal wagon crowned the caravan, its second level rising in elegant curves that defied typical dwarven geometric aesthetic.

Warding runes were carved into each door. They pulsed with subtle power, their meanings hidden in the secrets of dwarven literature. The magic within them created a web of protection that Lark could feel brushing against her consciousness strings.

Inside their assigned wagons, the space offered travelers not just shelter but comfort that bordered on luxury. A wooden stove bore marks of fire-blessing. Bunks held eight carefully placed sleeping nooks. A ladder climbed from the rear wall to a platform, a vantage point to survey the territory. Lark settled her pack at her feet as she sat on the smooth bench there.

Hardin emerged through the hatch. "Looks like we're in the same wagon."

Lark crossed her arms and fixed her gaze forward. The wagon lurched into motion as she attempted to ignore Hardin taking a seat next to her. As they left the crossroads, Lark's gaze found the three fur-clad figures. The same three rugged-looking men who'd been watching her from the stables. They followed at a steady distance, their weapons worn out in the open, metal clasps clinking in their saddles like warning bells. Lark gripped tightly, one hand on her pack and the other around a dagger handle.

12

LOOKING FOR ANSWERS

Lark maintained her vigilant watch as the afternoon sun cast long shadows across the rural landscape. She let Hardin's attempts at conversation wash over her like persistent rainfall, responding with terse nods and single words while her eyes swept the surrounding hills for any sign of their bearded pursuers. The hours stretched on without sight of them, but their absence from view brought little comfort. She sensed they were still out there.

A sudden warmth bloomed against her chest where the necklace lay, urgent in its warning. Her pulse quickened in anticipation of Nix's appearance, but when no familiar spark manifested, Lark's gaze was drawn northward toward the Everburning Forest. She expected to see the telltale anvil-shaped clouds that heralded a firestorm, but the sky remained a peaceful tapestry of azure and white. A flash of gold caught her eye, brilliant as the sun, before vanishing behind a cloud that drifted along a lazy yet constant path.

"Are you looking for the thunderbirds?" Hardin's voice pierced her concentration.

Lark kept her eyes fixed on the patch of sky where the

golden figure had disappeared, as if she could will it back into existence through sheer focus.

"You probably won't see one until there's a storm. My father says they're native to this region of Lamar."

Before Lark could respond, a shower of orange and red sparks materialized beside the wagon. Nix appeared, her red dress of flames lapping in the air. Lark felt relieved and let her muscles relax for a moment. Then she straightened and watched as Nix dipped below the edge of the wagon, her form floating ethereally just within Lark's line of sight.

"Hey, did you see that?" Hardin's sudden movement sent the wagon boards creaking as he leaned across her, trying to peer over the edge. The scent of leather and road dust clung to his newly acquired clothes.

Lark's arm shot out, pushing him back with more force than she'd intended. Her mouth twisted into a frown. *Can he see Nix?* The thought sent a chill down her spine.

Nix remained silent, but her presence felt like a held breath. Lark could almost taste the tension in the air.

"I think it was a fire fae!" Hardin said, his voice tinged with wonder and fear.

Lark made a show of searching over the edge. Below, Nix's orange-red hair danced as living flames in the wind. Nix pressed a finger to her lips in a gesture of secrecy before risking a quick glance at Hardin. In the next breath, she vanished in a pinwheel of sparks.

"I didn't see anything," Lark said, but the lie tasted sour in her mouth.

"Nobody ever believes me when I see them. You know that it's a bad omen to see one?" Hardin's voice carried an edge of superstitious dread.

"No."

"Oh, it's bad. Really bad luck," Hardin said, his fingers nervously working at the hem of his sleeve.

"How is seeing one bad?"

"Fire fae are of the dark court. They usually appear when the veil between our worlds is the thinnest, most commonly, when a mage is using forbidden magic and drawing it from the fae realm."

"Nobody here is using dark magic," Lark said.

Hardin's voice dropped to barely a whisper, as if speaking the words too loudly might tear that very veil. "Strong natural phenomena can trigger the veils to thin as well. Something bad always follows whenever I see one. A disaster, an attack, someone dying..."

"That can't be true. Bad things don't happen just because a fae being is nearby." Even as she spoke the words, memories flickered through her mind like shadows cast by candlelight.

"How do you know?"

"I've seen them a bunch of times and nothing bad has happened to me. Well..." The words died in her throat as images flooded back. Since the firestorm that had heralded Nix's arrival in Lark's recent memories there'd been some events that happened to her that were less than good luck. Now that she thought about it, the attack in the forest had come almost instantly after seeing her. Then there was Paq showing her the Hyalite, and the soldiers. Now, that Hyalite was the key to her understanding who she'd been before the amnesia.

That's why I need to bring the Hyalite to the Vermillion Keep. Paq said they'll know what to do. They'll know who I am and why I have it.

"See," Hardin said. "Now that you think about it, nothing good happens after you see a fire fae." Hardin leaned forward, his brown eyes bright with conviction. "Most people don't see them. People back home in Doran say seeing one means you're marked for death."

The wind whispered through the tall grass alongside their

caravan. "You're being ridiculous," Lark said, but uncertainty gnawed at her now.

"Yesterday, I saw one right after..." The color in Hardin's bruised face turned pale. "Well, after I had run-in with some trouble."

The wagon wheel hit a rut, sending a shudder through the wooden frame that seemed to emphasize the gravity of his words. "That doesn't mean someone died," Lark insisted.

"Someone did die. They said it was going to take someone's soul. I saw the sparks of a fire fae coming through and heard the person's death cry. I'm sure their soul was claimed for the conjuring. People were calling for help, but I knew it was too late for them."

"Nothing strange happens to anyone else whenever I see her," Lark said.

"You see a fire fae often?" Hardin's voice cracked, his eyes widening until they ringed with white. "Are you sure nothing strange has happened to you?"

"No," she insisted.

The memories she held sped through her mind. Her fingers found the familiar weight of her weapons, remembering with disturbing clarity how naturally she struck down the Nordraven soldiers. The blank void where her past should be yawned wide and empty. Then she thought of the dragon's gleaming scales in the woods the day before. Its presence was both terrifying and somehow right, like a piece of a puzzle she couldn't quite see.

"Wait, you saw someone use forbidden magic yesterday?" Lark asked, Hardin finally piquing her interest.

"I didn't see it per say, but it happened," Hardin said. "A girl I was spending time with was taken by Nordraven orcs and, they disappeared. Things like this always happen to people I get familiar with. That's why I'm going to Astral City. I need help from someone at the Keep."

"Someone was kidnapped right in front of you?" she asked.

Hardin recounted his tale, each word carrying the weight of fresh wounds. His story of Sasja spilled forth, the pain of loss evident whenever he spoke of this thief. The bruises on his face were a physical testament to his truth.

"So, yeah, she was kidnapped, which was right before I saw the fire fae. The fae was drawn near, I think, because a Northern mage used dark fae magic to conjure an illegal portal. Someone died because the orcs needed a person's life energy to create a portal. I was just lucky it wasn't me they grabbed for the soul energy. They stole Sasja away to who knows where," he finished, his shoulders hunched in defeat.

"That's why you're," Lark gestured to his mottled purple-yellow face.

"Hurt, tired, and pretty spooked by the thought of seeing another fire fae," he nodded.

"Why don't you try to find your friend?"

"I can't. They used a portal. That kind of magic shouldn't have happened in Lamar." He glanced to the side, as if ashamed. Then said, "Also, Sasja didn't seem to be taken so much against her will as I made it sound earlier."

"So, she wasn't kidnapped?"

"She was taken but, also, went willingly once she was caught."

"You believe she's being forced to work for them against her will?" Lark surmised. "Didn't she trick you and then steal from you?"

"Yes, but she only stole so the orcs wouldn't kill me. They have some pact that requires payment if they're attacked. Either blood or money."

"It sounds like your bad luck could've been avoided, and it's not the fae's fault."

"Sasja is so lovely though. I want to help her," he said.

"I don't know if you should go looking for this Sasja again. Maybe let her go and focus on whatever your initial mission was," Lark suggested.

"Maybe you're right, but I can't stop thinking about her..." Hardin's voice trailed off into the wind before he turned his questioning gaze upon her. "Enough about me, why are you going to Astral City?"

Lark tensed up immediately. She searched the deepening sky, hoping to glimpse again that massive golden form that had disappeared behind the clouds. When she spoke, she chose her words carefully. "I'm going to Astral City to find some answers."

"Answers?"

"Answers that I can only get from the Vermillion Keep."

"We have that in common."

"I thought you were trying to get help for your people?"

"It's more complicated than that," Hardin said, his words carrying the same mysterious weight as the secrets Lark held close to her own heart.

Lark let the conversation fade into contemplative silence. Though Hardin's recent trials matched her own in intensity, she couldn't shake the feeling that their paths, while parallel, were fundamentally different. Her fingers ghosted over the hilts of her daggers, remembering the inexplicable precision with which she'd wielded them against trained soldiers.

Above them, the sky deepened toward evening. Clouds gathered like conspiring courtiers as Lark searched for another glimpse of that mysterious golden form. The necklace remained faintly warm, a reminder of her connection to Nix while the fae was elsewhere, possibly off in another realm.

On the first night into their trek, darkness settled over the camp like a velvet shroud. The protected circle of wagons stood sentinel against the night. Ezra's warding magic hummed with invisible energy, protecting the travelers while they slept. Lark moved stealthily between the vehicles. Her footsteps were silent on the packed earth as she conducted her nightly inspection.

The crack of a twig shattered the quiet like a thunderclap. Lark froze, every sense suddenly crisp. Through the gloom beyond the protective boundary of the wards, a horse's silhouette materialized like a shadow. Its outline was blurry as it faded into a cluster of brush.

Is that one of our horses that wandered off? The thought barely had time to form before Lark's body was in motion. She pursued, each step taking her farther from the wards.

The horse stood quietly grazing between some bushes. "What are you doing out here," she said, advancing carefully. The words had barely left her lips when the trap was sprung.

Three shadows detached themselves from the darkness like ink bleeding through parchment. It was the bearded men from Stormwatch. Moonlight caught the edges of their weapons, two axes and a short sword that whispered as it cleared its sheath. They moved with coordination; the two axe-wielders shifted to her flanks while their leader advanced from the center.

Ash, the curse burned in Lark's mind as she back peddled. The necklace suddenly blazed with heat, no doubt responding to her surge of adrenaline. Her hands found her daggers, the hilts sang as she drew them.

Then the weapons left her grasp like silver fish darting through dark water, their trajectories perfect and inevitable. The sound they made as they struck their targets was soft, almost gentle as her steel parted flesh. Both flanking men staggered, their expressions twisted with identical masks of confusion. They stumbled into their leader's path.

The remaining attacker's advance faltered as a result. His sword tip wavered in the darkness as he watched his companions fall. Lark backed into the open grassland, the starlit plain stretching behind her like a vast arena. The protective boundary of the caravan's ward was just beyond reach, the energy raising the fine hairs on her neck.

"Give me that pack and I won't kill you," the man said, pointing with his drawn blade.

"No." The word emerged from her throat hard as stone.

"You don't have any more weapons. Give it up and I'll let you live," he said, but he sounded uncertain.

The tall Hawthorne brush behind him shivered, though no wind stirred the night air. The man straightened; his posture suddenly rigid as prey sensing a predator. "Guthrie, Lambert?" The names fell into the darkness without answer.

Lark shifted her weight, muscles coiling as she prepared to disarm him. The sword's lethal edge demanded perfection. One miscalculation would paint her life's ending across the moonlit grass.

"Hold it right there," he commanded, catching her subtle movement.

The attack came with terrible swiftness. Something vast and dark erupted from the brush, its movement so fluid and quick that even Lark's trained eyes could barely track it. The man's body went rigid as a statue; his half-drawn breath froze in his throat. Then he was simply... gone, ripped backwards into the Hawthorne thicket by the strange force.

Lark didn't wait to see more. She fled back to the wagons, each stride carrying her closer to the wards. The magical barrier washed over her like a warm current as she crossed its threshold, her heart hammering against her ribs. She pressed herself against a wagon's rough wooden side, eyes fixed on the distant thicket.

Through the darkness came a haunting sound. The slow

drag of something heavy across grass, the rustle of branches bowing to unseen passage. Lark knew with a certainty that she was hearing the departure of both predator and prey.

The night grew long, filled with the ordinary sounds of the sleeping caravan that seemed suddenly fragile against the darkness beyond. When dawn finally painted the eastern sky in brushes of pink and gold, Lark ventured back to the scene of the ambush. Morning revealed the dark stains that had soaked deep into the thirsty earth and were already beginning to brown at the edges. Her daggers lay carefully cleaned beside the Hawthorne bush, arranged with a deliberation that sent goosebumps up her arms. She retrieved the blades with swift efficiency, the familiar weight settling into their sheaths.

Over the following days, a feeling of unease watchfulness settled over Lark. Her eyes constantly searched the western front of the Astral Range, seeking shadows of Nordraven assassins. The threat remained dormant, yet its presence tugged at her subconsciousness. Hardin's ability to perceive Nix forced the fae to keep her distance.

The caravan's evenings took on a familiar rhythm. The wagons circled for protection, the aroma of fire-cooked meals mingled with Hardin's ballads of valor and heartbreak. Yet beneath the veneer of normalcy, Lark's attention to the shadows remained.

On the fifth day, as the sun reached its zenith and cast harsh shadows across the rutted dirt road, a breath of movement behind the wagon caught her attention. Lark spun in her perch, heart thundering against her ribs, expecting to face fur-clad warriors or copper-cloaked orcs advancing upon them. Instead, she found only empty air. Her keen eyes noticed a fresh disturbance on the road. A set of unfamiliar tracks.

Making sure not to disturb the wagon driver, or group inside the wagon, she descended silently onto the road. Worn into the dirt were the expected scars of their passage. She saw fresh hoofprints and deep lines from the wagon wheels. But there, a hundred yards behind them she found something else: a set of tracks.

As she crouched to study the massive oval print, Nix materialized beside her in a dance of sparks, her dress rippling liquid flame.

"What are you doing?" she asked.

"Look at this," Lark said, pointing at the large oval print.

"Those are tracks," Nix replied.

"Yes, but what kind?"

From the lead wagon now some distance ahead, Ezra's gruff voice called after her, "Lark, don't trail too far from the wagons. We're nearly to Fletcher's Passage."

Lark signaled to the dwarf that she heard him.

"And look at this," Nix said, flowing closer. "There are four smaller tracks in an arch in front of the main oval pad."

"Those aren't smaller tracks, Nix. Those are the toe pads to this foot." Lark searched the hills again, her necklace tingling with warmth.

"It's the dragon," Nix voiced her thoughts.

"Lark," Ezra called. "We're leaving you behind."

Reluctantly, she hustled back to the wagons. Hardin emerged, curious as ever.

"What were you looking for?" He asked.

"Answers," Lark replied.

13

ZORJAN'S LAIR

"Venrick," Zorjan's voice rasped, the name becoming something else entirely in the goblin's mouth. "What are you doing here?"

The goblin's unsettling question reverberated through the cave just a few days' ride into the mountains west of Astral City. Every scrape of the goblin's claws echoed back into the crushing darkness. In the heavy silence that followed, Zorjan's sharp teeth clacked together in predatory anticipation; the sound was unnaturally loud in the confined space.

"I've come to you for a service, Zorjan," Venrick announced from the mouth of the cave, where darkness wrestled with sunlight. He attempted to shade his eyes to be able to see into the black hole, to no avail.

Then the goblin emerged from the shadows like a nightmare taking form. His face shone first, a network of scars etched into wrinkled green flesh, dominated by a hooked nose that seemed to test the air like a serpent's tongue. His slender body followed, a masterwork of natural camouflage in mossy green mottled with earthen brown; the source of countless tales claiming goblins were creatures capable of invisibility.

Purple scars latticed across his chest in a testament to a life of violence. His arms were long and corded with sinewy muscle. They hung low enough for his sharp claws to graze his knobby knees. His leather shoulder holster, housing six long blades, creaked softly as he moved.

Though barely four feet tall, Zorjan's wiry frame buzzed with coiled energy, promising unnatural speed and strength. His egg-shaped head tapered to a knife-edge chin. His black hair was slicked back to emphasize a dramatic widow's peak. Golden rings weighed down his large, drooping ears, the metal singing softly with each movement. He had jagged yellow teeth and eyes like twin full moons.

He moved fluidly, his torn brown trouser legs whispering against each other as he slipped across the cold granite floor. His narrow feet made no sound, but his claws clicked against stone like dropped coins.

"Where is Tel Roan?" Zorjan demanded, his hand finding the grip of one long knife.

"Tel Roan is dead," Venrick said, choosing to take an honest approach, as Tel would've.

"Then why are you here?"

"I need a favor," Venrick replied.

"I don't do favors for you."

"You've done favors in the past."

"I owed Tel Roan a debt. One that I no longer need to pay if what you say is true. I don't owe you anything. Leave now and you might get off this crag alive."

"Do you recognize this?" Venrick asked, revealing the wooden chest they had used to store a Hyalite, its raised runes shimmering with magical energy.

"An enchanted chest." The goblin's eyes widened with intrigue. Zorjan's purple tongue licked at the corners of his mouth, before he answered, "If you intend to purchase this service from me, you're a fool. Bringing something of value to me, here in my lair, and all alone... why wouldn't I kill you now and take it for myself?"

When Zorjan snapped his fingers, magic crackled through the air like static electricity. A stone door slid down and the mouth of the cave sealed with a sound like a tomb closing. They were plunged into a darkness so complete it seemed to have no beginning or end. Feet whispered across stone in a deadly dance. Venrick drew his sword, the steel singing as it tasted air. A whoosh of movement cut through the blackness. Venrick's elven senses were keen. He leapt backward, sword rising in one hand while the enchanted chest became a shield in the other.

The impact of Zorjan's knife against the chest sent sparks into the pitch black, each one illuminating a demon-mask of rage that twisted across the goblin's face. The chest's protective enchantments vibrated now like a taut bow string as they deflected the blade. The force drove Venrick back until stone pressed cold against his spine. He was trapped against the sealed entrance. His counterstrike cut through open air, the whistle of movement mocking him in the midnight blackness.

Venrick stilled himself, each breath controlled as he strained his senses against the suffocating dark. Tel's training came to mind, the memory as clear as mountain water. "Fighting in total darkness may seem unimportant now, but it will save your life when one day you are a Knight. Monsters that escape the North seek refuge in caves. This is why we train."

He could almost feel the breath behind the words, as though Tel stood beside him, saying them again. "Use all of your senses. Your elven blood may have been a disadvantage in your past, but here, when it comes down to being in touch with your surroundings, your instincts are a great advantage. Tap into your abilities. Feel the energy of where the attack is coming from. Hear the movement. Trust your senses."

The whisper of disturbed stone came from his right. Zorjan's footfalls painted a picture in sound. The subtle stretch of leather betrayed the goblin's arm drawing back for a killing stroke. Venrick dove left as the knife cut through the space where he'd been, steel screaming against stone when it found the cave entrance instead of his flesh. Venrick's counter-attack caught something solid. It was a glancing blow rather than the finishing strike he'd intended. Suddenly Zorjan was there, tangling with him, all wiry strength and serpent-like wriggling.

"Got you," Venrick declared, his arms locked around the goblin in an iron embrace.

But Zorjan wormed in his grasp like an eel. With each twist, he threatened to slip free. The goblin's foot hooked behind Venrick's ankle with devastating precision, and they toppled backward. The impact against the sealed entrance sent fractures of light lacing through Venrick's vision. The door cracked and a sliver of sunlight broke through to illuminate their deadly dance. Venrick maintained his hold, the goblin's back pressed against him as they struggled against the stone door.

One arm slithered free of Venrick's grasp. Metal rang as another knife appeared, arcing backward in vicious stabs. Once, twice, three times the blade stuck the stone as Venrick weaved aside, death a possibility with each passing heartbeat. Venrick's defense found the fourth strike, his grip halted Zorjan's arm, the blade mere inches from his face.

Zorjan tucked his chin, and Venrick's battle-trained instincts screamed a warning of an incoming headbutt. Instead, needle-sharp teeth sank into his forearm, burning like molten iron against his flesh.

"Ahh!" The cry tore from Venrick's throat as his grip loosened. Zorjan melted into the cave's depths becoming the shadows, his movements fluid and predatory in the darkness. The attack Venrick braced for never came. Instead, the goblin's cursing cut through the stale air, his native tongue sounded harsh and guttural as it bounced between the stone walls.

"You bit me!" Venrick shouted as he watched in horror. Vermillion tendrils of poison spread beneath his skin like spilled ink, leaving a decaying numbness in their wake.

"Augh," the goblin spat, his voice thick with disgust. "Foul, tainted blood."

"You bit me!" Venrick repeated, incredulous, his world tilting as the venom worked its way through his veins like ice water, each heartbeat carrying the poison deeper.

"You vile elf-man, you're cursed," Zorjan spat, dragging his tongue across the wall with such violence it left streaks of saliva on the weathered stone.

The chest lay on the cave floor like a beacon in the gloom. Venrick stumbled toward it, the strength in his legs betraying him as he fell. His fingers scraped against the rough ground as he pulled himself forward, curling his wounded arm around the artifact. The runes carved into its surface awakened at his touch, releasing ribbons of celestial green light that writhed like living things. They coiled around his arm in spectral ribbons, drawn to the wound.

Where the light touched the bite, Venrick's flesh sizzled and steamed. Pain lanced through him, sharp enough to cut through the fog brought on by the venom. His muscles seized as the magic burrowed into him, hunting down every drop of poison. The sensation was like lightning trapped beneath his skin, excruciating yet clarifying. Through half-closed eyes, he watched the toxin rise from his flesh and dissipate into nothingness. Strength flooded back into his limbs, the weakness of moments before nothing but a memory.

Venrick rose in one fluid motion, the chest secure in his injured arm while his other hand found the familiar weight of his sword. The blade caught what little light filtered through the entrance.

"You have a curse on you. Be gone," Zorjan said.

"I came here for a service, Zorjan. I'm not leaving until you agree to what I ask," Venrick replied, his voice steady despite the lingering memory of pain.

"Soiled, tainted blood," Zorjan growled, spittle flying from his lips. His lunge carried the coiled tension of a viper's strike yet stopped short of commitment. The thin shaft of light from the doorway allowed enough illumination for Venrick to keep his blade trained on the goblin's throat, creating a delicate standoff.

Venrick risked a glance at the chest, marveling at how its magic had purged the goblin's paralyzing venom from his system with such incredible efficiency.

"Be gone before you pass your curse onto me," Zorjan insisted, his voice carrying the weight of centuries old superstitions. The space between them grew heavy with the lingering scent of spent magic and cave moss.

"I'm not leaving here until you show me how I can track down the person who opened this case last."

"No," Zorjan hissed.

Venrick stepped forward, pressing the sword against the goblin's skin. "I know you can do it. I've seen you create tracking charms for Tel. You said you only needed the trace of magic. The last person to open this chest did it by magical force to steal Tel's Hyalite. Make a tracking charm for me; lead me to the person who cast the last spell on it, then I'll leave. You'll never see me again."

A change washed over Zorjan's scarred features, subtle yet profound. "Your curse hinges on the retrieval of a Hyalite?" The goblin's smile spread across his face like a fresh wound, teeth gleaming wet in the dim light. "One that's ownership is already claimed by someone other than the Vermillion Keep?"

he chuckled, a sickly sound. "You should've let my poison kill you. The only way out of a binding curse like this is by either killing the mage who cursed you or by completing their mission. Either of which you alone do not have the skill to do. You're a dead man walking."

"That's right, Zorjan, I am a dead man walking. And right now, if I were you, I'd be afraid because I don't have anything to lose. I'll do whatever it takes to force that tracking charm out of you."

Zorjan's expression curdled like milk in summer heat, the lines deepening across his face. His clawed fingers twitched at his sides. "Tell me, Venrick, if you find this Hyalite, what will you do with it? Will you be an honorable servant of Lamar and bring it back to the Vermillion Keep or will you use it to your advantage?"

Venrick's response was measured, each word carefully chosen. "Why do you assume that my curse has bound me to the Keep? Curses are outlawed in Lamar, but not in Nordraven."

"The Keeps have overlooked you, haven't they?" Zorjan said, eyes narrowing. "Never given you a chance. Now they see a way to get rid of you."

"Will you perform this service or am I going to have to force you to?" Venrick pressed the sword, forcing Zorjan to lean back.

A strange look kindled in Zorjan's eyes. "No. I never did like Tel or his dragon. You, however, have been put in a curious position."

"If you won't help me—"

"I'll help you," Zorjan interrupted. "But just this once and not in the way you've demanded. I will leave you with this: A curse has forced you to begin, a quest unclear where hope is thin. Follow the flame that guides the way, for if you ignore it, your death will come that day. Track the fire, winged and bright, or lose yourself to your curse's plight."

"How does that help me?"

Zorjan's bloodied teeth flashed as he snapped them at Venrick in warning.

Venrick stumbled backward, ready to feel the goblin's weight on his sword. Zorjan didn't attack, however. With the snap of his fingers the door exploded inward. Sunlight crashed through the opening like a physical force. The searing wall of radiance blinded Venrick momentarily. He twisted, walking away as his eyes slowly adjusted to the daylight. His boots scraped against stone as he felt the air open around him. Suddenly, the mountain breeze whistled past his ears as he teetered on the precipice. He'd nearly forgotten that the cave opened to a deadly fall. Desperate, he caught himself as loose pebbles cascaded off the edge of the crag.

The cave door thundered shut. Venrick's eyes adjusted. He was standing alone on the narrow ledge outside the cave with the box under his arm.

"No!" The word tore from his throat as he hammered against the unyielding stone. He wedged his fingers into barely visible seams, pulling until his tendons quivered form the effort. Finally, the door yielded with grinding protest, creating just enough space for him to squeeze through. But the shadows had already swallowed any trace of the goblin.

"Zorjan!" Venrick cried futilely into the empty chambers.

The cave's depths beckoned with branching fissures. Each offered a possible escape route. The openings gaped like hungry mouths, leading deeper into the heart of the mountain. Venrick's experienced eye recognized Zorjan's advantage underground. Venrick couldn't find him now.

With his plans in ruins, Venrick tucked the enchanted chest under his arm once more and sheathed his sword. The treacherous mountain path demanded his full attention, the weight of failure added to the burden of the box.

Thunder and Giant still grazed peacefully in the meadow when he returned to the wagon, their calm presence a stark contrast to the tension he felt. The six-wheeled armored wagon accepted the chest back into the confines of its warded cavity. As Venrick retrieved his medical kit, the same one he'd used countless times in Tel's service, he examined the bite with growing awe.

"That bite should've incapacitated me. Ash, it probably should've killed me," he muttered. He knew full well that adult goblins could control their venom as precisely as an archer controls each draw.

He used sterile water to attend to the wound. Where there should have been blackened flesh and corrupted veins, he found only clean punctures. The healing salve he applied sank into the wounds with a cooling sensation, but Venrick's attention was drawn to the three empty chests.

The combination of elven magic bound within the dwarven runes had done more than simply dispel the toxin. It had rejected it entirely, as if the venom had never existed. "How?" His question went unanswered.

A decade of serving alongside a Paragon had taught Venrick the fundamental truth of magic used ethically. Spells spoken by magical races required power, and that power came mostly from Yogo Sapphire, and less frequently, with significantly more powerful Hyalite Orbs. The magical races of Sataran, magi, elves, dwarves, and orcs, were born with the ability to channel this power. The production of Hyalites and Yogos in Lamar only happened in the Everburning Forest. While the Paragons and Knights of Lamar and Nordraven held contests to retrieve the powerful objects, war to dominate the forest persisted in the east. As long as dragon-bonding offered the only path for humans to gain magical power over the other races, war between Nordraven's four kingdoms and the Kingdom of Lamar would be everlasting.

To Venrick's knowledge, the only thing other than Hyalites and Yogos that could permanently contain magical energy were runes. His half-elven heritage whispered of untapped potential, power that Tel had dismissed, insisting proper training could only come through the Paragon Academies' rigorous path to Knighthood based at Lamar's three great Keeps.

Venrick gathered the leather reins and climbed aboard the wagon, guiding his team back out of the mountains. When he reached the intersection of roads, one traveling north/south along the eastern front of the Astral Range, the other heading from the mountains due east toward the region of Lamar where the King's armies were thick with operations and training camps. He considered bypassing the war camps and trying to escape across the sea to Gambria, where elves reigned. He knew they wouldn't accept him as one of their own, but being an outcast was better than being cursed. If he abandoned his search for the Hyalite, however, the curse would kill him. Venrick resigned himself to the fact that if he wanted to live, he had to find the Hyalite.

The wagon wheels cut fresh trails into earth still damp with morning dew. For days, he rode blindly north hoping something would offer a sign of where to look. Zorjan's prophecy haunted his thoughts throughout another week as he wandered Northern Lamar, until one day, something in the air changed. Venrick pulled the wagon to a halt. The sudden silence was broken only by the gentle snorting of Thunder and Giant, their breath creating small clouds in the cooling air.

"Did Zorjan already know something had happened to Tel?" The words fell into the space between him and his horses, an old habit born from years of travel on lonely roads. Sometimes, in moments like these, the horses' ears would twitch with almost human understanding. Thunder's tail swished, cutting through the air with a whisper of horsehair against leather.

"He knew that I was cursed when he tasted my blood." Venrick's fingers absently traced the now-faint punctures on his arm. His flesh remained tender from the goblin's bite. "Curses in Lamar are illegal, so why didn't Zorjan assume it was the Nordraven Kings who were sending me to retrieve the Hyalite?"

The puzzle pieces shifted in his mind like pieces of a complex lock finally finding alignment.

"Zorjan might not have known that I was forced into going after the Hyalite for the Vermillion Keep, but once he tasted the curse in my blood, he figured it out." The words came faster now, each revelation building on the last. "We need to go back to the beginning."

With newfound purpose, Venrick pointed the wagon toward the Everburning Forest. The wheels ground against loose stone as Thunder and Giant responded to his urgency. Their hooves struck the earth with renewed vigor. As they approached the crossroads where opposing signs pointed toward Fletcher's Passage and Stormwatch, something in the road caught his eye.

A pattern in the dirt made his heart skip a beat. He descended from the wagon. His boots crunched on scattered gravel as he knelt to examine the massive impressions that marred the earth.

"Is that..." His fingers hovered over the print, feeling the residual warmth that only dragon claws could leave in their wake. "It is. These are fresh dragon tracks!"

Thunder and Giant's reaction was immediate and unmistakable. Their nostrils flared wide, drinking in the familiar scent that had followed Tel's golden dragon for years. Thunder's hoof struck the ground with military precision, while Giant's repeated snorts relayed his recognition of Ingamar.

Venrick's gaze swept the late afternoon sky, searching for any sign of golden scales glinting in the sun. The trees around him seemed to hold their breath, but no massive silhouette broke the endless blue canvas overhead.

Back in the driver's seat, the wooden planks creaking beneath his weight, Venrick guided his team eastward toward Fletcher's Passage. His mind raced with possibilities.

If it is Ingamar, and I could coax him back, his instincts could lead me to the Hyalite, he thought, the idea burning bright as forge-fire in his mind.

Then, another realization hit. "Ingamar has Tel's scabbard strapped to his harness. That means the brismil blade is still on him."

The tracks led him perilously close to civilization, an unlikely choice for a riderless dragon. Something about this felt wrong, like a song played perfectly but in the wrong key. At the edge of town, where wildlands surrendered to settled earth, the massive prints simply vanished.

"Ingamar?" Venrick called across the wind-touched grass, hope making his voice rise at the edges.

The trees to his right swayed, their branches lifting on the winds. No golden scales gleamed between their trunks; no familiar roar answered his summons.

"Ingamar!" The second call held more command, born of years serving alongside a Paragon, but still he was met with silence.

A bitter taste coated the back of his throat as Venrick recalled his years of strained interactions with the proud dragon. Ingamar had always viewed him with barely concealed disdain, tolerating his presence only out of loyalty to Tel. Now, standing at the dragon's launch point where massive claws had gouged the earth, Venrick studied the fresh wagon tracks that dominated the path into Fletcher's Landing. His hand rose to his chin, calloused fingers scratching against rough stubble as a thought took shape.

"Ingamar, who are you following, and why?"

14

FLETCHER'S PASSAGE

The weathered sign swayed gently from the oak's gnarled branches. The faded message etched in the wood read: Fletcher's Passage, population 1,304. The sign was clearly outdated. The town had swollen beyond those modest figures, with newly constructed cottages pressing outward from the valley's confines like desperate seedlings fighting for sunlight. The dwellings climbed the surrounding foothills in defiance of the steep terrain, their wooden frames adorned in a palette of colors that somehow maintained harmony beneath distinctive northern Lamar red clay shingles. Those rust-colored tiles, catching the day's dying light, created a rippling sea of crimson that flowed up the valley walls. At the heart of the city, a proud steeple pierced the sky, its shadow stretching long across the settlement below.

The caravan wheels ground to a halt in a frost-kissed pasture at the edge of town. Crisp evening air carried the mingled aromas of forge-fire and hearth-smoke, weaving through the orange-gold tapestry of sunset. The scent of woodsmoke danced with hints of cardamom and roasting meat, drawing an involuntary growl from Lark's stomach as she descended from the wagon, her boots crunching against the frost-hardened grass.

"Welcome to Fletcher's Passage, our stop until morning," Ezra announced. "You're welcome to have your meal here at the wagons as we have enough food, but I, for one, will be partaking in the town's offerings. Fletcher's Passage has the best food fair, entertainment, and trade this side of Astral City. We've been out on the road for five days. Maybe some of you can wait a few more before a meal out, but not me. Life's too short not to enjoy the little gems like this town. For any who'd like to come along, I'll be at the Bear's Tooth Tavern." He adjusted his belt before setting off toward the town center, his footsteps sure and purposeful.

"Hey, Lark," Hardin said, his voice carrying a note of hopeful invitation. "Do you want to head into town and get a bite? I'm going to see if performing at the tavern will pay for my food and drink. I wouldn't mind doing a few extra songs to pay your way."

"That's kind, but there's something I want to check out before I go in for the evening. Maybe I'll catch up with everyone after," she replied, her mind already racing with thoughts of the dragon's proximity.

Despite their shared journey from Stormwatch, the easy familiarity Hardin displayed remained unreciprocated, a one-way window into friendship. Besides, the possibility of a dragon's presence pushed all thoughts of comfort aside.

"Suit yourself," Hardin said, slinging his lute across his back before hurrying to catch Ezra.

Lark shouldered her pack, its familiar weight a comfort as she diverted from the stream of travelers heading toward the main thoroughfare. Her pendant stirred with warmth. Nix materialized in a shower of sparks, her tiny form glowing against the deepening twilight.

The darkening streets wound before Lark as she made her

way along the edge of town, each step carrying her farther from the comforting bustle of the caravan. The cobblestones beneath her feet had been worn smooth by steady travel through the area.

"Where are you going?" Nix asked with the innocence of a child. Though Lark now knew the innocence was feigned.

"I think that dragon has been following us since before Stormwatch." Lark said. "I thought I saw it flying overhead that first day. Then I think it hauled those bearded men off. Now, we've seen tracks following the caravan."

"Why is the dragon following you of all people?" Nix asked, assuming her characteristic pose of contemplation, tiny fiery fingers pressed against her red chin.

Lark frowned, "Isn't it obvious?"

"Maybe it is to you, but fae don't think the same way as you humans."

"The dragon's following us because I have the Hyalite," Lark said.

"And now you're going out to meet it, alone?" Nix gasped.

Once Lark rounded the final corner, she took in a sight that caused her steps to falter. Near the towering oak that bore the town sign, a group of broad-shouldered figures stood in hushed consultation. Their gray travel cloaks hung heavy around their imposing frames. They appeared to be encrusted with the dust of a long journey. One gestured toward a map held by his companion. His movement revealed a broadsword, its worn hilt emerging through the gap in his cloak.

As Lark froze, Nix noticed them, too. She darted toward the group, vanishing in a burst of sparks as one of them lifted his head. The sight of his blue skin, stark against the twilight, sent a jolt through Lark's core. Yellow eyes, sharp as a predator's, fixed upon her position. Two ivory tusks curved up from his lower lip, their points gleaming like pale daggers against the blue flesh.

Are they orcs? Her question lingered as the others turned to face her, moving like seasoned warriors despite their massive frames.

Something primitive and instinctive raised alarms in Lark's mind. She retreated into the street, her boots silent against the stones. When she dared to peer around the corner of the nearest home, the group of four had vanished from their position by the sign. They moved away toward the west, their massive bodies melting into the shadows.

Nix burst back into view beside her in a shower of sparks that momentarily pierced the gloom. One of the towering Morsythians halted mid-stride and turned. His yellow eyes swept the town, piercing through shadow and stone alike before he continued on with his companions.

"Why did you fly toward them and disappear?" Lark demanded.

"Those are Morsythians!" Nix said breathlessly. "They can see me. I was trying to act like a normal fire fae, drawn by something before disappearing. If I hadn't, they might've known we were together. It's not normal to see them down here. I disappeared because I felt one of them trying to draw me in."

"Draw you in? People can do that? Morsythians, too?" The concept made her shudder independent of the cool evening air.

"The right person, yes. You can," Nix replied, her light dimming slightly as if the very memory of the sensation drained her energy.

"Were they trying to harm you?" Lark asked, feeling protective, though what protection she could offer a being from another realm, she wasn't sure.

"I don't know, but I'm glad they turned around. I get a bad feeling from them."

"Morsythians," Lark breathed, the word tasting of half-forgotten memories on her tongue. These blue-skinned orcs were much more imposing than the bulky green orcs she'd learned were more common around Nordraven and Lamar. The Morsythian orc's predatory gaze was unsettling.

"That's what they are," Nix confirmed, her glow strengthening with urgency. "Come on, let's go find the others. I don't think we should be out here alone. Especially if a dragon is nearby, too."

Reluctantly, Lark turned back toward the town center, her mind churning as she tried to grasp her memories of the Morsythians.

A river-borne breeze cut through the main thoroughfare, carrying with a reminder that they had traveled north. Above, the first moon hung like a copper coin in the evening sky, while its siblings, the second and third moons, painted the horizon in shades of silver and gold. The sudden crack of a door slamming jolted her from her reverie, its frame rattling with the force. Lark tensed, her fingers tightened on her pack as she whirled around. A figure was moving slowly and deliberately behind her. Whoever it was maintained their distance, keeping a dark gray hood drawn up like a shroud. When the figure realized she had noticed him or her, the person froze, the stranger's face masked by the hood.

Her heart thundered against her ribs as she hastened toward the nearest building. Golden light spilled from the Bear's Tooth Tavern, warm and inviting as the wooden sign creaked gently in the breeze. Inside, a cacophony of voices and laughter rose becoming a shield against the night's growing threats. Hardin's clear tenor cut through the din, his song weaving a spell of its own, offering a lifeline in an increasingly uncertain evening.

The heavy wooden door yielded, and the warmth of the light and thunderous applause washed over her. To her right, Hardin stood on the raised landing as if it were his stage, his grin as bright as polished silver as he executed an elaborate bow, fingers lovingly curved around his lute's worn neck.

The space between them bloomed with life. The round tables were like islands in a sea of humanity, each one a microcosm of Fletcher's Passage itself. Local townsfolk rubbed shoulders with weathered travelers and familiar faces from Ezra's caravan. Their collective energy charged the air. From behind the swinging saloon doors, a cloud of aromas wafted forth: spiced meats crackling over charcoal and vegetables kissed by flame until their edges blackened and sweetened. Each swing of the doors released a fresh wave of mouthwatering smells, the servers' movements acting as a bellows to spread the intoxicating fragrance throughout the room.

To watch the service from the doorway was like attending a choreographed dance. Barmaids' skirts swirled and waiters wove through the crowd. To Lark's left, the bar stretched like a fallen tree, its surface polished to a mirror sheen by countless elbows and spilt ales. Amber light refracted off the forest of bottles behind the bar.

Lark had barely shifted her weight toward an empty table when a young woman materialized before her, brown hair tamed into a practical ponytail. She moved with the efficiency of someone who had mastered the tavern's battlefield. Silver utensils appeared from her apron as she asked, "Which dinner will you be having tonight, pork or chicken?"

"Chicken?" The word emerged from Lark's lips with the hesitancy of someone unused to such simple choices.

"Are you okay with spice?"

Lark's shrug spoke volumes in its uncertainty.

"The meal comes with risotto, charred veggies, and your choice of ale or mead," She recited, clearly having said this more than a few times already this evening.

"I'll have water," Lark replied.

"Are you paying now or later?"

Lark's fingers searched her empty pockets, her eyes drawn to Hardin on his landing. "He'll be paying for me tonight," she said, gesturing toward the bard.

The waitress gave her a knowing glance that flickered between them, a smile playing at the corners of her mouth. "I better let him know he owes us a handful more songs then." She vanished through the swinging doors, her voice rising above the kitchen's orchestral chaos.

Lark found a chair at an empty table. The worn wood creaked as she settled in. A few moments later Hardin joined her. "I thought you might not show," he said, setting his lute in the chair next to him, his faithful companion.

"I was going to stay back, but then I imagined this place and a room full of people judging you, and thought, heck, it might be fun to see how you perform for an audience that isn't forced to listen to your voice every single day. Always playing the same old so—"

"Whoa, whoa, whoa. Nobody's forcing you to listen."

A rare smile cracked through Lark's normally stoic expression. "Hardin, I'm joking."

"Oh," he said, leaning back with theatrical suspicion, his chair protesting beneath him. "I don't know if you should make jokes. That one wasn't very good." His hand rose to catch a passing waiter's attention. Within moments, a frothy mug materialized before him, its contents releasing tendrils of rich, hoppy aroma. The waitress followed next, setting Lark's water down in front of her before returning to the stream of people moving through the tavern.

"Not a good joke? Give me a break, it's my first try," Lark said with an innocent shrug. "I guess I'll figure it out as I get more experience."

"You've never told a joke before?"

"Not that I can remember."

"That's right, the whole memory-loss thing," he said.

Then he broke their eye contact as if losing interest and searched the room. He raised his mug to his lips.

"You'd have trouble, too, if you couldn't remember anything. At least I don't repeat the same verses over and over, like some bards I know," Lark said with a slight rolling of her eyes.

Hardin choked on his drink and grinned. "That was much better. Still room for improvement, but your sarcasm is coming along."

"Sarcasm," she repeated. "Now that, I do remember. Never was a huge fan."

"Where did you say you were from again?"

"I didn't."

"You're intriguing, and a little mysterious. The night we met you looked like you'd just fallen off the turnip wagon. Then the next day, you come out looking like that," he said gesturing to her. "Looking all cleaned up and wearing tailored clothes. Sometimes I think you're pulling my leg when you say you can't remember things. But you're so serious all the time... Also, there's this layer where Ezra trusts you to be his rear guard for the caravan, which is no small task. And at the same time, it's like you are clueless about so many things that people consider common knowledge. For example, you say things like..."

"Like what?" she prompted, annoyed at his comfort in pointing out her flaws and then holding back.

"Like how you didn't know fire fae are bad luck."

Tell him why you don't know these things, Nix's voice sounded in her mind.

Lark's emerald eyes cast out across the tavern. With so many lanterns glowing, she couldn't spot the fire fae right away but finally found her hovering in a windowsill across the boisterous room.

"I guess it doesn't matter too much since we'll be going

The Lost Dragonrider of Lamar

our separate ways in a few days," he said, taking a long sip from his mug. "What kind of answers are you hoping to find in Astral City?"

"I, ahh..." she stared. A chair skidded on the polished wooden floor right behind Lark, distracting her for a moment and creaking as it accepted someone's weight. She started to turn her head to see who it might be, but Hardin's question lulled her back in.

"I don't really know," she said, her hand drifting to the pack nestled between her feet, ensuring that the mystic orb was still in her care. As her hand drew close, a comforting pulsing passed through to her. The Hyalite was still safe.

"What makes you think you'll find the answers you're looking for there?" Hardin insisted.

"I have my reasons."

"You claimed you were a fire wheat harvester," he began, speaking his thoughts aloud, searching for answers of his own. "Given the competition in harvesting, that might explain why you have a grudge against Nordraven, but not why Ezra trusts you as his security detail. You are always armed with those daggers..."

"Hardin, stop digging," Lark warned.

"And you keep that backpack suspiciously close to you. In fact, I don't know that I've seen you leave it anywhere."

"Hardin," Lark's tone darkened.

"You bring it with you everywhere. At the start of the trip, you hinted that you were going to the Vermillion Keep as well. I think—"

The waitress slipped in and placed the plate of chicken, rice and vegetables on the table in front of Lark. "Careful dear, the plate's hot. Enjoy." She twisted, taking the order of the person who had sat down behind Lark.

"I said I have my reasons, so leave it at that," Lark responded. She grabbed her plate, hands singing with pain from the heat, but she wasn't going to let pain stop her. She stood, saying, "Thanks for the meal, bard."

"Ashes, you don't have to be so standoffish. I thought we were becoming friends?"

"Now you know that we're not. We're just acquaintances who happen to be stuck on the same wagon."

He frowned. "Are you leaving?"

"I want to be alone," she said, not sure if she believed what she was saying, but she had already stood up to make her point. She gathered her pack and moved to an empty seat near the glowing window where Nix perched.

Why did I do that? she wondered, the savory food falling second to the questioning of her reaction. She glanced at the pack, feeling the Hyalite's energy within. It was as though the energy there was harmonized with her. If she was being honest with herself, bringing the Hyalite to the Vermillion Keep and handing it off like she thought she should do was starting to feel wrong. *That's nonsense. I told myself I'd take it to them. They know what to do with it. Nix didn't want me to let it fall into Nordraven hands, so I need to keep going. The Keep may know who I am. They could tell me who I was before.*

She found herself looking toward Hardin again. Across the room, Hardin's hands wrapped around his mug as he met her eyes. Confusion crossed his face. Lark averted her attention, focusing on the contents of her plate as if they held answers.

I should trust him more. He's done nothing to harm me. Should I apologize? The thoughts tangled in her mind as she scraped the last morsels into her mouth.

When she risked another peek at Hardin, her breath caught in her throat. A young man sat beside him. The sight of his face sent a jolt of recognition through her body.

It's him, she thought, her pulse racing.

Who? Nix's voice whispered in her mind.

The elf from my vision, Lark replied.

She couldn't tear her eyes away. In the flesh, he was arresting and very much alive, not like the hollow shell she'd witnessed in her vision. The flickering tavern light played across his handsome features, bringing warmth to what she had only seen through her dreams.

He's not dead, she thought, her relief mingling with rising apprehension.

He cut an imposing figure next to Hardin. His presence demanded attention. His dark gray cloak, finely woven and travel-worn, parted to reveal form-fitting light armor. A sword hilt protruded from the wool fabric. On its worn smooth pommel, there was a blue sapphire alite with magical energy. Every line of him spoke of lethal grace: broad shoulders tapering to a warrior's build, a strong jawline and hard-edged features that gave him an air of stern nobility. His thick brown hair, less wild than Lark's own locks, fell in waves around his face. It hung slightly longer than military tradition dictated. With his hood drawn back, the distinctive tips of his slightly pointed ears emerged. But it was his eyes that held her captive. They were like emerald pools flecked with gold, seeming to pierce through to her soul, just as they had in her vision.

Horror crashed over her. This was the stranger tailing her. The hooded figure who had stalked her through the streets after that bone-chilling encounter with the Morsythian. Her hand unconsciously moved to her throat, to finger the lark pendant that hung there. Around his own neck glinted a gold chain of familiar craftsmanship, the pendant tucked away unseen beneath his layers.

He was the one who was following me here. He had been the presence that had sat down directly behind her. He'd overheard what Hardin nearly guessed at.

Does he know what's hidden in my pack?

Deep in her chest, warmth bloomed; not the magical heat

of her necklace, but something more primal. It was instinct mixed with adrenaline, the fighting instinct that had kept her breathing when Nordraven soldiers and grizzled bandits had tried to claim the Hyalite for their own.

She strained to catch their words through the noise of the tavern, but distance and crowd chatter rendered their conversation to meaningless murmurs. Still, she watched their lips move, trying to decode their exchange through gesture and expression alone. Did he know who Lark was? Her vision suggested their paths had crossed, though the memory of it was lost. That vision though, of her with the Hyalite, brismil sword in hand, and him on the ground, eyes wide open but not stirring. Clearly, he had something to do with the prize hidden in her pack.

Her heart nearly stopped when Hardin's finger jabbed in her direction, and his next word needed no sound to comprehend. "Her?"

Their eyes locked across the room again, and the intensity of his gaze struck her. His expression gave nothing away, it was calculating and devoid of emotion. She felt pinned, like a moth drawn to a flame, unable to look away from those forest-deep eyes. When she finally wrenched herself free from their hold, she stood with such haste that her chair scraped against the wooden floor and nearly tipped over.

The cool night air hit her face as she burst outside, but she found herself frozen once more. Her necklace flared with heat, much warmer than Nix's presence had ever triggered. She'd come to trust these sensations as a warning.

Nix materialized beside her, trailing whisps of flame. "I can feel it, too."

"Do you know what's causing it? Is it him?"

"I'll try to find out," Nix promised before vanishing into the darkness.

Lark knew this energy coming through the necklace. It

mirrored the pull she'd felt while watching the firestorm, but this was slightly different. This time, the call came from the depths of the forest. It settled in her heart like a stone dropping through a mountain lake. The dragon was reaching out, beckoning her to pierce the mysteries fogging her mind and come to him.

15

NO MERE HAPPENSTANCE

Venrick traced the wagon tracks to the edge of Fletcher's Passage. The afternoon sun cast long shadows across the rutted path as he spotted the caravan ahead, its wagons arranged in a defensive circle. The dragon tracks that had led him here troubled him more than he cared to admit. They were too purposeful, too deliberate for a wild dragon. Whatever had drawn Ingamar this close to civilization had to do with what had happened in Tel's final moments.

The air seemed to still with a peculiar quiet as Venrick guided his carriage toward a weather-beaten stable across from the town Commons. Parking outside, Venrick studied the silent wagons across the way, searching for any hint of what might've drawn Ingamar's attention. A whisp of magical energy pressed against his temple, hinting that a supernatural essence was nearby.

He turned to look back toward the huge oak tree on the edge of town. Four massive, blue-skinned Morsythians huddled around a map. Their rippling muscles belied a strength that could shatter stone, while their measured movements were those of trained warriors. All at once, they set out on the road in a line. Shortly after departing, one turned, fixing Venrick with its yellow eyes, before continuing west.

What brings the far Northern clans this far south? Venrick wondered.

Their departure lifted an invisible weight, but before Venrick could breathe easy, his reality fractured. A figure wreathed in living flame materialized across the street, its dress flowing like liquid fire. Hot blue flames erupted from her skin, turning yellow, orange, and red as they materialized around her body. The tiny figure's red hair flowed like the dress, embroiled in the same fire that was her form. Her otherworldly beauty was a clear mark of the fae, perfect in proportion, as small as a meadow lark, and as whimsical as a child. Venrick knew the creature at once, fire fae.

As fast as she came into focus, she disappeared behind a nearby dwelling.

Zorjan's riddle whispered in his head, "Track the fire, winged and bright, or lose yourself to your curse's plight." The words carried new weight now, as if the very magic in the air responded to their utterance. The convergence of these signs: fresh dragon tracks, Morsythians in the lowlands, and now a fire fae bold enough to manifest in the dwindling daylight. These were more than a mere coincidence. Power was stirring nearby. Venrick was close. He could feel it.

A stable boy materialized from the shadows, his voice cutting through Venrick's contemplation. "Will you be staying with us here at the inn this evening?"

"I only require the stables," Venrick responded.

"There's an extra fee if you plan on staying in your wagon," the boy said.

"Fair enough." Venrick produced a silver mark and dropped it into the boy's palm. "Take care of Thunder and Giant for me. I'll be back later this evening."

"Yes sir, Lord Knight," the boy replied, respect in his voice.

"Good lad. But I am no Knight," Venrick corrected.

"A Paragon then," the boy's eyes went wide with anticipation.

"Don't let the armor fool you. I'm as far from a Paragon as one can be," Venrick said lightly, hopping off the wagon and setting out after the fire fae.

Crossing the street, he fell in behind the fae, watching it drift down the alley. Its form was more defined than any fire fae Venrick had witnessed before.. These beings were of the night court in the fae realm, they had access to powers that were forbidden in Lamar. Their source of magic was what Archmagus Hierro had used to bind the cursed amulet to Venrick's neck, tying his soul to the curse. The fae's presence sent ripples through the veil between realms. The creature's very existence here, flying in plain sight, hinted at foul play or something else born of desperation.

Venrick drew his hood closer, to conceal his ears. The gift of his mixed blood allowed him to perceive what human eyes would dismiss as tricks of the light. Yet even with this advantage, the sight before him challenged everything he knew about the laws of the fae courts.

The fire fae's hair cascaded as living flame, each strand a ribbon of crimson and gold that danced in perfect harmony with her dress of pure rippling fire. She moved in perfect synchronization with a young woman whose presence demanded his attention, even without supernatural accompaniment. Her raw umber hair and pale skin complemented her travel cloak that shifted between blues and greens like the depths of a river winding through an old forest. A colorful pattern of autumn leaves adorned her shoulders, individual leaves of yellow, orange, and red trailed down the length of it as though they were falling behind her as she walked. Each stitch had been sewn with careful consideration and spoke to the craftsmanship with which the rest of her outfit had been tailored.

When the fae suddenly winked out of existence, Venrick felt a subtle shift in pressure on his temples. Had she passed into the fae realm, or had she gone elsewhere? He continued to follow the young woman alone, his footsteps barely disturbing the packed stones on the street. Despite his stealth something gave him away, causing her to turn.

The force of her gaze stopped him in his tracks. Deep green eyes, bright with intelligence, locked onto him across the distance. The world seemed to hold its breath. Her face, now fully revealed, carried the kind of beauty that poets struggle to capture in verse. Her features were almost elf-like, not physically perfect, but profound enough to hint to a goddess' touch. High cheekbones cast subtle shadows across light skin that glowed with inner beauty, framing a noble nose. Her supple lips were pressed into a tight line in warning. It was the same look the woman in his dream had given him.

Instead of confronting him, she turned sharply toward the tavern across the street. The fire fae chose that moment to reappear, her flame-bright body slipping through a shuttered window.

He entered a short time later. The Bear's Tooth Tavern engulfed him in a wave of warmth, conversation, and aromatics mixing with spiced meat and aged ale. The fire fae had positioned itself like a sentinel on the windowsill, her attention fixed on the mysterious woman who now conversed with a well-dressed young man. A finely crafted lute at his side marked him as a bard. The lute's strings stretched tight on a wooden neck of fine handy work.

Friends with the bard, he thought, trying to remember if he'd ever met a bard he liked.

Venrick navigated the crowded room, settling at a table that allowed him to listen in while remaining unobtrusive. A dwarf with storm-gray eyes met his gaze across the room, recognition flickering in their depths.

Ezra, Venrick realized.

Ezra had been an instructor at the Astral City Paragon Academy, where supreme soldiers were chosen for a special path separate from commanding a unit in typical war strategy. The academies were designed to create special forces that waged a different war against Nordraven, a constant struggle to be the first to collect sapphires and orbs containing fragmented energy from the gods. Venrick recalled that Ezra had retired from his position at the Vermillion Academy. He glanced away, hoping the dwarf wouldn't approach.

The conversation between the striking woman and the bard flowed in a friendly way. He discerned what he could. Their destination, Astral City, seemed simple enough, but discussion of the purpose of the journey, that's when the undertones of their conversation grew tense. Clearly the nature of her quest brought up strong emotions.

"What will you have, chicken or pork?" The waitress's question cut through his observations, her practical tone a stark contrast to the mysteries unfolding behind him.

Venrick's eyes tracked the dark-haired woman as she left the table. Though feminine, she moved with the poise of a trained warrior, control evident in every line of her body. She chose a seat near the window where the fire fae had perched, the magical creature's light casting subtle shadows across her features.

"I'll have whatever you recommend," Venrick replied absently.

"Spicy pork with mead it is," the waitress announced, spinning away and returning to the kitchen.

With deliberate casualness, Venrick relocated to the table the bard now occupied alone. This young man's earlier confidence had been noticeably diminished by the strained ending to his conversation with the young woman.

"Excuse me," Venrick said, standing across the table from the bard. "I couldn't help but overhear you say you were headed for the Vermillion Keep?"

"What's it to you?" the bard responded, not lifting his eyes from his mug to look at Venrick.

"Nothing to me really, I'm just eager to make conversation after being on the road for so long. Do you mind if I join you?"

The young man now looked up, his expression softening with interest upon seeing Venrick's attire. "Sure," he motioned. "Pull up a chair. I still have a few minutes before I need to go back on."

"That Vermillion Keep business seemed a touchy issue for your friend." Venrick pointed his chin toward the woman who was now eating in earnest.

"With Lark?"

Venrick's brow lifted.

"Ash, she's always acting so serious. I wish she'd lighten up a bit. I guess I might be a little touchy, too, if I couldn't remember anything,"

"You said her name was Lark, that girl with the green eyes?"

"Her," Hardin said, pointing directly at her.

She turned. The world seemed to still around them as their eyes met across the tavern's hazy expanse. The ambient noise of clinking tankards and boisterous conversation fell to a distant whisper. Her expression transformed, the earlier sharp awareness melting into a look of recognition that shouldn't have been possible.

Venrick felt the steady rhythm of his heart fracture into an erratic beat that sent waves of warmth through his chest. It was like sensing powerful magic on the air, only this feeling carried none of the usual warning signs of danger. The lantern light emphasized the perfect arch of her brow, the subtle parting of her lips. Even the shadows seemed to caress her face with a gentleness, suggesting nature itself acknowledged her beauty. A connection between them seemed to buzz as he stared into her emerald eyes.

"Yeah," the bard continued. "She said she was a fire wheat harvester, but I've never met a farmer who dressed as a Lady or looked like, well, I mean look at her. You see, it don't you?"

"She is striking," Venrick admitted, reluctantly pulling his gaze away from her. "You said she can't remember anything, why is that?" he asked.

"Don't know. Some horrific accident or something that she doesn't want to talk about. Apparently, it happened before she left this village where she was supposedly harvesting fire wheat."

As he spoke, Venrick watched Lark leave the building.

She must have something to do with the Hyalite. That stern, yet beautiful face had penetrated his dreams. He'd thought he'd conjured her in his mind somehow, but now that he'd seen her in the flesh... And the way the fire fae was following her... He pondered, mulling over the goblin's riddle again.

Venrick's gaze drifted toward the window to catch another glimpse of— Venrick flinched, his sweeping eyes interrupted by Ezra's pointed stare. The dwarf's stoney glare held him captive for a moment. Venrick forced himself to relax, shifting with the practiced nonchalance of a perfect stranger, hoping the dwarf wasn't about to spark up a conversation with him.

The bard's voice continued weaving through the noise of the crowd, washing over Venrick like a cascade. "Anyway, that's why I'm headed to the Vermillion Keep. Need to try and find a Knight or Paragon to help me. You don't happen to know of any do you?"

The Lost Dragonrider of Lamar

The last question pierced through Venrick's thoughts. "Yes," he replied.

"Really?"

"What was your name again?" Venrick asked.

"Hardin Morningstar."

"Good to meet you, Hardin. Mine's Venrick, just Venrick," he said, reaching over the tabletop to shake Hardin's hand.

"Do you really know a Knight or Paragon who might help me?"

Desperation wove through Hardin's voice, his earlier tale of theft and a village in need coming into focus. The specifics blurred at the edges of Venrick's memory as he hadn't been giving Hardin his undivided attention moments ago. He had said something about stolen coin, and a girl, some orcs or something? But what resonated, was that Hardin was in desperate need of a hero. The opportunity presented to Venrick was his for the taking. This was his way into the caravan. He could go with Hardin, keep a close watch on the woman and her fire fae companion. The plan was still taking shape as his words spilled out, fully committing himself.

"Yes, as it so happens, I have gone on hundreds of quests for the Vermillion Keep. I can help you with yours," Venrick said.

"Are you serious?" Hardin asked.

"Yes, even now I'm returning from having driven a goblin from his lair in the Astral Mountains."

Hardin's gaze narrowed to questioning slits.

"I can prove it," Venrick added, lifting his sleeve to show the puncture wounds where Zorjan had bitten him. The marks were scabbed over enough that he no longer kept it wrapped.

"Wicked," Hardin gasped, examining the wound. "You survived a goblin bite?"

"With the right spell, you can survive almost anything," Venrick announced, repeating a phrase Tel Roan had said to him in his first year as his Squire.

"Like I was saying, I don't know if I have enough to compete with the rates you're used to receiving."

"That's fine. I'm between contracts now and am not bound to the Keep. I'll even make you a deal; I'll do it for half. I'll help you and your friend, Lark," Venrick said.

"Lark, too?" Hardin said, scratching his head.

"Why not?" Venrick replied, leaning back in his chair.

"Yeah, she might hear you out since you know more about the Vermillion Keep. Maybe you can answer her questions."

"Sure, so I'll join you and the caravan in the morning. We can resupply in Astral City and be on our way." As he spoke, the waitress slipped him his meal on a warm plate and set down a tankard of mead with a clunk. Venrick smiled, quite pleased with himself.

"That sounds great," Hardin agreed.

"Then it's settled." Venrick forked a mouthful of the pork, took a bite, and washed it down with the sweet mead.

A voice like boulders rolling down a mountainside crashed through Venrick's moment of victory. "Hardin, introduce me to your friend," Ezra said, suddenly appearing beside their table.

He pulled out the chair next to Venrick, spun it round, and settled in on it backwards. He draped his beard over the edge of the chair and glared at Venrick as he set his mug down on the table with force. It splashed, some of the ale sloshing out onto Venrick's plate.

"This is Venrick," Hardin said, sitting tall with his chest pushed forward.

"Why does that name sound so familiar, Venrick?" Ezra asked, pointing his meaty finger at Venrick. "You look familiar, too. Have we ever met before?"

"No," Venrick lied.

"Ever attended Astral City Paragon Academy?"

"Venrick says he's gone on countless missions for the Vermillion Keep," Hardin said, folding his arms across his chest.

"Funny, I've helped train every Paragon that held a contract with the Vermillion Keep for the last fifty years, and I don't remember seeing you."

"It must've been after you retired, then," Venrick said.

"I didn't retire," Ezra growled through clenched teeth. "I resigned; there's a difference."

"I didn't realize it mattered," Venrick shrugged.

"It does. What are you doing sniffing around Hardin and Lark?"

"I'm not sniffing. Just making conversation," he said calmly.

"Venrick, why does that name ring a bell?" Ezra asked again, measuring Venrick with his stoney glare. After a moment, he snapped his fingers with the answer. "I know why. You had something to do with Tel Roan."

"Yes, well, I was Tel Roan's Squire for nearly eleven years," Venrick said.

"That's it, you're Tel Roan's Squire. I knew I recognized you," Ezra said, satisfied. He took a swig of his drink. "Shouldn't you be dead?"

"That's what everyone keeps telling me."

"You were trained by Tel Roan himself?" Hardin gawked.

"I was," Venrick said.

"Why does that seem to be so important to you?" Ezra asked, turning his scarred head toward Hardin.

"Because he's agreed to help me with my problem. He might be able to help Lark, too," he answered.

"Help? How exactly?" Ezra growled.

Venrick tried to wave the question away, but Hardin answered before he could reply.

"Because he's a Knight of the Vermillion Keep."

"Is that what he told you?" Ezra chuckled. He leaned in, facing Venrick squarely. "And how did you manage that while being Tel's Squire up until last month? Training at the Academy alone takes four years, and you need to be accepted with previous experience."

"I didn't say I was a Knight, exactly," Venrick said.

"You said you have gone on hundreds of quests for the Keep," Hardin accused.

"All true," Venrick said.

"He's got a sword, some armor, and look at his arm. Recently survived a goblin bite while banishing it from a mountain lair," Hardin said.

"Is that so? Which goblin was that and in what mountain range?" Ezra almost demanded.

Venrick cleared his throat. "Zorjan, in the Astral Range."

Ezra barked a laugh. "Zorjan? That slippery eel of an informant? I don't believe it for a second. Tel probably saved you after that green ash-stain bit you."

"This was a few weeks ago, after Tel's demise," Venrick said. *Although, it was Tel's enchanted chest that saved me,* he conceded to himself.

"Don't buy what he's selling, lad," Ezra said.

"He's not a real hero?"

"Looks can be deceiving. Plenty of silver-tongued swindlers lurk on the edges of the Keeps. We'll come across more the closer we come to Astral City. They'll take your money faster than you can give it to them and run. Better come over to our side of the tavern and let Venrick eat in peace before he heads back out onto the road."

Hardin scowled at Venrick, his somber demeanor returning.

"Hardin, I can help you. And I'll do it for much less than what a Knight under contract will charge. I'm very highly trained. I fought alongside Tel Roan for over a decade," Venrick pled.

Ezra stood, placing a calloused hand on Hardin's shoulder. "Come on, lad, you can find better men to spend your money on."

Hardin's back rounded, his head stooped, shoulders sagging as he took his mead and joined Ezra with the rest of the caravanners.

Venrick finished his meal alone. Embarrassed, and having seen no more signs of the fire fae, Venrick left. The tavern's warmth fell away behind him as he stepped out into the night. Hardin's melodic voice weaved its captive spell over the crowd, fading as the cobblestones passed under Venrick's feet.

If they won't let me in, I guess I'll just have to force my way in, he thought.

The signs were there, demanding his attention. The dragon tracks, the Morsythians, the fire fae paired up with a human, it was too much of a coincidence. This was no mere happenstance. Venrick couldn't let them pass him by without knowing more. Regardless of being bound by the curse, he was going to follow the fire fae. He wasn't going to give up his hunt for the Hyalite.

16

MORSYTHIAN

As she walked away from the Bear's Tooth Tavern, the night nipped at Lark's cheeks with winter's first bite. Behind her, heavy footfalls broke the silence. Her keen hearing immediately assessed them as deliberate and measured, like a predator's. She wasn't more than a block from the Tavern, when she noticed the shadowy figure, darker than the dimming night, moving in her wake.

"Hardin?"

The name died on her lips as she focused, knowing that whoever was tailing her was no friend. The being that stalked her dwarfed even the half-elf who'd been staring at her. The figure's shoulders were as broad as a smith's anvil; they stretched the fabric of his storm-gray cloak. Though a deep hood shrouded most of his features, moonlight caught the curved ivory of two massive tusks jutting upward from a blue-tinged jaw. It was the unmistakable mark of a Morsythian warrior. At his throat, a ruby amulet shone with an inner light. Its strange glow seemed to thrive on the darkness around it. Then, a metallic whisper hissed in the night, a blade being drawn from its scabbard.

He's come for the Hyalite, she thought with terrible certainty.

Lark quickened her pace, each heartbeat thundering in her ears. The Northern monster's strides rapidly ate the distance between them. She veered sharply into a side alley, boots scraping against the ground as she emerged onto the next street. There she pressed herself against a darkened wall, her breath coming in silent gasps as she watched the intersection. The Morsythian appeared like a phantom, massive frame moving with unnatural ease as he cut across her trail, now out in the open.

How does he know what I have?

Her feet carried her through the maze of streets and alleys in a desperate dance, doubling back and weaving unpredictable patterns that would have lost any normal pursuer. But each time she paused to listen, to hope, those heavy footsteps returned, as if the ruby around his neck could taste her scent. Ahead, golden lamplight spilled across the street from another tavern's windows, carrying with it the hope of safety in numbers. Sounds of laughter and song beckoned. Lark slipped through the door like a shadow, positioning herself by a shuttered window to peer through the gaps.

Did I lose him?

Terror sank its claws deeper as the Morsythian rounded the corner, moonlight revealing him in his full, terrible glory. Muscles rippled beneath his cloak, while black tattoos writhed up his neck like creeping vines. The ruby amulet bounced against his chest with each step, its unnatural lure growing stronger, hungrier.

From the center of the street, he raised one massive hand toward her hiding place. The ruby's glow intensified, bleeding into the night like fresh-spilled blood. The world tilted sideways as Lark stumbled back from the window, the tavern's boisterous crowd becoming a suffocating discord. The walls seemed to breathe, to close in. Darkness funneled at the edges of her vision. She pressed her hands against her ears, forcing her way through the crowd that parted around her like water, their cheers and applause a dull roar as she fought toward the rear door.

The night air slapped her in the nose when she burst outside, clearing away some of her tunnel vision. A woman's song still drifted through the walls. Lark shook herself, reset to flee, and froze. There he stood, close enough to touch. The ruby light painted his tusks the color of fresh gore.

"It is you," he rumbled, massive hands closing on her shoulders, one grabbing hold of her pack.

Instinct took over. Lark's boot came down like a hammer on his foot, followed by a strike to his Adam's apple. He gagged and staggered backward, his grip still tight on the pack. She drove her shoulder into his massive chest, fighting for space, but his hold remained iron-tight. The pack's strap stretched between them, growing as taut as a bowstring. She kicked his knee with brutal force. He buckled. But even as he fell, his free hand moved to his side, drawing a curved dagger from the hidden folds of his cloak. Steel rasped through the air between them.

Lark's eyes widened at the wild swing as it just missed. Her fist connected with his temple, the impact jarring through her arm.

He groaned, refusing to let go of the pack, readying himself with the dagger. His yellow eyes gleamed with determination and focus. They were fixed on the pack. Her punch to his head had rattled him, but these orcs were clearly warriors, their skulls thick as stone.

Back on his feet, he reset his stance and moved his blade for a killing strike. In one fluid motion, Lark released the strap, freeing her arm to snake around and capture his wrist. Something took over, a motion guiding her hands to find the exact pressure point that would make steel kiss the alley floor. As the dagger fell, she caught it from the air. The Morsythian cared nothing for the lost blade, his massive hands now claiming the pack as a prize. Moving faster than thought, she flowed behind him, lifted his chin, and pulled. The orc's eyes flew wide, understanding blooming too late. As his lifeblood painted the front of his leathers, his brows drew together in confusion. His fingers fumbled at the ruby amulet even as he cast the pack aside, as though the prize he'd died for meant nothing and the ruby was everything. Unable to grasp the jewel, he toppled forward onto the tavern steps. The ruby's glow faded with his final breath.

Lark stepped back, horror replacing battle-calm as her trembling hands reclaimed the pack.

What did I just do?

She scanned the alley with wild eyes, but the shadows held no witnesses. The Hyalite remained safe in her possession, though its weight seemed to have doubled. Lark understood now that she couldn't let the Hyalite out of her possession without knowing what it was going to be used for. Fear steered her down the only course she could see, forward to the Vermillion Keep where she would get answers. She was close. She just needed to make it to Astral City.

"Nix," she said. The fae didn't appear. "Nix, I need you!" But the fire fae was not there and the pendant on her neck had gone cold.

Panic rose like bile in her throat, so she did the only thing she could think of. She ran, leaving death and questions bleeding on the tavern steps behind her.

17

IN PLAIN SIGHT

Dawn arrived in bloody hues as Lark climbed to her perch atop the wagon bench, her fingers absently tracing the worn wood of her seat. The morning was bitter cold, a stark reminder of the night's events that still haunted her.

"Nix?" she whispered, her voice barely carrying above the creaking of wagon wheels and the stirring of the camp around her.

The necklace warmed against her skin, its heat a comfort. Within moments, Nix materialized beside her, her red dress seeming to trap the early morning light in its flame.

"There you are," Nix said, the flame embroiling her wavering like a candle in a gentle breeze.

Lark glanced furtively at the other wagons where people were beginning to emerge, their shadows long in the growing daylight. "What happened to you last night? I could've used your help," she whispered, tension evident in every line of her body.

"I found it," Nix replied. "I found the dragon."

"What? You did?"

"Yes. It hid from me." Nix balled her fists in frustration. "I followed it as best I could, but it wouldn't let me get as close as we were before. By the time I returned to town, I couldn't find you."

"Because I had to hide here, I needed the protection of the wagons." The words tasted hostile to Lark, memories of fight still fresh in her mind.

"Why did you do that? You know I can't come into the wagon because of that dwarf's magic."

"A Morsythian attacked me," Lark responded, her actions fully sinking in.

Voices drifted up from the wagon ahead, carrying news that made Lark's blood run cold. "A Morsythian? Are you sure? They're in the deep North. The only Northern people to have successfully separated from the four kingdoms in Nordraven. They have their independence, so why would a Morsythian be all the way down here?"

"I don't know. I heard from Ezra this morning that they haven't seen one in Lamar for decades."

"What business does a Morsythian have coming into Lamar unannounced?"

"I don't know, but he was murdered. Stabbed right here in Fletcher's Passage."

"Really? Killed by who?"

"I heard Ezra say it was likely that half-elf who was at the tavern last night. He tried to swindle Hardin, you know. Ezra thinks it happened shortly after he left..."

Lark closed her eyes thinking she could shut out the memory that way. The look on the Morsythian's face, the way his thick blue fingers had fumbled for the amulet in those final moments. The vision played behind her eyes in merciless detail. The glint of steel catching moonlight, the terrible dance of muscle memory of an assassin that moved through her with ease. Her fingers tingled with phantom sensation, remembering the precise pressure needed to handle the blade just so.

What were they even doing here? She questioned, seeking to displace the blame. *I thought they'd left, shortly after we arrived.* As if triggered by the raw emotion of the moment, a memory from her past burst forth.

She was no longer perched atop the wagon in the cool morning air, but standing in a home built among the trees, fabricated into the canopy as if grown rather than built. The massive branches cradled the structure, their snow-laden boughs creating a cocoon of pristine white.

A fire crackled in the stone hearth. Lark stood at a table. An assembly gathered around the heartwood slab, a group that would've given even the most seasoned diplomat pause. A silver-haired elf woman commanded the space with natural authority. Her presence bent the room's energy around her like light through a prism. A white hawk sat perched on her shoulder, a creature that was more sentinel than pet. The elf held a wooden staff, its Yogo Sapphire head writhing with rhythmic blue light.

Beside the elf stood a human woman. Strikingly beautiful, she had ice-blue eyes and thick blonde hair like spun gold, that had been woven into two braids and hung past either shoulder. She was leaning forward, her hands planted firmly on a map that covered the table. Across from them, three Morsythians stood proud. Their ceremonial armor reflected snow-filtered sunlight with subtle blue undertones that matched their skin. Their lack of weapons spoke louder than any blade could have. This was a meeting that transcended the usual boundaries of trust and suspicion.

Lark felt a weight of importance pressing against her. She was holding a golden medallion that seemed more crucial than the strange assembly gathered around the table. The artifact was a masterwork of smithing. It was round as the full moon, three saucer-shaped wheels fit inside one another. A collection of scripts were carved into it, written on silver bands that trimmed each nested ring.

Lark leaned forward and placed the medallion on the map of the Everburning Forest.

"The Magi Order won't help us and we can't count on the riders alone to stop the rimeshade," one of the Morsythians said.

"The riders are bound to their contracts. Most will not break them and risk losing the bonds with their dragons," Lark confirmed.

"Rimeshade?" the blue-eyed girl said. "That's what we're doing this for? I thought they were monsters of myth, made up to scare kids to return home before dark."

The elf shook her head, saying, "Rimeshade are very real. They threaten all Kingdoms of Sataran. Nordraven, Doran, Gambria, Lamar, and Sojax, are all under threat of corruption," the elf said.

"Which is why we need a rider of our own," the Morsythian said. "You're sure this will help?"

"Positive," the elf replied.

"We didn't go to all of this trouble just to try and set you up," the blue-eyed girl said.

The Morsythian in the middle met Lark's gaze. He reached across the table as she accepted his grip in hers. "We have a deal," he said as they shook.

The memory faded.

"Lark, did you hear what happened?" someone asked.

Lark blinked, her surroundings coming into focus. Nix was gone.

"Lark, are you okay?" Hardin asked.

She flinched. Hardin's face appeared unexpectedly nearby as he emerged through the hatch to join her on the perch.

"Ashes, Lark, I didn't mean to startle you."

"No, it's okay. I'm just tired. What were you saying?"

"Did you hear about what happened?"

"About what?" Lark said, feigning ignorance.

"There was a murder. Ezra wants us gone before the Town Watch starts poking around the caravan."

"A murder?" Lark said, trying to sound surprised.

"Yeah, it wasn't what you'd expect either. One of those Morsythians from the North, a blue-skinned orc."

"How was he killed?"

"Apparently with his own dagger. They found his neck," he ran his finger across his throat and grimaced. "Right outside a different tavern late last night."

"Do you know who did it?" Lark asked, her hand instinctively shifting to the edge of the wagon, as she mentally prepared to run.

"No. Nobody saw it happen, but those orcs are known for being tough. They've kept their independence as a tribal nation separate from the rest of Nordraven's monarchies. They haven't fought for the North, or against Lamar since the four Northern kingdoms made their alliance hundreds of years ago. Morsythians are known for being mean though. A true warrior culture. Whoever killed him was well trained. Could have been another one of their own kind who did it. That's what some are saying, but I think I might know who did it."

"Who?"

"Venrick," he said.

"Venrick? Should I know who that is?"

"Oh, that's right, you left just before he introduced himself," Hardin said.

"He was the elf?"

"Only half-elf, but yes. Venrick was Tel Roan's Squire for a decade. If anyone in this town could've killed a Morsythian, it's probably him."

Lark felt a rush of relief. She was glad to have the suspicion thrown from her, but guilt darkened her heart. She couldn't help but wonder, though. The Morsythians' and Venrick's arrival in Fletcher's Passage at the same time could not be coincidental. *Is the half-elf leading these Northern orcs? And why didn't he try to kill me himself? Was he waiting to see how dangerous I am?*

"Venrick was the one who tried to talk you into hiring him?" she asked, having just overhead the news.

"Yeah. He bid the job for half what the Knights of the Vermillion Keep would charge. I almost agreed until Ezra intervened."

Why would he do that unless he was trying to distract us while he came after the Hyalite?

"I'm sorry if I offended you last night. You kind of stormed off," Hardin said.

"I honestly had already forgotten about it."

"Really?"

"Trust me, you were the least stressful part of my night," Lark said.

"Is that why you didn't you sleep well?"

"Who said I didn't?"

"You said you were tired a moment ago."

"It was the chicken. It didn't sit right with me," she lied, grabbing her stomach.

"Should've had the pork, it was delicious. Though, I don't know how that spice will feel coming back out today," Hardin said.

Lark shook her head.

"Is that a smile I see on your face?" Hardin said, nudging her with his elbow.

"Did you have to share that image?" she said, unable to hold back a grin.

"You were the one who started it with that bad chicken talk."

"Everyone, load up," Ezra called out along the string of wagons. "We're moving out before more watchmen come asking questions."

Lark took one last glance over her shoulder as they left Fletcher's Passage. A lone rider in a hooded gray travel cloak drove a bulky six-wheeled wagon pulled by two impressive draft horses.

Lark nudged Hardin. "Is he following us?"

"Yeah, I think that's him." Hardin said, shifting to get a better look. "It is, that's Venrick. I guess the Watch let him go?"

"He's following us," Lark said, her grip tightening around a dagger handle.

"Maybe, or maybe he's going into Astral City. He mentioned something about having to resupply."

"Do you believe he really worked with Tel Roan?" Lark asked, watching him keep his steady pace about a hundred yards off theirs.

"Ezra recognized him. So, yes, he was Tel Roan's Squire. Who knows how useful being a Squire for a Paragon is, though. Usually, Squires are accepted into the training academies the Keeps sponsor after a year or two of experience. Sometimes they take soldiers who are exceptionally skilled, have potential for using magic, and don't have strong desires to lead a large army. When Squires don't make it in after a few years, they tend to go into another branch of the military to advance their careers. I've never heard of anyone squiring for a Paragon for over ten years, although he is half-elf. Since Lamar is a human-dominant kingdom, they tend to frown on anyone without pure bloodlines. I've never understood why," Hardin continued, chewing his lip in thought. With a shrug, he said, "Maybe Venrick will camp near us tonight. Last night I told him he might be able to provide some answers for you."

"You talked about me to him?" Lark said, snapping her attention to Hardin.

"Well, yes."

"What did you tell him?"

"I didn't tell him much. He was the one who wanted to know about you."

"He asked about me?"

Hardin nodded, and said, "The way he was looking at you usually can mean one of two things, and I don't think he wanted to kill you."

Lark's cheeks flushed at the notion that Venrick was ogling her. She quickly struck down any idea of romance. His intrigue was likely directed at her because of the Hyalite, not her appearance.

"Yeah, he overheard some of our conversation and wanted to know why it made you so upset."

"He overheard our conversation," Lark repeated, remembering that Hardin almost suggested out loud what he thought was in Lark's pack.

"It's no big deal. We'll be to Astral City by tomorrow and he'll be off our minds."

"Yeah," Lark said absentmindedly. Questions swirled like vortexes formed in a river eddy, bubbling with new information emerging from her memory and the knowledge of who Venrick had squired for.

Venrick won't get his hands on the Hyalite if I have anything to do with it. I'll keep my daggers close, she thought while watching the tall Squire sitting comfortably on the wagon rolling behind them.

∽

Venrick pressed the cool brass of the spyglass against his eye as he studied the caravan.

"There's something unusual going on with this lot," he said to Thunder and Giant, his trusted steeds.

They snorted in response, their breath forming tiny clouds in the crisp morning air.

"And why would Ingamar be following them?"

Thunder's iron-shod hoof struck the frozen earth with a resonant tamp at the mention of the dragon's name.

"The Morsythians, too. What's their reason for traveling this far South?" he questioned. "Odder still was that fire fae... she was with that girl; Lark was her name. Follow the spark, meaning her?"

He paused, considering the impossible. "I've never heard of a normal human bonding with a fire fae. Does that mean... No, she can't be, can she?" he considered, dismissing the thought that the unknown dragonrider who had come to Tel's aid would be tormenting their dragon by traveling via caravan.

He focused the spyglass on Lark. She sat perched atop the rear wagon, her face buried in her hands as though she were contemplating life choices. The bard, Hardin, emerged like a ground squirrel from the inside, popping through the hatch to join her on the roof. Moments later, they were moving along the road to Astral City. He collapsed his spyglass and kissed the two draft horses into motion.

Venrick followed, the familiar rhythm of hoofbeats beneath him a counterpoint to his racing thoughts as he tried to put the pieces of this puzzle into place. What he couldn't understand was why the town authorities in Fletcher's Passage had pointed the finger of blame at him for the Morsythian's murder.

He glanced over his shoulder at the town, glad to be leaving. Had fate not placed that stable boy in their way, verifying Venrick's presence at the Inn before the Morsythian's murder, he would be stuck behind iron bars.

"Who struck down the Northern orc? And why hadn't his

companions helped him?" Venrick's thoughts drifted to Ingamar lurking in the forest. The dragon could've easily intervened, but he wouldn't have left a body.

"Could all these strange events be because of the Flashover?" he asked himself. "It's coming up this year and people always say strange things happen around the Flashover," he mused. "Or is it because they have the Hyalite. No other Hyalites have been won since. If they are carrying a Hyalite with them, which one of them has it?"

Venrick didn't know who all was in the caravan, but he contemplated those he'd seen last night. "Ezra seems capable. He was an instructor at the Academy for decades. He could be trying to get back in the Keep's good graces. Or it could be the bard... No, Hardin needs to hire a hero. He's not one himself. There's Lark, she could be hiding secrets, but why? Why keep something so powerful a secret? Its energy is enough to forge a bond with a dragon, fusing the dragon's magical essence with that of one of the gods, forming an increased form of magic that can only be channeled by sharing it via a bond with the one the dragon chooses as its rider. Why would anyone in possession of a Hyalite pass up such an opportunity?"

A part of him wanted to drift back to where Ingamar might find him. The dragon's presence would be more than invaluable, even just for a second set of eyes. Ingamar shared a connection with all Hyalites as he had used the power of a god to bond with Tel. By now, Ingamar should've known Venrick was in the area. If it was Ingamar, he was keeping himself hidden and did not want Venrick to find him.

If Venrick let the Hyalite slip away because he fell too far behind to observe the caravan, he would never forgive himself. He and Ingamar never got along anyway. If the dragon wanted to keep his distance, then he could do so. With no other leads, Venrick continued to keep the caravan in plain sight.

Hardin's gaze traced Lark's hunched shoulders as she huddled near the wagon edge, her fingers absently working the slightly frayed hem of her cloak. The girl who had finally started sharing fragments of her past over campfire meals now seemed to fold inward with each step toward Astral City. It was as if the looming spires on the horizon were pressing down upon her soul. Today's silence cut deeper than yesterday's tentative words after Fletcher's Passage, when she had at least met his eyes while declining soup that evening. Now she stared at the road, her jaw set, the shadows beneath her eyes darker than the approaching dusk.

At least I don't have to keep trying to jolly her along after today, he thought.

Her leather pack rested against her leg, worn but well-oiled, its ivory toggle shining dully in the daylight. He'd never seen her let it get out of an arm's reach. Not while eating, not while sleeping, it was either on her shoulders or at her side. Whatever secrets that pack held they seemed to weigh on her more heavily than the pack's physical burden.

What could possibly be in there?

Hardin's eyes lingered on the pack, his mind spinning with possibilities. Precious Yogo Sapphires were a possibility considering the way she guarded it. His thoughts skipped toward a more sinister prospect before he forced them back. A Hyalite, one of the mystical orbs of power, could be nestled in those leather folds. The notion sent a chill down his spine.

No, he thought, shaking his head.

Hardin would sense that kind of raw energy, would feel it humming in his bones like a struck bell, wouldn't he? That kind of power would be impossible to ignore, right? Yet the question of what she carried gnawed at him.

She is so mysterious. Why does she pretend that she can't remember anything?

Hardin contemplated Lark's behavior since they first met. The way she tracked her surroundings, how she responded to questions with careful consideration rather than confusion. Saying she suffered from memory loss had to be a way to keep others from asking her too many questions. Amnesia alone couldn't explain her secretive nature. The truth lay elsewhere, locked behind those guarded emerald eyes.

Unless... Is the reason why she can't remember a side effect of a spell?

The pieces didn't align. Fire wheat harvesters might bear scars from their dangerous trade. The occupation would leave physical wounds, but magical memory loss? Those afflictions belonged to mages who'd drawn too deeply from forbidden wells of power. No, something more sinister lay beneath her carefully constructed story.

Lark's neck twisted again to scan behind them, her muscles clearly tense. The afternoon sun caught a sheen of sweat on her brow not caused by heat, but from the constant vigilance that had her head snapping around at every distant sound, every shadow that shifted in her peripheral vision.

She acts like someone who is used to being hunted, Hardin thought.

"Still back there?" he asked her.

"Yeah. He is most definitely following us." Lark said, furrowing her brow. Her narrowed eyes constantly combed the area, her lips pressed in a tight line.

"He's probably returning to the Vermillion Keep for reassignment or something," Hardin said, though he did find it odd that Venrick hadn't joined them, yet he'd chosen to maintain a steady distance behind them rather than riding around the caravan or falling farther behind over the last day and a half.

"I don't trust him," Lark said.

Hardin sighed, facing forward. The valley unfurled before them. The mountains thrust skyward, their snow-capped peaks piercing white clouds.

"There it is, Astral City," he said.

At their feet sprawled Astral City, its crimson spires and domes vibrant in the sun's rays. They cast shadows across the valley floor. The city shone with its own luminescence, the legendary wells of power within its foundations still burning bright after a thousand years.

They left the rural serenity, the lush fields and rich farmland, and passed into the organized chaos of civilization. Thatched roofs gave way to tiled ones, then to the angular geometry of urban architecture climbing the valley's gentle slopes. Above it all, the Vermillion Keep dominated. Its blood-red towers rose defiantly against the backdrop of the Astral Mountains. The fortress loomed over its domain, separated from the rest of the city by a dark, water-filled moat.

"We're coming up on the Vermillion Keep?" she asked.

"I've never seen an equal," Hardin said, in awe of the castle.

"Even Storm Keep?"

"Storm Keep is big, but not nearly as impressive as that."

Lark's features froze, blood draining from her face. It was the same haunted look he'd witnessed from her back in Fletcher's Passage.

"Are you okay?" he asked.

Lark's shoulders relaxed at his question. She took a deep breath, the color returning to her cheeks. She ran a finger over the golden lark on her necklace, something she'd been doing more often over the last few days. "Did you know the gates at the Vermillion Keep are guarded by runes infused with draconic magic." Lark said it as though it were common knowledge. "Once infused, the runes hold the energy powering them until tested. After centuries of dragonriders adding their own power to the wards, the Vermillion Keep is arguably the strongest magically protected fortress in Sataran."

"I knew they had runes powering their wards, but I didn't know it was draconic magic. I assumed it was elven or magi like the others. Hardin said.

"Have you been here before?" he asked.

"I think I have," she said, the faint quiver in her voice hinting at her self-doubt.

"You must have if you know about the runes."

"The runes were carved into the stone by the dwarves who mined the Vermillion stone from the Astral Mountains. The spells cast into them recognize only those who have been granted access or truly intend no harm. They automatically bar anyone else from entering. The moat surrounding the Keep, with the azgron crocks, is mostly for appearances," Lark informed him.

"Really? How do you know all of this?"

"Just how I know that a guard is posted at each of the city gates and they change locations every three hours. How there's magic warded throughout the entire castle to protect it against dragon attacks but only a few outdated systems that safeguard the city. Only the dragons who've been granted passage by the Paragons can fly in and out from the dragon's perch at the top of the Keep," she continued without hesitation.

"Which part is the dragon's perch?" he asked.

"That long, flat, anvil-shaped landing near the top is their landing area."

"I can see the dragons now!" Hardin said enthusiastically, joy swelling his chest at the long-awaited moment. His initial awe at the legendary Vermillion Keep suddenly soured. The structure before them matched Lark's eerily precise descriptions. They were details no common fire wheat harvester should know. The exact height of the towers, the number of arrow slits per merlon, the precise depth of the moat, her knowledge went beyond the norm. "You know all this because you've been here before?" he asked.

She shrugged.

"If not, you really did your research. Strange that you don't remember why."

"There's something about this place," she said. "I don't know. It's giving me an unsettled feeling."

That's odd, he thought.

"The other night when you left the Bear Tooth Tavern, what did you do again?"

"I went back to the wagons." Lark said, her voice carrying an emptiness to it.

She's lying.

"What's in that pack?" he asked.

"I don't like the way you're asking these questions, Hardin."

"Lark, why are you really going to Astral City? Is it to find answers or is it because of whatever is in there," he asked, pointing out the pack.

"I'm going to the city because everything I knew was stripped away into a dark void of nothing. I have nothing, no clues, no memories about why. This," she said, clutching the leather, "is the only thing connecting me to my past. By bringing it here, to the Keep, I'm doing the right thing. What any honest citizen of Lamar should do. The Paragons here are the only ones who can help me," she said with finality.

Hardin studied her a moment, waiting to see if he could detect a lie. He understood the passion in her voice. "I think, you're telling the truth."

She nodded.

Hardin watched her, measuring her truth against his instincts. Sasja's betrayal had taught him the harsh price of trust given too freely to a beautiful face. Yet something in

Lark's raw desperation rang true. The Northern soldiers' pursuit, Ezra's calculated risk in transporting her. It painted a picture of genuine flight, not calculated deception. Still, he kept his guard raised, even as his heart whispered that her quest for aid mirrored his own.

"I'll stop asking what's in there. If it's that important for you to keep it hidden from everyone, then I won't be the one to demand to see it," Hardin said.

Lark sat back, surprised by his level-headed response. Hardin hadn't realized it until now, Lark's hand was wrapped tentatively around one of her worn dagger handles. She let her hand fall away from the weapon. "Why do you trust me?" she asked.

"Because we're friends."

"Friends?" Lark asked, perplexed.

"Yeah, I think after the week we've been through, we can call one another friends," Hardin said.

Suddenly, sunlight glinted off Venrick's wagon trailing behind them, seeming to warn Hardin like a signal fire. His jaw tightened as the pieces of Lark's puzzle began to fall into place. The Morsythian ambush, Venrick's shadow on their trail, the Northern soldiers. They were all threads of a web with Lark's mysterious pack at its center. Whatever power that leather bag contained drew danger like moths to flame.

18

UNEXPECTED ACQUAINTANCE

As the caravan rolled deeper into Astral City, an unsettling weight pressed down on Lark's chest. While she tried to pay attention to her surroundings, flickers of memories danced through her head, like ghostly sails of a forgotten ship drifting through a foggy sea. She could sense them, vague, elusive, but whenever she focused, the images dissolved into the mist.

The streets of Astral City were filled with smithies, taverns, and stables that stretched before her, new yet familiar. The déjà vu was relentless.

The caravan pulled off the main thoroughfare, passing under a brick archway. Its mortar lines shimmered with the light of faintly carved elven runes. The passage between the two sprawling buildings gave way to a stable yard, a lavish necessity for the urban estate.

"This is the end of the line, Elks Lodge," Ezra announced. "My associate, Cheyanne and I, would be happy to give any of you a discounted rate to stay in the Pour House's sister inn. Everyone else, have a pleasant stay in Astral City." He made a point to hoist his war hammer over his shoulder, as he added,

"Any loiterers will be charged extra or forcebly escorted off the grounds."

Lark's necklace warmed a moment before a flash of light near a window stole her attention. Nix, who had been careful to remain out of Hardin's line of sight for a week now, openly hovered just outside a window at the inn. Her fire rippled against the window as she peered inside.

Lark checked to see if Hardin had seen Nix, but he was stooped over, back rounded, as he fished for something inside his lute.

Nix dropped away from the window, her usually pristine dress ruffled as she darted toward Lark. A word began to transform on her lips, then magic crackled around her form as she flared, darting away from the inn. Heat brushed Lark's cheek when Nix shot past, trailing sparks that dissolved into nothing. The fae continued as if fleeing from something invisible, her movements sharp and desperate as she disappeared around the corner of the archway.

"Nix?" Lark called out. A ball formed in the pit of her stomach. Something about this place didn't feel right. Something about bringing the Hyalite here didn't feel as solid as she'd imagined it would've.

"What's that?" Hardin asked, snapping to attention.

"It's... nothing," she replied.

"Ezra promised he would take me to the Keep," Hardin said, relaxing. "You're welcome to join if you'd like."

"The Keep," she repeated, her focus clinging to what could've made Nix transform and rush off like that. Her stomach churned with an unsettling feeling as doubts crept in. The idea of passing off the Hyalite without Nix there, it felt wrong. Nix was the one who initially pushed for her to keep the Hyalite and bring it with her on her quest.

This must be the right thing to do, she told herself. *They say this Keep is host the best Paragons of Lamar. They wouldn't miss-use a Hyalite, right?*

"Yes, Ezra says he can show us to the Vermillion Keep. The one you seem to suddenly know so much about," Hardin said.

If I don't do this now, I may not learn more about myself. Who I was and how I got this orb, she thought.

The crimson spires of the Vermillion Keep housed the elite guardians of Lamar; the Paragons. These champions of magical warfare were not just honored heroes. The highly trained warriors were living legends. The Paragons of the Vermillion Keep hosted the single largest collection of dragonriders outside Nordraven. How they agreed to follow their contracts with the Keep, Lark could only guess at. Money, power, control, these seemed like things a dragonrider, or group of dragonriders could gain on their own. Yet, Nordraven's dragonriders seemed to hold true to their kingdoms leaders as well.

Lark's questions spun as doubt that these heroes would take the best care of this Hyalite's power crept into her mind.

While she was standing near the wagon lost in thought, Hardin slung his lute over his shoulder, approached Ezra. Lark checked one last time for any sign of Nix.

"I will see to it that the both of you make it to the Vermillion Keep," Ezra said.

"That's not necessary, for me," Lark announced, feeling the stress mounting. "The Keep is hard to miss. I can manage to locate it on my own." She didn't know what the Keep would do with the Hyalite once they had it. She imagined they'd present the Hyalite to an unbonded dragon and allow the dragon to pick their rider.

But what if that's not how they do it here? What if they take the energy inside the Hyalite and use it for something else, like powering a new defensive or offensive ward for the Keep? Wards could hold power if left unused, but once the spells they were designed to protect were tested, the energy charging them drained. Without recharging runes with magical energy from Yogos, or one massive charge from a Hyalite, wards for a place as expansive as Astral City and the Vermillion Keep would die. With an enemy as cunning as Nordraven, surely the wards for the Keeps were probed and tested. Lark understood this as fact, just like she'd understood the layout and rotation of the Keep's guard. *Why do I know that?*

Over her journey, Lark felt there was a strange attachment that she'd grown with the Hyalite, like it shared piece of her soul. The question of whether she should go the Keep or avoid it weighed heavily on her conscience.

"Don't you want the answers you're looking for? Isn't that why you came all this way while keeping that," Hardin said gesturing to the pack, "a secret?"

Lark went rigid. She tilted her head, her breath came short and fast. She tried to wordlessly shout at Hardin to keep his mouth shut about her pack. "I think I'll manage. Ezra was kind enough to bring me this far. I'm not going to put him out anymore if I can help it."

"I'm already going to the Keep, but if you want to find your own way that doesn't bother me any," Ezra said.

"See, it's not out of his way. And he's not charging you extra," Hardin said, raising a brow at the dwarf and adding, "Right?"

"It's a one-time offer. Take it or leave it," Ezra said.

"I'll take it. Come on, Lark, what's the harm in saying yes every once in a while," Hardin said with a grin.

Lark's shoulders sagged. Hardin was relentless. "Fine, if it gets you off my case and encourages you to go annoy another person, let's go."

As they walked out past the inn and up the cobblestone street toward the Keep, Ezra continually checked to make sure they were still in tow. His visual check-ins worried Lark, *why has Ezra been so accommodating? Does he know what I have and is he making sure it is delivered?*

Hyalites contained powerful magic that once tapped into became an eternal well of energy for the users. Depending on which god it came from, the energy gave the user control over elements like earth, fire, water, or air. Others granted the users physical strengths, manipulation of emotions, power over gravity and healing. The strongest power born from a Hyalite, though, granted control over celestial powers; commanding elements of beyond those found on just one world.

A glimpse through the fog of Lark's memory hinted that a Hyalite's godly energy, though uncommon, could be forged to uses beyond the increased abilities it gave dragons and their bonded riders. Yet, the how, eluded her. She understood that Yogo Sapphires contained a finite amount energy that could be used to fuel spell crafting. Runes held spells cast by that energy until enacted on. Hyalites, however, were an everlasting source of magic. The key to controlling that amount of power, however, lay in the secrets of a dragon's bond. A bond that, in that moment she knew could be just as fragile as it was strong. Without the bond, the energy would burn through the wielder, killing them after tapping into the source. These powers were dangerous, but awesome and they warranted sums of money that rivaled a Kings ransom.

I'll keep my distance from Ezra in case he tries anything, she thought warily.

The cramped streets assaulted her senses. Waste-filled gutters competed with smoke from tavern spits and the sweet perfume of fresh bread. Market stalls overflowed with wares while smithies rang out their endless symphony of hammers and bellows. Through it all wound the city's lifeblood: humans haggling over the price of grain, dwarven metalworkers shouldering past with ingots, and elven artisans displaying intricate leatherwork, woodwork and pottery.

Astral City never rested, never quieted. Its endless commerce was constant as a beating heart.

Lark searched for Nix, stretching her mental connection outward seeking the familiar warmth of the fire fae's presence. Yet, she wasn't anywhere nearby. Even the lark pendant on her neck held no internal warmth.

Nix always chooses the worst times to disappear, she thought.

A burst of orange sparks crackling out from a nearby chimney drew her eye, raising her hopes for an instant. But instead of finding her friend's flame-cloaked silhouette, Lark's attention settled on another presence that added to her concerns. Venrick was there. The tall, dark-haired, green-eyed Squire from her vision followed, matching her pace like a shadow. He fixed her with that look. The one that sent flutters through her chest and made her pulse quicken. Hardin had warned her that look only meant one of two things. Lark knew which one burned in his eyes now.

Is he waiting for an opportunity to jump me?

As they approached the outskirts of the Keep, Ezra veered onto a narrow path. Magic from the Keep's wards hummed with an almost indetectable sensation. The strength vibrating off the outer walls sent prickles across her skin. She froze in a bustling intersection. Something about it wasn't quite right.

I shouldn't be going this way.

Reality shifted, back into place. Ezra and Hardin were far ahead, already turning onto another path. She panicked. She would lose them if she didn't hurry. She glanced back. Venrick was still there, stalking behind her. Alone, she would be vulnerable to his attack.

Lark took one step forward before an immovable force blocked her path. A hulking orc materialized before her, rivulets of sweat carving paths through the soot on his green skin. The blacksmith's hammer in his meaty grip seemed absurdly delicate, like a child's toy. His brown leather apron bore the patina of countless hours toiling at the forge. Eyes like molten copper locked onto hers as he spoke, his tusks lending his words a distinctive rumble.

"They didn't say you would come here. Why have you come?"

Lark retreated a step, her mind finding no trace of familiarity in his presence.

"What are you doing here?" he repeated.

"I don't know. I don't know you," she insisted, pushing past him. The residual heat from his forge-warmed apron brushed against her arm as she hurried after Hardin and Ezra.

At the next intersection, Lark rose onto her toes, straining to see over the sea of heads. Her eyes darted along the twisted streets, searching for any sign of her companions through the press of bodies and competing magical signatures.

"Hey," a new voice cut through the crowd's murmur. A dwarf emerged from the throng, his beard neatly braided and shimmering with fresh oil. The display case of jewelry he carried sparked with enchanted runes of protection. Waves of exotic perfume rolled off him like an invisible fog. Thick eyebrows knotted together as his face contorted into a scowl that seemed to deepen the very shadows around him. "You shouldn't have come! What were you thinking?"

Lark stared at the dwarf, her mind probing fruitlessly for any trace of recognition, any echo of a past encounter with him or the orc. But her memories offered only the unsettling void where her past remained hidden.

"Where is she? Is she here?" he asked, his gray eyes darting around the intersection.

"Nix?" she asked, confused.

"What does this mean? Is it because of the rimeshade? I must know why you came now."

"Do you know who I am?" Lark asked.

The dwarf's eyes widened. He wrung his hands nervously, backing away, and muttering to himself. Without another word, he disappeared into the crowd.

"Hey, answer me," she said, but the dwarf had dissolved into the throng of foot traffic. "Ash," she cursed, trying to find any sign of Ezra or Hardin.

The two were no longer in sight. Her eyes settled on Venrick again. He stood a safe distance behind, watching her with curiosity.

He wouldn't try to kill me, here in the open, would he? she wondered.

Lark hustled through the crowded streets, her steps guided more by instinct than thought, each stride carrying her farther from Venrick's threatening presence. Faces in the crowd flooded around her, until one among them made her pause. It was the blonde girl from her memories. Her glacial blue eyes and twin, sun-kissed braids were exactly as Lark envisioned. The only difference in her appearance now was the red stone bouncing from a chain around her neck. She cut through the crowd, each quick step taken directly in Lark's direction.

Their gazes met and the bustling thoroughfare seemed to be suspended around them. Those piercing blue eyes, cold as midwinter frost, unlocked another memory. Unlike the overwhelming torrent of her previous recollection, this memory seeped in gradually. In it, Lark and the blonde girl huddled, speaking in confidence, their voices low and urgent. Between them, the golden device from the map in her earlier memory was held firmly in the blonde's hands. The memory carried with it a weight of importance, though its full significance remained tantalizingly out of reach:

"Do you know what this, what it means that you took it?" Lark asked her.

"Yes, that's why I stole it from him. We can use this. It will

tell us where the next firestorm with power will be," the blonde responded.

"You should've consulted me before you took the astral lathe. Do you know what he'll do to us if he finds out you stole this?" Lark hissed.

"Relax. I covered my tracks. This will help us with what we're trying to do. We wanted to help get dragonriders to oppose the rimeshade. This will help us accomplish that goal."

"I meant recruit, not foster an order of newly bonded riders."

"You still believe focusing on taking out the rimeshade is the right thing to do, don't you, Ella?"

"Sasja, of course, I—"

The young woman's shoulder slammed into Lark with enough force to shatter the memory, reality rushing back in a dizzying wave.

"Hey!" Lark called out, her voice threading through the marketplace din as fragments of the vision slipped away. Her hand shot out, catching the young woman's arm. The contact sent a jolt of recognition through Lark. But the blonde wrenched away with such violence that Lark stumbled, her boots scraping against the cobblestones. "Wait, Sasja!" The name burst from her lips with unexpected certainty.

Sasja's head snapped around, those ice-blue eyes disclosing something darker than recognition as a light within her ruby necklace flashed. Then she was gone, her form blurring into motion as she darted through the crowd with uncanny speed. In her hand, azure glamor caught in the light. The bulky object glowed with an ethereal blue radiance, its energy leaving ghostly afterimages in the air behind her.

Lark's hand flew to her leather pack, fingers searching desperately for the familiar weight, the resonant hum of power that should have been there. Instead, they found only the soft rustle of spare clothing. The absence hit her like a collapsing mountain.

She has it. Sasja stole the Hyalite! The orb's absence left a physical ache, like a phantom limb.

Something primal awoke in Lark then. It was a desperate, burning need that consumed all other thoughts. She launched herself after Sasja, her feet barely touching the ground as she ran. Any lingering sentiment from their shared past evaporated. The Hyalite called to her, a siren's pull that demanded response, and Lark knew with bone-deep finality that she would tear through any realm to reclaim it.

Hardin whirled, "Ezra, I think we lost her."

"Let it go, lad. She was hard-headed and determined to go it alone. We did what we could, now it's time to solve your problem. I can talk you through the gate but after that you're on your own."

As he turned back, Hardin caught sight of a blur of golden hair and eyes like frozen sapphires brushing past him. Hardin startled and did a double-take; the back of the woman's hair was parted in the middle to form two braids.

"Sasja," he called. "Hey, Sasja!"

She turned just enough for her profile to remain backlit, the movement precise and deliberate as if not to give herself away. The gesture carried an echo of longing.

"Hardin, you need to go to the Keep now if you want to be seen today," Ezra said.

"But I just—" Hardin gestured toward the blonde's retreating form.

An elf materialized between them, his tall form elegant yet impenetrable as an iron door. When he cleared out of the way,

Sasja had vanished. The absence left Hardin with a bitter taste in his mouth.

"Let her go," Ezra commanded, his voice resonating with wisdom. "We can't help those who don't want it. There's a group of Knights and dragonriders in the Keep renegotiating their contracts but that window of opportunity is closing. Most of them will have already signed on with the King and will be tied to their duties here in Lamar. This is your only chance to line up a quality hero for anything close to what you can afford."

"I have—"

"I know about your stash in that lute. And don't think I didn't see you collecting tips from those on the caravan. You're still going to have to use that silver tongue of yours to convince a Knight of the Vermillion Keep to leave their posting in Lamar and to go with you to the Kingdom of Doran."

Hardin adjusted his lute, its weight betraying the treasure hidden within its hollow body. The streets offered no sign of Lark, and the memory of Sasja running past left an ache in his soul. The Keep's imposing silhouette grew larger with each step, its warded outer walls thick with draconic warding energy. Minutes later, they crossed the moat, the dark waters rippling as azgron crocks disturbed the surface. Ezra approached the guard post with the confidence of one returning home, he spread his arms wide in greeting to the familiar face standing watch.

"Ezra, where are you coming from, the Steelbinder Clan?" the man said, meeting Ezra with a warm embrace.

"Olaf, my friend, I'm afraid I have yet to be accepted back into the good graces of my family. The Steelbinders will have to wait a little longer for me to join them."

"Are you still working with Cheyanne?" Olaf asked.

"That's right. Cheyanne and I are still running a caravan back and forth between inns," Ezra said.

"Is that really what you wanted to do after you resigned from the Academy? You must be making pennies compared to what you were making. Why don't you stay in the city awhile? I'm sure the Keep would find a place for you," Olaf said.

"As nice as it would be to stop covering the same ground over and over, I made a deal with Cheyanne. I won't go breaking my word to her for a job guarding an already protected castle with a host of highly trained warriors inside."

"Ah, but that's the beauty of this gig. Nothing comes after the Keep. And if it did, there's a whole series of ancient dragonrider runes protecting us," Olaf said, finally noticing Hardin standing behind his old friend. Olaf measured Hardin with a less than friendly eye.

"Anyway, this here is Hardin. He's an honest lad looking to contract for some help with a little problem in his town back in Doran," Ezra explained.

"Doran, you say? Why didn't you go to Stormwatch for that?" Olaf asked Hardin.

"For the best, everyone knows you must come to the Vermillion Keep," Hardin replied, somewhat flustered.

"Right about that. Well, you'll need to hurry, if you want to submit your petition. They're just about to close out on the last of their contracts for the season. Go to the castle now and maybe you'll get a word in before they all sign. They should still be gathered at the Great Hall. Right straight through the main door. You can't miss it."

Olaf gave Hardin a quick pat down and let him past. As he was leaving, Ezra offered the guard a cigar and said, "There's a matter of importance I need to discuss with you know who about you know what."

"Now?" Olaf said, Ezra's response fading into the distance as Hardin made his way to the castle entrance.

Hardin stepped into the Grand Alcove. The passageway opened into the Great Hall like the throat of some magnificent beast. Paragons and Knights in surcoats bright as captured rainbows gathered. Their house sigils, each stitched on with golden thread, marked their allegiances as clearly as branded flesh. They moved between long tables overflowing with delicacies, their conversations reverberating off the vaulted ceiling.

Above them, candles hung in defiance of gravity, their flames dancing with unnatural colors that cast ever-shifting shadows across the assembled nobility. Yogo sapphires adorned throats and fingers, each gem containing its own captured constellation of light, their blue depths holding slivers of a god's power.

Hardin's fingers found their position on his lute strings, the instrument wound tight with potential energy as he prepared to unleash a telling melody that would plead his case for a hero. But before he could strike the first note, the temperature plummeted.

A figure emerged from the shadows as if borne from them. The dark-haired man's presence seemed to drain the warmth from Hardin's surroundings, his body too thin, too angular to be entirely human. He positioned himself in the entrance like a gatekeeper of the underworld.

"What are you doing?" The words slithered from his lips.

"I need to get in there. If you'd move, I'll be—"

A wave of cold magic pulsed from the figure, making the air ripple between them. "You can't go in there. This hall is reserved for the honored warriors of the Vermillion Keep. They do not require any services from a bard. This meeting is strictly business."

"That's why I'm here. I need to hire a Knight."

"No. I'm afraid you can't. That isn't how things are done at the Keep anymore."

"Excuse me, but who are you?" Hardin said.

"I am Joc, the Archmagus Hierro De Vonte's apprentice.

But what I want to know is who you are and how you got in here?" said the demonic-looking man countered.

"If I could just speak with General Ashbrook for a moment," Hardin said, seeing the woman in the background speaking to a Knight in a light blue surcoat. "General Ashbrook," he called out loud enough for his voice to catch her attention.

General Ashbrook looked over at them. The mage nodded to her, then wrapped his arm around Hardin and pulled him surprisingly forcefully for what his frame suggested was possible, out of view from the Great Hall. The doors shut without anyone touching them.

"Get your hands off me," Hardin said, resisting the tall man's attempt to control him.

"I don't think you know who you're addressing," Joc said.

"Some puffed-up wizard with a complex about who can go into the castle Great Hall. I was admitted by the security guards *and* the wards. I'm not here to harm anyone. I'm here to seek a contract with a Knight. It is my right to petition the Keep and let them decide if they want to accept my offer," Hardin said.

"Some puffed-up wizard," Joc repeated through clenched teeth. The alcove darkened. The sunken pits of the man's eyes grew deeper for an instant before he regained his composure. "I will have you know that I am the right hand to one of the most powerful among the Magi Order. The Archmagus and I were sent by his Majesty, King Agadorn himself, to oversee the goings on in this Keep. When I tell you Lord De Vonte is no longer doing business with private, third-party contracts, then it is law. No Knight will contract with you as they are all on assignment now to serve the King and the best interests of Lamar."

"The negotiations are still ongoing, are they not? It is my right," Hardin insisted.

"Are you a citizen of Lamar?" Joc asked.

"I am a human in need."

"You are not a citizen of Lamar, are you?" Joc countered.

"I hail from Doran."

"Lamar's Keeps no longer contract out to protect or fight for any group or domain outside our kingdom. If one did work for you in Doran, they would be voiding their right to serve as a Knight for any of Lamar's Keeps and they would forfeit any chance they might have of rising to the title and rank of Paragon. You wouldn't have been able to contract with a Knight even if you had arrived on time," Joc said. He took Hardin by the shoulders and pushed him from the castle.

"This isn't justice. I must speak to General Ashbrook or the Archmagus Hierro De Vonte," Hardin insisted.

"Be gone with you Doranian minstrel," Joc said.

Just then the doors to the hall opened. A man dressed in dark robes similar to Joc but older and more skeletal walked out with General Ashbrook at his side. The two looked with concern at Joc. Hierro asked, "Is everything okay out here?"

"I was just informing this Doranian that he is unable to petition for a contract to hire a Knight or potential Paragon from this or any other Keep in Lamar," Joc said.

"Right you are," Hierro said.

"If you would just hear my story. Thorgan the Relentless cursed our—"

"Did you say Thorgan, as in the Northern mage who has proclaimed himself the Warlock King of Doran?" General Ashbrook asked, now engaged.

"Yes, he's placed our town under a horrible curse," Hardin said.

"Good work, Joc," General Ashbrook confirmed. "We're not going to allow smut like these lies be heard in our halls. Thorgan was defeated long ago."

"Did you call me a liar?" Hardin asked, incredulous.

"I know you are lying for two reasons. First, Tel Roan killed Thorgan twelve years ago. He lost his Squire in the fight. And second, if you truly were cursed, you wouldn't have made it this far. You couldn't have told us. Curses cast without precautions like that aren't curses, they're hexes and for that you can go to any warlock to be cured. Now be gone and don't come back."

"But," Hardin said as they retreated into the Hall, the doors sealing with a magi's touch.

"You heard them. Leave now or the guard will escort you out," Joc said. An instant later something invisible caught his attention and he peeled away, his dark cloak billowing out as he stalked down the hallway.

With dashed hopes, Hardin left the Keep. Heartbroken, defeated, and confused, he retreated to the gatehouse where Ezra waited with Olaf, sweet cigar smoke curling lazily around them.

"That was quick. Must have gone well for you," Ezra said. His almost-smile fading to a frown upon looking more closely at the young man.

Hardin stopped at the edge of the bridge and stared out across Astral City. He wanted to answer Ezra's question but something far more pressing had arisen. A dragon appeared like a falling star, its scales reflecting the sunlight and throwing it back a thousandfold. It flared out, speeding fast over the city.

"What's wrong, lad?" Ezra asked.

Hardin's trembling finger pointed out the beast's descent as it plummeted toward the city below. The dragon's riderless form moved with vengeful purpose. It crashed into the buildings, the resulting impact sent a ripple through the wards at the Keep. The collision point erupted in a maelstrom of splintered wood, shattered stone, and fractured enchantments.

19

TORN ASUNDER

Lark sprinted after the blonde-haired thief, each footfall pounding like drumbeats of rising dread. She felt lost without the Hyalite. The orb's presence had become as natural as her own heartbeat. In an instant, it had been torn from her, but she could sense it in the distance as it moved away from her. Lark threaded through the marketplace chaos with unnatural speed. Her body wove paths between merchant stalls, past traders whose wares blurred into streaks of color, and around clusters of citizens.

The rage building within her transformed into something more primal. She had but a single focus, the Hyalite. It was the only thing that mattered. Sounds faded to a dull roar, as if she were underwater, every sense focused on the retreating figure ahead.

Sasja slipped through a gap between a weathered cart and a cluster of women shopping, the copper pots ringing at her passing. Her golden braids trailed her before she vanished into an alley. The entrance she ducked into gaped like a wound in the stonework leading to darkness.

Shortly afterward, Lark hurled herself through the gap. Her shoulder met centuries-old oak with a thwack. Pain ran up her arm with blinding force. The door's hinges snapped, giving way to her frenzied push. She stumbled into the shadows where a dozen orc warriors huddled. Their copper cloaks were visible enough in the gloom. The figures were all green skin and rippling muscle. Ivory tusks as long daggers jutted from their menacing jaws.

Behind the wall of Nordraven orcs stood Sasja. The Hyalite illuminated her shocked expression with its ethereal light. She stood next to a Morsythian who dominated the space like a brewing storm. His black hair twisted around a face that was scarred from a lifetime of fighting. The same ruddy amulet that Sasja wore dangled at his throat. It blazed with the deep crimson glow of freshly spilled blood. When he spoke in his guttural language, a shimmer of energy wept from the amulet.

"Fire fae!" The warning cry from the street outside came too late.

The Morsythian's outstretched hand cupped the air as he turned an invisible doorknob. Smokey trails of amber sparks carved an oval in the air. They twisted, spinning into spirals, moving faster and faster until they came together to form a vortex. The vortex cut a hole right through reality with a terrible screeching sound. The hole revealed an entirely different place. A forest covered in snow.

The sorcerer's chanting leveled off until a deep repetitive song fueled the dark magic he was performing. The massive Morsythian grabbed Sasja by the wrist. Her skin blanched white under his grip as he dragged her through the portal. The moment they crossed the threshold, Lark's connection to the Hyalite's presence wavered. The warmth she'd felt from it in her soul stretched thin, then snapped with an almost audible crack that arrived with waves of nausea.

A molten fury erupted from her chest where the pendant lay, nothing like the gentle warmth from before. The fury spread through her core.

"No!" she snarled, as she drew her daggers. The steel sang against their sheaths, eager to taste orc blood.

Pounding footsteps sounded as someone darted through the alley, stopping directly behind Lark. A shadow stretched across the threshold, distorted by the portal's light. The figure's hand gripped a broadsword, its edge drinking in the strange colors. Lark sidestepped instinctively, making ready to defend herself, but recognition froze her in place. Venrick stood framed in the doorway, his striking features illuminated by the glowing light.

Is he in on this? The thought barely had time to register before he moved, confident in his posture as he took up a defensive stance alongside her.

The portal's edges began to curl inward. The orcs surged forward toward the pair, their massive forms moving with surprising speed. Lark dodged a blade, saving herself from decapitation, but her movement brought her directly into another's fist. It hit like stone. She stabbed out. Her dagger found flesh, drawing first blood, but the victory was short-lived. Venrick's blade flashed in her peripheral vision, sinking deep into green flesh with a wet thud.

Each blow she avoided carried enough force to shatter bone. Her daggers deflected strikes meant to disembowel her, the impacts jarring up her arms. These weren't the undisciplined swings of any common thug. These orcs moved as trained killers.

Her dagger found the soft spot under one orc's chin, the

blade sliding home with a spray of dark blood. Without pausing, she pivoted, burying her other blade into a broad chest. But for each opponent she felled, two more seemed to take their place, an endless tide of muscle and fury.

The portal behind them was shrinking with each passing heartbeat. Venrick's voice cut through the chaos, his elvish words rolling from his tongue. The Yogo Sapphire in his sword pommel blazed, its blue light burning so intensely that it left afterimages dancing in Lark's vision. With the last of his words, the gem's power burned itself out. Its glassy prism transferred pure magical energy from the Yogo out through Venrick's palm. The spell cast forth, striking the portal's edge. It slowed, the closure, the vortex of sparks became sluggish in its inevitable collapse.

Now's my chance, Lark thought. The Hyalite's energy was growing fainter by the moment. She had to get through the portal or all would be lost.

She spun, her heel connecting with an orc's jaw in a devastating arc. The impact left a spray of blood and broken tusks in its wake. Massive bodies lay still on the stone floor while more emerged from the shadows. Pain exploded through her ribs as a fist caught her side. She folded inward, instinct alone saving her from the knee that whistled past where her nose had been an instant before. A hammer-like fist crashed down between her shoulders sending sparks of white across her vision. She didn't let it stop her. The orcs pressed in tighter, becoming a forest of muscle and steel, as she tried to work her way into the diminishing portal.

Venrick's blade flashed in and out of view, a desperate dance of silver against the encroaching darkness. But even his elvish gifts were failing against the onslaught, each parry coming slower than the last, each step less certain.

Lark found purchase on a thick leg aimed at her chest. Instead of resisting the force, she redirected it, using the orc's own momentum to send him crashing backward. He dropped as hard as a felled tree, taking two others with him in a tangle of limbs and curses. The breach in their line was all she needed.

A grunt of pain drew her attention. Venrick's sword met a war hammer with the sound of clashing steel. The impact sent him stumbling backward, and before he could recover, a boot caught him square in the chest. He disappeared through the doorway, copper-clad shapes pursuing him into the alley. The moment his concentration broke, the portal resumed its closing pinwheel.

Lark surged forward, crossing the distance in desperate bounds. Through the shrinking oval, she caught a glimpse of the North. Snow-laden trees stood like silent ghosts in an endless winter. Sasja was among them, her glacial blue eyes widening with horror as she realized Lark might actually reach her.

But then the Morsythian pulled himself back through, the closing portal sealing the winter world away behind him. His ruby amulet glowed as if lit by the tortured souls it had used to generate its dark magic. Lark couldn't tell if he controlled it or it controlled him. A red mist began to form, its spell taking hold as invisible chains wrapping around Lark's limbs. She struggled against the magical binding, her dagger hovering mere inches from the orc's throat, close enough to see the pulse beating beneath his skin.

He stepped away, letting the Nordraven orcs descend upon her. They lifted her as though she weighed nothing, then brought her down against the unforgiving stone. Boots and fists rained down, each impact carrying enough force to shatter stone. Even after the magical restraints dissolved, she could do nothing but endure as her world narrowed to the bursts of pain from the impacts.

The world collapsed around Lark. Her connection to the

Hyalite had been severed. Though the orcs kept up their pummeling, beneath her pain something else stirred. Her rage burned, sizzling through the lark pendant around her neck. It blazed against her skin; a living flame trying to escape. The undeniable power within it begged to be let out.

When she cried out, the word emerged not from her mind but from somewhere deeper. It crackled through the void, lighting up a sliver of her forgotten past for an instant. The knowledge vanished from her memory as it left her lips, but its effect rippled through reality. She hadn't really even heard what she'd said, but at that moment power erupted from her core, bringing with it both blessed relief and terrible hunger.

The air around her began to thicken as ethereal vapor coalesced from nothing. It swirled around her. Flames exploded throughout, setting the vapor ablaze with an impossible blue. It wasn't the gentle azure of summer skies but the devastating cold-fire of stars. These flames formed a cocoon of protective fury around her, and through its rippling curtain, she watched in horror and relief as the orcs' massive forms blackened and crumbled.

The spell spread lines of flame-wreathed vapor across the room, consuming everything in the fire's path. Each surge drew more deeply from her essence, turning her own life force into fuel for its hungry flames.

"End the spell!" Venrick's warning cut through her fading consciousness.

She fought to rise, to resist, but she couldn't. She didn't know how to control whatever this terrible power was. Lark felt her body had become leaden and unresponsive. The magic fed on her, each pulse of power drawing her closer to oblivion.

"End the spell before it kills you, too!" Venrick shouted.

Lark could barely form words, let alone remember the one that had started this cascade of flaming energy. "I'm trying," she whispered, feeling as though she was speaking with a throat full of ashes.

Through the haze of blue fire and encroaching darkness, Nix appeared as an image of salvation. "Olancia," she said. The word she offered resonated deep within Lark's fading consciousness. "Lark, say the word, Olancia. Say it now!"

"Olancia," Lark repeated, her voice a hoarse rasp.

The supernatural flames vanished as though they had never existed, taking with them the terrible drain on her life force.

The roar that followed shook more than the walls; it resonated with Lark on another level, vibrating through bone and soul alike. Even in her weakened state, she recognized it.

That sound, she thought as she neared fainting. *I know that sound.*

20

THE THIRD RIDER

Venrick's sword hung in his sweat-slicked grip, the Yogo Sapphire forged into the pommel offering him nothing that could help Lark in her collapse. He jumped when the dragon's roar shattered the air, buzzing the windows in their frames. His instincts screamed at him to flee, but deep within that earth-shaking bellow, he recognized the tone. It was that specific pitch he'd heard countless times before.

Ingamar burst through the ceiling of the hideaway in an explosion of splintering wood and breaking tile. Each of his massive foreclaws, the size of wagon wheels, ripped through centuries-old timber and slate as if they were parchment. The debris rained down upon the surrounding streets in a deadly hail, forcing terrified onlookers to dive for cover. Venrick stood his ground, knowing the precise distance to maintain. The great dragon's neck, corded with muscles and adorned with scales, descended into the building. Ingamar's breath came in hot, sulfurous gusts, washing over Venrick in plumes.

"I am not going to harm her," Venrick said steadily, still holding his blade. "I am here to help, just the same as you."

Ingamar peeled back his upper lip in a deliberate snarl, each ivory fang like a polished blade waiting to sever him in half. The growl that rumbled from the dragon's throat carried tones too deep for human ears to fully perceive. Ingamar swung his horned head away, each movement precise despite his rage. His foreclaw cupped around Lark's unconscious body as he cradled her gently. The dragon's crowned head swung like a battering ram, his spiral horns smashing through the stone wall as if it were made of sand. Debris cascaded down in a waterfall of stone and mortar, but Ingamar's barbed tail swept away the chaos, preparing his launch pad.

Ash, I can't lose her like this, Venrick thought.

Ignoring the screaming protest of his battered muscles, Venrick surged up the mountain of broken stone Ingamar had created. Each step sent more debris skittering beneath his boots, but he found purchase in the rubble, letting his innate elven speed guide his feet. At the crest of the ruined wall, he launched himself into empty air, arms outstretched toward Ingamar's back. His fingers met the smooth, scaley surface. The impact knocked the wind from his lungs as he scrambled for a handhold on the living armor. Each scale was a polished surface that offered no grip.

He panicked as he slid downward, his fingers finding no fissures in the pristine scales. In desperation, he grabbed wildly at anything within reach: scale edges, ridges, even the spaces between them. Above him now, Ingamar's wings unfurled like vast golden sails, blocking out the newly exposed sun. Then Venrick's fingers finally caught onto something solid. A leather strap from an old saddle, half-hidden between the scales. He locked his grip with the strength of a drowning man.

Ingamar's launch shook the very air, each downbeat his wings rattling windows throughout this section of the city. The force of their ascent threatened to tear Venrick's arm from its socket, sending white-hot bolts of pain through his shoulder. His teeth ground together as he endured, suspended like a desperate flag in the turbulent wind. The city shrank beneath them, its proud spires reduced to toy blocks as Ingamar carried them north, climbing higher into the cooling air.

How? The question echoed in his mind, nearly drowned out by the cacophony of warning bells and sirens that had begun to wail below, across Astral City. The sound marked the death of any hope for a peaceful resolution. The Vermillion Keep's crimson banners seemed to wave in accusation as the unlikely trio soared past. Venrick knew the King of Lamar would see this invasion of Nordraven orcs, Morsythians and a riderless dragon as nothing less than a progression of their war. Word of the opening of a portal to the North would travel along the streets and up the hill to the Vermillion Keep within minutes. The full might of the kingdom would set out after them. The elite Knights of the Keep, battle-hardened dwarves, elves and magi wielding powerful spells, and the legendary dragonriders themselves would come hunting. Although they would not know exactly what they were looking for, since Venrick and this woman he'd been tracking didn't actually know what they were after either.

Ingamar trembled violently, nearly dislodging Venrick's white-knuckled grip on his sword. Somehow, dangling there on Ingamar's side, he managed to sheathe his blade and immediately grab the saddle with his freed hand. The dragon's movements became deliberately erratic, each shake a calculated attempt to dislodge this unwanted passenger, making Venrick's grip on the leather straps all the more precious.

"Ingamar!" The name tore from Venrick's throat, harsh and raw against the wind. "You really want my death on your conscience, too!"

The dragon's response came in a burst of orange flame that illuminated the clouds around them. Before the fire could dissipate, Ingamar plunged through his own inferno, the superheated air washing over Venrick in a searing wave that stole his breath and singed his exposed skin.

"Hey!" Venrick's shout was half protest, half pain as the heat rolled past him. It was a mercifully brief blast that left him scorched but not seriously burned.

Despite Ingamar's attempts to be free of him, Venrick's years of combat training served him well. Each movement was calculated, each grip tested before he committed his weight as he pulled himself up the dragon's flank. The golden scales beneath his hands still radiated heat from the flame-bath as Venrick pulled himself onto the familiar curve of Ingamar's back.

Tel's saddle waited there like a ghost from the past, its sophisticated engineering a stark contrast to Venrick's current predicament. His legs found the armored holsters, sliding into the open-backed stirrups. The quick-release strap, an innovation that had saved countless riders' lives, lay ready at the back. The padded chest rest beckoned, designed to cradle a rider's upper body during the howling speeds of dragon flight, while the tether ring stood ready to secure a proper riding harness.

Venrick's armor of steel plate and padded leather served him well in ground combat, but now it worked against him. It lacked the specialized attachments and anchor points of proper dragon-riding gear. Left with no choice, he wrapped his hands around the two handles positioned ahead of his knees. The worn leather felt like the hilt of his sword as he locked his grip, preparing himself for whatever aerial acrobatics Ingamar might attempt.

"What are you trying to do, Ingamar?" he called to the dragon.

Ingamar shook again, his golden scales rippling with his hide.

"Instead of trying to shake me, why don't you fly outside

the veil of protection before the Keep traps us inside with their wards?" Venrick shouted over the wind.

That shimmering barrier hung before them like a curtain of clear iron, its magical resonance creating ripples in the air that caught the morning sun. The veil, a masterwork of magical engineering, offered Astral City a protective layer. Its enchantments were woven through centuries of spell craft and had protected the dragonriders of Lamar for as long as anyone could remember.

"You realize if the wards have been changed, we're going to boil from the inside out once we pass through the veil," Venrick shouted, his voice tight with the knowledge of exactly how such a death would feel. The magical barrier was designed to recognize friend from foe through complex enchantments tied to each dragon's unique magical signature. These enchantments could be altered with terrifying speed by skilled a magician.

Ingamar showed no hesitation, driving forward with increasing speed toward the shimmering wall. Venrick's muscles tensed involuntarily as they approached, preparing for pain he desperately hoped wouldn't come. The veil enveloped them in its ethereal embrace. A moment of tingling pressure, like passing through a curtain of static electricity, washed over him. Then they were through, alive and whole. The vast expanse of Northern Lamar opened before them. They headed directly for the legendary Everburning Forest, an ocean of trees that was home to the contested territory between Nordraven and Lamar.

The city's warnings echoed behind them, tolling bells and wailing battle horns carried their message. Venrick twisted in the saddle, scanning the skies for the telltale silhouettes of pursuing dragonriders. The Vermillion Keep's response should have been immediate and overwhelming, yet the sky remained empty except for clouds. The absence of pursuit was nearly as unnerving as had there been one. The chill he felt had nothing to do with the altitude.

"Why aren't they coming after us?" The question slipped from his lips, heavy with suspicion.

Lark's fire fae materialized beside him, her presence matching the dragon's speed. Her hair writhed like living flames in the wind, her dress flickered with pure fire. Her words carried a grave warning.

"The Archmagus knows they don't need to chase you. That amulet you wear will warn him if you complete your mission. If you want to help Lark in getting back the Hyalite, you must not share the same path. It's too dangerous. She doesn't remember how to control our power."

"Why should I listen to you? You weren't there to help when that woman stole the Hyalite."

"I want Lark to come back to me, but I can only be away from him for so long before..."

"Before what?"

"He knows I'm not there. I have to go," she said.

"Wait, are you coming back?" Venrick asked.

"He is suspicious. If he knows where I've been sneaking off to these last weeks, he'll stop me from being able to help her. Don't let Lark fall victim to your curse," she warned, then vanished in a spray of sparks.

She's right, Hierro will know where we go unless I can go somewhere that's hidden from the Magi. We need to go somewhere with protective spells that only a rider can create.

"Go to the Floating Islands.... Ingamar, did you hear me?" he said louder. "Go to Tel's safety zone."

The world twisted as Ingamar spiraled through the air, the horizon spinning like a potter's wheel. Despite his secure position in the saddle, Venrick's insides lurched with each rotation. Bile rose in his throat. As the dragon leveled out, sliding behind a towering storm cloud, nausea won out. He leaned out to avoid fouling Ingamar's scales. His fingers brushed against something that changed everything.

The object jutting up near his left leg was something he hadn't noticed, with its hilt and pommel resting in line with Ingamar's shoulder. The instant his hand touched it, a tempest was unleashed. Divine electricity surged through Venrick's arm, a current of raw power that flooded every nerve. It thundered through his chest, each heartbeat a drum of pure energy that echoed through his being. Venrick's eyes flew wide open, seeing what true magic was for the first time. Everything around him became vibrant with life. The patterns of the world swam around him. He could access true strength far beyond any that he could've imagined. With this power, Venrick felt he could reshape the world.

The connection broke as he yanked his hand away, leaving him gasping as the world returned to its mundane state. The abrupt loss felt like plunging into darkness after staring at the sun.

"Stormbreaker," he breathed, recognition dawning on him as he identified Tel's brismil blade still secured to Ingamar's saddle.

This time, when his hand closed around the hilt, he was ready, or thought he was. Nothing could truly prepare him for the flood of energy that crashed through him again. Power surged through his being like a celestial river breaching its banks. The blade sang with energy both creative and destructive. Within this blade forged from an ancient dragon's claw was a god's might. The sensation was so complete, so all-encompassing, that part of him believed if he jumped off Ingamar he could fly.

Ingamar rolled again, but Venrick no longer feared falling. His legs gripped the dragon's sides with supernatural certainty as they inverted, hanging upside down beneath the clouds as casually as walking on solid ground. When they righted themselves once more, Venrick released the sword with a laugh of pure joy. The blade vanished in a trail of smoke, rematerializing in its sheath like a magic trick.

"Amazing," he grinned, traces of power still tingling in his fingers.

After an hour of hard flying, the Floating Islands materialized in the distance. The massive chunks of earth hung suspended, defying the laws of gravity. They hovered in majestic silence hundreds of feet above the heart of the Everburning Forest. Venrick continued to scan the horizon behind them only to see empty skies, untouched by the silhouettes of pursuing dragons.

They banked around a towering cliff face among the westernmost islands, Ingamar's wings cutting through cloud-wisps with surgical precision. The dragon suddenly angled right, then barreled straight toward an imposing wall of stone. Venrick's heart hammered. He knew of this hideout from the weathered lines on Tel's maps. It was one of many sanctuaries the Paragon had warded with layers of protective enchantments against prying eyes and hostile magic.

"Ingamar, the cliff," Venrick called, his knuckles whitening on the saddle handles. The dragon's only response was a dismissive snort that carried traces of smoke.

"Ingamar, watch out for the cliff!"

Venrick clamped his eyes shut, muscles tensing for impact. Instead, they passed clean through the illusion of rock. Ingamar's wings cupped the air as they descended. Venrick opened his eyes. They were gliding over a pristine meadow nestled into the forested hillside.

"The cliff was a fake," he breathed, equal parts relieved and impressed by Tel's masterwork of magical deception.

Ingamar landed smoothly in the soft grass. As he carefully set Lark down, Venrick went to work loosening his legs from the saddle. His hands shifted to the worn clasps securing the dragon bone scabbard. Without warning, Ingamar's shoulder dipped, the motion sending a tremor through his entire frame. The subtle shift in the dragon's muscles beneath the saddle was all the warning Venrick needed. The intent was clear in that deliberate tilt. Ingamar meant to roll, with or without his unwanted passenger free of the saddle.

Venrick launched himself away from the rolling dragon, but he got caught in one stirrup. His boot was wedged firmly in the reinforced leg sleeve, the metal edges biting into his ankle as he twisted. The momentary snag was all it took.

"Hey! Ingamar, stop!"

Ignoring him, Ingamar continued to roll. The weight of his side pressed down. The ground rushed up to meet them. Venrick's leg was pinned there between the ground and Ingamar. The pressure built instantly, bones creaking under stress they were never meant to bear. The saddle's intricate metalwork dug into his flesh, transforming from safety equipment into an instrument of torture.

"Ahh!" Venrick cried out. "Stop, my leg, you're breaking my leg."

The pressure let off slightly. Ingamar held himself partially on his side, still trapping Venrick there. He wriggled like a fish on a hook, finally wrenching his foot free so he could scramble away from the dragon.

"What the ash is wrong with you? Are you sick in the head or something?" The words had barely left Venrick's mouth before Ingamar's head snapped forward, jaws clashing like metal doors a few feet away. Spittle carrying the scent of brimstone sprayed across Venrick's face and body.

The dragon coiled protectively around Lark's unconscious form, one membranous golden wing spread over her like a living pavilion. Every movement was calculated, every gesture a clear warning for Venrick to keep his distance.

"I'm not the bad guy here," Venrick protested, hands

raised from his sides. "We all want the same thing, to get that Hyalite back before Nordraven taps into it. I'm just trying to do it before I'm killed by this curse. Maybe then I'll finally be seen for what I am and become a Knight in training," he said, then considered what Ingamar's motive were. "Why are you doing this anyway? She's not Tel. I don't know where you went off to after he died, but it sure as ash wasn't to help me. Selfish beast," he muttered, settling on the grass dozens of yards away.

Ingamar cocked his head back and sent a burst of flame at Venrick, igniting the grass at his feet, and forcing Venrick to roll away. The fire crept through the grass without wind to drive it, creating a natural boundary between them.

"Thanks," Venrick's sarcasm drifted through the still evening air. "It's almost dark and I'll need a warming fire."

Two perfect rings of smoke drifted from Ingamar's nostrils in reply.

As darkness drew in around them, Venrick busied himself with tending a small fire fueled by the dried branches he found along the edge of the meadow. The whole while, Ingamar never took his gaze off him. As he sat down to bathe in the warmth of the fire, Venrick leveled his stare at Ingamar's unwavering golden eyes. The dragon released a low growl that sent vibrations through the ground, a constant reminder of the fragile truce they'd established.

"I'll stay over here, and you stay over there. And you don't have to worry about the glow from the fire. Tel has this place masked into the rock to look like a cliff and I'm sure the wards would turn around anyone who thought they smelled smoke," Venrick said.

Ingamar seemed to accept the words, easing into the grass as he lay his muzzle on the ground.

"I saw your tracks outside Fletcher's Passage. Did you know she had the Hyalite then?" Venrick asked.

Ingamar's eyes narrowed to slits.

"I wasn't sure of it until I saw that other woman steal it," Venrick admitted. "But I'm sure you felt where it was the whole time. It's the one Tel had, isn't it?"

Ingamar raised his upper lip, showing the fronts of his teeth.

"A different one? But what are the odds of that. Hyalites don't go missing and then we find a random woman who is hiding one just a few weeks after ours was stolen. You know the Nordraven kings haven't found it yet either. Or at least they hadn't when I went to pry information from Zorjan."

Ingmar perked up at the mention of the goblin's name.

"That's right. I faced that slippery goblin on my own. He bit me, you know," Venrick said, showing his healing forearm to the dragon.

Ingamar hummed, almost like a purring, and put his head down again.

"You think that's funny? I would've died had it not been for the elven magic imbued in that chest, you know the one I'm talking about."

Ingamar shifted, his muscles relaxing.

"Zorjan told me to follow the fire fae. You led me to her. After I found the fae, I just followed her," he said, nodding toward Lark's still body beneath Ingamar's wing. "Had I known that she had the Hyalite, we could've avoided that mess with the Nordraven orcs in Astral City. You could've helped me had you revealed yourself back at Fletcher's Passage."

Ingamar sighed, blinking lazily.

"Do you think she was the third dragonrider that day?"

Ingamar's gaze drifted away from Venrick. He lowered his head, peeking at Lark under his wing.

You do, don't you, Venrick thought.

"It makes sense. She had the Hyalite. She doesn't have her dragon anymore. She can wield magic. I've never heard of a rider being able to use magic once their dragon has been killed but maybe she's formed a new bond... I mean, you were vulnerable from having just lost Tel and she was in a similar position having lost her dragon. I wouldn't blame you if you two," he suggested, meshing his fingers together.

Ingamar's tail whipped through the air like a golden lance, striking the earth between them with enough force to leave an impression in the soil. His growl resonated through the clearing, teeth bared on display, their razor edges flashing in the darkness.

"I take it that's a hard no," Venrick said, understanding in his voice. "I guess you're right. You didn't form a bond with her, intentionally."

Before Ingamar could summon another vengeful fireball, rustling under his wing caught their attention. Two delicate hands emerged from beneath the membrane, pushing the light golden barrier aside with surprising strength. Venrick's breath caught in his chest as he set eyes on her perfect features. Her face held a symmetry that seemed almost carved rather than born. Her face was framed by reddish-brown hair that fell in waves. But it was her eyes that truly captured him. Those sharp green irises that hinted at distant elven ancestry held wisdom even as they blinked in confusion.

She moved carefully, like someone waking from a deep sleep, as she took in her surroundings. Her realization seemed to arrive in stages. First, her eyes took in the scaled tail stretched across the grass, then the wing she had just pushed aside. Her gaze traveled upward until she met Ingamar's large head directly above her, his golden eyes now fixed intently on her face.

"Ah!" she shouted, springing out from Ingamar's warmth.

"Calm down. You don't want to startle him and get on his bad side, trust me," Venrick said, rising beside his nearby fire.

"What the? You!" she said as she adopted a defensive fighting stance.

Venrick placed his hands on his hips, trying to project an air of calm despite the magnetic pull of her presence. Each movement he made was conscious, slow, like someone approaching a spooked horse. "Relax, I'm not trying to kill you. I just saved your life, well, I tried and then he did ultimately." He gestured toward Ingamar with a slight tilt of his head. "I more or less gave you time to get through that portal. Ingamar was the one who carried us here. Despite his wishes, I hopped on for the ride."

Even as she fixed him with a gaze sharp enough to cut glass, her hand hovering near the dagger at her belt, Venrick couldn't look away. Her beauty was unparalleled, wild, and natural. Questions burned in his mind like embers. Who was she really? Why had Tel's dragon chosen to protect her? What power lay behind those forest-green eyes that seemed to hold compounding secrets? How was she not severely crippled after the beating she took from those orcs? But he swallowed them all back, sensing that one wrong word might send her fleeing, or worse, drive her to violence. The tension between them was palpable, waiting to see whether it would loosen or slowly ease to resting.

"Where the ash did you take me?" she said, her fists clenched tight.

"Not me, Ingamar. I merely hitched a ride to escape with you. Ingamar is too pleased that I jumped on his back and tagged along, aren't you, buddy?"

Ingamar snorted, thumping his tail hard enough to send a tremor through the ground in warning.

"You two were following me," Lark said, her bright green eyes moving from Ingamar to Venrick and lingering on him before they examined the burnt ground around his fire. "I lost it, the thing you were hunting, so there's no reason why you should've saved me."

"Why didn't you take it to the Keep right away? You don't work for the Northern Kings, do you?" Venrick asked.

"I would never. They took everything from me and burned it to ash. They separated me from those who actually wanted to help me. No, I hate the North," she said.

"We have that in common then. But you should've picked up on that when I risked my life to help you escape those orcs."

"You could've called your dragon sooner," she replied.

"I didn't call Ingamar down, he did that all on his own."

"Ingamar, that's his name?"

Ingamar purred at the sound of Lark's honey voice saying his name.

"He took us to one of Tel's safety zones near the heart of the Everburning Forest. This place is protected with wards, hidden from the rest of the world by magic. We should be safe here, for now."

Lark relaxed slightly, letting her hand come away from the daggers on her belt. She measured Venrick with judging eyes. "Why did you so willingly jump into a fight at my side?"

"You were being attacked. I couldn't stand by and let it happen without helping. That goes against the Paragon's code."

"But you're not a Paragon. Ezra told us about you."

"No, not a Paragon or a Knight."

"But you have a dragon?"

"I already explained it. Ingamar is not my dragon, he was Tel's," Venrick said.

"You're serious? You don't have any influence on him?"

"No. Ingamar doesn't care for me."

"So that burn patch near you, and your distance, it's not just an argument, he genuinely wants you gone?" Lark said.

"Ingamar, for whatever reason, found you after, let's call it our event, and was following you. I only caught on around Fletcher's Passage. He decided to break all kinds of laws and tear that building apart in Astral City to get to you."

"And he wasn't there for the Hyalite?"

"Apparently not. You must've imparted something on him from before, because that spell you cast was—"

"I cast a spell," she said, seeming to remember as she said it.

"An extremely powerful one. It nearly devoured you. If your fire fae hadn't given you the words to end it, both of you would've died."

"You know about Nix?"

"That fae who appears to you as the small flaming woman in the red dress?"

She nodded.

"Yes, I'm half elf," he said, narrowing his eyes.

And a dragonrider like yourself should know that, he thought.

"It caught me off guard at first," Venrick continued. "I'd never met a human who had bonded with a fire fae before, but now... considering what happened with our event, it makes more sense."

She scrunched up her face at him, "Sasja escaped through the portal."

"That's her name, the blonde girl who stole our Hyalite?"

"Our?"

He nodded slowly. "You do know who I am, right?"

"Tel Roan's Squire," she said.

"Yes. And yes, she escaped with that Morsythian sorcerer, which is odd in more ways than one. I wouldn't have expected one to be this far south at all. And until the other week, Morsythians didn't show any signs of ever wanting to use dark magic to create a portal. For centuries they've been opposed to using magic at all. And it's strange that they've picked now to suddenly be working with Nordraven."

Lark's brows pinched together, and she looked down.

"Are you feeling okay after what's happened? I mean, you took quite a beating and then cast a spell that drained your energy so much you passed out, hard."

"I have to get that Hyalite back," Lark said.

"Trust me, I know the feeling."

She frowned at him.

"We could work together. I used to help Tel with this kind of thing. You and Ingamar have something going already, I can lend a hand."

"Why do want to help me?"

"I'll tell you if you tell me why you need that Hyalite back," he said, hoping she wouldn't make him lie to keep his life.

"I just— I just do, okay? It's important to me. At least I think it's important to me."

"What do you mean by that?"

"I," she groaned in frustration. "I don't know who I am."

Venrick met her eyes. Those beautiful, bright, dazzling eyes, and couldn't find a hint of deceit in them. "You're being serious."

She nodded.

"Your name is Lark, Hardin told me."

"That's the name Paq gave me," she said, taking a seat in the charred grass near his fire.

"Paq, as in, the god of air?" Venrick asked, cautiously sitting down near her. He glanced at Ingamar, checking to see if the dragon would object to his being closer. Ingamar's eyes followed him, but the dragon didn't object.

"No, not that Paq. It's a long story…"

"Tell me about it. We don't have anywhere to be and we definitely can't leave here anytime soon."

"You already know about the Hyalite, Nix, and the dragon. I guess there's nothing left for me to hide."

The firelight flickered across Lark's face as she unraveled her tale. Her voice grew quiet when she spoke of the village and her friend, Paq, of the fire wheat harvest and of the mystical fire fae. A shadow crossed her features as she recounted the Nordraven attack. Guilt etched lines around her eyes despite the lives she'd helped to save. The Hyalite's presence weighed on her as she described Nix's insistence that she keep it, her journey to Astral City, and the fateful meetings with Ingamar, Ezra, and Hardin.

"And after Ingamar saved me on the way to Fletcher's Passage, you'll know everything from then on." Her silence stretched into the night.

"You really can't remember how you got the Hyalite?" Venrick leaned forward, the fire warming his cheeks.

"No. Clearly it has something to do with the Northern Kings, and now apparently Tel Roan's death if his dragon's been following me this whole time."

Beneath his armor, the amulet pressed against Venrick's chest felt icy cold. The weight of the cursed metal had never been so uncomfortable. The truth clawed at his throat, desperate to escape, but he knew the price he would pay. Instead, he watched her across the flames, his mind racing for ways to help her remember without triggering the curse that would end his life.

Because of the conditions of my curse, I must be careful of what I say. I can't tell her exactly what happened or I'll die, but maybe I can help her remember, he thought.

"Venrick, do you understand the connection between me, the Hyalite, and Ingamar?" she asked, picking up on the unspoken words he couldn't offer.

"How much about Tel's death do you know?" he said, testing the waters.

"Hardin read a news article aloud to me about it as we traveled with the caravan. A rider, Marcel Heartfell, attacked Tel. Another Paragon from the Vermillion Keep was there to help. Tel was slain by Marcel, Marcel's dragon was wounded and eventually recovered by Nordraven, but the third rider's dragon was killed. Both surviving riders have been missing ever since."

"The thing is," Venrick began, choosing each word with painful precision, "the Vermillion Keep didn't send another Paragon there. They hadn't commissioned another dragonrider anywhere near the area where Tel was slain." The firelight caught the tension in his jaw as he continued. "I remember Tel being worried about the upcoming contract renewal. Something to do with the Magi Order becoming involved. When we went out for that storm, Tel was the only dragonrider anywhere near the Vermillion Keep."

"One of the other riders couldn't have shown up?"

"All the riders from the Vermillion Keep were accounted for on that day. None were close enough to get involved." He leaned forward, shadows deepening around his eyes. "Regardless, nobody knows where this rider came from or where he or she went after their dragon was killed. They would've had to be very strong to have prevented Marcel from taking the Hyalite. Something no dragonrider of Lamar has ever done."

Understanding crossed her face. "He or she... you don't think that I?"

Venrick nodded slowly. "You can spellcast, you're bonded with a fire fae, you had a Hyalite on you, and Ingamar broke all ties with the Keep to save you."

"What are you saying?"

"Lark, I think you're the third dragonrider."

21

PROMISE ME

Was I really a dragonrider; a Paragon? Lark wondered.

She sat silently, exploring her memories through a new lens. The signs were crystal clear, if only she'd had eyes to see them. From the beginning of her time in the village, the way she survived the harvesters' attack and had gone on to collect more fire wheat than even the most experienced among them. Combat came to her as naturally as breathing. Then there was Nix, a creature that non-magical people couldn't see, let alone bond with. Most telling of all was the raw power that had answered her call in Astral City. She had wielded real magic without drawing any from a Yogo and all without conscious intention.

A chill ran down her spine as she recalled the spell, its power erupting from deep within like a geyser of pure energy. The words had torn from her throat in a language she couldn't remember. Death could've consumed everyone in that room. Lark had nearly followed her victims into the void, her very essence draining away until Nix desperately intervened, offering her the word to break the flow of power.

"Lark?" Venrick said, drawing her back to the present. She looked at him, seeing the same features that had appeared in her dreams. She'd analyzed that face in countless moments of paranoid speculation, certain his sharp eyes would be the last thing she saw before he claimed the Hyalite. Now, concern flickered there, not for her power, but her safety.

"I need some room to think about all this," she said, rising on shaky legs.

Lark paced to the edge of the meadow to gaze out over the cliff. Below, the forest stretched like an ocean. Her pendant rested cool against her skin, devoid of any warmth or Nix's resonance. Her fingers traced the golden lark.

Nix, she projected the thought into world. *I need you. Where are you?*

Lark wondered if she had been a dragonrider, as Venrick suggested, which of the three Keeps was she meant to serve? Hardin and Ezra informed Lark on their journey that the Vermillion Keep was the castle with the most dragonriders. But Ezra and Venrick would've recognized her if she'd trained there. And Storm Keep had no dragonriders. *What about the Capital, Lamar City... Surely the King would host dragonriders at his Keep.*

When she turned back, Venrick stood sentinel by the fire. The flames deepened the shadows of his form, highlighting the strength he had developed, not just because he was half elf, but from having fought at a Paragon's side for over a decade. Her heart fluttered when he looked up at her and smiled, his warmth almost matching that of the fire.

Don't let yourself get distracted by him, she chided herself, even as the warmth spread through her chest. *He was hunting you for the Hyalite and the power it holds.* Yet the memory of him charging in to help her against the Morsythians replayed in her mind. He didn't do it for any Northern vendetta, but purely to aid her when she stood outnumbered. Even if

Venrick had a selfish reason to help her prevent the Hyalite from falling into Nordraven hands, the fact that he desperately tried to save her from her own parasitic spell showed his true character. But was that enough for her to trust him now?

"How did you know that I had the Hyalite?" Lark asked.

"You don't know?"

"If what you say about me is true and I am this dragonrider who was there to help Tel Roan... Whatever happened to me between then and me being in that village was so traumatic it left me with amnesia. Assume, for now, that I don't know anything about everything."

"Is it because you can't remember, or because you don't want to remember?" he challenged.

"I can't remember," she insisted.

"If you can't remember, how do you know who to trust? How can you know to trust me?"

"Nix. She has been my rock through this since I lost touch with the only other person I trusted. Nix isn't here to help me now and I don't know who to trust. I don't know if I can trust you. The only other person I've recognized from my past just betrayed me by stealing the Hyalite," Lark said, not wanting to admit to Venrick quite yet that she had visions of him before Fletcher's Passage.

"I thought you said you didn't remember anything from before?"

"I don't, mostly, anyway. Some things do rise to the surface now and then. But they're usually murky and too out of context for me to understand. What I remember about Sasja was that we were working together on something."

"How did she know you had the Hyalite with you and that you'd be in Astral City?"

"I don't know, but I think it was the same Sasja who robbed Hardin before we left Stormwatch."

"Hardin was robbed in Stormwatch?"

You're letting him distract you and giving him too much information, she thought.

Lark closed her eyes and took a deep breath. "You didn't answer my question," she said, meeting his emerald eyes. "How did you know I had the Hyalite?"

A muscle twitched on Venrick's jaw. She thought she saw that look again, the one where she thought he might attack. Then he calmed and said in his smooth voice, "I can't tell you that."

"Why not?"

"Because. I just—" he grew tense, his shoulders bunching, fists balling, jaw gripped tight.

"You have to tell me, or I will never be able to trust you. For all I know you are just going after the Hyalite for your own personal gain. You could be hoping to sell it to the highest bidder."

A stillness settled over Venrick like the quiet before a storm. He moved forward with fluid purpose. His gaze pierced through her mask of carefully constructed barriers warding her heart.

Lark's breath stilled, each heartbeat reverberating through her chest like distant dragon wings. Her chest warmed, but not from the pendant. Venrick's calloused hands enveloped hers with an unexpected gentleness. "I promise you that I would never give a Hyalite to someone who was offering me a King's ransom. I wouldn't take that away from the dragon and rider who it was destined for. Tel made sure he instilled his most honorable traits in me. My word is my bond. I swear on my life," he said, letting go of her hands and placing his right hand to his chest, "that I would never voluntarily give a Hyalite to a Nordraven King, dragonrider, Paragon, or otherwise."

Lark looked up at him, her heart opening, just enough to let her guard down. "Promise me," she said.

"Promise you what?"

"Promise me now that if I let you in, you won't betray me and take the Hyalite for yourself."

"Lark, I—"

"You say your word is your bond. Break that bond and you will break this alliance we're forging. Promise me you won't betray me, and I will work with you to get this Hyalite back."

Ingamar rose to a seated position, his eyes intent on Lark like a dog waiting for a command.

"You want to know how I found you and the Hyalite. This is how: 'A quest unclear where hope is thin. Follow the flame that guides the way, for if you ignore it, your death will come that day. Track the fire, winged and bright, or lose yourself in your plight.'"

"That's not a promise."

"I need to tell you something, Lark. I must follow a very specific set of rules," he said. A flash of pain flickered in his eyes, and he clutched his chest, wincing.

"I know. You told me. It's the code of honor Tel instilled into you."

He bowed his head, seeming unable to say what he intended. "I was coming back to Tel's... where he. To the place where..."

"Marcel killed him," Lark said.

He nodded. "Afterward, when I was looking of Ingamar, I found a set of tracks, but he was gone. When I saw those tracks again outside Fletcher's Passage, I knew it was him. Why he was following you, I didn't know. When I saw the group of Morsythians, I got suspicious. Then I saw your fae, Nix. Seeing her with you fit too well into a riddle Zorjan, the goblin, said to guide me. I know Zorjan was intending for me to be killed by following through, but I couldn't ignore it. Ingamar, the Morsythians, and then the fae acting like it's bonded to you. I knew I was getting close. I wasn't sure until Sasja took it from you."

"You weren't trying to help, you were just after the Hyalite," Lark said.

"No," he said, pinching the bridge of his nose and taking a moment to gather his thoughts. "We can help each other. I have to go with you. If I don't," he said, the words catching in his throat. A shadow darkened his features, and something unseen seemed to constrict around his words, turning them into a strangled whisper. His hand moved to his throat, fingers finding that gold chain around his neck. The metal links disappeared beneath his light armor, concealing whatever pendant or token lay against his skin.

"I want to help you, but—"

The way he looked at her, pained, but determined. She wanted to help him, but she couldn't. She needed to keep her distance. She had to stay firm.

"Promise me and I'll agree to letting you help," Lark said.

"I promise," he said, the smooth richness of his voice returning. "I promise that if we find it, I will not take the Hyalite for myself." Venrick relaxed, his body loosening as though he'd just dropped a heavy weight that he'd been shouldering.

"I'll hold you to it," she said seriously. "Break this promise and I will never forgive you."

"I won't."

"Since you were close to Tel and probably know more about dragonriders than anyone, I need you to help me answer some questions that have been burning in my mind."

"I'm not sure I know all there is to know about dragonriders, but I'll do my best," he agreed.

"You know about magic. I saw you use it to stun the portal. How was I able to use it if I didn't have the Hyalite or any Yogo Sapphires?"

"I was just as surprised as you were. It didn't make sense at first, because without a bond with a dragon, the only ways to conjure magic are by sourcing it from a god's energy, such as a Hyalite or a Yogo Sapphire. Or by tapping directly into an energy source from another realm, which is extremely rare. Another option is dark magic. I know because I saw you do it, that isn't a possible explanation for how you were able to use your power because you didn't harvest a living soul to power your spell. The Morsythian on the other hand, did. If you didn't use dark magic, and you didn't have any anchor to draw power from another realm, and without any slivers of godly power stored in runes or Yogo Sapphires, you actually had only one option. You used your bond."

"My bond?"

"Yes," Venrick's eyes lit up. "You are a dragonrider, so you have used your bond before. Without realizing it, I think you and Ingamar formed a bond when you met. You must've tapped into it when he was near enough for you to form the link and call him in somehow."

"But I never bonded with Ingamar. I only saw him clearly the one time in the forest. Our next meaningful encounter was when he ripped open that building," Lark said.

"Your other dragon died, was killed by Marcel. Riders can't tap into the flow of magic without their bonded dragon. Death severs that magical bond, but the powers linger, searching for a new host to channel them despite the mourning period for dragon or rider. Ingamar must've let his control slip after Tel died. If he presented himself to you in the forest, that could've been the moment when you bonded."

"I don't think that's how it works," Lark said. Her instincts told her that much of that explanation wasn't accurate.

"You had already lost the Hyalite. It was taken through a

portal to another place. I'd already used up the only Yogo I had, the one in my sword pommel."

"Didn't you say Nix arrived right around then?" Lark asked.

Venrick frowned. "She did, but what you did wasn't dark fae magic. Trust me. The Morsythian who created the portal used evil magic. That's what the screams in the street were about. But not you, you tapped into a bond with a magical creature."

"That's what happened to him, too," Lark said.

"You remembered something?"

"Not in the way you mean. Hardin told me after Sasja disappeared with a group of orcs," Lark said, wincing at not having realized it sooner, "a fire fae appeared and he heard screams. I should've known that Sasja was with the Nordravens when I recognized her. Hardin told me, but I didn't realize it until it was too late."

"You can't blame yourself for what happened. Those Nordraven soldiers shouldn't have been allowed in the city. They would've needed to bypass the wards without triggering them. Nordraven orcs or Morsythians don't practice that level of magic. It just, doesn't make sense."

"How exactly do wards work if they aren't using a bond or soul-harvesting magic?"

"Through imbuing a rune with energy. Spells cast into runes retain the power until its intended purpose is met. They are critical for creating wards, or protecting something," Venrick said.

"Rune magic, you didn't mention that one before."

"Because you still need to use power from a Yogo or a Hyalite or the bond of a magical creature to cast the spell that goes into the rune," he said.

"What about the gods or the fae, don't they use magic?" she asked.

"They are beings of magic and do not require an external source to draw upon to access their powers like the other races of Sataran. Yogos and Hyalites are a sliver of the god's power they send through the veil. And the fae... They're something different. Their magic is still foreign to most of us here in our world. Dragons are the only known creatures who've migrated en masse from the fae realm to Sataran and remained here."

"Can anyone with a Yogo or a Hyalite use the energy to power magic spells?" she asked.

"Yes, and no. The amount of energy is immensely different between what's in a Yogo and what's in a Hyalite. Obviously, Hyalites hold vastly more power, so much so that a dragon needs the bond of a rider to control it. Amounts of energy aside, the magician needs to be trained in the language."

"Magic has its own language?"

"Not necessarily a language, but more an innate understanding of how to use the language. The right inflection, emphasis, and emotion are essential when binding it with the power. It can be done in any language, but learning how to do it takes years of training. Tel had been training me for ten years and my use is still very rudimentary."

"But you stopped the portal."

"I momentarily stunned it. The spell is a basic level of magic any warlock or amateur mage could do. It was lucky that it worked. And that's just basic magic that sorcerers can shape from a Yogo. That energy is nothing compared to what comes from a Hyalite. But those channels of power that come with the bonding of a dragon are specific to the god that sent the Hyalite through the veil," he said.

"Like what?"

"Well, you mentioned your friend from the village's name was Paq."

Lark nodded, remembering him saying he was named after a god, but clearly, he was a human child.

"The god Paq, for instance, is the god of air. If you bonded with a dragon that had won a Hyalite with Paq's power, you could control air."

"That doesn't seem very impressive. What do you mean?" Lark said.

"Removing the breath from someone's lungs with a single word or increasing the air density to a crushing weight on an entire group of enemies or funneling a stream of wind so strong it cuts a hole through a man doesn't seem impressive to you? You could make the air so thin that enemy dragons couldn't fly. It's a huge advantage and one of the less common powers."

"I didn't realize," Lark said. "Tel's magic must have been fire."

"That would be Tia's, the goddess of fire. I don't know, though," Venrick winced. "Tel never revealed his gift in front of me. In all the years I knew him, he relied on other tactics and only used his and Ingamar's gifts if needed."

"And with one word, I used mine to kill half a dozen orcs," she said, the hollowness of it cutting through her.

"More than that, but yeah. That spell is why I think you and Ingamar have bonded. A spell like that must've come from something as powerful as a dragonrider bond; it had to be from Ingamar. And in that case, you could ride him."

"I can?" she said.

"Yeah. The only reason Ingamar put up with me on the ride here was because he was trying to keep you safe. He tried shaking me off the whole way, but he was more focused on getting you here. It's the only way I was able to hold on."

"He tried to make you fall off?" Lark said, frowning at Ingamar. The dragon lowered his head and looked up at her with wide eyes.

"Ingamar and I were always at odds when it came to which of us Tel spent his time with. Ingamar rarely does anything I tell him to. You, though, you should be able to control him. Guide him."

"How do I do that?"

"Climb into the saddle. Tel used to say, the dragon responds to you, and you respond to the dragon. You are as one in flight. Other than that, I don't know. If I were you, though, I'd wait until tomorrow. Wouldn't want to get dragged into an aerial battle your first time back in the saddle."

"Right," Lark said, her attention now fixed on Ingamar. The dragon watched her every move. He awaited her response or direction as though he owed her his life, and Lark hardly knew him, that she remembered.

"I'm going to try to get some sleep," Venrick said, settling beside the fire.

"Smart," Lark said, curling up on the opposite side. The distance between them felt both vast and fragile.

Shifting scales clinked around her as Ingamar settled in at her back. The warmth radiating from his body was more consuming than the fire. His wing unfurled, creating a living shelter that enclosed her in a cocoon of dragon-warmth. Tension melted away from her bruised muscles as sleep approached. She entered her dreams soaring through calm blue skies on the back of the golden dragon, imagining the flight she was going to take first thing in the morning.

22

FORCED FLIGHT

Lark traced her fingers along Ingamar's foreleg, each scale a masterwork of the gods. The overlapping plates felt like weathered granite beneath her touch. Ingamar remained perfectly still, his posture stoic as he patiently waited whatever was to come next. The sky painted itself in layers of rose-gold and amber, like molten ore.

"With his tail fully extended, he's twenty-six feet in length," Venrick said, admiring the dragon with a halfcocked smile.

Her hand fell away from Ingamar's shoulder, the lingering heat of his body still warming her palm. Standing beside the dragon, she found herself dwarfed by his magnificent form. The junction where his wings met his back rose to her eye level. Each wing membrane held patterns like sheets of hammered gold, veined with darker ridges of his magical blood.

"On all fours, with his neck straight up, he's twelve feet to the crown of his head," Venrick said.

"That's a proportional height for his length," Lark said,

regurgitating the compliment as it emerged from the fog of her memory.

"His wingspan is twenty-eight feet."

"That is..." Where did she learn that that wingspan was seven feet longer than average for a golden?

"Impressive," Venrick finished her thought.

"Exactly."

"Are you sure you want to do this?"

"Yes. I'm still struggling to wrap my head around all this. How I know that those sizes for a golden are standard, except for the wingspan. How it will make him faster. He'll have a longer range with that glide, yet his compact body will allow for quick maneuvering. How do I know that larger dragons, like an onyx or albino, are more destructive on infantry? Yet, these larger breeds are outmatched when it comes to aerial battle. Ingamar is a versatile size, especially for a rider with an adaptable set of skills," she said.

"Ingamar was a perfect match for Tel. They paired at the end of Tel's first year in the Astral City Paragon Academy, a full year before the students are presented to non-bonded dragons looking for riders," Venrick remembered.

"He must be heartbroken that Tel is gone," Lark said, looking up at the magnificent creature.

Venrick nodded sharply.

She stood next to Ingamar, admiring his golden scales. They varied in size. Some were large and rugged like those across his shoulders, chest, and back, while other smaller and finer scales surrounded his pointed muzzle, his intense eyes, and flexible joints. Each paw was armed with retractable claws. Rounded knobs traced the length of his spine, threatening to erupt into spikes, but never quite reaching the jagged sharpness of those crowning his head. Like a lion's mane, spines overlapped in layers, forming a fearsome beard and cape. Two imposing horns bowed back from either side of his head. His eyes shone with a gold richer than his scales, set deep above his armored snout. Around his brows, spiked nodules accentuated his intense gaze, giving him fierce resting glare that was almost wolf-like.

"Majestic, isn't he? What I would do to get a chance to train at the Academy in Astral City," Venrick said wistfully.

Ingamar flexed, taut corded muscle rippling under his armored hide. Smoky tendrils seeped from his nostrils, as he sported a soft but present growl.

"Why doesn't he like you? And don't give me that bull spit you told me about vying for Tel's attention like you tried to play off last night. This is deeper than that," Lark said.

Venrick's lips drew into a line.

"You two have known each other for ten years, right?" she said, motioning toward Ingamar while looking at Venrick for an answer. "How can he be so abrasive toward you?"

"Dragons do not forgive easily. They can sense things within us that aren't apparent on the surface. I can think of a few reasons why Ingamar isn't warming to me. The first being that he could blame me for Tel's death as I wasn't able to help prevent it. The second, which is what I believe more strongly, is that it's because I'm half Gambrian wood elf."

"What would that have to do with it?" she asked, genuinely perplexed.

"A long time ago, I'm talking several Flashovers, something happened between the elves of Gambria and the dragons. There was a war because of which both species' survival were threatened. Though I didn't have anything to do with causing this rift, I still have elven blood. Dragons hold grudges," Venrick said.

"I don't think that's it. His anger feels fresher than age-old hatred or prejudice. His discomfort has become more intense since you mentioned that academy," Lark noted.

"I wish he could speak. Then he could tell us," Venrick said.

"Dragons can communicate with their riders," Lark said.

"But they can't talk. It's more of an emotional pushing and pulling," he confirmed.

"When a rider is with their dragon, they're in sync. Their thoughts meld, and they don't need words to let the other one know what they intend to do. In flight, it's as though they are one," Lark said.

"Your memory of dragons is quickly improving. It's clear that you at least trained with dragons in your past. I'm curious to see how Ingamar will react to you riding him."

"My memory is fickle. I seem to pick these facts out of the fog as we talk," she said, rubbing her temples. "It's like I'm saying things without fully processing what it is I'm talking about. As soon as it comes out, I'm left wondering how I got that information in the first place. Was I really a rider or was I a Squire like you?"

"I don't know. I don't recognize you from the Vermillion Keep or the Academy in Astral City. I didn't know any from Keep Lamar or the Academy there. What I do know is Ingamar chose to save you all on his own. I believe that means something."

"Can I really do this, just hop on him and ride?" she asked.

"The only way you'll know is if you try," Venrick responded, urging her on. "Ingamar wouldn't chose to save you if he didn't believe you were special. The question you need to ask yourself is if you're ready to find out why."

"Even if I wasn't a rider, this could make me one," she said.

"Lark, you're strong, capable, and tenacious. Others would've abandoned the Hyalite if they were in your position. But not you, you're different. Ingamar believes you are worthy and so do I."

Lark's cheeks flushed as she realized she was leaning closer to Venrick. That same warmth burned in her chest. She blinked, realizing that warmth wasn't coming from her emotions, it was coming from the necklace. Lark held her breath for a moment, waiting for Nix to appear.

Where is she? Lark thought.

"There's a storm building," Venrick said, following her gaze.

Ingamar's attention had turned toward the storm, distracting Lark, and drawing her toward it too. That sensation to drop everything and go to the storm nagged at her.

"Ingamar can sense when a storm has power," Venrick said. "Once a dragon takes in the power of a Hyalite, they share a connection with others that come to Sataran from Thalindor. The firestorms thin the veil between our realms, offering opportunities for the gods to force their power through to our world. If they are nearby, dragons can sense when a god's power is preparing to come through," Venrick said.

Lark rolled the metal necklace between her fingers. A familiar warmth bloomed from the metal, seeping into her skin, spreading through her veins in waves that matched her heartbeat. The sensation rippled outward, a rhythmic pulse that resonated in her bones. That pulse mirrored the energy emitted from the Hyalite when she had had it. Each beat seemed to pull at something deep within her, as if the two sources of power were calling to each other across some unseen divide.

"That storm building within view is all the more reason to get out there and try this flight while you can. If Hyalites or Yogos arrive with that storm, you know there will be Paragons, Knights, and their troops moving in. All kinds of attention you don't want."

"You? Didn't you mean to say we, right?" Lark said.

"We? No, I said you for a reason. You need to take this flight, not me. Last time I was on Ingamar he tried to kill me, multiple times."

"What if I can't bring him back?"

"He will return if you want him to," Venrick said.

"What if we aren't bonded and he doesn't listen to me. I don't know if I can find this place again. Once we leave this floating island, he might decide not to come back for you. You said it yourself; he doesn't like you."

"I could see him leaving me up here..." Venrick mused.

"You have to come with me," Lark said, a sense of relief washing over her. A part of Lark didn't believe that she and Ingamar had formed a bond strong enough to tap into yet. He clearly wanted to protect her but was that just because he was after the Hyalite? What if Ingamar decided he didn't need her anymore and shook her off?

"Do you think you can you keep him from throwing me?" Venrick asked.

"I can't promise anything. He might try throwing me, too," she replied.

Venrick's jaw worked, grinding like millstones as he weighed his options. Face certain death in Ingamar's vengeful talons or embrace the slow decay of starvation.

Before them, Ingamar patiently waited at the edge of the drop. Lark's heart thundered in her chest, each beat reverberating through her body like a war drum, the weight of what she was about to do coming into focus.

"I'm going to climb into the saddle," she said, her voice hollow and distant.

Her fingers found the worn saddle handle. She gripped the rear with her other hand, testing the ancient leather with careful pressure. The saddle melded to Ingamar's form as though it had grown from his scales. Lark's eyes narrowed as she searched for any sign of a securing strap. There was nothing. How was it secured? The puzzle pieces clicked into place in her mind. *By magic.* Ingamar's chest expanded beneath her in a great sigh, scales shifting like golden plates in intricate patterns, yet no physical binding revealed itself.

"I think he'll let you on," Venrick said.

Drawing in a breath, Lark leaped. She hauled herself onto the seat, sprawling across Ingamar's back like a discarded cloak. She stayed there, every muscle tense, waiting for any sign of rejection. Instead, he merely turned his serpentine neck, fixing her with single golden eye.

"Get your foot in the stirrup," Venrick called.

"I know," she responded, her foot searching blindly below until it found the loop.

The leather creaked and adjusted, responding to her weight with surprising flexibility. She swung her left leg over Ingamar's broad back, feeling the warmth of dragon's body heat rising through her clothes. The second stirrup welcomed her foot, and the leather straps balanced themselves like scales finding equilibrium.

Standing in the stirrups, she hovered above the seat. As she lowered herself into place, her hands found the twin handles flanking the chest pad, their grip both reassuring and terrifying. Her legs slipped into the armored sleeves as if they had been crafted for her alone. Ingamar stepped forward, his wings unfurling with a sound like ship sails catching the wind.

"Whoa, whoa, whoa," Lark called, her legs tensing against Ingamar's sides. The dragon's response was immediate, like a current of understanding flowing between them. Yet that mental connection flickered, threatening to break at any moment. "Venrick, hurry up and get on before he goes."

"Is he going to let me on?"

"Just get up here before I lose control," Lark said, panic threading her voice. She held herself rigid as steel, every muscle locked in place, afraid the slightest shift would send them plummeting over the edge.

Venrick scrambled up, using Ingamar's wing joint as a ladder. The membrane trembled beneath his touch. Lark remained frozen, fighting the thing that was beckoning Ingamar forward.

"I think there's a clip or something back here," Venrick said, his fingers searching the straps behind her, separated only by the padded leather that cushioned her. "There it is," he announced, pressing himself against her back as a metallic click sang out, sounding his security. His arms wrapped around her core, their warmth a comfort to her. As Lark's focus softened, Ingamar moved forward, setting his talons on the cliff edge. He tilted forward, muscles coiling like springs beneath his scales.

"Hold on!" Lark shouted, her body tensing as she released her tentative mental grip on the dragon's will.

Venrick's arms constricted around her as Ingamar pitched forward, surrendering them to gravity's embrace. The world became a howling tunnel of wind and vertigo. A primal groan escaped Lark's throat as they plummeted, the jagged cliff face bleeding past in a palette of earth tones until suddenly, they dropped into open space. Pure, endless space spread out like an unending sea of clear sky. Her heart thundered against her ribs, but euphoria bloomed across her face in a wild grin. The wind transformed her burnt umber hair into a banner streaming behind them, each strand dancing with electricity as they fell.

They plummeted toward the carpet of green below. Then Ingamar's wings snapped open, catching the air and transforming their death-dive into a graceful arc. As they leveled out, Lark became acutely aware of every point of contact between her body and Venrick's, every shared tremor of adrenaline. Something shifted in her connection with Ingamar. A mental doorway swung open, inviting her to take the reins of his consciousness. Venrick's grip relaxed marginally as he said, "He hasn't killed us yet."

"Yeah, I think he wants me to fly us."

"You can do this."

"You might want to hold on tightly again," she said, moving his forearm back over her navel. "Are you ready?" she asked.

"As ready as I'll ever b—"

Lark's intentions flowed through the mental link like water finding the path of least resistance. Ingamar dipped his left wing, using three powerful beats of his wings to send them climbing through the air in a sweeping bank. She felt every ripple of muscle beneath the saddle as they corkscrewed out of the turn, the world spinning around them in a dizzying dance of earth and sky, before leveling out, only to mirror the maneuver to the right. Then Lark sent him up, climbing straight toward the sun. Gravity tugged at them like a jealous lover and Lark pressed herself against the chest pad, fingers white-knuckled on the handles as the force threatened to tear her away.

"You're secure with a strap?" Lark called to Venrick.

"Yes," his rich voice resonated against her ear.

"Good," she replied, her legs slipping free from the stirrups' embrace. Venrick's chuckle vibrated through her as his legs followed suit. They hung suspended in the thin air, their bodies floating a foot from Ingamar's warm scales, connected only by Venrick's grip on her waist and her hold on the saddle handles. The void below beckoned to Lark, tempting her to release her grip and surrender to freefall, trusting Ingamar to swoop down and catch her like a falling star.

She pushed the thrill aside, pulling herself back into the saddle as Ingamar's ascent slowed. Their momentum bled away until they hung nearly motionless in the sky. Then

Ingamar took command, nose dipping earthward, teaching her the boundaries of his trust.

Suddenly, her necklace flared with a heat that cut through her euphoria. "Stop here," she commanded.

Ingamar's wings beat steadily as he held them aloft in the thin air. A familiar sensation crawled up her spine. That same electric anticipation she'd felt when witnessing the firestorm. It pulled at her very essence, drawing her attention to the distant pyrocumulonimbus. She leaned forward, willing Ingamar to break their hover and dive, but like before, he stood firm against her command. She pushed harder with the mental connection but met an immovable wall.

"It's beautiful, but frigid," Venrick observed.

"I want him to go down over there. He's not letting me guide him," Lark said, frustration in her voice.

Ingamar's resistance carried its own flavor of tension. Through their connection, she sensed an invisible cord pulling at him, too, as if whatever lay hidden in the forest below the clouds had cast lines of power around both dragon and rider, drawing them toward some unknown point.

"Why won't you go?" Lark asked.

"He isn't listening to you anymore?" Venrick asked.

"No. He won't go toward that storm. There's something that's causing him to hesitate. I don't know why, but I think he wants us to fly south, back toward the City," she said.

"The City? Don't let him. We need to find wherever Sasja."

What if this sensation I'm feeling is coming from the Hyalite.

Disagreement emitted from Ingamar like rank fruit. Lark tried to overpower him with her sheer will. Then in an instant, the connection was gone. Ingamar fell back into a dive, rocketing back toward the south, toward the border of Lamar.

"Ingamar," Lark struggled to speak aloud over the roaring

wind. She gasped for air as it assaulted her almost too fast for her to catch any in her lungs. Panic set in.

Oh ash, is he going to try to throw us?

The more Lark fought to regain control, the more impenetrable Ingamar's mental walls became. She couldn't sense anything from him now. He angled downward, speeding toward the southern reaches of the forest. The strange pull that had been drawing her east gradually weakened, as did the warmth from her necklace. Eventually it was gone entirely. Soon, they were dangerously close to risking exposure to the towns near the edge of the forest.

"We're going to be seen," Lark said, the puffs of smoke from rooftops coming into view.

"Ingamar, what are you doing?" Venrick asked.

Suddenly Ingamar folded his wings and dove, slicing through a gap in the canopy. Trees blurred past, branches snapping off his scales as he hurtled forward. Lark tried again to seize control, commanding him to land, but Ingamar ignored her. He weaved through the dense forest, his speed so dizzying that Lark struggled to keep track of the narrow spaces between the trees. All she could do was cling tightly to the saddle.

"Ingamar, set us down," Lark said, nausea starting to set in from the constant turning, blurring trees rushing by.

Without warning, Ingamar tucked his wings tightly against his body and hit the ground at full gallop. Lark braced for impact, lifting herself in the stirrup as they slammed down. Behind her, Venrick thudded into her back, bouncing wildly. His grip broke, and for a second, he fumbled with the saddle strap at her rear before being thrown free. She felt his warmth disappear as he hit the ground with a heavy HARRUMPH.

Ingamar slowed to a trot, slinking lower as he continued to slow, walking, then stopping altogether. Lark hurried out of the saddle, landing firmly on the ground. Her legs felt wobbly, the ground still felt like it was moving beneath her, but she was standing still. She braced herself against the dragon's foreleg and said, "What the ash was that, Ingamar?"

Nearby a masculine voice called to hush another. Lark froze, the realization that it wasn't Venrick speaking hitting her all too quickly.

She bristled, wondering if an army was traveling through the forest to get into position for the firestorm. She went for a dagger on her belt as Ingamar slunk down onto his belly lowering his head and tasting the air with his tongue.

Why did you bring us here? To get us killed? She shouted her thoughts at the dragon, but he didn't hear, understand, or care. He simply waited, tail swishing in the ferns behind him.

A whistle sounding like a timber lark sounded at her back. Lark twisted, seeing Venrick, approaching with his sword drawn. Blood trickled down the side of his brow, dirt smeared across his cheek, twigs and brush stuck out from chinks in his light armor.

"Nice landing, Ingamar," he said in a whisper.

Lark put a single finger over her lips, silently shushing him.

"What happened back there? I thought he was giving you control?" Venrick asked in a voice so quiet only Lark could hear.

"I don't know. He shut me out," she replied.

"We're close to the road," Venrick said, pointing through a gap in the trees. "Someone approaches."

Lark held still, sensing Ingamar lurking behind them, low and out of sight. When crouching, he could become half Lark's height, somehow easily hidden in the brush.

The voices continued as the sound of wagon wheels rolled on the ground.

"I think you're just paranoid," a youthful-sounding male said.

"I am not, I'm cautious. You don't reach my age without

being cautious. Especially when we're in the Everburning Forest," the gruff older man replied.

Do I know those voices?

"And exactly how old are you, dwarf?" the younger said.

"Old enough not to answer that question," he replied.

"I do know those voices," Lark said, sliding out from behind the tree.

Through the gap, Lark saw Hardin's face. Seated at his side with a war hammer in his lap was Ezra. They rode a six-wheeled wagon being pulled by two enormous draft horses.

"Hang on," Venrick said, lowering his sword and emerging beside Lark. "Is that? It is. That's my wagon."

Ezra tugged on the reins, stopping the wagon and gazing into the forest. "Lark? Venrick?"

23

READY OR NOT

"Where in the world did you two come from?" Ezra asked, rising next to Hardin on the wagon.

"See, I told you these horses knew where they were going," Hardin said, a smile growing to his eyes as he patted Ezra's back.

Ezra pulled away from Hardin, saying, "Thought they'd lost their minds when they refused to go any other direction than north from Astral City. And again, when they wouldn't budge unless we continued north of Fletcher's Passage. I was questioning my own sanity right up until now."

Lark waded out from the undergrowth onto the road, Venrick emerging at her side. She glanced over her shoulder, sensing Ingamar there but not seeing him. Something about the bond Venrick insisted was there didn't feel right. Ingamar's presence was distant and wild.

"I could ask you the same question," Venrick said, a twinge of anger in his voice. "How did you manage to steal my wagon. It's warded."

A line formed on Ezra's brow, and he stuck his thumb toward Hardin saying, "You want answers to how he bypassed your Paragon's wards, ask him. After your catastrophe with Tel's dragon, someone made the connection that Lark came from my caravan. The guard impounded my wagons before we could return. It wasn't until Hardin recognized yours that he opened it."

"You did? How is that possible without magic?" Venrick asked.

Hardin shrugged, "I didn't use magic. I just opened it up, checked the interior, then climbed into the driver's seat. Thunder and Giant led us here."

"You just waltzed into the wagon without doing anything to destroy the wards that Tel Roan created to protect his own wagon?" Venrick asked again.

"Yeah," Hardin replied. "I don't understand why it's such a big deal. Maybe they finally faded after his death?"

"No, that's not possible. The magic was imbued into these runes. It can't be changed or surpassed, unless..." Venrick trailed off. "I hadn't considered that."

"It seems there's more to our bard than meets the eye," Ezra said, nodding.

Lark cocked her head, trying to discern what they were hinting at.

"Him, a Walker, really?" Venrick asked.

Ezra nodded.

"Look at him. There's no way," Venrick said.

"It's the only explanation. There just isn't any other rational way to explain how Hardin could walk right through the wards," Ezra said.

"For my sake, will you just speak plainly, and tell us what you think is so special about him," Lark said, nodding toward Hardin.

"He's a Ward Walker. I hadn't mentioned it as a form of magical being because you'd need to be a demigod," Venrick said.

Ward Walker, I know that term, she thought.

A clear memory burst through. A conversation she was having with Sasja about the ringed device that predicted which firestorms would produce which god's power during a firestorm. Sasja's words were muddled at first, then she said clearly, "If we're going to break in to get it, we're going to need a Ward Walker. I can steal almost anything, but I can't get through wards like they can."

Lark had responded, "Where are we going to find a willing demigod on such short notice?"

"Cheyanne might know."

"I should be the one to go to her."

"No, if he finds out... Do you know what he'd do to you? To us and what we're trying to do with that device? No, ever since..." Sasja said, her voice in the memory turning to the underwater noise again before clearing one final time. "Cheyanne hasn't been able to trust you. But she still trusts me. I need to be the one to go to her."

The memory faded.

"No, I'm not a demigod. I have human parents. For those of us who don't know, what's a Ward Walker again?" Hardin asked, drawing Lark back to the discussion at the weapons wagon.

"A Ward Walker is just that, they can walk through wards without triggering them," Venrick said.

"That's right," Ezra said. "Their powers come from a direct bloodline of a god."

"I think I would know if one of my parents was a god," Hardin said.

"Would you?" Ezra asked.

"I think so," Hardin frowned.

"Ward Walkers are rarer than Hyalites. Because the laws of magic don't apply to them in the same way as others, they're usually executed when their abilities manifest. Keeping it a secret is key to their survival. I can think of two times Tel Roan crossed paths with a Walker during his time as a Paragon. The first, he killed. The other was working for the King of Lamar and protected by the Magi Order, otherwise Tel would've killed him, too," Venrick said.

"But I'm not a Ward Walker," Hardin said defensively.

"If you were, would you admit it?" Lark asked.

Hardin shrugged.

"How could someone not know if he or she was a Ward Walker?" Venrick asked.

"I suppose it's possible for someone to grow up not knowing that one of their parents had lain with a god or goddess. The parent could shield the child from ever knowing, especially if they didn't grow up around magic. It would have to be somewhere interior and far away from the borders where magi, dragonriders, elves, and dwarves wield magic," Ezra said.

"I'm not a Ward Walker," Hardin insisted. "I'm just a regular guy. I can't use magic and never have been able to."

"Yet you were able to take Tel's wagon without doing anything special, something that shouldn't have happened," Venrick said.

"We can test his ability, prove it to him now," Ezra suggested.

"I think we're going to have plenty of opportunities if we're going to get this Hyalite back," Venrick said.

"What Hyalite?" Ezra said.

"The one that Sasja stole from me and is probably in Nordraven hands by now," Lark said.

"Sasja, as in my Sasja?" Hardin asked.

"She was as you described, blonde-haired, and blue-eyed, and she portaled away after retreating to a group of orcs," Lark said.

"I knew it," Hardin said. "About what was in your bag and

that I saw her in the crowd on the way to the Vermillion Keep."

"Hold on. Are you telling me that you," Ezra said pointing to Lark, "had an unclaimed Hyalite with you this whole time?"

"Yes, but she doesn't have it anymore," Venrick added.

"And we're going to get it back," Lark said.

"How do you know that the Hyalite hasn't already been tapped?" Ezra said.

"Trust me, I'd know. It hasn't been used," Venrick replied, sounding sure of himself.

Lark eyed him curiously. *How would Venrick know if that Hyalite's powers had been used?*

"Let's say that it's still intact. Sasja teleported away with it. Unless you or Lark is a dragonrider, there's no hope that you'll find it. You would need a dragon, and despite what happened in Astral City, I don't see one here with you now," Ezra said.

Venrick looked at Lark. Ezra glanced between them, then settled in on Lark, his head cocked. "Are you a?" he started, then shook his head.

"Lark, we should bring them up to speed. A Ward Walker would be useful to have on a crew that is trying to steal back a Hyalite," Venrick said to Lark.

"What are you two planning?" Ezra growled.

Lark smiled, responding to Venrick. "It sounds like Hardin made a connection with Sasja, which could help."

"You're right. And I think it might even work with forging a tracking charm," Venrick said.

"I don't like the way you two are talking," Ezra said.

"If only we knew a warlock who could craft one," Lark said, folding her arms and looking at Ezra.

"Oh no," Ezra said, shaking his bald head. "Whatever half-brained plan you are concocting, leave me out of it."

Hardin scratched his head and said, "Hang on, Lark, how did you end up with a Hyalite in the first place?"

"Lark wasn't a fire wheat harvester, she was a dragonrider," Venrick explained. "She was there fighting Marcel when Tel Roan died. Somehow, she got the Hyalite off Marcel and escaped, but in the process was hit with some kind of spell that gave her amnesia."

"Well, ash," Ezra cursed.

"What, isn't this good news? We have a Paragon with us. We have this whole time," Hardin said.

"I would've liked to remain in a position where I didn't know all that. Now if another dragonrider or a mage catches up with us, we can't claim ignorance. They'll scramble our minds for having known and helped since Stormwatch," Ezra said.

"Are there people coming after her?" Hardin asked.

"They have been this whole time," Ezra replied. "There were those bearded men following us when we left Stormwatch who disappeared. The Morsythian in Fletcher's Passage. Then Sasja. And now we're party to it. Ash, even the Paragons would condemn us if they found out."

"There's nothing we can do but move forward," Venrick said.

"Right then, out with it. Let's hear the whole story," Ezra said.

"Lark is a dragonrider?" Hardin said, somewhat delayed in his response to the disclosure.

"We don't know that for certain," Lark said.

"So Ingamar didn't just follow you for the Hyalite?" Ezra said.

"No, Lark cast a powerful spell when the orcs were attacking. Moments later Ingamar ripped the roof off that building and stole her away. I managed to grab hold of the saddle, which was the only reason I have not been locked up or executed," Venrick said.

"Is that so?" Ezra asked, his focus on Lark.

"If it hadn't been for my fire fae, I would've died from exhaustion," she said.

"I was wondering about that fae. I wasn't sure if she was following you or Hardin," Ezra said.

"You can see her, too?" Lark asked.

Ezra nodded.

"You can all see her then?"

"I couldn't, only the once," Hardin said.

"You can see her," Lark said. "After that first day on the Caravan she hid from you so you wouldn't see."

"That confirms it. He is a Ward Walker. Magical folk like riders, elves, dwarves, and, yes, Ward Walkers, can see fae folk. Regular humans can't see them unless it's in the moment before someone near them dies," Venrick said.

"What happened to Lark's dragon?" Hardin asked.

Lark proceeded to fill them in on exactly what she could remember starting from the village.

"And you flew here on Ingamar, while maintaining control?" Ezra asked.

Lark waffled her hand, "I started out in control, but halfway through the flight, he took over and brought us here."

"He took over and brought you here, to us?" Ezra asked, stroking his beard.

"Maybe that just means that your bond with him is weak," Hardin suggested.

"That's not it. Lark should've been able to feel something through the bond if it existed," Ezra said.

"So, she isn't a dragonrider?" Hardin asked.

"Maybe she is, maybe she isn't. And if she is, she wasn't trained in Astral City or with anyone associated to the Vermillion Keep or Storm Keep," Ezra said.

"But she did use magic. She had a Hyalite. Ingamar chose to save her over the Hyalite. Why would that happen if she wasn't a rider? Ingamar must've bonded with her when they met in the forest," Venrick suggested.

"That is not how bonding with a dragon works. It is a monumental event. One that you hope never to forget," Ezra explained.

"If I'm not a rider, how do you explain the spell. I didn't use the magic from the Hyalite, it wasn't even with me. It was already through the portal, and we didn't have any Yogos," Lark countered.

"There is only one explanation that I can think of. That being, you are still bonded to another dragon," Ezra said.

"What dragon? Lark's dragon died right next to Tel. I was there, I saw it," Venrick said.

"And you say she took the Hyalite from Marcel?" Ezra asked.

"I can't remember doing that," she said.

"How else would she have gotten it? Marcel was the one who stole it off me when I was in and out of consciousness. He came right up to me in his black brismil armor. I remember seeing a glimpse of him holding it," Venrick said.

"You must have been a powerful rider to have taken a Hyalite from Marcel Heartfell. Maybe from Lamar Keep in the Capital. It's curious that I've never heard of you," Ezra said.

"That's what I was thinking. She probably came up in Lamar City after you resigned," Venrick said.

"In that case, with your dragon slain, it is possible that you formed a bond to the unhatched dragon that will be produced from that mystic orb," Ezra suggested.

"Can that happen?" Lark asked.

"I've never heard of it before, but that doesn't mean it isn't possible. Unless your dragon is still alive somewhere. If Venrick is right, however, your dragon was slain. Being bonded to another dragon is the only explanation I can think of, unless you used dark magic."

"She didn't. Lark's magic came from a willing source," Venrick said.

"Ingamar and I can't bond because I'm already bonded?" Lark asked.

"I don't see why bonding with more than one rider at a time or one dragon at a time for that matter isn't possible. It's not been done before, but you have something of a bond with that fire fae."

"Is it a bond? She hasn't shown herself since Astral City," Lark asked.

"You were taken away to a warded location," Ezra said. "She probably couldn't locate you."

"She showed herself to me while we were in flight," Venrick said. "She seemed afraid of being caught by someone."

"Probably the King of the Night Court back in her realm," Ezra suggested.

"No," Lark said, playing with her pendant. For some reason, Lark knew Nix was still in their realm. "Nix is still here in Sataran. I think that might be what I felt coming from the east."

"What do you mean, felt something? Describe it as best you can," Ezra asked.

"I get this burning desire to be near that firestorm building in the distance. It's an instinct, this urge that tells me to go there. Sometimes, it sends a sensation through my necklace," she said.

"You're necklace?" Ezra asked.

"This one," Lark said, showing him her golden pendant.

He examined it, humming to himself. "No Yogos or

anything that could store power... This feeling you describe, the desire to go toward the storm, have you felt it before?"

"I have."

"Is it with every storm?" he asked.

"No, some give me the sensation more than others."

"And you always feel it through the necklace, too?"

"Not every time with the storm, but it does give me the strange sensation right before I see Nix."

"That's curious. I think I can help you. What you're describing with the necklace is different than the sensations you get from the firestorms. Your necklace almost sounds like a cursed object. But if it was a curse, there would need to be a rune, or a jewel capable of holding power, like a Yogo. I don't see any on your golden lark. It also doesn't seem as though you're constrained by any external force acting on you. I'm not sure what to make of it that you feel it before this Nix appears."

"Got it, she's not cursed," Venrick said.

"What about the firestorm?" she asked.

"What you have described concerning the storms is the calling a rider feels when there is power within a storm. Once a rider has bonded with their dragon, they share a connection with the realm of the gods. When power is being forced through the veil between our realms, you can sense it," Ezra explained.

"As in Yogos and Hyalites?" Lark asked.

"Yes, one or the other. Yogos are the most common, though sometimes a Hyalite is produced."

"You said you felt this to the east, but Ingamar brought you here. Why?" Hardin asked.

"Maybe Ingamar knew the storm was going to attract unwanted attention and happened upon us?" Ezra suggested.

"Where is the dragon now?"

"Ingamar is here. He's not far off the road now, watching us and listening to us. He brought us here intentionally," Venrick said.

"Is that what he is doing? Making us work together to find the Hyalite I lost rather than seek out a new one?" Lark asked.

"Ingamar knows we have a better chance to find what we lost as a group than by working alone," Venrick said.

"You mentioned that Ezra could be useful with a tracking charm?" Hardin asked.

"I can't perform that level of magic," Ezra said.

"So that's out," Venrick said.

"I can't, but I do know an elf who can. And I think she might be interested in helping us find a Hyalite that's not been claimed by Nordraven or Lamar," Ezra said.

"We shouldn't waste time. Tell us where to go. Lark and I can ride to her," Venrick said.

"This elf isn't like most of her kind. She will require payment for this service."

"I have my money, but is it enough?" Hardin offered.

"Her organization has enough money. What she will want is magical energy," Ezra said.

"I don't have any on me, I used my last Yogo on the orcs in Astral City," Venrick said.

"I can't give away my power if I can't remember how to use it," Lark said.

"Which is why we're going to use Lark's abilities to find some more," Ezra said.

"You mean I go into the firestorm?" Lark asked.

"Isn't that a risk we shouldn't take?" Hardin asked.

"Time is ticking," Venrick said.

"Every day that passes the Hyalite could pass into enemy hands," Ezra said. "This may seem a distraction but if we get the tracking charm to lead us to Sasja it will be worth it."

"How sure are you this elf will help if we find more Yogos?" Lark asked.

"Positive," Ezra said.

Ingamar emerged from the forest. Lark felt a faint sense of positivity from him. She sensed that now he was willing to go whether Lark was ready or not.

24

MOTIVATE TO DOMINATE

"If you're going into a firestorm, then you're going to need some improved level of protection," Ezra said to Lark as she examined her wares. They were a far cry better suited to a fight than what she'd been given back in the village, but for a real battle, she doubted the traveling cloak would protect her against more than a chilly breeze or light downpour.

"I thought the dragon was the extra protection?" Hardin said, eyeing Ingamar warily.

"She might not be able to control him. If she gets knocked off her mount, it won't just be other Paragons, their Knights, or Northern monsters that pose a danger. The firestorm itself is dangerous enough. If she goes in wearing some light riding leathers and a wool cloak, she'll have less protection than the standard infantry. At least those young lads have some padding under their plate and leather to insulate them from all that heat."

"I'll have Tel's brismil sword," Lark said, remembering what it felt like to have the blade in her hands. Its power had transferred into her own stores for use.

"The blade offers you a great advantage, but like Ingamar, if you lose hold of it, you'll be another set of boots on the ground without proper protection against the flames," Ezra insisted.

"It's a good thing then, that we've brought a Paragon's mobile armory," Hardin said.

"Tel's sets of armor are in there, excluding the brismil scale," Venrick said.

"Are you sure?" Ezra asked.

"It's locked in an enchanted chest that only he could open," Venrick said.

"Only Tel could open it?" Ezra asked.

"Yes, unless one of you has a power strong enough to break ancient elven magic," Venrick said.

"Could I open it?" Hardin asked.

Venrick opened his mouth, then hesitated. "Follow me," he said, a curious expression wrinkling his face.

Lark followed Venrick and Hardin, walking directly at Thunder and Giant. Both horses reared suddenly and stamped their hoofs as Lark neared them.

"Whoa there," Ezra called, trying to steady them with the reins.

The draft horses pinned their ears flat back, snorting at her. Lark hopped out of the way, veering wide around the side of the wagon.

Venrick immediately reacted, splaying his arms out to the side as he blocked Lark from the horses. "It's okay," he said in a soothing voice. "Calm down. It's just me, Giant. No need to worry, Thunder."

The two horses calmed, their eyes still wide as Lark passed behind their blinders. Venrick moved in to rub the sides of their jaws.

"That's it, settle down," he said as Lark stood back.

Ingamar nuzzled his nose up against her side, lifting her

arm as he nudged her forward, almost like he was encouraging her to keep going to the back of the wagon.

"What got into them?" Hardin asked.

"Don't know, that's the first time they've shown any emotion since we've had them," Ezra replied.

"It's probably Ingamar. Like me, they've always had a bit of an issue with him," Venrick said.

Lark continued around to the rear and eased the door of the wagon open. Sunlight streamed through the gap, casting a warm, golden hue over the vast array of weapons and armor. Tel's arsenal was an impressive sight, with racks bristling with melee weapons. She saw gleaming swords, wickedly curved scimitars, heavy battleaxes, and an assortment of daggers, knives, and maces, each polished to a deadly sheen. Spears stood tall in their racks, their razor-sharp tips glinting in the light. The selection of ranged weapons was equally formidable. Longbows and short bows rested against the walls, alongside intricate crossbows and rows of carefully balanced throwing axes and javelins. Shields of various shapes and sizes hung neatly on hooks in one corner, their polished surfaces also reflecting the sunlight. Toward the front, a cluster of trunks and stands that showcased armor of all kinds. They ranged from light, flexible riding gear to imposing suits of heavy plate, each piece meticulously maintained and ready for battle.

"It can be overwhelming at first glance," Venrick said, popping in next to Lark. "It all has its purpose and believe me that they have all been used at one time or another on Tel's missions."

Lark's attention drifted to three small chests laying closed in the back corner.

"That smallest one was where Tel always kept the scale when he wasn't using it," Venrick noted.

Lark retrieved the chest, examining it closely. The ornate

box was covered with runes. The raised marking flashed with a blue sheen as she ran her finger over it. The markings felt familiar to her, though they were written in a language that she should know but didn't recognize. She handed it off to Hardin as he climbed inside.

Hardin met Venrick's eyes. He nodded and Hardin moved to open the lid. The chest clicked, unlocking for him. He lifted it open.

Venrick let out a chortle, passing his hand through his thick hair. "I can't believe it's right here."

The scale was simple, nothing more than a palm-sized, deep blue dragon scale.

"Out of all the advantages in this armory," Venrick said, a smile gracing his handsome face, "that is the one that will put you above all the others, if it's there."

Venrick's jade-flecked eyes met Lark's. She held his gaze, her lips parting slightly, heart beating faster at their proximity in the enclosed wagon.

"I'll be outside if you need anything else," Hardin said, feeling awkward at the moment.

Lark didn't take her eyes off Venrick's as Hardin left the wagon.

"This brismil scale was instrumental to Tel's success as a Paragon," he said, seeming reluctant to take his hand away from it.

Lark's memory jogged, producing an insight to the precious artifact. Brismil scales were not only rare, but extremely powerful. When touching exposed skin, the user donned a plate armor suit made of dragon scales. Brismil scales varied in size depending on which ancient dragon they'd come from. Brismil armor was nearly impenetrable. It enhanced the user's sight, hearing, strength, and stamina. The extent of this enhancement varied with the individual wearing the armor. When worn in combination with a brismil sword, whoever was in the suit wielded strength akin to a god. The one in brismil was difficult for any dragonrider to destroy. For a Knight or a common soldier, it was next to impossible.

"I can't accept this," Lark said, offering the chest back to him.

"You should be the one to wear it. It will only increase the abilities you already have and yours are more valuable than any of mine."

"Venrick, this is worth more than a set of Yogo Sapphires. If I lose it—"

"You won't lose it. Tel has scale harnesses you can wear."

"A harness?"

"This scale needs direct contact with the user's skin to work. Wear the harness under your shirt but leave it unclipped, where it won't touch your side. Only clip it in if you need to use it."

"I'm not going in alone; this will be too much."

"You think I'm going with you?"

"I just assumed you were. You are, aren't you?"

"I mean, maybe, but I can't just go up against a dragonrider and expect to survive. And what if there are Northern troops there? Am I supposed to face them on the ground alone?"

"I'll be there, too, and so will Ingamar. You have to go with us. What if I need support?"

Venrick hesitated in his response.

"I'm not Tel Roan and I don't know if I can do this alone."

"I don't know if Ingamar would be too keen on letting me ride with you. With this," Venrick rapped his knuckles against a chest plate on the suit of armor, "I might be about as useful as a Knight, though I lack the formal training. But that means I'll need to be ground support for you if you want me to go into the firestorm with you."

"What if there isn't an armed force outside this storm?" Lark suggested.

"That's a dangerous way to think. If there's power in this storm there will soldiers ready to fight for their Kingdom's claim on the right to collect the power. But it's not like I haven't seen this kind of action before, just not with these odds. I do have a decade of training with one of the most powerful dragonriders in the Kingdom, so I'm not completely lacking when it comes to knowledge of the battlefield. Squiring for Tel wasn't all just jockeying weapons."

Lark imagined two small armies facing off around the edges of the firestorm, Venrick in their midst, this time without Tel's Honor Guard or a squad of friendly soldiers to help watch his back. This time, if he went on the ground, he'd be alone. She tried to push the chest containing the brismil scale back into his arms.

He wouldn't accept it.

She clenched her jaw, meeting his eyes and said, "If you're not going to take the scale, you won't be able to keep up with us from the ground. You will take Tel's brismil blade. It will give you the speed needed."

Venrick's expression widened, two lines forming on his forehead. "Stormbreaker is meant to be used with the suit of dragon-scale armor. You will put it to better use than I can."

"I protected the Hyalite for several weeks with nothing but a few daggers. Now I have Ingamar's help, and with this," she said, tapping the brismil scale case, "I bet collecting a few Yogo Sapphires will come naturally."

"If you're concerned for my safety, and that's valid, but yours is paramount. Yes, we're both on Lamar's wanted list now, but I am not the one that everyone will be looking for. You will capture everyone's attention," Venrick said, leaning in closer, measuring her with his gaze, locking in on her parted lips. "You should have the sword and the scale."

Lark lifted her chin, her heart racing as she leaned in to meet him. The wagon rocked as a shadow broke the light streaming in from the doorway. Lark stopped herself by palming Venrick's chest, catching herself before her balance tipped all the way into him. She felt something other than the firm sculpted muscles under his armor. Something at the end of the necklace that he kept tucked under his light armor

"Oh, I didn't realize you were, um, having a moment," Ezra said, shielding his gaze and backing out of the wagon.

"We weren't having a moment," Lark said awkwardly.

"We weren't?" Venrick asked.

"Well, no, we were arming ourselves for the storm. Then we—"

"You're right, we were about to agree on me taking the sword, you using the scale," he said. "You'll need this," Venrick added, picking a leather harness off the rack on the wall behind Lark. "It holds the scale in place, allowing you to take the armor on and off in the blink of an eye. Clip this latch into place and the scale presses tight to your skin. Remove it and it's suspended away from your body. You'll want to put the harness on under your shirt. Any other weapon you might need is here, too, all at your disposal, obviously. I'll give you some privacy." He started out of the wagon.

"Venrick," she said, stopping him by grabbing his arm. "I didn't mean for it to—"

"No, no need to make it clear to me, Lark. I thought I was... never mind. Let's forget it happened."

"But," she said.

"You're a rider, Lark. If you didn't have amnesia, you wouldn't be giving a no-name half-elf Squire any kind of attention," he said.

"That doesn't mean we can't be friends, or..."

"I made a promise to you, and I intend to keep it. We're going to get that Hyalite back and getting Yogos to pay for a tracking charm is the fastest way," he said, taking a heavier suit of armor from the rack and putting it under his arm.

She frowned.

"We should be focusing on the firestorm. I'll give you some privacy to get changed." Venrick hauled the fresh set of armor out and closed the door behind him.

Lark slid out of her traveling attire, fitting the leather brismil harness on. After several tries, she used the cloth in the scale's case to secure it into place. It hung a few inches away from her ribs. A circular hole cut into the leather allowed it to press tight to her side when cinched down into place. Every other piece of armor she tried on was too large. Tel's frame might've been close to Venrick's but was much too broad in the chest and tall for her. With the magically charged armor at her disposal, Lark returned into her shirt, fitted leather vest, and wool travel cloak. She picked through the racks of weapons, finally settling on a sword. It was smaller in size than that of the oversized brismil blade, but larger than the average broadsword. With her brismil armor at the ready if the need arose, and the long sword strapped on her back, Lark felt as formidable as she ever had.

Emerging from the wagon, Lark stood before Ezra, Hardin, and Venrick, who had already managed to get Stormbreaker and the scabbard off Ingamar's saddle.

"You didn't put any of the armor on," Hardin noted, folding his arms across his chest.

"Oh, she did," Venrick said, cinching the brismil blade to his sword belt below his chest plate. The additional leash that attached midway down the scabbard up to his belt was the only way to keep the long sword from digging into the ground as he walked.

Lark couldn't help but stare at him in the form-fitting armor. His broad chest was pronounced in the plate, his shoulders padded and large. The way he looked at her with those green eyes made her heart flutter.

"Go on, show them," Venrick said with a grin.

Lark palmed the clip on her side. When she snapped it into place, the brismil scale surfaced snug against her skin. Instantly she felt a chilling sheet of energy that coated every inch of her body. It was buzzing with raw power, like the blade, but more direct. It vibrated through her core.

"Whoa!" Hardin shouted, stumbling back.

Lark saw them staring wide-eyed through a wide slot in the armor's visor.

"You look like..." Ezra said.

"A bona fide dragonrider," Hardin overrode him.

"The brismil armor fits to the shape of your body. It's as light as normal clothing, strong as dragon scales, and fireproof. It supercharges all the abilities you already have," Venrick said.

Lark examined herself, seeing the black brismil plate on her arms, legs, and torso. She squatted, jumping slightly as she rose. She lifted her legs, twisted and bent. "That's wild," she said. "It looks so strong, but I don't feel any restraint. It's as though I'm wearing nothing at all."

"How do you feel?" Ezra asked.

"I feel," Lark said, sensing power in her. Magical energy flowed through the scale and into her. She felt charged, like lightning was running through her veins. "I feel amazing!" and moved to unclip the scale. The lever was under the armor, the whole harness was under the armor, but her fingers somehow passed through the armor, unclipping the lever that held the scale down against her side. The deep blue plate armor instantly disappeared. She moved around now, feeling the same mobility but without enhancements.

"Are you ready to go find out what it's like to fly a dragon into a firestorm?" Ezra asked.

Lark met Venrick's eyes, locking in on them for a moment. He smiled, then gave her a nod.

"Motivate to dominate" she said, the phrase coming through from the fog of her past.

"Motivate to dominate?" Ezra replied.

"I like it," Hardin said.

Venrick smiled. "Me, too. Motivate to dominate. Fitting for what we're about to do."

25

SEEING RED

Lark slipped her boots into the stirrups. Standing on the balls of her feet, she tested their length. On instinct, she checked over the saddle, ensuring that the straps were properly locked, and the chest pad was the correct height.

"Looks like you're a natural in the saddle," Ezra said.

Lark placed her hand on Ingamar's neck, trying to impart a sense of calm over him. "That fire is ten miles out through rolling forested hills without a clear path. Shouldn't you and Hardin have left already?" she asked.

"With how convinced you are that there's power with this storm, it will be safer for us to hang back. There will be troops just outside the fire fighting for their Knight, or possibly a Paragon, to harvest magical energy. We won't be able to get close enough to do anything helpful in time. We'll head that way, but your strategy to quickly retrieve any Yogos produced will be crucial. The longer you're in the fire, the greater the chance that you'll encounter a Knight or Paragon."

"It looks like the storm's picking up speed and heading

this way," Hardin pointed to the anvil-shaped cloud. "We may not have as far to go as we think we do."

"We'll offer what support we can. If you need resupply for some reason or a weapon, we'll be observing from a safe distance. But Venrick will be on the ground. With how fast he can move, he should be able to circumnavigate the fighting and sneak into the fire to aid you."

"I should be off then; Venrick's already gone ahead and I don't want him reaching the fire before Ingamar and I can scout for other Paragons," Lark said. "If we encounter one, I'm not sure we're ready to handle him or her. We'd need to pull out and think up a different way to track down Sasja."

"I wanted to discuss spellcasting before you go," Ezra said.

"Spellcasting, no, I won't rely on using magic I don't know how to control right now. It nearly killed me the last time," Lark replied.

"You might not do it on purpose. Your bond will allow you to use some magic instinctively, like deflecting an arrow, or tracking your sword to hit its intended target without uttering a word. I understand that some of your memories have returned, but whatever you do, don't speak a spell unless you fully understand what you're doing. You could kill yourself or your bonded dragon without meaning to."

"I won't cast a spell unless I truly understand the words," she promised.

"If you come across a Knight, they may be an elf or a mage, in which case they'll be practiced in their use of magic. The first thing they'll do is test your mental defenses."

"I don't have mental defenses," Lark said.

Ezra's stoic expression cracked with a grin. "If you really are a rider, you'll have them in place, even if you don't remember how. For a dragonrider, mental defenses come be as naturally as breathing. If you are who we believe you are, your instincts will guide you."

"Is there a way for you to tell if I have them in place?" she asked.

"I'm just a warlock. My skills are in crafting runes and imbuing them with a transfer of energy, not shaping that magical energy. My skills with mental attacks are so limited, it would take me too long to talk you through it, like how this exchange is becoming. For Venrick's sake, I don't want to keep you any longer. In the coming fight, trust your instincts. You'll be fine," Ezra said, backing away toward Giant and Thunder.

"Good luck, Lark," Hardin called from the wagon.

Lark focused on Ingamar. She felt a sensation from him. It was similar to the warmth that she felt from her necklace every time Nix appeared, only this touched her mind more and her body less. Lark focused on her mental directive.

It's just like talking to Nix with my thoughts, only he responds with actions, not thoughts of his own, she told herself. And as she did, she sensed a hint that Ingamar was ready for instruction. Lark pointed her internal compass to the direction of the firestorm, and with that thought, Ingmar shifted into action.

In the narrow strip of space between trees where the road passed through the forest, Ingamar coiled into a crouch. With his wings tight to his sides, he reared back. Lark held on as he launched himself upward, using his tail like a coil to spring them up over the canopy. The leathery membrane brushed the tips of the treetops before he climbed higher. A distinctive column of smoke rose to the east, dissolving into the growing thunderhead. Lightning cracked between the clouds, running horizontally as it fractured. Behind the storm, a wall of dark gray streaked to the ground. No smoke lifted in its wake.

"The Giving-Rain," she said, thinking of the fire wheat harvesters who would be heading out to the burn area the day after the storm.

The last time Lark was anywhere close to a storm, she had

been busy trying to prove herself by harvesting the rapidly growing wheat. Little did she know that proving herself would be more than just harvesting. She had had to make it through the first harvest and return not only with grain, but with her life. This time, Lark wasn't going in for the wheat harvest. She was going after gifts from the gods.

Ingamar leveled off even with the thunderhead. Lark spotted a dark mass moving through the forest from the south. Sunlight reflected off spears, shields, and armor.

"A Keep's troops are moving in from the south; those will be led by Knights or a Paragon. Unless there's another dragonrider, or Knight in brismil armor, we stand a good chance of beating them to any Yogos produced," Lark said to Ingamar.

She waited for a hint of response, but Ingamar's attention seemed focused on an individual passing through the forest with great speed. Speed imparted on him by brismil. Lark looked down to catch a glimpse of the dark blue streak that was faintly visible as Venrick rounded the troops to approach the edge of the burn. As they passed over him, Ingamar's attention focused on the storm and the power growing there.

"Can you see any dragons or riders in the sky?" she asked, not yet fully trusting her connection with Ingamar to provide clear communications.

She didn't sense any fear or danger rising within him. He was completely focused on the storm now. Lark scanned the sky, searching for any sign of another dragonrider pair. The tension in her seat lessened when nothing larger than a bird flew above the trees. Lark felt a nudge on her to look to the north.

Was that Ingamar? she wondered.

Her gaze followed, spotting more movement in the forest below. Green creatures moved en masse through the trees. Upon closer inspection, she noted orcs and pale-skinned, bearded men wearing furs marching in from the northeast. She didn't see any enemy riders flying over them.

"Nordraven has a force on the move, too," she said to Ingamar, confirming that she had noticed them, too.

Ingamar slowed to a hover just beyond the smoke column. The fire had spread to half-a-mile in width and was staying on the ground and out of the canopy. Occasionally it crowned for a short run atop the towering trees. The armies below maneuvered into their positions, having yet to engage with one another. Lark hoped neither force had sent their leading warriors into the burn.

Shouts rose to Lark's ears from either side of the fire, lightning crackled through the cloud ahead, fracturing hairline tendrils of light out from the main bolt. The pulse hit the ground, sending more energy rippling through the sky. It channeled back and forth through the veil, spreading out onto the earthly plain below. The white light flashed a final time, cracking and booming with thunder as it cleared. In that moment, the drive that fed Lark's desire to go toward the storm surged within her. The necklace burned hot as though it had been struck by the fire. She touched on her connection with Ingamar, but he was riding the same impulse. He dove from the sky, plunging into the smoky cloud at breakneck speed.

Lark struggled to hold herself flat against his back as the wind ripped around her. Her cloak whipped out behind her, slapping the air as they streaked through the storm. Water stung her face, peppering her with icy droplets that numbed her skin. An instant later, the chilling touch of the clouds turned into a blast of heat. Her face prickled, instantly thawing as they crossed into the smoke. She coughed, choking on the airborne ash.

The scale, she remembered.

The heat was beginning to blister her cheeks and knuckles

when she finally had the wherewithal to clasp it tight to her side. Icy bolts of lightning shot out through her veins, filling her entire body with the charged sensation that came from donning brismil plate armor. The smoke, the ash, even the heat vanished as Ingamar plunged into the flames. Orange and yellow waves of fire washed over them as they broke through the canopy. Ingamar flared, instantly slowing them down, the gust he created producing a blast of wind that fanned the flames, sending ash and debris scattering from the landing zone.

As Ingamar flapped his wings once more before landing on solid ground, three enormous sets of eyes emerged from the flames. These were followed by the emergence of long, bared teeth. Northern wolves with bodies as large as Ingamar's approached. Lark took hold of the sword, only getting it halfway out of the sheath before the giant wolves lunged at them. Ingamar swatted the first, flaring back as his hind legs touched down. At the same time, Lark pulled the sword free, but she lost her grip on the saddle. The momentum of his flare caused her to fall back.

The snarling and snapping jaws of dragon and wolf became muffled as Lark bounced off Ingamar's wing and landed flat on the ground. Ingamar clawed, connecting with fur-covered flesh. His tail hissed as he spun it over Lark, striking another giant Northern wolf that had snuck past his claws and was bearing down on Lark.

By the time Lark was on her feet, ready for the fight, Ingamar had released a furious torrent of fire, blasting out in the wolves' direction. One took the brunt of the heat, turning to ash as the other two disappeared into the smoke. Ingamar cut his breath of fire off, snapping his jaws together with a clack, then he roared before chasing after them.

Lark rose to a fighting stance, both hands on the long

sword, the armor feeding her energy and heightening her senses.

"Thank the gods I'm not on Ingamar's bad side," Lark muttered under her breath as she scanned her immediate surroundings.

Clusters of blue gemstones littered the ground all around her. This was where the lightning has pulsed, sending a god's power splashing down, crystallizing into the Yogo Sapphires as it was forced through the veil between realms. The sapphires were uncut and grouped together in prismatic patterns. They glowed like cobalt formations of quartz, the light brightening their hue as it pulsed in the same way the Hyalite had. In the same way the lightning strike that delivered them through the veil had.

Seeing no sign of Ingamar or the giant Northern wolves, Lark began gathering the Sapphires by the handful. She grouped them into piles among the soot for easy collection when Ingamar returned with the saddle bags. Lark momentarily unclipped her brismil scale to fill the leather pouch that was on her belt. Heat from the inferno blasted her skin while she untied it, quickly donning the armor before the radiant heat blistered her skin. She worked quickly, filling the purse with two large handfuls of Yogos. Faster than before, she unclasped the scale, exposing herself to the heat again as she secured the Yogos and reformed her armor.

Flames dwindled as the head of the fire rolled westward. Lark had piled up all the sapphires into two mounds.

This has to be enough to buy the tracking charm we need from Ezra's elven friend, she thought.

Each pile would easily fill a saddle bag when Ingamar returned. Lark stretched her thoughts out, feeling for the faint connection to Ingamar.

How far did he chase those wolves? she wondered, the thread of their connection so thin it was barely noticeable.

Low grunts sounded behind her. Lark spun, dropping into a fighting stance with her long sword pointed out. Six hulking Morsythians stalked toward her. These threatening orcs, known for maintaining their tribal independence from the Northern Kingdoms, were three times the size of an average human. They were even bulkier than the orc she'd faced in Fletcher's Passage. Black tribal tattoos covered their skin. Their wiry black hair was dreaded in thick sections and pulled back behind their torso-sized heads. Two ivory tusks as long as Lark's dagger spurred up from their lower jaws, rising between thick lips, coming to points just beneath their red eyes. All six wielded wide cleaver-like swords, chipped on the edges and reddened from recent use.

"Ashes," Lark cursed as they advanced through the smoldering flames wearing only leathers and fur to protect them from the heat.

Surrounding her, they closed in. One of the enormous Morsythians produced something from under his leather and fur vest, gripping it tightly as he spoke in a deep voice. The heavy sounding syllables ground out of him as though forced, though they were clearly in his native language. The spell tumbled out of him like boulders sliding down a mountainside. A red hue glowed in his palm. Lark's eyes went wide with recognition. This red wasn't like that of the coals burning in the tree trunks around them. It was deeper, like blood, like the red that came from the amulets of the others. Lark reacted too slowly. The power from the orc's spell cascaded out like water pouring through flood gates.

Ingamar's connection with her stiffened, nearly causing Lark to jump as he came thundering back into view.

"Ingamar," Lark shouted in warning.

The Morsythian sorcerer spoke the last of his guttural words with a sharp clap of his hands and a red plume expelled out. Lark dove, narrowly escaping it while Ingamar arched his neck to blast the Morsythian. Before he could breathe fire, the spell closed in around him. Ingamar released the fire, but it died instantly in the cloud of growing red fog. He thrashed, claws swiping at the red powder as it lifted him and suspended him off the ground. He pumped his wings, but the fine red smoke trapped him in place.

By the time Lark had risen to her feet again, one of the hulking Morsythians had moved in to attack. His massive blade swung in. Lark twisted faster than any human, but it wasn't fast enough. She failed to get out of the way. The blade slammed into her back, sending her sprawling.

How are they doing that? Lark wondered, as she gasped for air. The brismil plate protected her from being hewn, but the blow knocked the wind out of her. Lark scrambled to her feet, inhaling half breaths that failed to fill her lungs.

Another orc joined the first. When she faced them, both were mid-swing, their swords slicing in opposing side swings, leveled to snip off her head. Lark dropped to a knee, tucking her head as the swords passed a breath overhead. Both orcs were fully committed to their attack. Neither could stop his blade as they carried through toward each other. A sickening thud sounded as the orcs felled one another.

Lark slipped between the fallen orcs. Finally able to breathe deeply again, she met the next attack. The remaining Morsythians barreled into the fray while the orc with the amulet struggled to keep Ingamar contained in the red mist. Lark blocked a heavy-handed blow from one orc. She deflected another as she took a glancing hit across the front of her helmet. She planted her boot into another as he raised his sword aloft. Her enhanced kick cracked his chest, and she sent him flying. She spun out of the way, suffering a hit on the shoulder as another blade came crashing in.

The remaining two Morsythians peppered her with hits. Lark wove around them as best she could, blocking and keeping pace with their attack. Her instincts began to take over, seeing openings after the fact that she should've taken to end the bout. She had no idea where or when she'd learned to fight like this, but the more she moved, the more she understood what she needed to do. She blocked a choppy strike, stomping her foot into one orc's knee, causing him to fumble to maintain his footing. He thrust wildly and she caught his arm under hers. She thrust her sword under his jaw. The Morsythian went limp, falling into the ashes at her feet.

The remaining orc backed away, giving her space as he joined the orc who was attempting to join the fight after suffering her powerful kick. Lark vibrated with excitement, her necklace sizzling on her collar from the strength she wielded. The sensation urged her forward. This was a real challenge. These Morsythians were huge, even for their kind. Despite the advantage of their size and numbers, Lark's brismil plate allowed her to hold her own. As she pressed in on them, a smile spread across her face. The orcs couldn't see it through her dragon scale visor, but she bore an almost maniacal grin.

A figure in steel plate armor, stained with soot and blood came streaking in through the flames with unnatural speed. His enormous dark blue blade sliced clean through a Morsythian, cleaving one of the two orcs Lark had been confronting.

"No," Lark said, confused as to why this armored man was joining her fight and taking her kill.

She barely recognized him, a friend. It was Venrick. He'd caught up with her and was there to assist in the retrieval of the Yogos at their feet. Lark engaged again with the Morsythian, driving him back. Venrick continued past Lark and trained his brismil sword on the orc wielding the amulet.

No, Lark thought, deflecting her attention from the Morsythian she was facing to what Venrick was doing.

Being half elf, Venrick moved with a grace superior to

most humans. With the added advantage of the brismil blade, his speed was too fast for the Morsythians to comprehend. Lark blinked and the tip of Stormbreaker was sticking out the other end of the orc.

"NO!" she barked, somewhat irrationally. That orc was hers to slay. Hers to run through for attacking them and trapping Ingamar.

The red mist surrounding Ingamar faded. Venrick pulled the blade out and stepped away from the felled orc. Ingamar's breath of fire that had been stalled in the spell's entrapment blasted out. The fire torched the ground where the orcs had been, scorching the fallen.

A cocktail of emotions crowded Lark's chest, begging to get out. Relief for Ingamar flooded in, excitement at their near victory mixing in, and anger toward Venrick for taking what was hers igniting her adrenaline. The remaining Morsythian backed away from Lark as she focused on Venrick. She stalked toward him, head angled down, glaring through the slot of her visor.

Venrick dropped the blade, letting it vanish into his sheath. He slid up his visor, a smile crossed his face. The smile wavered and faded to a narrow line of worry when Lark continued to march toward him, her shoulders rolled forward, sword still gripped firmly. Rage rolled over the other emotions and all Lark could see was red.

26

ELLA

Tngamar stepped between them, his wings spread wide, blocking Venrick from Lark's view. The golden dragon lowered his horned head, teeth showing through the thin gap between his lips as he snorted at her. A sulfurous gust sprayed ash at her feet, washing her in a familiar scent. She stumbled, awareness returning.

What am I doing? Lark blinked, her desire to attack fading. *Venrick is here to help.*

She diverted her attention to the Morsythian sorcerer. His chest rose and fell in ragged breaths as he clung to his final moments of life. Sheathing the sword at her back, she came to the dying orc's side. His giant hand still gripped the dimly glowing amulet. Dropping to a knee, she asked, "Where did you learn this magic?"

The orc was muttering in his native language, keeping his red eyes skyward as life left his body.

Shaking him, she said, "Where does this magic come from?"

The Morsythian's voice trickled, then died. His chest stopped rising and he lay still.

"Lark, are you okay?" Venrick asked.

"I'm fi—"

Red light exploded out from the dead Morsythian sorcerer, funneling to two beams that blasted from his eyes, another streaming out his mouth. The body lifted for a single moment that caused the earth around them to tremble. Then the light cut off, his body fell, now limp, and the once-red amulet became a pale, almost colorless yellow.

Lark's gut reaction was to snatch the wasted amulet off the dead Morsythian, ensuring that no more magic would come from his corpse.

"Venrick, Ingamar?" she called, concerned for their safety.

"We're unharmed," Venrick said

"What happened to him?" she asked.

"Whatever that was, it's not good for us. The lightning strike that produced these Sapphires was on the northern side of the fire. If the outside forces of Lamar and Nordraven didn't know where to look for them, now they do. We need to collect what we can and get out of here," Venrick said, taking a leather bag from Ingamar's saddle.

She did a double-take. Ingamar had let Venrick touch him without a hostile reaction. Now that Lark was paying attention, she noticed that Ingamar was staying closer to Venrick than he was to Lark.

Was he affected by the spell?

She joined Venrick in gathering the Sapphires as quickly as possible. Within moments they'd filled one saddle bag. Lark retrieved the second, handing it to Venrick to hold while she filled it with the remaining Yogos.

"Take them on Ingamar and meet me back at the wagon with Ezra and Hardin," Venrick said, offering the bags to Lark.

Before she could accept the handoff, a hissing sound shot overhead. Lark scanned the smoke-filled sky. A vaporous trail of dark smoke twisted and swirled down from the clouds. Two rings of light formed, swirling green and silver. Robed figures adorned in flashy fillagree emerged from each ring. Both clutched long wooden staffs topped with glowing blue Sapphires. The one on the right had a long gray beard, speckled with more glowing Yogos. The smooth, youthful-looking man on the left had pointed ears ringed with Sapphire earrings.

"Reveal yourself imposter," the elf said, magic enhancing his voice to boom over the sound of the fire blazing around them. He pointed his staff at Lark, speaking spellcraft under his breath. A wave of power washed over her like a gale force wind. Even in her brismil plate armor she had to dig her feet into the ground and lean forward to maintain balance.

The bearded magi planted his staff into the ashen soil and spoke in a rumbling voice. Fire swirled around his body, turning into a vortex. It came on, aimed at Venrick and Ingamar. Venrick dove out of the way, the fire whirl spinning on past him. Ingamar roared, sending his own instinctive counter magic into the tornado of fire. The flames spun apart, but in the distraction, the mage's staff flashed from the light of his Yogos. The saddle bags tore free from Venrick's grip. They flew through the gap, landing directly in the wizard's awaiting arms.

Lark struggled to gain ground on the elf. She drew her sword, taking slow, drawn-out steps. The elf's eyes widened when his magic didn't render Lark motionless. He studied Venrick more closely as he struggled to drive Lark back.

"This can't be. That is Tel Roan's armor... His dragon, too," he said, in surprise.

Ingamar roared at them, the mage spellcasting another whirl of fire at Venrick and the dragon.

"Tel Roan is dead," the man replied.

"Give us back the Yogos," Lark growled, gaining ground as she worked to close the gap.

"The Vermillion Keep lost its right to claim powers in this region of the forest when Tel died," the mage said. "This treasure belongs to Storm Keep now."

"Like ash. Give us back the Sapphires or die," Lark said through gritted teeth.

"Don't make us drag the Keeps into conflict again," the elf warned, a vein in his head bulging in his struggle to maintain his spell toward Lark.

"Tell your General that Tel Roan's armor and dragon are worn by a new rider. One that will not bend to lesser Paragons or Magi," Venrick said.

"Venrick, I can handle this. Leave them to me," Lark said, the adrenaline that drove her to see red rising again.

"Venrick?" the wizard said. "You are no longer under contract with any Keep. As a former Squire, you have no right to be here and make such a claim. Rest assured that the Archmagus and the rest of the Magi Order will hear about this. You'll be marked for trying to claim these, hunted down, and prosecuted as a rebel operating against the King's contracts."

"No," Venrick hissed.

"I think he will be particularly interested to hear that you've been seen here, at a storm of power, with hopes of finding a replacement for what you lost."

Lark was nearly to the elf. Her movements were restrained, as though she was hauling herself through a vat of molasses. The Sapphires in the elf's staff began to flicker. One flashed faster than the others and winked out. The wind pushing against Lark eased ever so slightly. She extended her sword tip toward at the elf. A dark shadow spread over Lark as she struggled to propel the tip forward. Her necklace burned again, seeming to grow hotter as the ominous shadow grew.

Both magi turned their attention to whatever created it. Another of the Sapphires in the wizard's staff winked out, easing the tension that held Lark back. The two diverted their attention, gave one another a curt nod, then vanished in a swirl of green and silver.

Lark stumbled forward, her sword running through the vaporous cloud that now drifted away in the gathering wind. When she regained her footing, the darkness surrounding them became more obvious. The glow of the fire appeared brighter though the flames were flickering and blowing out in the growing gale.

"Lark, we need to go before the Giving-Rain hits," Venrick said.

"They took the Yogos," she replied.

"If this wall of Giving-Rain hits, we'll be torn to shreds. I don't know if the brismil scale will protect you."

To her surprise, Ingamar allowed Venrick to climb on him.

Lark couldn't feel any of the cues coming from Ingamar. The flush pulsed through her necklace, however. Then sharp and direct, Ingamar sent a rush of one pure emotion at her. It gave her a sour taste in her mouth. Fear. Whatever approached struck unequivocal and overwhelming fear into Tel's dragon.

She looked skyward. The shadow that had been growing beyond the smoke wasn't just from the approaching wall of the Giving-Rain. A massive set of wings spread wide; the shape of a dragon's body outlined against the storm clouds descended.

"Oh, ash," Lark cursed, realizing the look in the elf's eyes wasn't fear of her and Ingamar, it was fear of this new dragon and rider. A pair whose ominous presence was notable enough to scare away two Paragons from Storm Keep.

"Lark, come on," Venrick urged from Ingamar's back, glancing nervously at the sky. "It could be Marcel. I don't think Ingamar wants to have another run-in with White Eye. Let's go, Lar—"

Ingamar broke into a gallop, cutting Venrick off. He charged past Lark, tucking his wing and lowering his shoulder so Lark could grab hold. Her hand found purchase on the saddle handle as she was scooped off her feet. The strength from the armor kept her shoulder socket in place as she bounced against Ingamar's side.

"Give me your hand," Venrick said, extending his.

As Ingamar spread his wings to get airborne, a flash of light sparked into existence next to her. The tingling sensation she felt whenever Nix was near cut through the burning along the chain.

"Nix?' she said, seeing the small fire fae appear alongside them. She was in her fiery red dress like always.

Nix smiled slightly. A sickening look came over her angelic face before she said, "I'm sorry."

Lark frowned.

A breath later, Nix transformed into a haunted woman, dark rings around her eyes, black lips with long fangs, gray claws jutting from her fingertips as she expanded ten times her size and flew as if to attack.

Lark screamed, letting go of the saddle to block herself from Nix's shocking aggression.

Before Nix could strike, however, she flickered out of existence, a flurry of sparks cascading over Lark's armor. Lark's stomach lurched as she realized she was falling. Flaming branches broke against her back as she dropped fifty feet from the height of the forest and slammed onto the ground. The armor kept her body from breaking, but pain flashed white in her eyes, blinding her. Larks' kidneys, spine, and head throbbed with pain, her breath coming ragged as she struggled to inhale.

The ground shook as trees popped and fell, the old-growth timbers striking the ground around her with explosive energy. Her world spun. She struggled to her feet, trying to force herself to run. A gust of wind slammed her in the back and knocked her down again. Blistering heat stung for an intense second, flames crashing around her, then it was over. The throaty roar deafening from behind her confirmed Lark's fear. That blast of fire came from a dragon.

Rolling onto her back, Lark looked up at the towering beast looming over her. Its charcoal wings folded, revealing the dragon's size to be five times that of Ingamar. He stared down his long snout with pure milk-white eyes. Seated between six-foot-long spikes protruding from the dragon's spine was an armored figure. He wore black brismil plate armor and a helmet with wide horns that curled down beside his head. The man held a long spear, the tip as big as Tel's brismil blade. A copper cloak flapped from around his shoulders.

Marcel? she thought, this rider's appearance not quite fitting the image she'd crafted in her head.

In an instant, the black dragon's eyes flashed to a deep golden color. The rider rose from the saddle, standing atop the dragon's back as the beast took in its surroundings. Effortlessly the rider jumped down the twenty-five feet from his giant dragon's back, landing in a plume of ash. Hot soot rippled out like a thick fog around his feet as he stood well over six-feet tall in his impressive armor.

Lark found her footing. With her inferior sword, she settled into a defensive stance. Wind ripped at the rider's copper cloak as he dropped his spear. It vanished, brismil's hallmark afterimage of smoke tearing apart in the gale. Sparks formed in the air near his horned helmet. Nix appeared, hanging there in her flaming dress, her eyes angled down as if unable to look at Lark.

Lark's heart sank. The fire fae remained in the air at the rider's side.

"Nix, how could you?" Lark whispered.

"Ella," the rider addressed Lark in a rich, smooth voice.

That name. Sasja had called her that; the name that... her father called her? Lark furrowed her brow as the sound of his voice teased at a faint memory. This man was her... no, not her father, but a fatherly figure to her. She could see his frame outlined before her. Broad shoulders, proud chest, toned like a soldier. And his name. *His name isn't Marcel... His name starts with a B?* she guessed, unable to remember.

"I see you've claimed Tel Roan's armor as your own," he observed.

"What have you done to my fae?" she demanded.

"Nix? I haven't done anything to her. We do not own fae, we can, however, control them when they are in this realm. You've lost control of her. Now she does as I command."

"That's a lie," she said raising her chin at him.

"Calm yourself, Ella. We don't need things to turn violent again. We can go back to how they were, how they used to be."

"Stop using that name. My name is Lark."

"Lark? Ah, I see," he said, placing his hand to his clavicle.

"If you're here for the Hyalite, I don't have it."

"If you did, I'd already have taken it from you. No, I'm not here for the Hyalite you stole, or any powers you may have collected from this storm. I'm here to compel you, Ella. Compel you to tell me where it is. I want back the thing you stole from me," he said.

"I didn't steal anything from you," she said, catching Nix's droopy eyes. There was something different about them. Where they were normally the color of flames, now they burned white-hot, like the dragon's had when the rider had first landed. Nix quickly diverted her gaze back down to the spot near the rider's boots where she'd been staring.

"Oh, Ella, but you have stolen from me. You've stolen something very important to me and I need it back," he said, his smooth voice turning firm at the end.

Rain cascading from the sky sounded in the near distance. Lark flicked her attention to it for a moment, noting the dark gray wall crashing toward them. The rain that struck down so forcefully Venrick had said it could tear them apart, even with brismil armor.

"I don't want to fight with you," he said, checking over his shoulder to gauge the distance to the wall of monsoonal rain. "Give me back the gadget you stole, and I won't fight you anymore." He stepped forward, extending a hand and wrapping it into a tight fist.

Something prodded at her. She felt a faint familiarity with the sensation as she was forced to try to remember. The memory of the meeting with the Morsythians came forward. Her mind focused in on the golden device placed atop the map of the forest.

No, she thought, forcing the mental probe from her mind.

Rain slapped the ground around them, puffs of ash rising from the fist-sized droplets.

"Ella, stop playing these games. Give me the astral lathe," he ordered.

Lark's necklace warmed against her chest. "My name is not Ella." Something inside her began to stir. "And I'll never give it to you."

A source of power vibrated through her. Her necklace burned as it built from somewhere deep inside. She extended her mental arm toward it, feeling the bond. A presence tying her to the power of a god.

"Astra Rapi," she shouted, the words revealing themselves to her through the fog of her mind.

Raw magic burned through her, passing from the bond, channeling through her body and out her arm. A sphere, glowing bright white and chased with a tail of sparking light circled around her arm, growing as the power released. It flared, shooting forth, rocketing at the enemy rider.

"Fragmos," he countered.

A swell of stone ripped up from the ground to block Lark's attack. The comet of Lark's energy collided with this resurrected ore. The crash clapped, stone exploded, her sphere of gaseous light fractured. The energy fields melded for an instant, then tore apart, creating an ear-splitting KABOOM!

The resulting ripple of energy washed out in all directions slamming into her, sending her flying up and away. In an instant, Lark was shooting away from the wall of Giving-Rain, crashing out through the canopy. She reached a moment of weightlessness as she arched out through the smoke. After several seconds, she released a yell, feeling her trajectory turn as she headed back toward the ground. Clear sky came into view. She was whipping down through the trees. She hit the ground with her shoulder blades leading the impact. A wordless, HUGH escaped before the pain again blurred her vision, nausea rising in her stomach.

"Lark!" was all she heard before she fell unconscious.

27

LIKE A METEOR

"Turn around! Ingamar, turn back!" Venrick shouted, holding on for his life. He was completely subject to the whims of the dragon.

Venrick twisted uncomfortably in the saddle, trying to see through the thicket of smoke to locate the other dragonrider. But the smoke was too thick. He couldn't see below where Lark had fallen.

Venrick pounded his fist against Ingamar's neck. "You can't leave her like this! Go back, Ingamar."

Ingamar ignored him, flying away from the fire.

In the forest below, Venrick spotted Storm Keep soldiers who'd pushed beyond their territory to occupy Tel's region of the forest. They fled, Northerners and orcs chasing them as they retreated with their prize. Behind the storm, the black stain of fire glistened in the monsoonal moisture. No sign of the dragonrider or Lark.

Ingamar dipped, rolling into a dive for the ground, far too close to the fleeing soldiers.

"What are you doing now, Ingamar? We can't get to Lark from back here," he said.

Ingamar tucked his wings in, dropped through the canopy, then flared to slow himself before landing hard. Venrick jostled in the saddle, coming out of his seat and nearly falling off before the dragon trotted to a stop. Ingamar did not wait for Venrick to dismount. He dropped his shoulder, acting like he was going to roll.

"Whoa, whoa," Venrick shouted, leaping off, landing in a tuck-and-roll.

Thundering hoofs sounded.

"Ashes, we're going to be overrun by the Northerners," Venrick said, drawing Stormbreaker. Adrenaline rushed through his body. With the energy from the blade passing through him, he was much faster, stronger, and more powerful. "I can do this," he told himself, dropping into a fighting stance.

Curiously, Ingamar sat on his haunches, waiting for something as he scanned the sky above.

"Hee-yah," Ezra hollered as he and Hardin rounded the corner. Thunder and Giant galloped ahead, eyes wide, nostrils flared. Without receiving a command from the dwarf, Thunder and Giant drew to a halt before passing Ingamar and Venrick.

"Venrick, where's Lark?" Ezra asked, hopping off the wagon, scanning the trees, rolling the war hammer shaft in both hands.

"She fell," he said.

"Lark's dead?" Hardin gasped.

"No, she fell off Ingamar. There was another rider."

"I didn't see any rider fly within the borders of Lamar," Ezra said.

"It had to be a Northern rider because Storm Keep already had two Paragons there, an elf and a mage."

"Two Paragons from Storm Keep and a Nordraven dragonrider? There must've been a Hyalite," Ezra said.

"No, the Paragons from Storm Keep must've already been in the forest when this storm started. With Tel gone and the Vermillion Keep in the midst of contract negotiations, they were trying to expand the region that they patrol. The Nordraven rider, though, that was a shock to them, as it was to us. There were only Yogos with this storm. The Paragons fled at the first sign of him. The Northern's dragon was huge. From what I could tell of its shadow, it had to be four or five times larger than Ingamar."

A chilling howl rose in the near distance, a second quick to follow. Ezra snapped to attention, facing the forest to the north.

"Nordraven brought wolves," he said.

"I barely made it around the flank of their soldiers before entering the burn. I saw the wolves fleeing before I found Lark. She'd been fighting Morsythians, one of them was wielding power through a ruby amulet."

"Morsythians don't have any interest in magic. Why would they be here?" Ezra said.

"Where are these red amulets coming from?" Hardin asked.

"It's the third I've seen in a month," Venrick said, not letting on that the one he was forced to wear around his neck was of the same make.

Several soldiers ran past within view. A group of three stopped, veering toward the wagon until they spotted Ingamar staring up at the sky. The soldiers chose wisely and continued running.

"I have a feeling that we're about to see more in a moment," Ezra said.

"I have to go back for Lark," Venrick said.

"I'm coming with you."

"You'll only slow me down."

"You'll be torn to shreds by the Giving-Rain," Ezra said.

"She could be facing Marcel Heartfell for all we know, alone, and without a dragon's support. I'm going."

"My wards can help protect us. I'm coming with you, Venrick."

"Hey, what in the world is that?" Hardin said, pointing overhead.

A figure catapulted out from the smoke cloud, trailing tendrils of magical essence. Ingamar sprung from his coiled tail, launching himself into the air to chase.

"That's her," Ezra shouted, taking off after Ingamar.

Venrick sprinted off through the forest, dodging oncoming soldiers from Storm Keep. With the power of the brismil blade channeling through him, he sent a driving pulse of the dragon's power through his legs to leap high into the air. Ingamar was ahead of him, but Lark fell like a stone, streaking down and disappearing from view into the trees. Ingamar darted in after her. Venrick's heart skipped a beat. He knew Ingamar wasn't going to make it. Venrick couldn't bound there fast enough. In a fit of anger, he landed among the Northern orcs, letting Stormbreaker dispense his rage. By the time he reached Lark, Ingamar was shielding her with his wings. The green forest around him was charred black from his fire breath. The ground smoldered with the remains of the Northerners who had tried to approach.

Golden light ebbed from his body down onto her, glancing off the protective magic inherent to the brismil armor.

"Lark," Venrick said, seeing her limp body in Ingamar's claws.

Ingamar growled, his lip quivering in Venrick's direction.

"I know you're not mad at me," Venrick said, continuing to approach with his hands open, arms spread wide. "Why did you choose to save me instead of her?"

Ingamar snapped at Venrick, a glob of spittle landing near the half-elf's feet.

"By now you should know that I'm not trying to kill her. I might be able to help," Venrick said.

Ingamar narrowed his eyes, then recoiled his neck, allowing Venrick to approach.

Venrick scanned Lark. The brismil armor remained intact around her body, meaning she was still alive. Brismil armor returned to the single dragon scale if the wearer died. Venrick didn't know what to do. Lark's body could be shattered inside from the fall. He knew brismil armor protected against blows from mortal weapons and could only be broken by dragons or other brismil weapons.

Ashes, Lark, what happened to you back there? he thought.

Ingamar growled again, but when Venrick looked up, the dragon's attention was focused on Ezra and Hardin. Both were panting, having just passed around the edges of the fleeing armies. Ezra's war hammer was slicked with gore, Hardin's shirt spotted with his own blood where he'd narrowly missed being mortally wounded on his side and shoulder.

"I don't know how to get the armor off," Venrick said.

Ezra lowered his head as he approached, Ingamar growled but allowed them to continue. "Can you use her own hand to get a grip on the scale harness strap?" Ezra asked.

Venrick picked up Lark's limp arm, trying to run her hand in over the place where the brismil scale was secured to her side. Her hand passed through the chest plate but without her grip, he couldn't force the mechanism to open and release the scale from her skin. "It's not working."

Hardin placed a hand on Venrick's shoulder. "Let me try," he said.

"It won't work if she's not conscious enough to grip it. If she's paralyzed, she won't be able to get herself out."

However, Hardin didn't use Lark's arm. He searched with both hands at Lark's side, feeling for where the scale was located. Venrick watched in awe as his hand sank through the plate armor. A moment later, the brismil armor disappeared, the scale loose in the harness where he'd released the latching mechanism.

"Ward Walkers can breach brismil?" Ezra said in disbelief.

Venrick's attention was solely focused on Lark. He checked her for obvious signs of injury, not seeing any bones protruding through skin or puddles of blood, but that didn't mean she didn't suffer internal injuries from her fall.

His hand fell to her forehead, feeling her temperature with the back of it. He spread her eyes open, seeing the pupils dilate. He pinched her finger, the color returning instantly. As he watched her chest rise, counting her breaths, a weak voice said, "Venrick, my eyes are up here."

"Lark, you're alive," he said, cupping the side of her face.

She attempted a smile, then winced when trying to move.

"Don't move just yet. We need to make sure you didn't break anything serious," Venrick said.

Lark winced again, ignoring his advice and pushed herself into a seated position. "What, are you a field medic, too?"

"Squire for a Paragon, remember?" he said. "Now seriously, don't move any more until I'm finished examining you."

～

"Ouch!" Lark winced at Venrick's touch on her back. "Stop treating me like I'm porcelain and let me get up."

"Lark, you should be dead. You just launched out over the forest. You probably went over a mile and fell hundreds of feet. Look at the depression you made in the ground; you were like an ashing meteor."

"I was in brismil armor," she said, her body tender with pain.

"I've never heard of anyone taking a fall like that in brismil armor and surviving," Venrick said.

"This armor is like having a dragon's hide for protection. Dragons can still be broken by falling from the sky," Ezra said.

"Then why wasn't I?" Lark asked.

"Maybe she has Yita's gifts, isn't she the goddess of gravity and healing?" Hardin suggested.

"All dragonriders have some healing powers, but if she had Yita's, she could've controlled her fall."

"Right," Ezra confirmed.

"Clearly, it's because of the armor," Venrick answered.

"Exactly, I'll be fine," Lark said.

"The point we're trying to make is, it doesn't make you invincible," Venrick argued.

"Good to know now that I've already fought giant wolves, hulking Morsythians, an elf, a mage, and a dragonrider," she responded through gritted teeth.

"And it was all for naught," Venrick said. "We should've been focusing on where Sasja could take a Hyalite without Nordraven or Lamar knowing instead of nearly getting ourselves killed over Yogos to pay for this tracking spell."

She rose to her feet with some effort, untying the leather pouch from her sword belt. "Hold out your hands," she said. Venrick did, Ezra and Hardin leaning in as Ingamar stood guard over them. Lark opened the pouch and poured the soot-stained Yogos into his hands.

"You kept some hidden under your armor," Venrick said, blinking.

As they revered the Sapphires, Hardin interrupted, saying, "Didn't Lark just fight a Nordraven dragonrider?"

Venrick nodded.

"Are we in serious danger here? And I don't mean just

from the Northerners who could be marching back through here after chasing off the unit from Storm Keep," Hardin said.

"Hang on, some of these are used," Ezra said, checking through the Yogos. "Why did you collect spent sapphires?"

"They weren't spent when I collected them," Lark said, seeing that nearly half of the Sapphires she had bagged were without light.

Ezra leveled his gaze at Venrick. "You realize what this means, don't you?"

"That the power housed in Yogos is unpredictable?" Venrick guessed.

"No. She used them," Ezra said.

"You have to speak to coax the magic from them," Venrick argued.

"I didn't use them. I don't even know how to," Lark said.

"You mean, you don't remember how to," Ezra corrected her.

"Regardless, I didn't use them. I didn't say any spells after I was airborne."

"You spell-cast when facing that rider, though, right?" Ezra said.

"Yes," she admitted. "But I was channeling through a bond. I could feel the tether there connecting me to the power."

"It is as I have suspected for some time. The other instructors at the Academy said I was mad, but I knew the Magi Order was keeping this hidden," Ezra said.

"What are you talking about?" Venrick said.

"Lark's armor fed off the magic in the Yogos to keep her body from breaking," Ezra said.

"What? No, that's not how brismil works," Venrick said. "I didn't go to an Academy, but Tel schooled me on its origins. Brismil comes from the original twelve dragons who claimed residence in Sataran. When their long lives were drawing to a close, they shed their earthly forms, ascending to the realm of the gods. Their magical essence was transferred into their scales and bones, leaving behind armor and weapons for the future dragonriders. But brismil can't take on more power, only impart its eternal energy onto the bearer, right?"

"They are pieces of magical beings, though?" Ezra asked. "None of the original twelve were killed. They ascended to the realm of the gods, leaving behind these pieces of themselves. Who's to say if those fragments of the ancient dragons can be shaped into something new."

"This has been tried before and failed. Tel told me," Venrick said.

"How many years did you or Tel spend researching this very subject. Did you have access to a magical laboratory, testing the longevity and potency of magical objects created by Hyalites or other ethereal powers? Because I did. I spent decades researching and theorizing on this exact topic. Just when I was getting close to an answer, they forced me out."

"Why force you out over something that would benefit the Paragons?" Venrick asked.

"One door opens..." he said, staring at the Yogos.

"You're suggesting that the brismil scale absorbed the power from some of these Yogos and used it to heal Lark's body from the impact?" Hardin asked.

"Yes, but only what was needed to keep its host from being crippled," Ezra said.

"She's alive, which makes what you're suggesting possible," Venrick said. "But how can that be? Everything we know about the energy from Sapphires tells us the magician needs to speak for the magic to take form."

"In human riders, magi, elves, dwarves, and orcs, yes, but not dragons. Dragons are of a different realm than the other races and do not speak to use their magic; it stands to reason then that brismil would fall under the same class of rules," Ezra argued.

"This is all really fascinating, but I think we need to circle back to that question I asked a few moments ago. You know, about the enemy dragonrider who Lark was just fighting," Hardin said.

Lark felt her stomach drop as though she were falling all over again. The pain, the unconsciousness, the arguing, it was all distracting her from processing what had just happened. She was horrified at what she'd experienced. From Nix betraying her to the moment that she channeled magic through her dragon bond, it all flooded back.

"Ash, we need to get out of here," Lark swore. As she said it, she noticed the sensations that had driven her before, the ones emitting through her from the necklace were no longer there. The gold chain felt cool against her skin. In a panic, she tried to rip the chain free. She yanked on it, tugging her head forward, the chain biting into the back of her neck.

"What are you doing?" Venrick asked, trying to perceive the threat that Lark had felt.

"It's this necklace. I think it's linked with him because of Nix," she said trying to rip it off again. It didn't budge.

"Linked to who?" Ezra said.

"That rider."

"Describe him."

Lark gave them a play-by-play, getting the feeling that if the rider was going to destroy her, he would've given chase by now. She told them of Nix's betrayal, making her fall, the rider revealing that she was his fae sent to spy on her, or so Lark suspected. How he spoke to her as though they'd known each other. That he demanded the Hyalite from her. And how she'd channeled through her bond.

"Maybe the Giving-Rain got them," Hardin said hopefully.

"Wishful thinking," Ezra said. "That rider is gone for now. Otherwise, he would've attacked us."

"And you're sure he acted like he knew you?" Venrick asked.

"It wasn't just that he knew me. I knew him," Lark said. She struggled to remember what he looked like under that armor. "His voice was so familiar to me, but I can't think of how I know him or what his name is."

"Was it Marcel?" Hardin asked.

"He does ride White Eye," Venrick said.

"But the dragon's eyes turned golden again after landing," Lark said.

"The rider has warging powers," Ezra said.

Lark cocked her head at him.

"It means he can see through other animal's eyes, effectively controlling them for a period of time," Venrick explained.

"White Eye's eyes are rimed in gold, he's not being warged into like this dragon you faced. Marcel Heartfell doesn't wield a brismil spear either. I've never known anyone to have escaped Marcel's wrath. If Marcel wanted the Hyalite, he wouldn't have let you escape."

"He wasn't actually after the Hyalite. He wanted something called an astral lathe," Lark said.

"Curious. I wasn't aware that those were still in existence. Not much is known about them, other than that they came with the first twelve dragons who settled here in Sataran," Ezra said.

"Did you say he let her go? Or is she a powerful dragonrider who can stand up to Nordraven enemies?" Venrick challenged.

"Regardless, this means that Nordraven doesn't have the Hyalite," Lark said.

"You're right," Venrick said. "This means that the

Morsythians might not be acting with the Northern kings like we assumed. They may be acting in their own interests."

"Why now? What do they need this Hyalite for and where did they learn to use such powerful magic? These red amulets you say they used are not powered by Yogos," Ezra said.

"They're used for curses," Venrick said.

"All these Morsythians are under a curse?" Lark asked.

"Curses don't manifest as spell-casting abilities?" Ezra said.

"Maybe things have changed since you were at the Academy," Venrick suggested.

"Maybe they have, maybe they haven't. What makes you say this magic the Morsythians are using is a curse?"

"Intuition," he said. "I know it sounds unlikely, but what if they're being manipulated by corrupt magic. What if the magi figured out how to store power in them and taught the Morsythians how to use it?"

Ezra wrinkled his face and shook his head. "That wouldn't work. Besides, the Magi Order forbids curses. They wouldn't allow such a thing to happen among their group. Using curses is a Northern practice."

"What makes you so sure the magi won't change their ways?" Venrick asked, narrowing his gaze at Ezra.

"These amulets, what do they look like?" Hardin asked.

"I grabbed one," Lark said, searching the depression where she'd landed. "Here it is," she said, lifting the broken chain and wasted amulet. "I took it from the Morsythian. I guess I had a good grip on it. It's spent of magic, not the same color that it had been."

"This is just like the one our chancellor wears. His is redder, too," Hardin said, taking the amulet and examining it.

"You said your townspeople were put under a curse," Ezra said

"That's right."

"But it doesn't affect you because you're a Ward Walker?" Lark said.

He shrugged.

"Who is powerful enough to be placing curses that could affect entire populations?" Ezra asked.

Venrick stared at the ground near his feet, knowing the answer but unable to hint at it more than he already had. The Magi Order. If one was corrupted enough to curse him while the others watched, there had to be more that could do worse. Venrick noticed Lark observing his posture.

She's intuitive. Well, I guess you have to be when you're a rider strong enough to take a Hyalite from Marcel ashing Heartfell, he thought.

"We may find more answers while getting our tracking charm," Ezra said.

"So, you are sticking around. You'll join our cause?" Lark asked.

"I joined your cause the day I found you wandering the woods with a dragon in tow, a fire fae on your shoulder, and a Hyalite in your pack."

"Good," Lark said. "Tell me, who is this sage elder who can forge our tracking charm and who knows so much more than you?"

"She's an elf. She was cast out by her people and is feared by ours. She was one of the best instructors I ever saw at the Academy and now organizes something much larger. We're going to seek counsel from Cheyanne."

28

CHEYANNE

"So, what's the deal with this Cheyanne lady? You haven't told me much," Hardin asked.

Ezra glanced around as they rode deeper into the forest. His amber eyes surveyed each tree as though it may be watching.

"We're alone out here," Hardin said. "Ingamar is the most fearsome thing we'll see in this wood. As long as Lark's back there in the wagon, resting up, we're safe as can be."

"No safer than we were when those Northern soldiers came rushing through trying to scare off every last person from Storm Keep. Ingamar might be a dragon, but he isn't bound to any of us," Ezra said.

"He is to Lark though, right?"

A glimpse of golden scales flashed between the trees and out of Ezra's view.

"At least, she's used magic through the dragon bond, which is as close to being protected by a dragon as I suspect we'll ever get. I hope she is getting some rest with Venrick back there. They way they look at each other, am I right?" Hardin said, nudging Ezra with his elbow.

"That's a common misconception," Ezra grumbled.

"What, that those two are struggling to express their feelings for one another?"

"No, I mean the thought that a dragon will make things safer for you. If anything, it attracts more danger," Ezra replied.

Hardin hummed, drumming his fingers on the base of his lute. "I wonder what happened that Sasja became so in debt that she stole the Hyalite?"

"Is that all you think about, the fairer sex?"

"How do you mean?"

"All you can talk about since we left Astral City is that thief who stole your money and the Hyalite. If you mention her again, I'll know for sure that she stole your heart, too."

"What?" Hardin scowled. "I do not constantly talk about Sasja. And if I do, it's only because she ruined my opportunity to get help from a Knight of the Vermillion Keep."

"Yet, you forsake your village to go on this quest with Lark and Venrick," Ezra pointed out.

"And you," Hardin added. "But I'm not forsaking them. Those red amulets the Morsythians have been using are at the root of what's happening at home. By going on this quest with you, I'm pursuing a solution to the curse that's crippling my hometown. Once I learn the antidote for whatever control the red amulets have, all I'll need is Paragon or a brave Knight to carry out tasks I can't do myself," Hardin said.

"There might have been a time years ago when the Paragons and their Knights contracted themselves based on vanquishing evil, ridding Lamar of agents of chaos who lay waste in our society and promoting peace. Nowadays, though, they sign contracts with the highest bidder. It's all about collecting Hyalites and Yogos. The shift started when Nordraven and Lamar committed to full-scale war in the northeast region of the forest. Now, anyone like you who is trying to get a quality hero has to go to a Knight of a Keep, or a Paragon. It's nearly impossible to compete with the contracts they're offered. People like the King, the Dukes, and other High Nobles snatch them up in hopes they'll increase their stockpiles of magic. When real trouble comes knocking, everyone without deep pockets is effectively left to fend for themselves."

"I wonder what she's doing now?" Hardin said, lightly strumming his lute, leaning back in the bench and staring up at the sky.

Ezra shook his head at Hardin's lack of focus. As they rode, a white hawk flew past with a familiar beat of its wings. It perched on a branch a dozen yards ahead, overlooking the path. One glance at the brown and black spotted patter on her chest, the scar over her left eye, and Ezra knew.

"You said you wanted to know what the deal was with Cheyanne?" Ezra said, his voice gruffer than he intended.

"Yes, you keep mentioning her. That she is a partner in your business, but now you want to take us farther north, practically to the heart of the Everburning Forest where we could be caught up in another firestorm at any moment so she can craft a tracking spell? Couldn't we find some mage at the Keep to do it? Seems like it would've been closer and more convenient. There's barely a road here. We've been riding up and down these forested hills for days. I mean, we're practically directly under the Floating Islands. Who knows if Sasja even still has the Hyalite," Hardin replied, gently putting down his lute, and turning his full attention to Ezra.

"When I was your age and we wanted to go somewhere in the Everburning Forest, we had to dig a new mine shaft, hope to find a new cave system and maybe we'd get there someday. You should count yourself lucky we're able to travel overland. It could be worse, if Thunder and Giant weren't here, we'd be walking."

"You didn't answer my question."

"I'll let her answer your questions herself."

"Why not tell me?" Hardin's voice trailed away, his back straightening as the path before them widened.

The evergreens before them parted to reveal a singular oak tree, wide-trunked, the roots sprawling out around the grassy surrounding. From the ground, twisting bark swirled up the ancient base, dividing into forks and Ys with thick branches that reached upward toward the sun. Emerald light seemed to glow throughout its leafy canopy, casting a warm, imperial brightness to the ivory house in the treetop. A stairway wound its way up the trunk, leading to a landing that surrounded the elven craft home. Arched gables of bleached wood crowned the three main chambers. Heavy beams edged the sides with long glossy windows reflecting the light as though crystals had been embedded into the home.

A blonde-haired, green-eyed woman stood near the railing that lined the wrap-around deck. The white hawk flew off its perch and landed on her white staff.

"Is that?" Hardin asked, finding his voice again.

"Cheyanne," Ezra said.

"She's a wood elf, from Gambria."

"I've mentioned that she's an elf around you before."

"I thought you were joking, or maybe that she was like Venrick and not full elf, or possibly a different kind of elf, like a mountain elf. Don't the dwarves hate Gambrian wood elves? How are you in business with one?"

"Maybe you haven't noticed, but I'm not exactly your standard dwarf."

"Still, the rivalry between your peoples is legendary. You're sworn enemies."

"Not all mountain dwarves hold grudges," Ezra said, slowing the wagon at the base of the tree. He rapped three times on the wall of the weapons wagon, signaling for Lark and Venrick to emerge.

Ingamar stepped out of the forest, sunlight highlighting his radiant golden color.

Lark moved slowly, waking her stiff muscles, sore joints, and tender bruises as she exited the wagon. She stepped gingerly out into the grassy opening beneath the elven tree. Her gaze lifted to the stunning elven treehouse. It pulled Lark into another vision from her memories.

She stood at a treehouse just like this. Flames consumed the tree, fae creatures sparked as they fled the wooded home, disappearing into the forest. A dark column of smoke chugged up into the air above the trees. Lark hefted the weight of a blade in her hand, noting that the steel was clean of blood. The bond with her dragon vibrated fear and confusion through both of them. He stood beside her, the dragon's bulk just out of view. Lark blinked away the memory, again taking in the elven home before her.

"Lark," Venrick said, his presence at her side drawing her away from the chaotic vision. "Are you good? You look like you've seen a ghost."

"This place is familiar to me," she said, knitting her brows. "It didn't look like this the last time I was here."

"It's just like the homes in Gambria. Perhaps Cheyanne will have some answers. Gambrian wood elves are said to have long-lasting memories," Venrick said, joining Ezra and Hardin at the base of the stairs.

The white hawk glided gracefully down from Cheyanne's staff to the railing at ground level. Ezra approached it, speaking to the sharp-beaked hawk.

"I wouldn't have brought them here unless it was necessary. We need your help."

The hawk's head bent sideways at a ninety-degree angle, then she screeched.

Lark tugged on Venrick's sleeve and whispered, "I thought Cheyanne was the elf."

"She is," Venrick answered.

"Why is Ezra speaking to that hawk?"

"Cheyanne is warging into the hawk."

"Warging," Lark repeated the familiar word. She'd heard the others explain it in regard to the Nordraven dragonrider, but the experience she'd had with warging seeped into the edges of her memory. Warg magic was the ability of an individual to enter another animal's mind. They could see, hear, and experience what the animal was doing at that time, and some were powerful enough to control them.

"You remember it from before, don't you?" Venrick asked, his mouth turning into a quarter smile.

"I do," she replied, noting how his attention to her questions was improving.

I shouldn't trust him so willingly. It wasn't long ago that I believed he was going to kill me for the Hyalite. I need to work on not always showing my emotions on my face, she thought.

The hawk blinked and a creamy white film that had been covering its eyes cleared. They were now golden. It flew back to the deck overhead. Ezra motioned for them to follow, taking the lead on the stairs. Before Lark stepped onto the first step, she looked over at Ingamar. The golden dragon's eyes were fixed on them, but he appeared to be relaxed.

Breaking the plane of the decking, Lark set eyes on the elf woman who she'd seen in her memories. Just as she was in her vision, the elf woman appeared youthful. Her smooth face, high cheekbones, and button nose contrasted with the scars she bore on her eyebrow, cheek and neck. Her long ears were ringed with earrings, her narrow frame outfitted in light robes. She held a white staff with glyphs carved into it, a large Sapphire resting in the lattice cage at the top of the staff. Her green eyes were glued on Lark, even as Ezra approached her to speak.

She remembers me, but is she a friend?

"Cheyanne, thank you for diverting to meet with us here," Ezra said.

Diverting? From where? Isn't this her home?

"After the sighting during the last firestorm, I wasted no time in making my choice. I have others relying on me to keep them hidden. I don't need a Nordraven rider sticking around," Cheyanne said, her slitted green eyes watching Lark.

"You remember Tel Roan's Squire—"

"Venrick, yes," Cheyanne nodded to him.

"You know me?" Venrick asked.

"Yes, but we never met as you didn't attend the Academy."

"You worked at the Astral City Paragon Academy as well?"

"How else do you think an exiled wood elf from Gambria and a mountain dwarf of Lamar became friends?"

"I can't remember ever seeing you around the Vermillion Keep," Venrick replied.

"I didn't spend much time within the grounds of the Keep. I did keep a close eye on all future prospects who squired for the Knights and Paragons. I was sorry to hear the news of Tel Roan's death. Curious how you were able to stay alive, especially being half elf. Usually when a Paragon dies, regardless of the outcome, the Keep ensures the Squire meets the great equalizer."

"I laid my life down for Tel and Ingamar."

"I'm sure you did. If you hadn't, Ingamar would never have followed you," Cheyanne said, shifting her weight as she looked on in judgement.

Hardin approached, clearing his throat to fill the silence.

"We haven't met before either, but Sasja steered me toward the Pour House back in Stormwatch. My name is Hardin Morningstar," he said, extending his hand in greeting.

Cheyanne greeted him, her eyes growing wide and mouth turning slack-jawed when she gripped his hand. Hardin's face contorted in panic. Cheyanne was crushing his hand as she squeezed with an absent-minded expression. Almost as soon as it started, Cheyanne let go, saying, "Forgive me. You should've prepared me, Ezra. A Ward Walker?"

"Yikes," Hardin said, shaking out his hand. "You've got one heck of a grip, lady."

"Ezra, are you aware of the company you're traveling with?" Cheyanne asked, momentarily diverting her attention to Lark.

"Ingamar broke the pact and attacked a civilian residence in Astral City," she motioned to the golden dragon. "Tel Roan is dead," she gestured to Venrick. "And a Hyalite has escaped Nordraven and Lamar's clutches." Cheyanne pointed her chin at Lark. "Now, you show up here with those responsible for all of this and with a Ward Walker as well. The King of Lamar would execute every one of you if you were caught," Cheyanne leveled her glare at the Lark again, while addressing Ezra.

Lines formed between Ezra's brows as he looked from Lark to Cheyanne. "Do you two know each other?"

"How can you not recognize her? The Northern Kings are searching everywhere for her. She stole the Hyalite and fell off the face of the earth, until now," Cheyanne said, moving toward an entrance to one of the large chambers of the lofted home.

"Cheyanne, wait," Lark said, stepping forward.

The wood elf halted, her back to them with one hand resting on the doorknob.

"I've lost my memory. I only learned that I was a rider

recently, but my bond with Ingamar is all but non-existent. I don't know how I got it, how I came to be in the village, or what it meant to have it. I made a promise that urged me to bring it to the Vermillion Keep, but when Sasja stole it from me in Astral City—"

"You lost the Hyalite!" Cheyanne snapped, spinning on Lark with a look full of hate in her eye.

"She didn't lose it. It was stolen from her," Venrick defended.

"That's what Sasja does. She's a thief, she steals things. You shouldn't have trusted her with it," Cheyanne said.

"I never gave it to Sasja," Lark said.

"I was there, I saw the whole thing. Sasja stole it and escaped with a Morsythian. If it hadn't been for the Morsythian who created a portal with power from a cursed amulet, we would've gotten it back," Venrick said.

"Say that again," Cheyanne said.

"We would've gotten it back,"

"No, not that. What did you say about the Morsythian creating a portal and having a cursed amulet?"

Lark produced the drained, now yellow, amulet from her pocket as Ezra interjected. "Cheyanne, this is why I asked you to meet us here. Morsythians are using magic, powerful spells. We thought they were working with Nordraven because Sasja was with Nordraven orcs too, but none of the Northern Kings have claimed the Hyalite. One of the Morsythians was strong enough to trap Ingamar in a web of energy while his companions attacked Lark and Venrick. They're using dark magic to create portals; it's not like them."

Cheyanne took the amulet Lark offered and examined it. "You're sure there wasn't a magus near them, controlling them to make it appear that the spells were coming from the Morsythians?"

"This was not magic drawn from the power of Yogos or

Hyalites. We've seen them use a wicked combination of dark fae power and rune magic," Ezra said. "I've never seen anything like it."

"You said it was a cursed amulet," Cheyanne now looked at Venrick.

Venrick shrugged, scratching at the chest plate where his hidden, cursed necklace rubbed against his skin. "It seems possible. Hardin's seen them before."

"I have," Hardin chimed in. "My hometown has been cursed by a rogue magus, and our town Chancellor wears a similar-looking stone cast in an amulet."

"The Magi Order forbids curses," she said offhandedly. "How many of these magic-wielding Morsythians have you encountered?"

"There was the one from Astral City, one from the firestorm," Venrick started.

"Sasja portaled away from Stormwatch. That means there was most likely one there, too, " Hardin said.

"And there was the one in Fletcher's Passage," Lark added.

"I thought those didn't have the amulets?" Ezra asked.

"Lark said the one she took out did," Venrick replied.

"Lark?" Cheyanne repeated.

"She can't remember her name," Ezra said.

"And you call her Lark?"

"The necklace," Ezra gestured.

"You can't remember your own name?" Cheyanne asked, approaching Lark.

"No."

"And you were taking the Hyalite to Astral City, to turn it over to the Vermillion Keep?" she asked.

Lark nodded.

"I'm embarrassed to say that she had it right under our noses the whole way from Stormwatch. Ingamar and Venrick picked up on it before I did," Ezra admitted.

"Nix was the first to," Lark said.

"Right, the fire fae," Ezra said.

"Where is your fae now?" Cheyanne asked.

"She's gone," Lark said.

"How do you know about Nix?" Ezra asked. "You guys have a history, don't you?"

"She can tell you about it, if she remembers," Cheyanne replied. "But you've come to me about these amulets, and I presume, Sasja?"

"We need to find Sasja and get the Hyalite back. We think Sasja will try to sell it to clear her debt with whatever mess she's gotten into," Hardin said.

"Whatever Sasja's is doing with the Morsythians can be explained by her," Cheyanne gestured to Lark. "She and Sasja were partners. They tried bringing me, bringing all of those I represent in on it, but they betrayed me and it fell apart before we could go through with the plan. I got burned and walked away clean from the mess those two created."

"I told you, I can't remember!" Lark insisted. "Whatever it was, please help us get the Hyalite back."

"Answer this truthfully. If you get the Hyalite back, what will you use it for?"

"I'll let it guide me to the dragon it's destined for, allowing the dragon to choose its next rider," Lark said.

"And if that rider is evil, then what?"

"Dragons are not inherently evil," Lark said truthfully.

Cheyanne looked them over for an uncomfortably long moment, then said, "I will help you find Sasja, but only with a tracking spell. I will not aid you in your goal. Sasja has wronged me too many times for me to try to save her again."

Lark frowned.

"Ezra, I need to talk to you about who you're traveling with," Cheyanne said, leaving the deck as she stepped into the large living space of her home.

"Lark, the Yogos," he said.

She undid them from her belt and handed them to the dwarf.

"I don't know what it is you two have between one another, but whatever it is, it's not good. Cheyanne is not one to forgive and forget when it comes to wrongs she's suffered," Ezra said under his breath.

"She'll help us though, right?" Lark asked.

"Maybe when I'm alone with her, she'll trust in me and divulge more of the background. For now, go back down and wait with Ingamar."

They all nodded, venturing down to the opening below.

"Lark, how do you know Cheyanne?" Hardin asked.

"I said, I can't remember. Remember?"

"There isn't anything?" Venrick asked, his sharp green appealing to her.

"Well," Lark said, hesitating. "I've had a few memories. She and Sasja are in them, but the memories don't make sense."

"Lark, you should be telling us this stuff. We can help you try to decipher it," Venrick said.

Hesitantly, she described the visions of meeting with Morsythians in the North. Sasja was there. They were discussing the prediction of firestorms. Lark left out her most recent memory of watching a house just like this one burn. Cheyanne's comment about being burned didn't seem to be a euphemism.

What if I was the one who literally burned her?

"Well, whatever happened between you, Sasja and Cheyanne is probably why you can't remember anything. It's probably why Tel Roan got killed in the crossfire," Venrick said. "We just need to keep on it. Keep digging and we'll get some answers."

"You should try talking to Cheyanne in private. See if

she'll tell you anything she wouldn't say in front of us," Hardin suggested.

Lark knew he was right.

When Ezra emerged from the treehouse, he was alone, carrying a new cane at his side. Cheyanne didn't follow. He approached wearing a grim expression and avoiding looking Lark in the eye.

"What did she say?" Venrick asked.

"I have a way to find Sasja," Ezra said, offering the small cane etched with runes and dotted with three of the Sapphires.

"That's the tracking charm?" Hardin asked.

"The cane is a prop she used in a scam when she last encountered Sasja. The combination of Sasja's signature left on the cane and the spells woven into the runes will lead to Sasja. This is our charmed object because she was the last person to touch this cane. Yogos keep a flow of power to the runes on charm. It's only good for twenty-four hours, so we need to move," he said.

"Where's Cheyanne?" Lark asked.

"She had to leave," Ezra grumbled.

"She left, where?" Lark asked, her eyes darting around the base of the tree.

"She has other important issues to attend to. Ones that are more urgent than answering your questions about the amulet, unfortunately," Ezra said.

"What did she say to you about me?" she asked.

"It wasn't anything I didn't already know," Ezra said.

"Ezra, you shouldn't keep us in suspense about this. It's not fair to Lark," Venrick said.

"Cheyanne warned us to be careful around you, Lark. She says you're dangerous, which I already knew. She told me you were a rider, which I already knew. And she told me that you're more powerful than most, which again, I already knew."

"That's it?" Lark asked.

Ezra's gaze lingered on Lark long enough to let her know it wasn't, but he nodded, saying, "We need to be going if we're going to get to Red Lodge by tomorrow morning."

"That's on the northern side of the forest, in Nordraven. We won't make it in time unless we all ride on Ingamar and that's definitely not happening," Venrick said.

"I know a passage we can take under the forest. It will be faster, trust me," Ezra replied.

As they walked toward the wagon, Venrick sidled up to Lark. "There was something else about Cheyanne that you're not telling us."

She nodded slowly.

"You can tell me," Venrick whispered.

"I saw her house on fire."

"From a firestorm?"

She shook her head. "It was dragon fire. I think it was my dragon's fire."

29

SPRUNG

The dragon trailed behind the wagon as Thunder and Giant pressed deeper north into the forest. Lark sat atop Ingamar, while Venrick walked beside them. Lark glanced up, scanning for potential threats from an enemy rider among the floating rock islands in the center of the Everburning Forest. Carpets of green moss coated cliff walls, sending trickles of water cascading off jagged edges. The water vaporized into a fine mist far overhead.

"How does this tracking charm work?" Lark asked, sensing no immediate danger.

"The magician uses an item that's recently been touched by whomever you're trying to locate," Venrick explained. "The magic user collects a copy of the person's aura. That copy longs to become part of the whole once again. It will try to get back to its host. When trapped by a rune, the aura guides whoever holds it to the person whose aura has been tapped. The catch is these copies of auras don't last long."

"That's why we're hurrying to Ezra's underground passage," Lark nodded.

"Tracking charms only last the length of the day they were created."

"I still think we'd be better off risking the flight. I am strong enough to fight if needed," Lark said.

"If we knew where the Hyalite was, I would agree with you. But if Sasja had already sold it off, we might scare off any potential leads by arriving on dragon back."

"But this charm just points us north. How do we know that she's in Red Lodge and not farther north? I could fly ahead and find out."

"It's too risky. You could be seen, or you could spook whoever has the Hyalite. They could take it anywhere with their willingness to harvest souls to teleport. Maybe they would be reckless enough to tap into the Hyalite and try to use the immense amount of power before we can stop them."

"It seems risky to assume Sasja is in Red Lodge and not somewhere even farther north," she repeated.

"If you think you know where the person you're looking for could be, and you have a map of that area, you can hold the charm to the map. It will show a glowing dot if they're anywhere on it," Venrick added.

"And if you don't find a dot or they move?"

"The charm still points the way, but it only lasts the day or until the power from the Yogos runs out."

"I thought you said it was trapped in a rune?" she said, perplexed.

"The rune only binds the aura to the object, otherwise it would drift off through the ether and instantly return to the host. The magic from the Yogos keeps the charm active," he explained.

"Asking around in towns, or being a good tracker seems like a better way to locate someone. The Yogos could've been used for something else we may need. We don't know for sure that Sasja still has the Hyalite."

"Tracking charms have their place, but if the person wards against them, they're useless."

"You can ward against them?" she asked, nearly exasperated.

"Yes, most higher-ranking soldiers, and all Knights, their Squires, and the Paragons ward themselves against use of their auras. If they didn't, they'd be assassinated more easily by any enemy. I bet you're warded against them. If you aren't, one of the Kings' Paragons would've found you by now."

"They did find me, multiple times," she argued.

"I'd wager those were by happenstance. You probably would have been attacked by an enemy rider right away," Venrick said.

"Maybe it's you and Ingamar that have shielded me. The attacks stopped once I started to travel with you," she said.

"Maybe," Venrick said, raising an eyebrow.

Ingamar slowed to a stop alongside the wagon. Lark stood on the balls of her feet, raising herself in the saddle to see over the top of Ingamar's lowered head. Before them, set into the hillside, covered in ferns and overgrown with brush was a set of stone stairs. The thick granite slabs laid the path up to a twenty-foot crag that cut along the slope for fifty yards. The widely spaced trees here grew around the structure as though it were once well maintained.

"Welcome to the Gosmer Mine," Ezra said to them.

"A mine? That's your secret passage?" Lark asked, dismounting Ingamar.

"I knew there were mines under the Everburning Forest, but how will this lead us to Red Lodge?" Venrick asked.

"There are hills, rough terrain, and small mountains to cross if we continue traveling overland. The distance to Red Lodge from here, as the crow flies, isn't that far. Since flying will expose us, we can take the mine shafts. They're straightforward, have sturdy paths, and cut right through the rough terrain. I used to travel these mines when I was a young dwarf. I can lead us through to the entrance near Red Lodge. From there, it's a short way out from the northern edge of the forest to town," Ezra replied.

"Don't you need access to these entrances?" Venrick asked.

"As a former clan member, I have access to open the wards for entry. These routes will take us very close to Red Lodge. Traveling through the mine is much faster than going overland through all this timber," Ezra said.

"Maybe for you, but if we use brismil, couldn't we just meet you and Hardin at the other side?" Lark asked.

"When Cheyanne showed me her map, Sasja was in Red Lodge. Even with good pathways, you running there using brismil to aid your speed would be cutting it close. The forest here hasn't burnt as often; in fact, it's been decades. Consider the mountains and hills through this dense forest without a trail. Then you'll run the chance of running into group of Nordraven troops patrolling the northern parts of the forest. We don't have enough time with the charm without flying or taking these tunnels under the forest."

"If this is the fastest route to Red Lodge will we need to leave Thunder, Giant and the wagon here?" Hardin asked.

"Unless Ingamar wants to carry them," Ezra said.

Ingamar's upper lip quivered as he released a low growl.

"That's not happening," Venrick said.

"Then we'll need to leave them and come back. I don't plan on staying in Nordraven after we retrieve the Hyalite. Tel's runes warding the wagon and horses will keep them safe until we return," Ezra said.

Lark's necklace tingled. She glanced skyward. Clouds were building in the distance, threatening a firestorm. Something in her memory jogged and she recalled an anecdote. "Don't evil creatures lurk in these mines?"

"Not in this mine," Ezra said, hoisting his belt up over his waist. "The last time I was here, the mine was thriving. They were sending ores to both sides of the forest, to Lamar and Nordraven." Ezra cracked a smile. "No, there won't be anything that can breach a dwarven ward down below."

"When was the last time you were down there?" Venrick asked, scanning the area.

"How long has it been now?" Ezra said looking up in thought.

"It does look abandoned," Hardin said, pulling back a thick fern bowing over the doorway.

"This access point was never a main entrance," Ezra said.

"If the wards were breached, this shaft could be a death trap," Venrick said. "Tel never trusted traveling in the mines. He always chose another way for his troops to pass through the forest."

"Tel Roan was a sky boy. He didn't have the stomach for the tunnels, and we don't have much time to waste. If we want to retrieve that Hyalite before it gets into the wrong hands, then we need to go this way," Ezra said. "Now come on, I'll lead us in."

Venrick gently gripped Lark by the elbow and said to her, "I'm going to say farewell to Giant and Thunder. Make sure you either take the brismil scale from the wagon or Stormbreaker from the saddle before we enter the mine."

"Before we enter, I will," she assured him.

"Good. You should bring an enchanted chest. It could be useful beyond having it later to secure the Hyalite. Those runes contain powerful magic," Venrick said before turning to tend to the draft horses.

"Don't worry, Lark," Hardin said. "Ezra is a dwarf. He knows these tunnels better than any of us. Besides, I have a feeling that you're more dangerous than anything we could run into down there."

Lark gave him a weak smile. She approached Ezra, who

was cleaning the overgrowth away from the mine shaft door. "Are you sure this entrance has been used recently?" she asked.

"Look here, there's a deposit of some kind that's been spilled," Ezra said, pointing with his boot to an oily slick that pooled near the corner of the decorated door frame. "That tells us that a group recently brought some of the riches to the surface and harvested them."

Lark helped him scrape away the remaining greenery, exposing the liquid tar that spread from the base of the door. It trickled out, filling the cracks between stone slabs that formed the landing they stood on. Lark snapped off a branch from a nearby tree and poked it into the substance. The stick bent as she pushed it into the resin-like liquid. It hissed, smoke spewing from the tip of the branch that had prodded the sludge.

"I don't think this is something that you mine for, is it?" she asked.

Ezra was busy searching the stone with his hands, feeling it and muttering under his breath, "Where is that darn handle. I can never find it when the wards are acting up like this."

"Wow, check this out," Hardin said from behind them. "Is this the Hyalite?"

Lark's eyes turned to Venrick, who was rushing over from Thunder and Giant. His face contorted with horror as she shouted, "No Hardin, don't touch tha—"

The ground under Lark's feet opened up. Her stomach lurched into her throat as she caught a fleeting glimpse of Venrick, his arm outstretched but much too far away to grab her. The forest disappeared above the rim of the surface as she fell into the chasm.

～

Venrick blinked at the place where Lark and Ezra had been a fraction of a second earlier. The ground where they had been standing had stitched back together immediately, the stone slabs around the shaft knitting back together as if nothing had happened. Venrick dropped onto the stones, pushing on them but none so much as budged.

Ingamar was there an instant later. He bumped Venrick out of the way and clawed at the granite paving stones. In his panic, Ingamar should've easily been able to rip out the stones and dig into the soil. Nothing, not a single stone scratched or budged as a result of his efforts. Ingamar roared in frustration.

"Hardin, what did you do?" Venrick gasped.

Hardin dropped the emerald orb on the ground. "I don't know. All I did was pick this up," he said.

"They're gone. Where the ash did they go?"

"I... I didn't mean to. I grabbed it because I thought it might be the Hyalite."

"Hyalites are blue, not green," Venrick said brusquely, running a hand through his thick hair.

"How am I supposed to know what color they are? It was a glowing orb on the ground, so I picked it up."

"Try it again."

"What?"

"Maybe whatever triggered the trap door will do it again." Venrick looked at Ingamar, who had squeezed himself onto the landing ready to dive in if the trap was sprung again.

Hardin picked up the orb again; this time nothing happened.

"Where was it the first time?"

"Here," Hardin said, planting it down near the mine where it had been. Again, he picked it up, but nothing happened to Venrick and Ingamar.

"What's different?"

"I don't know," Hardin said, trying again and again. No matter where or what way he tried to pick it up, the opening did not reappear.

Ingmar started tearing apart the ground around the stone. After each claw strike, the disturbed soil moved back into place. "Those are the wards at work," Venrick growled. Venrick paced, his eyes working back and forth as he ran through every scenario he and Tel had experienced. Nothing like this had ever happened. If there was a trap, Tel would've spotted it, set it off or gone around. But this trap wasn't just sprung once. Venrick slowed.

"That's why Ezra couldn't get in," he said.

"What?" Hardin asked in frustration.

"Ezra said this entrance and the mine were warded by dwarves, but what if the wards have been broken?"

"Either way, I am a Ward Walker. All I need to know is where the latch is to open the door or set off this trap again. So why isn't this working for me?"

"Because this isn't warded, it's something else," Venrick said.

Venrick, Ingmar and Hardin now focused on a swirling light that took shape near the landing. For an instant, Venrick wondered if it were Lark emerging from the trap, but this swirling energy was familiar. It was the same swirling light that formed moments before the portal appeared to allow Sasja's escape with the Hyalite back in Astral City.

Ingmar growled, his lips parting as the doorway to the portal formed.

"Hardin, get back," Venrick said, grabbing his shoulder and pulling him out of the way.

An instant later, fire jetted from Ingamar's open maw. Venrick felt the blast of heat across his cheeks as he fell out of the way with Hardin. The numbing heat stung for a heartbeat, then faded as the stream of dragon fire vanished. With a roar,

Ingamar snapped his jaws at the closed portal. The dragon reared back and took off, bounding through the forest.

Venrick sat up, resting on his elbows, face still warm from the fire. His head swam trying to comprehend what happened. Ingamar had run off in a rage. They were alone, Hardin and Venrick, alone with the weapons wagon.

"Venrick," Hardin said from behind him.

He rolled up onto his feet. Hardin had Giant and Thunder by the reins and was leading them away. He waved for Venrick to follow. Wind sounded near him, though there was no breeze. A swirl of light formed; the portal reappeared before Venrick.

He cursed, setting out after Hardin. They ushered the wagon off the path, behind the trees.

Light shot through the portal. An attack at Ingamar, but the dragon was long gone.

Venrick hid out of sight, leaning up against a tree. He listened for movement.

Footsteps crunched on the charred ground. Venrick chanced a glance around the trunk, to see the young woman with blonde hair and bright blue eyes walking carefully across the burn.

"Impressive," a second person said from within the swirling light of the portal. Venrick wasn't at the right angle to make out their features, but that voice... He had heard it somewhere.

"The dragon is gone," Sasja said.

"The dragon is, but the rider is not."

"She won't make it through the mine," Sasja replied, looking down at the stone landing. "There are things in there that would scare even you."

"This one is tougher than you give her credit for. We'll see if she comes out the other end."

"And if she does?" Sasja asked.

"Then she dies for good this time," the other said.

Venrick glanced across to the tree where Hardin had been only to see that he was crawling his way toward Sasja and the swirling portal.

30

SHADOW TERROR

Lark fell into the darkness. A memory flashed through her mind's eye. In the vision, Lark was falling through open air, looking up at a great black dragon flying overhead. He stared down, his alabaster eyes, ringed with gold, were solely focused on her. Pain flared up her side. Lark's flight leathers were torn and slick with blood. As she continued to fall, death felt inevitable. Panic overrode all other emotions and the instinct to survive drove her to reach within herself to touch the vibrating energy that was their bond. She tugged on that tether of magic, channeling it like light through a magnifying glass, passing out of her with a surge of explosive power.

The vision vanished when Lark hit solid ground, slamming onto her back. Pain ripped through her once again, reminiscent of that she'd suffered earlier in the week. But she wasn't broken, not yet. Lark stomached the nausea with effort. To her left, a small flame ignited and for a split second, Lark thought Nix had returned to her. It was Ezra, however. He got to his feet holding a ball of fire from a rune-carved stone in his palm.

"Lark, are you okay?" Ezra asked, stepping over the broken beams that had supported a section of the mine shaft.

"I'm good," she said, checking herself once over again. "And you?" she asked, her eyes starting to adjust to the darkness.

"Not injured, but I am far from good," he said, sweeping his hand toward the tunnel they'd dropped into.

Timbers bolted with heavy lags extended down the length of the shaft. Discarded tools, thick canvas tarps, rope and pullies littered the sides of the tunnel. The shaft had collapsed in the area where they'd been swallowed by the ground. Rubble from the support beams lay strewn and broken before a mound of stone and dirt that clogged one side of the passage.

"What happened?" Lark asked, peering up at the seamless rock overhead, seeing no trace of the opening they'd fallen through.

"We set off a trap," Ezra said, shaking his head. "This shouldn't have happened. The last time I corresponded with my clan, the mines were thriving under the forest."

"How long ago was that?" Lark asked.

"Only five years," Ezra said.

"That may not be long in a dwarf's lifetime, but a lot can happen in five years," Lark said. "Can we get back up to Hardin and Venrick?"

"Working on it," he said, switching to his native dwarven tongue to enact his stored magic.

Using his war hammer and the runes etched into it, Ezra probed the rock, looking for a way out. Lark attempted to locate her bond with Ingamar. She felt nothing humming along that bond that she'd felt in her vision.

A cast of blue light cascaded out from a Sapphire embedded into Ezra's hammer shaft. The light rippled over the stone like the underside of water's surface. No trace of an opening remained. It was solid granite overhead.

"That's just my ashy luck," Ezra cursed.

Before Lark could respond, deep groans and a sound like claws grinding against stone drifted in from somewhere down the mine. Ezra stiffened at the noise.

"Ezra, what was that?" Lark asked, her imagination inventing a monstrous beast lurking within.

"That did not sound like the pounding of pickaxes," Ezra answered, aiming his glowing hand our into the darkness toward the sound.

"Your people reside down here, right?" Lark asked, with a flicker of hope.

"The way back to the surface is sealed with a spell too complex for my abilities, I'm afraid. If we're going to get out of here, we're going to have to pass through the tunnels."

"And what about Ingamar, Venrick, and Hardin. We're just leaving them?"

"A trap was set at this access. They will not be able to pass through. If they are wise, they'll continue north to Red Lodge. They have the map. Perhaps they will meet us there in few days, if we can navigate through these tunnels."

Lark brushed her hand over the side of her clothes, searching for the brismil scale. Her heart sank when she realized she hadn't put the scale in the harness when Venrick asked her to. The magical armor was still packed away in the saddle bag. Ezra shouldered his war hammer, advancing wearily into the darkness. A strange clicking sound echoed off the stone. Lark drew the sword from the scabbard she wore on her back, wishing she hadn't taken off the brismil. She followed Ezra.

Discarded tools, piles of wood and half-filled barrels of unrefined ore littered the shaft.

"Do the dwarves usually leave their equipment unchecked like this?" Lark asked.

"Not this clan," Ezra said, stopped to grab a smooth rock that was affixed into a lantern hanging from a timber supporting the shaft. He hit the stone hard on the rock wall. It clicked, a soft yellow light gradually brightening by the time he inserted it back into the lantern.

"Your rocks are imbued with glyph magic?" Lark asked.

"No," Ezra replied, headed down the tunnel off of the shaft, holding the lantern out in front of them to light the way. "This is lumistone, a rare ore in Sataran. This mine is one of the few where they are harvested. Lumistones glow bright at any depth. Their luminescence burns hot enough that dwarves in this part of the world use them not only for lighting but for cooking and heating their hearths as well."

Guided by the light, they followed the tunnel until it opened up into an expansive chamber reminiscent of a Keep's Great Hall. Lark continued to glance over her shoulder, peering back into the darkened tunnel behind them. She couldn't shake the feeling that something was there, lurking in the shadows, watching them.

At the center of the vast underground room a crack a few body-lengths wide split the floor. A stone contraption with gears and pullies had been constructed over the opening. A stone platform large enough to hold Ingamar was attached to it.

"What is that device?" Lark asked as Ezra inspected a broken stone gear.

"These are our platforms. They transport the dwarves up and down the shafts to access more tunnels deep in the mine. Normally, they run on magical energy from the runes," he said, passing a hand over the ancient lettering carved into one of the thirty-foot wheels. "Perhaps this is what caused the clan to leave this area of the mine."

"How deep do these shafts go?" Lark asked.

"Some say they go so deep that they enter the realm of the fae," Ezra said. "Cheyanne has told me that the elves believe these shafts dig right through to the underworld and creatures of evil use them to tunnel their way through to our side."

"Is that true?"

"We dwarves know better. The only evil that comes down here is hiding from the Paragons above. Some wild dragons have been known to take up residence in abandoned shafts. It's what gave rise to the human myth that dragons are treasure hoarders. But I'd challenge you to find a dragon's treasure hoard that was bigger than any belonging to the dwarves."

A groan echoed up through the opening in the chamber floor. The sound created enough of a rumble that rocks shifted and loose dirt fell from the ceiling.

Lark's expression gave her away, prompting Ezra to try and calm her down, "Not to worry. The groans of the earth are not to be feared."

"You don't think that could be coming from an animal?" Lark asked, looking down the hole into the pitch black.

"Nonsense. I think I would've heard from the clan if there had been something like a dragon or shadow terror that had moved in," Ezra said.

"Shadow terror?" Lark asked.

"Nasty creatures conjured by Nordraven magi to fight against fae creatures like dragons. They're winged and two-legged like bats. Their long, wolflike snouts are jumbled with sharp teeth. They can grow as large as an adult human. If you ask me, they look like winged devils with their blood-shot eyes. They can't spell-cast, but they have some levels of protection against magic. Someone must've given them goblin blood when they were created because all it takes is one bite and your life will never be the same."

"Goblins target dwarven mines more than any town or village," Lark said, the knowledge returning to her in confusing clarity. "They hate sunlight; mines are better suited to their kind."

"They have been known to take over other mines, but not those belonging to our clan. We're strong, and hardy, and our magical protections prevent such creatures from gathering in large groups," Ezra said.

"Is it possible that one of these shadow terrors has chased off the dwarves?" Lark asked.

Ezra glanced over the edge into the abyss below the disabled platform. "It's never out of the question," he said quietly. "But if that were the case, we'd have no chance at surviving. Best not to consider those things when you're trying to navigate through an abandoned mine."

They exited the chamber through another tunnel and continued on, passing through more expansive chambers with broken elevators, again noticing tools scattered haphazardly. Ezra's confident disposition and cheerful conversation cooled to a stone-hearted series of grunts and voiceless nods the farther they went. Whatever it was that had happened down here succeeded in clearing the inhabitants out and breaking the transportation platforms. It was evident that work had stopped abruptly.

Lark lost track of time, unsure how much of their twenty-four-hour window of access to the tracking charm they'd spent walking through the abandoned mine. Again, the walls opened up to another vast chamber, this one a more natural cave. The stone landing spanning the length of the giant cave jutted out along the entire left side and then ending abruptly in a drop-off. The chasm dropped deep into the earth. A waterfall, barely visible in the gloom at the far end of the cave, thundered out from the cliff wall, the water disappearing into the midnight abyss.

Ezra slowed to a stop before the stony outcropping. The light of the lumistone exposed a horrible scene. Mounds of corpses, dwarf and elf, littered the ground from an epic battle. Hundreds of soldiers from the struggle lay strewn about, every one of them killed in a conflict between dwarf and elf. Their skeletons wore ring mail armor, thick leather surcoats, and chest plates.

"They're dead," Ezra whispered, his hammer falling to the stone floor and dragging behind him as he was overwhelmed by the shocking scene. As though she had been present during the fight, Lark could envision clearly how the dwarves and elves had fought one another. It was clearly a melee.

"Gambrian elves?" Lark said, noticing that their clothing and weapons were of the same style as Cheyanne's.

"How did I not hear about this?" Ezra exclaimed.

"There weren't any survivors," she said, the only rational explanation that came to mind.

"But someone would've checked on them. Someone should've been expecting ore, smithy service, or something," he said. Ezra's reaction echoed through the chamber.

"They were so close to the exit," he said with a shake of his head, motioning with his hammer. As his motion parallelled the chasm, Lark spotted the dimly lit entry carved into the wall there. "Only a short exit tunnel away from the outside world. What could've driven them to this madness?"

A strange clicking sound like something tapping on stone sounded behind them. A low, throaty groan emitted from one wall. The hair on the back of Lark's neck rose. The sound was evil, a creaking forced through clenched jaws. Ezra flashed his light out at the creature, finding its horrifying form standing on bent legs, dragging long arms. The creature emerged from the shadows into the light of the lumistone. Wolfish in form, the hairy, black creature stood tall, it's claws as long as a daggers. It spread its wings wide, exposing the full width of its body.

"Shadow terror," Ezra said.

A fraction of a second later the monster lunged at them. Ezra spoke a shortly worded spell, but the magic went wild, missing its mark as the creature bounded from one side of the cave to the other in a single wingspread leap. Lark dodged, slashing at the air but missing. She reached for the power from the bond, but the magic wasn't there. She couldn't channel.

The creature came at them again. Her sword hissed through the air at the beast. This time the steel made a satisfying slicing sound on wet flesh as the shadow terror crashed by. Ezra only just barely managed to get out of the way as it passed them. A howl erupted, vibrating through the chamber like an earthquake.

"Lark, get to the exit," Eza called to her.

They ran, and the shadow terror giving chase.

Lark followed as Ezra wound through the fallen elves and dwarves. The duo charged across the landing, tired but too fearful to stop as they raced for the opening to the world above. Light from the outside world rimmed the stone doorway at the end of the short tunnel, highlighting their escape route. They were there, passing through the last short tunnel when the shadow terror caught up with them. Lark felt the air rush behind her back as it swiped, followed by a crunch. She looked back to see that it had been wedged in the tunnel entrance. Its claws scratched at the floor as the creature squeezed deeper into the narrow doorway, its snapping and snarling, its jaws just feet away from them.

"I thought you said they can only get as large a human. That one is a giant," Lark said.

Ezra attempted to spell-cast through the runes on his hammer. The door highlighted in thin lines from the sunlight lurched open a crack, then stuck, apparently wedged in place. Light streamed in from the outside. He reached the door, working his fingers into the crack, prying at it to force it open enough for them to squeeze through. Lark slid her hand in near Ezra's and applied her weight against the stone as well. It scraped against rock on the floor as they strained with all their might.

Fresh air from outside washed in over her. Ezra moved the door farther with a powerful push, exhausting the rest of the power from the Yogos on his hammer. Lark was just stepping through to the forest behind him when something snapped around her ankle. Sharp searing pain shot up her leg as she was ripped onto the ground and dragged back into the mine.

She clawed at the shadow terror's barbed tail, but its grip was too tight. She slid on her backside through the short tunnel, bumping across the rough stone in the chamber's landing, heading toward the chasm. Elf and dwarf skeletons parted around them as she stabbed and hacked at the beast. With one of its long claws, it sliced her hand, forcing her to drop her sword. The metal clanged against the ground a moment before she was pulled off the landing's edge. She hung by her leg wrapped in the shadow terror's clutches, peering straight down into the abyss below, an endless pit of darkness.

"Lark!" Ezra's frantic voice called from the stone landing in the chamber.

His voice was drowned out by the sound of wingbeats rapidly approaching. The shadow terror snapped its wolflike head to attention at something approaching from the cave roof. Expansive wings spread over them, and the terror's barbed tail let go of Lark's leg. She clawed through the air trying to grab hold of the winged creature, but the terror had let her go. Once again, she found herself falling.

31

OMIRRE

Lark was falling again. Looking up, she saw a pair of black wings flapping over her. It was the scene from her most recent memory, only this time there was no open sky behind the dragon. This time she was looking up at the domed cavern in a dwarven mine. And the dragon was no dragon, but the shadow terror that was trying to kill her.

Ezra's voice faded as she dropped below the lip of the landing into a seemingly endless crag.

As the shadow terror hovered in the moment before its descent, a whip-snap echoed through the chamber above. Dark liquid spattered out from the shadow terror's chest, a sharp sword-like tail driven through the nightmare. An instant later, the sharp spike retracted, followed by a fearsome roar. The bellow boomed as the terror hit the landing, now far above Lark. In the dwindling light, a winged, serpentine creature dove into the crag, streaking toward Lark with lightning speed.

Lark's fall halted with a whiplash. Warmth wrapped around her, coiling her ribs tight. Lark's trajectory changed; she was now being carried up by the winged serpent. She strained to see what it was, a dragon? No. This creature had scales like a dragon, its body, wings, and head shape all bearing a striking resemblance to a dragon, but this animal lacked arms and legs.

Amphiptere, the name sounded in Lark's mind in a mental voice unlike her own. The feminine voice was seasoned, raspy, and tense, like it was holding back a verbal assault.

The serpent carried her through the cavern at a dizzying rate. This creature flew much faster than Ingamar could've as they passed over the chasm toward the mouth of the waterfall. Lark closed her eyes, bracing for impact with the cliff wall. At the last second, the amphiptere hugged her close with her powerful tail. They darted into the narrow opening where the water came rushing out. The creature skimmed along the water's surface, dunking Lark into the cold river. After suddenly being submerged, they slid up onto a dry ledge. The tail uncoiled, letting Lark go.

She hacked up water, crawling on her knees like a drowned rat in the creature's lair. The amphiptere coiled herself like a snake, her swordtail raised just under her arched head twenty feet away. Her tan wings were folded in tight against her brown and black diamond-patterned back. She shot a red forked tongue out between sand-colored scaly lips. Her beady black eyes locked in on Lark, watching her every move.

The lair was cut out of a ledge alongside the underground river. The roof arching overhead was smooth and dotted with lumistone rocks that glowed a soft white to illuminate the cavern. A dark hole with smoothed stone showed where the creature entered a cave system at the back of the opening. With the river launching off into the abyss and the amphiptere blocking the cave exit, Lark had nowhere to go.

"Are you saving me to let me go or saving me for your own meal?" Lark asked, raising her voice to be heard over the rushing water.

"That depends on how you answer my questions, Ella," the creature replied, speaking aloud without moving her mouth.

"That's not my name."

"Lie to me again and I will send my tail through your chest just as I did to that shadow terror. I can let the water wash you into the depths of the underworld far below."

"Ella is not my name, anymore," Lark corrected. She felt for the dagger sheathed at her back. Finding it, she pulled it free in a reverse grip, ready to use if the amphiptere attacked.

The creature lowered her head, extending her barrel-sized face closer to Lark. She tasted the air with her tongue, saying, "You speak truth."

"Who are you and why did you save me? Or are you playing with me before you try to make your kill," Lark snarled.

"You don't remember who I am?"

"I can't remember much from before a few weeks ago." Lark said honestly.

"I am Omirre, but the name you knew me by back then was Clawless," she hissed.

Lark shook her head, "Doesn't jog any distinct memory for me.

The serpent hissed, striking the cave floor with the flat of her tail, causing Lark to flinch, dangerously close to the edge. Omirre slithered over to Lark, sliding her swordtail up to Lark's chest, holding the tip away from her by a few inches. "You really don't remember me?" she growled.

"I don't know what I did to you in my past life, but whatever it was, I'm sorry. I can't afford to stay here and sort out a disagreement or whatever we fought about before. I need to get to Red Lodge and fast," Lark responded.

"I swore to the gods above and below that when next I met

Ella, that I would slay her for the wrong she did to me and mine," Omirre said.

The vision of the elven fire burning the treehouse played out in Lark's head. Was this creature there, too? Did Lark and her dragon attack them?

"You're trying to remember."

"Were you there in Gambria as a friend of the wood elves?" Lark asked, not sure how it connected.

"If I were a friend of the elves, would I have let them destroy themselves with those dwarves right outside my cave?"

Lark frowned. "Who was I to you?"

Omirre retreated again to her coiled state twenty feet away. "If you don't remember what you did to me, what kind of person you were, then you are no longer that person. Until the time you do remember who you were, I cannot take my revenge."

Lark couldn't shake the feeling that she was combining the memory of the fire with this creature, but she was not sure how they were related. "Will you tell me who I am?" Lark asked.

"You know who you really are. People like you, like Ella, don't change. If you don't remember, you will repeat the mistakes of your past, becoming Ella again. When you do, I will be ready. When you do, I will come for you and your dragon, and kill you both," the creature said.

"My dragon... You knew my dragon?"

"I know your dragon. He lives."

Lark felt faint. "No, he was killed when I lost my memory."

The amphiptere shook her head. "Your dragon was injured but not slain that day. He yet lives. I was hoping to kill you, lure him here, and kill him myself. But it seems that by ignoring him, you're killing him yourself."

"No! I'm not ignoring him. I don't remember who he is."

I didn't know he was alive, right? Lark thought. She knew that a bond was necessary for her to have performed the magic she'd used, but she thought that bond was with Ingamar. It had to be from Ingamar. He was there, within range of accessing the bond. Lark had flown on him, touched his senses. But her connection with Ingamar wasn't right. She'd known that all along. She thought the disconnect was because they were both suffering their losses. If he was alive, Lark was betraying her dragon by trying to bond with Ingamar.

The realization of this, of what she was doing this whole time to her bonded dragon... Nausea welled up in her stomach, she thought she would be sick.

"You know that I am right. You can feel it in your bones that you have been crushing your dragon's bond by entertaining another. You never even went looking for him. You left him and started anew, the whole time crushing his life force by ignoring his existence."

"No, I didn't mean to. I didn't know," Lark stammered.

"You say you need to go help your precious friends, but they aren't the ones who truly need you. They don't know who you really are," Omirre said.

Overwhelmed by grief, Lark said, "That's not true! How is this happening? It can't be. This isn't..." She closed her eyes tight and searched herself, reaching back into the fog of her memory, hoping to find something that would tell her who she was. Omirre's words echoed in her soul, vibrating around her like... *like a thread of magic,* she realized.

"You should be going to save your bonded ones, not helping your so-called friends," Omirre said.

She's manipulating my emotions, Lark realized. This creature was like a dragon and had magical powers, one of them must be able to manipulate the emotions of its prey.

"You're evil. As evil as they come, Ella. Remember how you first got your powers. Where you got that necklace and what you did. There are more ways than one to channel magic through the veil on Sataran. Remember, Ella. Remember what you've done," Omirre said, her obvious resentment washing over Lark.

She's trying to get me to admit to her that I wronged her so she can feel justified in her revenge. "But I don't remember," Lark said honestly.

"You killed the only thing I've ever loved. How can you not remember," Omirre hissed.

Lark searched herself, drawing back into the recesses of her memories. She couldn't see who she had been, only who she was now, who she had been since she found herself in that village.

Lark shook her head. "No," she said, straightening up. She raised her chin to the winged serpent. "I am Lark. I am not evil. I am trying to help people I care for. I don't remember having a bonded dragon. If he is still alive, then I will go and find him. If he is truly mine, he will understand me. He'll know that what I've been through wasn't my choice and forgive my absence."

Omirre hissed, swatting the ground again with her tail.

"You can't get your revenge if I don't remember you or what I did to you. And despite whatever this is," Lark said, feeling the erratic jumping of anger, depression, and anxiety, acknowledging them for emotions that were not true to her. "Whatever you're doing to make me feel this way, I can't help you. You're looking for a confession or an admission of some kind that I can't give you. Either kill me or let me go but do it knowing that I don't remember you."

Omirre let out a wail, then snapped her head to attention. "Fine, I will not kill you now but know that your release comes with a cost. You might not have been the same person when you came here, not having known what it was you cost me and mine. Know this, Lark, the next time we meet, I will have my vengeance. You will find your memories, and when you do, you'll know that Lark is nothing like Ella. People can't fake who they are for long."

"How do I get to Red Lodge," Lark said through gritted teeth.

"Climb back around to that landing where your dwarf friend escaped. It's not far from there," Omirre said.

"That's a sheer cliff outside, provided I'm able to get to the crag wall without slipping into the river and being swept off that waterfall."

"Angle your fall right and you'll land in the pool below; if you survive the drop," Omirre said.

"Then climb all the way back out? It seems like you're setting me up for failure," Lark said.

"Surviving the fall into the pool is just the beginning. You enter there and you're no longer in this realm. You'd have to have your fae bond to help you."

"The pool is a doorway into the fae realm?" Lark asked.

"You really don't remember anything."

"How do you know about Nix?"

"The fae you're bonded to, and ignoring as well. You can remember her but not your dragon?"

Lark blinked, confusion dispelling any pain she felt when reminded that she had a dragon out there, alive and still bonded with her. "Where does that tunnel lead?" Lark said, pointing to the hole at the back of the cave.

"My den. The only way out for you is through the fae realm, barring that, you would need to scale your way across the cliffs to return to the dwarf's exit. I will not interfere again if another of the creatures inhabiting this mine attacks you. The choice is yours, Lark. If you make it out of this cavern alive, I will come for you again. When I do, you'll remember why I'm there to kill you."

Lark scowled, turning her back on the winged serpent.

Approaching the mouth of Omirre's cave, she looked out through the opening. Water gushed off the cliff, disappearing as it fell through the open air, to the pool of an unknown depth below. Lark tested her grip on the rock before climbing out of the cave. She focused on the ledges for her feet and hands as she traversed from Omirre's cave onto the crag wall. After a few yards, Lark came to a ledge carved into the stone. Testing it with a few kicks before trusting it with her weight, Lark stood on the narrow landing. It ended a few short strides later, leaving another wide space of cliff wall before reconnecting to another ledge. The far ledge followed a narrow path cut from the stone, leading down to stone stairs. She followed the stairs with her gaze, seeing they came out on the platform where the shadow terror had attacked. The exit lay just beyond.

She breathed in deeply, gauging the distance to the next landing where the path formed. Lark had jumped at least that far before when she was wearing the brismil scale. The enhancements of the scale, however, were not an option here. Lark was forced to rely on her natural athletic ability. The gap was at least twice as wide as she was tall, but half that distance lower as well. She didn't have enough space to make a running leap. She only had room to take one long step before jumping. Her gaze searched the cliff. Here, the granite was smooth, offering no holds but for one small crack in the middle.

"Omirre must've crushed this trail with her tail so nobody from the mine could easily scale over here," she told herself.

Lark still had her dagger. It appeared to be a similar width to the crack in the smooth granite face between her and the far ledge. She had no way to know if it would hold, but if she were to wedge the dagger in, she might be able to use the handle to vault herself the rest of the way.

If I could just get one more step out, then I could make it, she thought.

With the dagger in her right hand, she laid down flat on her stomach on the ledge. She stretched her arm out, holding onto a crimp with her left fingertips. Her shoulder reached out past the edge, her face now half-way off, nearing the point where she would fall if she went any farther. She strained to see her target for the dagger placement. Her hand was near the crack now. She angled the dagger, finding the slit with her point. She eased the point into the rock, stretching as far as she possibly could. Lark pushed down with the blade until it stopped, wedged into the bottom edge of the crack.

"If this doesn't hold, I'm dead," she told herself.

Gathering her courage, Lark took a running step off the ledge. Her right foot landed on the handle, and she jumped. The dagger held long enough for her to use it and continue on her angled trajectory toward the lower ledge. As she jumped, the blade snapped, breaking and sending the handle clinking off the stone, soon to be swallowed by the darkness. Lark dropped forward, hit the opposite ledge with speed, crouched and rolled over her shoulder before springing up to her feet. She slid to a halt, teetering on the edge before finding her balance. She shuffled back, placing her back flat against the cliff wall, heart pounding.

"Holy embers that was close," she swore, peering back at the shorn end of the dagger blade sticking out of the crack, the handle gone entirely.

Calming her adrenaline, she continued carefully onto the narrow path and down the stone stairs. With a sigh of relief, she walked out onto the expansive landing where she'd last seen Ezra. The door was still open a crack. As Lark made her way through the skeletons of dwarves and elves, a short figure appeared near the light streaming in.

"Ezra?" Lark asked, recognizing the stout body.

As her eyes came into focus, however, she could see that in place of the dwarf's beard was a smooth, dagger-tooth smile.

The being's eyes were reddened, and the light revealed long green ears ringed with piercings.

"Not Ezra," the goblin replied, his voice cracking with excitement as he edged his way around the light filtering in through the door.

Lark reached for a weapon, but she didn't have any.

"If I ever cross Ezra's path again," the goblin said. "I'll be sure to give him your condolences."

He rushed forward, stabbing at her with a long knife. She moved, but the blade cut through her shirt, narrowly missing her body. She managed to spin away, quickly retrieving a blade of elven make from a pile of armor and bones. Lark's necklace warmed an instant before she sliced out across the darkness with a sweeping swing. The sunlight caught on the blade as it came around and a line of rippling blue flame carried out behind the blade's path. A scream shook through the cave as the goblin who narrowly missed being cleaved by the sword was engulfed in flames.

Lark nearly dropped the sword in shock, but the training of a lifetime forgotten willed her to hang on. She backed away as the goblin rushed wildly at her, burning with the blue flame and shouting at her in garbled speech. She backed away, closing the distance between her and the open doorway. The goblin, dropped to his knees, the fire claiming him as he tipped forward in a pile of burning flesh on the landing.

Lark held the sword out, seeing more red eyes, snapping teeth hissing at her in the darkness. Steel caught in the strip of sunlight as they jabbed forward, far enough away that there was no danger of them reaching Lark. She felt behind herself for the opening, her skin warmed by the rays sunning the lip of the stone. She backed through, pulling the door shut behind her. Muffled cries and vicious screeching sounded from behind the door, but with the protection of the sun now beaming around her, she was safe from the goblin horde.

Lark backed away from the mine, taking in her surroundings. She was in the forest again. The trees were narrow, taller, and more tightly packed. A fresh coating of snow covered the ground at her feet and the needles above. A pair of wide-set footsteps tracked away from the mine shaft, heading out toward a snowy field beyond.

Ezra.

32

RED LODGE

"Hardin," Venrick whispered, but his voice couldn't carry over the portal's swirling vortex.

Hardin crawled between trees, directly behind a tall, slender magus in flowing copper robes, who had emerged behind Sasja to examine the dwarven mine entrance. Hardin rose to a crouch, side-stepping in a squat position, then crab-walking his way closer to the portal.

"What is he doing?" Venrick thought. If Hardin tried to go through the portal, the mage who created it would sense him, wouldn't he? There would be a clear pull on the warding that was sure to be aligned with the portal... "He's a Ward Walker, though. He'll go through without setting it off."

Venrick got to his feet. Smoothly and quietly, Venrick passed from tree to tree until he was just behind Hardin. Hardin caught Venrick's eye, motioning with his head toward the open portal. Venrick drew this sword and gave Hardin a nod.

From where he stood with his back against the tree, he could see a half-moon sliver of the location where Sasja and the mage had come from. If Cheyanne's map was to be trusted, the other side of that portal was the Northern city of Red Lodge.

"Sasja," the magus called to her.

Venrick's heart skipped a beat as he froze. He stood as still as he could against the base of the tree. Through the corner of his eye, he could just see a bit of Sasja's figure. She lifted her head, her attention on the mage. From where she stood, Venrick wasn't sure if she could see Hardin in her peripheral vision or not. Hardin paused briefly in front of the portal, completely exposed.

"This trap was set by the wood elves for any dwarves who might come through the mines. Since the fall of the clan, I've been monitoring the entrances. It's been years since any dwarf has come to this door," the magus said.

I know that voice, but which Magus is it? Venrick thought, trying to place him without seeing his face.

"Didn't you say that the group you stole the Hyalite from included a dwarf?" he asked.

"They did, my Lord," Sasja replied.

"And didn't he drive a caravan?"

"Supposedly," she said.

"Go and see if there is a horse and wagon nearby. Maybe their companions are still hoping to get away."

Sasja turned, sweeping her gaze across where the portal stood open. To Venrick's surprise, she didn't stop to call out Hardin as he stood frozen before it. Venrick's attention had locked onto the magus and Sasja. When he checked, he saw Hardin was gone.

Did he?

Sasja distanced herself from the portal, her back to them now. The magus continued to examine the mine door. Nothing stopped Venrick from moving to the portal. His heart raced, mentally preparing to close the gap.

A shaggy brown head popped out through the other side

of the portal. Hardin's face twisted toward Venrick, a grin upturning his mustache. He waved for Venrick to come. Without a moment's hesitation, Venrick ran. Hardin took hold of him and pulled him through.

"Sasja? What was that?" the magus said.

Venrick saw he was turning around, perhaps bothered by a strange sensation that might've alerted him from the portal's magic.

Before Venrick could see his face, Sasja responded diverting his attention. "I found the horses and wagon. It's warded shut. Nobody seems to be here."

"Bring them with us. Whoever sprang this trap will have to pass through the abandoned mines. With those shadow terrors, I doubt they'll make it through to the other side."

Venrick stumbled out into a high-ceiling stone room. On the walls hung banners rimmed in the Nordraven copper which displayed the symbols of varying orc clans. Tapestries painting the struggle for Hyalites hung over the crackling fire in the hearth. Before the fireplace sat a large wooden desk. Several upholstered chairs faced the desk and the dynamic tapestry hung over the mantle. Illuminated by natural light coming through the large, framed window to the right, Venrick could see the dragon's destruction. All of it, the chairs, the desk, the banners on the wall and tapestry were charred, still smoldering form Ingamar's breath of fire sent through the portal.

"They're coming back. We need to get out of here," Venrick said.

"They don't know we're here," Hardin said with a grin.

"The wizard felt something strange when you pulled me through. They're coming back," Venrick warned.

As Venrick quickly examined the room, the air swooshed. He swiveled, catching the last lines of the portal closing.

"I thought you said they were coming back?" Hardin accused.

"They were, with the…" and he realized it.

"Is that a fire fae?" Hardin said, pushing open a window. A moment later he jumped back, cringing as a shrill shriek echoed up from the street below.

"They're coming back with the horses and wagon," Venrick said, finishing his thought.

"These portals are going to be the death of us. I've seen three fire fae since I left Dagger's Landing," Hardin said, his mood changing.

"Odds are, staying in this room is going to be the death of us," Venrick said, moving to the open window.

The second-story window looked out onto the snow-dusted city below. A mix of wood- and brick-sided homes clustered around the area. Chimneys poked out of every slate roof, wood and coal smoke adding to the hazy inversion layer that clung a hundred feet over the narrow valley. Snowcapped peaks rose out along the northern edges, feeding a steaming river that wound through the center of the city. Venrick looked south, toward a stone fortress. It looked almost like a Keep, butted up against the southwest edge of the orc city. All along the southern edge of Red Lodge, the frosted tips of the Everburning Forest emerged, transitioning from snow-ghosted trees to a sea of dark green evergreens that expanded out across the southern horizon.

Green orcs with two tusks sprouting from their lower jaws walked the streets. They wore furs and thick, hooded cloaks as they bustled about their day. Several ran for the dying orc whose life had been claimed by the creation of the portal. For a moment, Venrick thought the others were going to attempt to help the orc. But when they reached him, the group peeled off his clothing, stole his boots, and fought over the twin axes tucked in his belt.

A tall male with short, filed tusks capped with copper rings and tightly braided black hair spotted the chaos from across the street. He bellowed a throaty roar at them, shouting, "Hey you, stop what you're doing!"

The three who'd stripped the dead orc bolted down the cobblestone street. The short-tusked orc pulled a club from his belt and chased after them, calling, "Thieves! Stop those ruffians!"

Directly under the window, Giant and Thunder walked into view. Sasja led them, her blonde hair covered with the thick blue hood of her cloak. Once stopped, she tossed out several flakes of hay from under a covered alcove, then disappeared.

"Hardin, we need to get down there now right now," Venrick said as he tossed his leg over the windowsill and searched for a way to climb down the outside of the building.

"Did you see the way that one orc chased after the others for stealing?" Hardin said, still watching down the street.

"Yes, we all saw it happen, now it's time to go."

"Do you think that buck was trying to enforce their laws?" Hardin asked.

"Of course he was. Just because this is the North doesn't mean it's lawless," Venrick said, climbing out onto a stone ledge barely wider than his feet.

"I never thought of the Northern cities as being, well, like ours."

"Nordraven has four Kingdoms, Hardin. Of course they have laws. They probably have more laws than we do."

"None of that's in any of the songs I sing about them. It's always, big bad orcs in the North causing chaos in the South because that's what they do," Hardin said as he joined Venrick on the ledge, snow scuffing off the stone.

"That's what they do in the South because those who venture south tend to belong to their organized crime syndicates. Those criminals target us in Lamar. If everyone did that here, they wouldn't have a flourishing society now, would they?" Venrick responded, edging his way to the corner.

"This is really peeling back layers to a place I always imagined to be harsh and rugged, not with its own culture," Hardin said, lowering the window behind his back before following Venrick.

"Can we please stop talking about how life-changing it is being here in enemy territory and focus on getting down before that magus sees us and kills us?" Venrick said.

"Oh, yeah, good idea," Hardin said as though he just remembered whose portal they had traveled through.

When Venrick reached the corner of the building, he carefully worked around to face toward the wall. He then carefully lowered himself to hang off the ledge as he searched with his foot for a hold on the window framing from the first floor. Finding enough to apply friction, he used the cracks between stones to slowly make his way onto the ledge of the first story. He looked up at Hardin and waved for him to follow.

"How am I supposed to do that?" Hardin said.

"Just do it," Venrick replied.

"I'm a Ward Walker, not a cliff climber."

"Just get your butt down off that ledge. I'll support your feet."

Hardin maneuvered himself over the ledge, hanging by his grip only.

"There's are windows to your right and left; spread your feet wide and press your toes up against the framing."

"Venrick, help me. My grip is slipping."

"Put your foot here," Venrick said, reaching up to put Hardin's foot in the right position. "And your other the exact same but on the right."

"I'm going to fall, Venrick," Hardin said as he shimmied his way down. When he got close enough to him, Venrick helped support Hardin as he huffed and grunted through the descent onto the first story landing.

"That wasn't so bad, was it? Only one more to go," Venrick said.

"Aren't we going to break in again, right here?" Hardin asked.

"What for? The wagon is right there. We need to get it and go find the mine shaft Lark and Ezra were trapped in. It was a through passage."

"But the Hyalite, it has to be here, right?" Hardin said.

Venrick's face slackened. If he found that Hyalite, this cursed amulet that threatened to end his life with any misspoken word, or the expected failure of this mission would end. He'd be free to be himself again.

"No. Lark is trapped in there. That magus said—"

"That wizard said he has the Hyalite. The one Lark needs back. We could get it here and bring it back to the mine shaft."

"There are shadow terrors in the mine. Lark will need help," Venrick argued.

"Lark already has help down there. Ezra is with her. He's also a warlock, which is more than most dwarves can claim with their magical abilities. He will be able to help. If we go in there, we'll probably get lost and put ourselves in harm's way. Then nobody gets the Hyalite back for Lark," Hardin said.

"But we don't know if this is where it is."

"Sasja brought it here. I know it. They don't know we're here yet. That's not going to last forever, especially with Cheyanne..." Hardin's face slackened.

"Especially with Cheyanne, what? Hardin, don't make me dig it out of you," Venrick threatened.

"Ash, I wasn't going to say anything until we knew the Hyalite was here for sure," he said, clutching the bricks of the stone wall they stood on.

The second story window opened above them, and they

both went rigid. "Sasja," the magus' voice said. "Did you leave this window open?"

"No, you must've," she replied.

There was a long silence before the man hummed to himself, then closed the window. Hardin looked up at the window with a slight smile on his lips. Venrick narrowed his eyes at him, and whisper-shouted, "Hardin, you want to go back so you can see Sasja!"

"What?" he said with a flush. "No. Why would you say that. She stole from us, twice."

"Right. She isn't on our side."

"But don't you think it's odd that she hasn't handed it over to any of the Northern Kings?" he said.

"Who do you think these people are working for? More than half the crime that goes on back in Lamar and Doran is funded by the Nordraven."

"I'm not convinced that she's all bad," Hardin admitted. "Yes, I want to talk to her, but I know that will get us killed. So, I won't. I know how important it is that we recover this magical object. I say we do it now."

"If it's here and if it were me that had the Hyalite, I'd be keeping it stored in that castle-like building over there," Venrick said, pointing to the fortress that was now visible from their expanded view of the city.

"The magus said they have it. That must mean it's here. Lark hid it in plain sight for the whole trip to get to Astral City. Maybe that's what they're doing."

"Fine. If it gets you to stop talking me off this ledge, then I'll help you. Any wards we come across though are your responsibility. I'm not having my hands severed by reaching out to touch something that's magically guarded."

"And if we do recover it for Lark, you'll be in charge of the storage."

"I'd need to get down to the wagon for that. The chest is in the wagon."

"It's not that far of a jump down to it," Hardin suggested.

"How are you going to stand there and say that right after you just grunted your way off that ledge?" Venrick replied.

"You're half elf. It's easier for you."

"Why do humans always say that? You know it's because of that kind of thinking why I'm treated differently."

"I didn't mean it like that. I just meant that you're better physically at this kind of thing than I am."

"In this case, you're right, I am. I can get down and back up, but you'll need to leave the window open for me," Venrick said.

"I'll be in this room," Hardin said.

Venrick wasn't sure if his ability to channel would work with the uncut Yogo Sapphire he'd pocketed before fleeing the firestorm with Ingamar, but he had to try. He reached for it, feeling the energy vibrating through the stone. He cast the basic unlocking spell. The first story window clicked, then opened a crack.

"It worked," he stammered.

Hardin pulled it wide open. "Ven, this one was open," he said giving Venrick a thumbs up.

Venrick nearly rolled his eyes before leaping down and landing lightly on top of the wagon. Thunder and Giant stirred as he walked across the roof and climbed down the side ladder. Glancing around quickly, he slipped inside the safety of Tel's weapons wagon. Once inside, Venrick retrieved the enchanted chest, the one Lark was supposed to take into the cave with her. He ran his fingers over the raised runes embossed onto the ironwood.

"Am I a fool to be listening to Hardin right now?" he asked himself. "Why would the Hyalite be here and not in the fortress?"

He pulled the red amulet out from under his armor. The circular amulet, rimmed in gold, held the ruby red stone. He saw unfamiliar runes etched into the sides. The red light moved within, tracing tendrils of light that arched and fractured through the red stone. It was eerily similar in looks to the Hyalite.

"Should I be going to find Lark now or risk this chance at finding the Hyalite?" Venrick asked himself. "I could go back up to the window, get Hardin, and we could be on our way in moments."

He nodded to himself, making up his mind, and lowering the chest. The wagon rocked to the side, causing him to stumble. When he regained his balance, the wagon lurched into motion.

His heart sank into his stomach. Venrick rushed to the door and tried to open it. It wouldn't budge. He was trapped inside, being taken to an unknown location in an unfamiliar place across enemy lines.

33

LIKE A BOULDER

Hardin slid open another drawer, the last thread of hope unraveling like twine under pressure.

"It's empty."

Like every other drawer, chest, shelf and closet in the room, the Hyalite was not there. Stepping to the window, he checked again to see if Venrick was still outside with the wagon. His head snapped as he did a double-take.

"Wha-the?"

He watched Giant and Thunder lurch into motion and saw that the wagon was being driven by someone other than Venrick. The rear door flexed as something on the inside pounded to open the wagon from within, but it wasn't budging.

"Ven, he's been caught."

Footsteps squeaked against the floorboards in the hallway outside the door. He froze. The footsteps approached. Hardin searched the room for somewhere to hide. His options were less than ideal; behind the desk or curtain, or back out the window onto the narrow ledge. He dove behind the end of the desk.

Oh ash, did I forget to close the drawer?

The door opened a second later, footsteps clicked into the room and then paused.

"Sasja," a smooth voice called from down the corridor.

The door creaked on its hinges as it closed partway. A second set of heavier foot falls approached, and the door creaked wide open again.

"We've dealt with the intruder, but something has me second-guessing that that's the extent of the intrusion. A part of me questions whether he was actually alone. Tel's Squire shouldn't possess the magical ability to get past my wards. Either I missed something when I created them, which has never happened before... or he's with someone capable of slipping through without so much as a hint of triggering an alarm."

"Why would he have come here and not gone to the fortress if he had access to such power?" Sasja replied.

"The only thing I can come up with is that he somehow snuck through my portal. Did you have eyes on it the entire time?"

"No, I didn't because you commanded me to search for the wagon," Sasja said through gritted teeth. A moment later sounds of distress came from her, though Hardin couldn't see what was overcoming her. He nearly stepped out from his hiding place when they suddenly stopped.

"When you use that tone with me, I question where your true loyalties lie," the man replied.

"It's bad enough that I have to live like this. Now you want to control my thoughts and emotions, too?" Sasja argued.

"I let you go out into the world; you have more freedom than the Morsythians," he answered.

"I'm as free as a boulder rolling down a mountain. My fate is set, the paths I can take are defined. I can't escape."

There was a long pause where Hardin thought the mage might've left. Then he said, "Be thankful you are still of use to the Order."

"I'm not of use to you now. I don't know how Venrick was able to get through your wards."

"He has the genetic marker that my Master spoke of, but that wouldn't give him the strength to break through my wards."

Hardin leaned in, hoping to hear the mage explain.

"But you caught him?" she asked.

The man's voice shifted to a condescending tone. "The fool went out the window, scraping the snow off the ledge. I've sent him to the fortress, where the Morsythians and I will handle him," he replied.

The mage caught Venrick and took him to the fortress, Hardin's eyes went wide as he realized he was all alone now.

"He didn't find it, did he?" she asked.

"Of course not. I wouldn't keep the Hyalite in an unguarded building. It's still secure where nothing can get past the protection I have set around it. Not even the Archmagus could take it," he replied.

"What about Ella. She could, couldn't she."

The mage didn't answer aloud. After a brief pause, he asked, "Didn't you say you saw the Doranian in Astral City?"

"He must've continued on his quest undeterred to the Vermillion Keep."

"Was he traveling with the dwarf?"

"How would I know?"

"You saw him near the Keep, but was he with the dwarf?"

"Hardin didn't have the funds to contract anyone from the Vermillion Keep. Your plan to steer him away from Lamar was still intact. He would've had to go back to Stormwatch to afford a Knight."

Hardin nearly gasped aloud but held his breath. *Sasja was in Doran to stop him from coming to Lamar?*

"He shouldn't have continued beyond Stormwatch if you had done your job. It was imperative that he not make it to Astral City, yet you saw him there."

"I did my job. I tried to convince him to go to Storm Keep. When that didn't work, he was beaten by your orcs, then robbed because of me, all by your design," she said.

"Continue to search the estate. I want to verify that my wards have not been compromised before you join us for the event."

"As if I had a choice," she muttered under her breath.

"Say that again," he threatened.

"I do as your will commands," she said, venom lacing her voice.

"It does, and don't forget, Sasja. I know about your past with that dragonrider. Do anything to aid her and you'll meet the same fate."

"How could I? With this amulet, I am a boulder rolling down a mountain while wishing to break free and fly," Sasja repeated, struggling to keep the pain out of her voice.

"As are so many. Count yourself lucky I don't make you serve as the Morsythians do," he said, leaving her in the entrance.

Hardin remained still. In his heart he longed to step out from behind the desk, to see her again, but he wasn't sure that he could trust her. *Wouldn't she out him to the mage as soon as he approached? But Sasja had answers to questions that had brought him here. She had targeted Hardin since before they met, stolen his coin according to this mage's design to throw him off course, to distract him from going to Astral City. Why?*

I have to know!

Hardin rose from behind the desk just as Sasja stepped out of the room and into the hallway. Hardin slipped over, catching the door before it closed. Sasja whirled, her blue eyes widening as she faced him. Her shock faded into a grin, before horror contorted her perfect features. He wrapped his arm around her waist, pulled her into the room, and closed the door behind them.

As he held her, Sasja's lips parted to say an apology? or... She drew in a sharp breath.

She's going to cry out, he realized.

Hardin's instincts took over. With his hands full, holding her still and keeping the door shut, he did the only thing he could think of that would keep her mouth shut. He pressed his mouth against hers, locking lips and kissing her. Hardin squeezed his eyes tight, hoping Sasja's voice wouldn't blast through his lips.

Her exhale cut short as she let out a slightly alarmed mummer that faded into a simmering hum. Sasja's rigid posture relaxed. Her lips worked against his, kissing him in turn. She ran her hands into his hair inviting him in. Hardin melted into her, their ebbing and flowing rising with equal passion. He brought his hand away from the door, gently cupping the side of her face, as he held her closer. She ran her hand into his hair, pushing him in, deepening their kiss.

The time apart, the unspoken attraction between them, the desire he felt for her all coalesced into this moment. A moment he didn't want to end. Whatever was going to happen after this kiss, Hardin didn't want to factor in. He couldn't think those thoughts. He wanted to remain there, in that moment, immersed in the throes of their passion.

Fluttering tickled his heart as the kiss came to a natural end, leaving both of them panting as they held one another. Hardin waited for Sasja to speak, ready to throw himself right back into the kiss to keep her from shouting an alarm.

"Hardin, I wanted to come back to you. I wanted to explain, but this," she said motioning to the circular amulet around her neck. "I wish I could explain to you how much it pained me. How hard I was resisting his power."

"Sasja," he said, quieting her. "I understand."

"You do?" she said, her bright blue eyes narrowing.

"This curse," he said, running a finger gently down the amulet. "It's why I was traveling to Astral City. It's why I still have to find a way to help the people in my town."

"But you aren't," she said, pressing a hand against his chest, feeling for an amulet like hers.

"I don't have it because I walked away from it," he said.

She shook her head. "That's not how this works. If you had, you would be dead."

"I didn't die because I'm a... Well, apparently, one of my parents is a—"

"You're a Ward Walker."

He nodded.

"That's how you and Venrick were able go through the portal without him knowing," she said, nodding toward the door.

"I pulled us through the portal. We're here to find the Hyalite."

"I..." she stammered.

"I know the conditions of your curse. I was victim of a curse like you, but because of what I am, I didn't die when I disobeyed. You don't need to risk your life to answer my questions. Just nod or shake your head when I ask a question. You didn't want to steal the Hyalite from Lark, did you?"

She shook her head, a quarter of a smile coloring her cheeks slightly. "Lark, the name suits her far better than Ella."

"The whole time I've known you, you've been under a mage's curse and forced against your will to do his bidding," he said.

She nodded.

"The amulets the Morsythians wear are his, too. They are all under his control."

She nodded.

"This mage has discovered a new way to wield power through the curses in the amulets."

She nodded.

"But not all Morsythians wear them."

She shook her head.

"So, something else is binding the Morsythians to this mage's will?"

She nodded.

"But what could that be?"

Sasja shook her head. "If I tell you, it will kill me."

"It must have something to do with the Hyalite. Something they can do with the power from it."

She nodded.

"But if he's had it for this long... He's waiting for something else," Hardin said.

She nodded.

"You do know what it is."

She shrugged.

"You have an idea but you're not sure."

She nodded.

"Do you know where they took Venrick?"

She nodded.

"That's where the Hyalite is. You need to take me there," Hardin said.

"I will take you, but Hardin, if they find you... If he finds out you're here, he can turn everyone under his control into a slave who will carry out his desires. He can use me to work against you," she warned.

Hardin kissed her again. Sasja's lips moved against his, kissing him back. Their passion rose. Hardin wanted to remain in that room, just the two of them, but he knew they couldn't stay for long.

When they came up for air, he said, "The mage won't know I'm there. He can't feel my presence through his wards. I can get the Hyalite and Venrick out of there. You just need to take me to the Fortress."

Sasja took his hand, leading him to the closet door. "Here," she said, pulling a fur cloak and matching hat from the rack. "Put these on. You'll blend in as one of the warlocks who is often present to assist the Magi Order."

"Won't the others suspect me?" he asked.

"Nobody but the mage knows when a warlock has been summoned. As long as he doesn't see you, you should be able to get around without much trouble," she said, pausing as she bit her upper lip.

"What is it?" he asked.

"You'll need to lose the Doranian accent," she said. "How's your Sojax accent? The warlocks are almost always from the kingdom south of Lamar."

"I've tried before but my Sojax is abysmal. I could try a Gambrian accent. Are there ever any warlocks from the East?" he said, switching to the eastern accent.

"No human ones, but that will have to do. Just don't say anything if you don't have to. I'll get you in. Once we're there, it's on you to find it and take it."

"It being the Hyalite," Hardin confirmed.

She nodded.

With the disguise donned, Hardin followed Sasja out of the office, and down a hallway. She paused, checking down the stairs to make sure the main floor was empty. She led him out from the bottom of the stairs, past the entryway and into a mudroom. From there, they exited a side door and went out to the stable. She harnessed a single black mare to a buggy and took up the driver's seat. Hardin climbed on next to her, hoping the magi robes with their deep hood would be enough to disguise him.

34

NO CHANCE

Lark trailed Ezra's fresh tracks through the snow. Red Lodge came into view beyond the trees. The buildings sprawled across the bottom of a river valley rimmed by snow-covered mountains to the north. A sprawling stone fortress with turrets, thick protective walls, and a large open courtyard just within the gates jutted out from the southeastern edge of the predominantly orcin city. By Lark's estimate, Red Lodge was roughly half the size of Astral City or Stormwatch.

The knowledge that Omirre, shadow terrors, and a goblin horde were lurking just beneath the surface of the forest, not more than a few hundred yards away from the fortress and edge of the city, raised the hairs on the back of her neck. She shivered, not just from the chill of the northern air, but also with the realization that there must be even worse creatures here in the North to keep these monsters confined to the underground network of mines.

Ezra's tracks led Lark out of the long shadows of the Everburning Forest, away from and around the far eastern edge of the city until they settled on a snowy hilltop in the shadow of the mountains. From this vantage point, the dwarf had a perfect view of the city. Brush blanketed the hillside under a small snow ghost forest skirting the mountains.

Lark kept her footfalls light, tracing Ezra's and hoping these weren't the wayward tracks of a creature from the mine. The tracks ended in a cluster of thick brush ten feet in height. As she followed the tracks toward the opening, she was unsure whether she should announce her presence. Then she heard a crunch behind her. Lark swiveled to see the snarling bearded dwarf, with a white-knuckled grip on his hammer. He was arching it back and then caught himself.

"Lark?"

"Ezra, it's me, don't—"

"Lark?" he repeated, the hammer falling to his side. "I must be hallucinating because I saw you die."

"You're not seeing things. It's me. I'm here. I didn't die," she said.

"But, how? I watched the shadow terror drag you off the edge and drop you into the chasm as the amphiptere struck. You fell."

"I fell, but not to my death, obviously. Omirre, the amphiptere, caught me. She flew me into her lair."

"Omirre? But that can't be. Omirre was an agent of chaos, an evil creature with no remorse. Her rider was slain, and she disappeared from our realm over a decade ago."

"She knew me. Knew who I used to be," Lark said, dipping her chin.

"Why did she save you and how did you escape?"

"She let me go."

"You didn't kill her?"

"No, does it matter how or why I got out or that I'm out? I'm here now," she said.

"I won't prod at fresh wounds. You're here and that's what matters. Come," Ezra gestured for her to join him under the cover of the bush. "It's warmer in here. The snow insulates and traps in the heat."

He led her to the base of three hawthorns that formed a small hollow covered by branches that intertwined overhead. Thick snow clung to the bushes, creating a barrier from the elements. Looking out through a gap, they had a good view of the larger-than-average Northern city.

"How long have you been observing this place?" Lark asked.

"Long enough to have gathered some useful information we can share with our allies," he said with a smile.

"Hardin and Venrick?" Lark asked, hope rising that they had made it through the forest.

Ezra shook his head. "I'm afraid our lads may not have made it this far. They might have assumed that we died in the fall into the mine and turned around. Hardin doesn't have the stomach for this kind of work. It's why he was going to Astral City in the first place. To find a hero, not become one."

"But Venrick wouldn't turn back," she said.

"Now that Venrick and Ingamar have reconciled, why wouldn't they turn around. Go back to the Keep and enroll in an academy. From what I can see, he's more than capable of being a great Knight. If he bonded with a dragon, he'd have a good shot at becoming a Paragon, too," Ezra said.

"He wouldn't leave us just because we set off a trap and got stuck in the mine. He would keep trying to find us. And Ingamar," she said.

"You and Ingamar have not bonded," Ezra stated flatly.

"How do you know?"

"It's true then."

"We share a connection. Of that I am certain."

"But you did not bond with Ingamar after he found you. You used magic, but not through his bond," Ezra said.

"How do you know that he didn't bond with me?"

"In that firestorm, Ingamar chose to save Venrick and leave you behind," Ezra said. "While you were resting, Hardin and I spoke with Venrick. He told us everything that happened. He said there was a moment in the flames where you were looking like you might turn on him, Ingamar stepped between you two, to protect him. Fortunately, you came to your senses."

Lark remembered the event as though it were a dream. It really did happen that way. She tried to deny it, but she had no excuse.

"I know soldiers can go blind with rage in the heat of a battle, especially when the odds are stacked against them. But Ingamar chose to protect Venrick and continued to do so from then on. He flew him out to safety before going back for you. That was telling enough. When I asked Cheyanne during our encounter—"

"I thought Cheyanne only told you what you already knew about me?"

"She did. And more. She knew who you are. Or rather, she knew who you used to be," he replied.

"Did she tell you? Does she know where my dragon is?" Lark asked.

"No, she wouldn't say. Lark, your dragon died that day in the forest. Marcel killed him."

Lark shook her head, turning her mental probe in on herself. She tried to dig through the fog of her memory. "He didn't die, Ezra. He was wounded, but somehow he survived. How else can you explain how I'm still able to wield magic through our bond?"

"Venrick was there. He saw the corpse of the dragon. He wouldn't lie about that."

"The dragon's body was gone when Tel's Honor Guard returned to the scene."

"Yet, those same Knights verified the dragon's death."

Lark shook her head again. "Something isn't right. I wish I could remember," she said.

Ezra bowed his head, letting the silence grow. A snow flurry swirled around them, stirring them to search outside. "Is there a storm coming?" Lark asked.

"None that I can see."

A white and golden dragon flew in behind them, landing in the snow. His features mirrored Ingamar's, only his coloring was off. Ingamar didn't have any white scales, yet this dragon's head, neck, shoulders and top half were a crystal white that blended in perfectly with the snow.

"Is that?" Ezra said.

"Ingamar?" Lark said, sensing the connection she felt whenever he was near.

The dragon shook. The ice shot off his scales, revealing more of Ingamar's gold underneath.

"It is!" Lark said, running to him. He bowed his head, folding in the spines around his mane and welcomed her in with a curl of one of his wings.

"If you two aren't bonded, why is he so loyal to you?" Ezra asked, scratching his bald head.

"He must know I was truly trying to help him and Tel before I lost my memory. That's the only explanation. The connection we have, is no bond, but it's as close to one as another rider can have with a dragon," she said, hugging Ingamar around the neck. "Ingamar, you found us."

Ingamar hummed in his throat, the sound akin to purring.

The sun passed behind the mountains as they returned to the cover of the brush. Ingamar nuzzling his snout into the entrance behind them, his breath sulphury but warm in the early evening.

"I've been watching the movements of several groups in the city," Ezra said, pointing through the boughs toward Red Lodge and the fortress. "Several groups of orcs patrol the outskirts. They move between outposts. With the snow, it'll be easier for them to tell if anyone's arrived from anywhere else but a main road."

"Unless we fly in," Lark said.

"True. But that would be risky, seeing as we don't know if this city has wards like Astral City or Stormwatch. Also, I've seen two other dragons in that fortress."

"Two?" Lark's jaw dropped in surprise.

"They emerge from it every once in a while, mostly staying behind its walls and out of plain sight. It seems they've been distracted by something inside as Ingamar approached without them becoming alert. You also were lucky to miss being seen when following my path."

"They don't know we're here?"

"If they do, they don't see us as a threat. But my guess, is they don't know."

"I see a fire burning in the center of the fortress. It looks like it's coming from a courtyard," Lark observed.

"That's been burning since I got here. Must be getting rid of something. The dragons have re-lit it twice since I reached this spot. Whatever it is, it's not burning very well."

"That fortress is almost like the Keeps in Lamar, only smaller, not quite so grand-looking," Lark said, examining the thick stone structure.

"They are just like the Keeps in Lamar. Red Lodge is an outpost on the border between the Northern Kingdoms Wintermire and Skol. There should be a magus, dragonrider, or perhaps a powerful orc sorcerer in there. They'll have a training facility here that's meant to prepare the troops the Nordraven sends into this region of the Everburning Forest on their quests for Yogos and Hyalites."

"It's heavily fortified. I can see ranks of Morsythians down there."

"Morsythians?"

Lark nodded.

"This is not traditionally Morsythian territory. They've resisted Nordraven for a long time. I wonder why they'd be aiding them now?"

"I can only guess at this from what I can see of the courtyard. The rest of Red Lodge seems to be inhabited by common orcs. A few humans are mixed in."

"That tells us the Morsythians are only helping the Northern Kings in their quest for more Yogos and Hyalites. They've not settled here with the others in the community."

"And the two dragons, are we to assume both have dragonriders?"

"At least one of them includes a dragonrider. I saw a saddle on one of the black dragons that's been reigniting the fire in the square. As for the other one, I have not seen enough of it to determine. They're both grounded for now, staying somewhere withing the walls."

Lark focused in on the center of the fortress. She could see the head of a dragon, but nothing more. Her necklace tingled, causing her to flinch. She wished she could just take it off, but no matter how hard she tried, it wouldn't give. The discomfort was generally tolerable enough to ignore. "They're hiding something powerful in there," Lark noted.

"Exactly. Now we just need to wait for Cheyanne and her rebel force to arrive and we'll—"

"You never told us that Cheyanne was coming with a force to aid in this Hyalite retrieval," Lark snapped, cutting him off.

"Cheyanne is a powerful magician. She commands a force of rebels who've based their center of operations out of the Everburning Forest for almost a decade."

"When were you planning on telling me about this?"

"I meant to before, but with the mine and being separated, then the shadow terror."

"I thought our plan was to locate Sasja, make sure she still has the Hyalite without raising suspicion, and figure out a way to get it back. Not attack the fortress with an elf's rebel army?" Lark said.

"Cheyanne is my truest friend and ally. We've been working together to try and expose corruption in Lamar's Keeps since long before you entered my life. The Kingdom of Lamar's Noble Class has been using this competition for powers to line their pockets for centuries. They get richer while the Common Class is oppressed. Citizens are incentivized to try and become something greater through the Academies and the Keeps. The nobles pay them with such exuberant contracts, it's become the peak of social status in our society. The people believe they're fighting against evil, but the reality is the Nobles are using the Paragons and Knight like players on a continental gameboard where there is no end in sight and peace is impossible. I tried for years to make change from the inside, but eventually learned, to expose what's really going on will take a revolution. A revolution Cheyanne is trying to build."

"That's why you left the Academy," Lark said. "It wasn't to become a simple businessman."

"The inns and caravan route are just a cover so I can get supplies to her and her organization without either side of this war knowing. I've long suspected that Nordraven's Nobility is playing the same game that Lamar's is. This conflict is more complicated that it seems at face value. We need allies and Cheyanne is on our side here. She would never do anything to jeopardize what we're trying to accomplish. We can trust her."

"Can we though?" Lark asked. "Did she tell you about the meeting with the Morsythians that we had. The one where Sasja, Cheyanne and I made a deal with them?"

"Since when are you making deals with the Morsythians?"

"This was before the amnesia. The memory came to me after I saw Sasja the first time. I've had a few more memories surface that included Cheyanne. We disagreed about something. I think it was about this Hyalite," Lark said.

"You should've told us. We could've—"

"Could've what? Told Cheyanne more of my secrets so she could betray me again?"

"You don't know that she did anything to you."

"You don't either. Cheyanne said Sasja and I burned her. What if it was her who sent Marcel after us, knowing that we were trying to get this Hyalite. It could've been her. All of this could've been because of her."

"She isn't like that," Ezra said.

"Even her own people don't accept her. How honorable can she be?"

"She is honorable. You would know that if you could remember who she is," Ezra said.

"The Hyalite has to be down there, and you want to wait for her? For what, so she can steal it from us?"

"No. Lark, so we can take it back. There could be a whole legion of Morsythians in that fortress. On top of that, we're in Nordraven territory. People here will not take kindly to a couple of Southerners invading their city. The people of Red Lodge certainly won't provide refuge for us. Besides, there's at least one dragonrider down there, maybe two. There's no way to know if the fortress is a trap," Ezra said.

"And Cheyanne can tell us if it is or not?" Lark said.

"She is powerful. More than I am. We could use her and her—"

"I'm going down there," Lark announced.

"We should wait for assistance. Venrick and Hardin might be coming, too."

Lark's necklace warmed uncomfortably. The same feeling that drew her into the firestorm pulled at her now. The sensation that Ingamar shied away from. It called to her and this time she wasn't going to ignore it. This time, she was going to act.

"The Hyalite is down there. I know it in my bones and I'm going to get it back whether you come with me or not," she said, getting to her feet and turning to leave.

Ingamar backed out of her way, the frost still coating his scales from his flight through Northern winds. Lark unstrapped the brismil blade from his saddle and secured the sheath to her back. Sliding the giant sword out from the sheath for practice, she swiped the powerful blade through the air several times. The resulting pulse of energy flowed through her veins like the brismil armor, only slightly differently. She dropped the sword, and it reappeared on her back. Lark headed out to make for the ravine. Ingamar moved to walk with her.

"No, Ingamar. You can't come with me this time."

The dragon tilted his head sideways. He snorted at her, motioning with his head at the fortress.

"If there really is more than one rider down there, we could be taken before we get a chance to see if the Hyalite is there. You are too large and obvious with your golden scales. The cover of darkness will help, but I'm surprised that the other dragons and rider haven't noticed you already."

Ingamar sat, obedient, but the growl in his throat suggested that he wasn't happy about it.

"Stay here with Ezra. You have my full permission to fly down there if something happens to me. Okay?"

The dragon nodded his large head in response.

"Lark," Ezra said, pleading. "If you'd just wait, you won't need to take this risk alone."

"I'm not willing to pass up a chance to recover the Hyalite. Besides, I'm not alone. I have Stormbreaker and Ingamar for backup," she said, turning to leave.

35

THE FORTRESS

"No, no, no," Venrick said, working his way to the rear. He tried to open the door, but it wouldn't budge. He tried again, pushing harder but the door wouldn't open.

"Ash," he swore, searching the wagon for a way out. He tried the hatch on the roof. Nothing. He tried to wedge open the boarded and barred windows. Nothing gave.

"Not good, not good," Venrick said.

In his indecision, Venrick had squandered their opportunity to escape and find Lark. "And there is no way Hardin would've locked me in here," he told himself.

He took a deep breath, searching the interior of the well-stocked wagon. *I can't imagine that there's anywhere better to be than in Tel Roan's weapons wagon if I want to spring forth from a trap, ready and armed,* he thought. His eye was instantly drawn to the brismil scale.

"She doesn't have it," he said, his heart sinking, but he now knew what he had to do. He had to do what Tel Roan would, fight.

Venrick stripped off the leather armor, slung the spare

scale harness on. He secured the brismil scale into place. A flash of energy spurred throughout his body. Crystalizing ice, and crackling fire tore through his veins. Everything increased around him. His senses heightened, his strength surged, his focus honed. He drew the largest great sword from the rack and strapped it to his back. He belted two shorter swords to his sides. Throwing daggers he attached around each leg. In one hand, he took a star mace, the other now held a loaded triple-headed crossbow. Then he hunkered down as much as he could with all this gear in the center of the wagon to wait.

When the wagon finally stopped and a powerful charge of red light ripped the wagon door off its hinges, Venrick was ready. He let the bolts fly, two Morsythians dropped. Venrick erupted from the rear of the wagon like a wild animal. With a wild swing, he crunched the mace from one hulking Morsythian to the other. One glance told him the stone-walled courtyard where they'd parked was full of the blue orcs. As they crowded in around him, he noted some had the cursed amulets around their necks. Many were bound against their wills, just as he was. All had glowing red eyes and black winding tattoos.

A red mist like the one that trapped had Ingamar ripped through the air toward him. He rolled, taking a throwing dagger and landing it on its mark, between the rib and pectoral of the orc with a glowing amulet. The mist evaporated as the orc fell from the dagger in his heart. Venrick rolled to his feet, sliding a short sword from his belt. With the mace in one hand and a short sword in the other, he launched his attack. They came at him as fast as he could strike.

There are so many, he thought, wondering if he were fighting against an entire army. *Tel always said a man in brismil plate armor was a walking legion.*

Venrick didn't stop moving, knowing the strength from the brismil would carry him on. He weighted his entire body behind every hew of his mace, crashing it into multiple nine- and ten-foot-tall Morsythians at once. The blue bodies dropped, yet his strength did not wane.

He swung the mace, twisting his hip hard into the throw. It crunched against the target. A crack sounded and Venrick nearly tripped. Glancing down, he realized that the handle was all that remained of his mace. A weight hit him from behind and Venrick rolled forward. A Morsythian moved in, but he jumped up, stabbing him through with his short sword. Drawing the other short sword, Venrick set to work again.

Time blurred. He couldn't tell if he'd been fighting for a few minutes or hours. The Morsythians continued to press him. Eventually, the swords, like his mace, broke. He flung the dagger into one of the orcs wearing an amulet. The only sword Venrick had left was his two-handed great sword. Energy from a Morsythian spell-caster exploded around him, clearing space on the floor of the courtyard for him.

Suddenly a single clap sounded throughout the courtyard. All the Morsythians stopped, arms instantly hanging loose at their sides. In unison, they straightened into the same posture, a blank stare crossed their faces as they peered forward like puppets held tight on strings. Venrick remained in a fighting stance, two hands firmly gripping his great sword. A door swung shut at the other end of the courtyard, drawing his attention.

A slow clap from a single set of hands sounded again. The applause from the individual continued as the Morsythians cleared to the sides of the square at once.

"Venrick, well done," that familiar voice said.

Venrick's eyes widened as he recognized the face of the mage apprentice approaching him. Magi Joc, the Archmagus' pupil, clapped at him, his copper hood falling back to expose his identity.

"You," Venrick hissed through gritted teeth. He coiled to

launch his strike, determined to kill the mage who had cursed him so the curse would end.

Joc raised his hand as though to cast a spell, but instead of casting, he simply closed his fist into a tight grip. Venrick halted immediately mid-stride. The brismil armor gave him more energy as he demanded, urging him to resist, but Venrick couldn't move.

"I thought you might actually do it. Tel would be proud of you," the mage said with a cynical smile.

Venrick struggled to speak, to say something to resist whatever spell had ahold of him. But this wasn't a spell. Joc had never spell-cast on him.

"I bet you're wondering how you could possibly be stuck in place right now, even while wearing your Paragon's brismil armor?" the mage asked, walking so close Venrick could feel this man's awful breath on his face. The great sword stuck straight out next to him, it's killing blow just out of reach.

Joc casually glanced at the sword and said, "It is remarkable what this power can do to those who are captured by it."

Venrick's fingers betrayed him, prying open against his will. The sword clanged to the ground. There was nothing he could do to stop himself from reaching in and unclasping the brismil scale. The armor vanished from his body.

"I'm sure you noticed by now that there are others who wear an amulet like yours. Ones who can suddenly cast amazing magic, without the use of a Yogo or a Hyalite," Joc said.

Venrick's arm disobeyed all his bodily will, removing the scale and handing it over to Joc.

"It's because of this," the mage said, taking the scale from Venrick and holding it with a long sleeve of his robe. "Lamar has not been ready to experiment with brismil the way Nordraven has. The Four Kings are desperate. They know what's coming from the deep North. They've fought the rimeshade. They know what will happen when the Flashover begins."

The flapping of wings pounded the air above the courtyard as a pair of smaller dragons dropped down and landed among the dead bodies. A third massive dragon followed but stopped to perch on the thick wall above them.

"You've just delivered to me what was right under my nose," Joc tsked. "And I would wager that the woman is not far behind you. It's a shame. All that work. All that effort you, Tel Roan, and the rest of your haggard rag-tag group have invested in trying to get it back."

He sighed dramatically, "And now you've led them all right to me. Wrapping you up in chains will make a nice present for them, don't you think?" he snapped his bony fingers. "Better yet, you can be their executioner." He grinned, exposing a wicked yellow smile. "Best keep that big sword. We have some heads we're going to set rolling."

Venrick willed himself against the power, but the curse controlling him was too strong. He couldn't break free.

Lark worked her way down through the snowy ravine, staying out of sight of the city until the moonless night covered her movements. Once she reached the edge of the forest, she steered toward the road, tracking it close enough to the city that she could see the orcs on patrol. The few stationed at the outposts sat by fires, chatting loudly and laughing. She waited as three passed along the road that apparently circled the valley and watched them enter the next outpost. Soon after, three different orcs emerged to continue along the loop to the next post. Once they'd gone, she passed across the road behind them, entering Red Lodge among a few rows of houses to the north. The chill of the night air cut through her fall weather cloak. She shivered and took the first opportunity she came across to duck into a covered building where no one was visible in the room.

"Olrug, is that you?" someone called out in a thick Northern accent.

Lark rubbed her shoulders. A rack of thick fur-and-leather coats hung near the door. She grabbed one and threw it over her shoulders as she silently opened the door and headed back out into the snow-dusted street. The weight of the fur coat enhanced her ability to conceal her features in the dark. Lark moved more freely now, trying to get a sense from her necklace about where the Hyalite might be hidden. The pendant burned as it had when a source of power was close by. She would be greatly surprised if it wasn't here.

As she drew close to the fortress, she noted that the entrance was begin guarded by two armored Morsythians with massive poleaxes. Their matching tattoos denoted that they belonged to the same tribe. The black ink rose up their beefy arms to points, that ended on either side of their necks.

Lark crossed the street in front of them, her head bowed, covered by the large hood. She peered through the open gates of the entrance and into the courtyard beyond. She paused when she noticed the wagon, Tel's wagon. Giant and Thunder were tied to a chain in the wall. The draft horses snorted, stamping their feet, clearly under some kind of duress. The rear of the wagon, though warded by powerful magic, had been ripped apart.

She couldn't help but stop to stare through the opening. This drew the attention of one of the guards at the entrance, who tilted his head slightly as he looked at her. His voice was barely audible as he spoke to the orc across form him. Now they both took notice of her. One made a move toward her. Just as Lark thought she might be sniffed out, the orc's posture relaxed. His face slacked and his arms sagged. He suddenly completely lost interest in Lark and returned to the gate. She heard them mutter something about a shift change, and then they turned to enter through the raised portcullis and disappear around the corner.

Lark's heart sank. *Venrick and Hardin, they could've been captured.*

Before the gates could close, Lark sprinted through into the open fortress. She passed by without hitting any wards that would alert the guards. Giant and Thunder calmed at her touch.

"Shhh, it's okay. I'm going to get you out of here, but I need to know if Hardin and Venrick are somewhere inside?"

The horses whinnied, bobbing their heads up and down.

"Are you sure?"

They bobbed again.

"Good boys," she said, untying them and slapping them lose. They charged out through the gate, snow flying up behind the wagon wheels. She heard orcs gasp as the unmanned wagon flew past.

Lark slipped off the fur and drew her blade. Power tingled as it coursed through her. She darted farther into the fortress at breakneck speed. She slid into the courtyard. Morsythians lined the walls, all standing at attention. Each one wore the same slack-jawed expression as the two outside had. The black dragons were nowhere in sight. The burn pile they'd been torching all day was a heap of Morsythian bodies.

Lark charged back through the halls of the fortress, searching for any sign of animate life. Each soldier or guard she passed by was flaccid, staring straight ahead as though their minds were not attached.

"*What the ash is going on?*" Lark thought.

She burst through another door, this one opening into a long great hall. At the far end was a throne. Morsythians lined the open-air throne room. Venrick sat in the center in front of the throne wearing the same expression as the Morsythians.

"Venrick," she said, using a burst of power from Stormbreaker to slide right up to him. "Venrick, come on, let's get out of here!"

He didn't respond.

"Venrick?" she said, shaking his shoulder.

He didn't move, didn't blink, didn't even acknowledge that she was there.

"What's happened, Venrick? Say something," she demanded. "Is the Hyalite here? Is Hardin alive?"

No reply.

"Venrick, wake up!" she said swinging to slap him awake.

His hand shot up lightning fast, catching her wrist before it landed. Lark's eyes widened in horror as he turned his expressionless face toward her, a red glow cast on his features from the amulet around his neck. His grip tightened. He blinked, his expression changing ever so slightly to fear as he struggled with his words. "Lark, you should not have come here. I'm..."

"What, Venrick. You're what?"

"Sorry," he forced out before the emotionless slate replaced his pained expression.

"Venrick?" she said.

With the same speed, he snatched her hand holding Stormbreaker. She tried to pull away, but his grip was powerful. Too strong to be his own. He twisted and a gut-wrenching sound echoed through the hall. Her wrist snapped, the bones breaking clean through. She screamed as she dropped the sword. Something slipped under the strap holding the blade on and cut it free. The weight of the sheath on her back was lifted.

Nausea and pain blurred her vision. Another familiar figure moved in from behind the throne to stand beside

Venrick. The rider in the brismil plate armor, his helmet sporting two curling horns. Lark's heart dropped. She recognized him from the recent firestorm. Venrick's grip tightened on her broken wrist, increasing her pain. Just before she passed out, Lark saw a robed man with black hair and slender features walk in, his grip in one hand formed a tight fist. In his other hand, he cradled the Hyalite.

36

ON THE INSIDE

Hardin sat next to Sasja as they drove along roads that passed through Red Lodge. They were headed to the fortress near the edge of the forest. As they approached, a large dragon stretched its leathery black wings out over the thick stone walls.

"The mage is working with a dragonrider?" Hardin asked, his heart racing at this added layer of complexity. One wrong look from a dragon and he could be transformed into a pile of ashes.

"This I can speak on. Joc's Order, which I think has its base in Wintermire, made an alliance with Greggor Emberhelm, the King of Skol. They've brought several unbonded dragons to this fortress, but whatever they've been trying to do with them isn't working. I'm not sure what they're planning, but it seems like King Greggor's Emissary, General Barrik, is the only dragonrider here now."

"King Greggor sent General Barrik, as in, the Nordraven rider who is said to have trained Marcel Heartfell?" Hardin asked.

Sasja nodded.

"But Nordraven's been claiming they don't have the Hyalite. So, Joc and Barrik are acting without the King's knowledge?"

She nodded again.

"And they've claimed they haven't found Marcel since his run-in with Tel Roan. Could Marcel be here, too?" Hardin asked.

Sasja shrugged and said, "White Eye isn't here."

The black dragon within the courtyard at the fortress stretched its neck, exposing its horned head and revealing two white eyes.

A chill crept down Hardin's back as he saw them. "Whose black dragon is that with the white eyes then?"

"All animal eyes look like that when they're being warged," Sasja said.

"Does that mean Marcel's dragon has always been under someone else's control?" Hardin asked.

"I don't know. White Eye's eyes are said to have a golden ring around them, not truly all white like animals who are being warged. But I wouldn't be surprised if a Nordraven rider is forcing his dragon into action, an action the dragon might not agree with," Sasja said with a shrug.

"Why would a dragonrider warg its own dragon like that? Don't the dragons have the control to reject their rider's will?" Hardin asked.

"Not always. Some riders are stronger in how they control animals when warging. Some can only see what the animal sees while others can manipulate what the animal is doing. I guess it's kind of like this," Sasja said motioning to the amulet around her neck. "It all depends on how strong the magic wielder is."

Hardin sat with his head bowed, hood up as they passed under the watchful eyes of the white-eyed dragon.

Two hulking Morsythians crossed their poleaxes, blocking

the horse before Sasja could continue through the entrance. "What's with the extra baggage this time?" the one on the right said, red eyes locked on Hardin.

"I don't have to answer to you, orc," Sasja replied.

"Joc didn't say anything about a warlock coming."

"He's not accompanying the mage, he's accompanying me. Do you really think that Joc would accomplish a breakthrough in magic without an understudy to observe or take the fall should something go awry?"

The Morsythian chewed on the idea. "That seems possible, but that doesn't sound like him."

"Let us past and I will ensure that you stay on your guard post for a day longer before you have to rotate back into serving," she said.

"You have that kind of authority?"

"Just look at me, I can get him to do what I want with some pulsation. If I really want to, I'll make it so," she said.

"Make it so. I would like to make it through this night so I can return to my little ones at home."

Sasja drove into the portcullis, turned down the corridor, and ventured out along the edge of the courtyard. Hundreds of corpses littered the yard, all Morsythians. Venrick's wagon waited on the side of the stone yard, its two driving horses untied and missing. The rear of the weapons wagon had been torn or blown off.

Hardin blinked, trying to comprehend, what had happened here. A massive melee. *Perhaps Morsythians against Morsythians*, he wondered. The fighting had been violent.

"What could've done this besides a dragon?" Sasja asked, repulsed.

As they rode by, Hardin looked into the open wagon. The hook where Lark had hung the brismil scale was empty. Lark didn't have it with her. "Brismil plate armor," Hardin whispered.

Sasja nodded.

"This whole fight was to contain Venrick," Hardin realized.

"Not just to contain him," Sasja said. "He had something Joc wants."

"Tel's brismil?" he said, hearing the insinuation in her voice. She was trying to tell him something without breaking her curse.

She nodded.

"That's why they've been waiting to use the Hyalite. It has something to do with the brismil."

She nodded again, tapping her nose.

"But that brismil is part of a set. It's not to full power without the sword."

She tapped her nose, nodding again.

"They're using Venrick to set a trap for Lark, so they can get the other half of the brismil. Then what?"

Sasja tightened her lips.

Hardin was close to figuring it out. Yet he couldn't quite connect the dots. "What does the magi need a brismil set for when he can bend people to his will with a curse? Why not just curse the person with the brismil and use them as a weapon?"

A door opened across the courtyard, echoing though the expansive square. The mage entered the far side of the courtyard, leaning in and speaking intently with a Morsythian. Hardin rolled off the edge, hiding behind the buggy.

"Hardin," she said in a hushed tone, meeting him alongside the buggy.

Hardin stared into her dazzling eyes and kissed her for the length of a single breath, then pulled away.

"I forgot to tell you, that outfit looks great on you," she said with a wink.

"Thanks to you," he said, smiling back.

"Stay alive."

"I'll do my best," he replied, then slunk away into a nearby hallway.

Hardin's heart pounded as he walked with purpose through the corridor. Knowing he could open any door without setting off wards gave him the confidence to hunt for Venrick and the Hyalite. Door after door led to offices, chambers, a massive kitchen. He had worked his way around the entire first floor and was heading up to the second when he heard the screaming.

That voice, it sounded like... *Venrick.*

Hardin took off at a run. No armor, no weapons, but his sheer will to help. He burst through the room at the end of the hallway where he thought the scream had come from. There, sitting on lone pedestal was a chest with embossed runes on it, just like the one that Tel Roan had. Light swelled from under the lid, a pure blue light that pulsed like a beating heart.

Hardin stepped closer when a sound at the end of the hall tickled his ear. He spun upon hearing the approaching footsteps.

"Ash," he swore, searching for an escape.

The room, however, was completely bare, offering no exit but the one door Hardin had come in through. The feet clacking against the stone grew closer. They were nearly at the room. Hardin pressed himself flat against the wall just behind where the door would swing open. The door opened.

Please don't close the door, he thought, as it swung in, stopping a few inches from smashing him against the wall.

The person entered, leaving the door open. Hardin peeked around the edge. A rider in black brismil armor strolled up to the chest. A fire fae trailed behind him. The rider took hold of the chest. The fae turned back, staring directly at Hardin. His heart sank as he ducked back behind the door.

The armored boots walked toward him, the door handle clicked on his gauntlet, then swung shut, closing with a click.

The fire fae staring at him whispered as she passed by, "I'll be back to deal with you." Then she disappeared.

Hardin sagged, relief washing over him after narrowly escaping detection. He didn't understand what the fae meant with her hushed warning but she hadn't alerted the rider gave him hope. He turned the door handle. No, not turned. It didn't budge. He frowned, trying again, but again it didn't turn. He pulled on the door, frantically trying to force it open.

"No," Hardin said in a panic. He tried again and again but the door wouldn't budge.

Hardin was trapped and the Hyalite was gone.

37

THE BINDING STONE

When she awoke, blurry figures moved around the throne before her. The throbbing in her arm had dulled to a consistent ache, her skin had swollen tight from the break. She moved slightly, and the stabbing pain immediately radiated out from the break to just past her wrist. Lark bit down and forced herself to focus.

Venrick was standing next to her. Careful not to move her arm, she sat up, taking in Venrick in his current state. His face was a drawn tight into a firm expression as though internally he was struggling with something painful. His body twitched slightly as he stood stiff as a board.

She now looked ahead toward where she'd seen the throne. Five shallow steps led up to a dais. The throne had evidently been moved and in its place, someone had produced a single slab of onyx granite.

A binding stone, she realized and remembered the repercussions the instant she saw it.

Behind the stone, tall stained-glass windows depicted scenes of dragons gathered around similar stones. In one picture, glowing mystic orbs hovered above the dragons. The colorful windows reached up almost as high as the fortress wall, the clear night sky open above. Crisp cold air filtered in from the open-air dais. Two live dragons peered in, their claws gripping tight to the perch the barrier wall provided.

On either side of the binding stone stood the mage and the enemy rider. The mage was wearing a new white robe with a pattern like frost stitched in black thread, adding texture to the fabric. His pale, glossy head was shaved bald, hood pulled back to expose him to the cold night air. The rider, the same rider Lark had faced in the storm, stood stock still. He wore black brismil plate armor, a copper cape hanging loose at his back, and a horned helmet that disguised his features. Nix hovered next to him, her flame-hot head bowed in shame. She glanced at Lark, revealing that her eyes were no longer the white they'd been when this same rider had evidently controlled her in the firestorm. She shied away when she noticed Lark glaring at her.

Together the rider and the mage placed the brismil scale and Stormbreaker on opposite ends of the binding stone.

Nix, Lark thought toward the fae.

She looked up, her flame red eyes leaking tiny drops of liquid fire.

Nix, help me stop them.

Nix bowed her head. Then she scratched her clavicle, an act that seemed out of place.

A woman in a hooded fur cloak emerged from behind the dais. Her two thick blonde braids fell below the edge of her collar, a pair of glacial blue eyes peered out from the hood. She carried a chest embossed with runes , similar to the one Venrick had in the wagon. A blue light glowed under the lid, pulsing in time to the beat of her heart.

Lark now pushed herself up to her feet, ignoring the pain in her arm. "Sasja, don't do this," she implored.

The mage's attention flicked to Lark, while the red light

on both Sasja and Venrick's amulets flared. Venrick's arm shot out, his hand locking around Lark's bicep to hold her in place.

The necklaces are controlling them. They cannot tap the power from them on their own, she thought. *It's been that way all along. Is that what you were trying to tell me, Nix?* Lark directed these thoughts toward the fae, knowing she could still hear her.

Nix returned a sad smile.

"Stop," Lark shouted, taking hold of the amulet around Venrick's neck with her good arm.

"Ella," the rider said, his tone somber, scolding even, almost like a disappointed parent.

The mage held up two fingers to silence him. "If I may," he said.

The rider nodded.

"Take it off him and your sweet Venrick will die," the mage said with a sinister note.

Is that true? Lark checked with Nix.

Nix nodded.

Lark pulled tight on the chain, threatening to break it regardless.

"Go ahead, take it off him. You'll be doing me a favor. I was going to kill him eventually anyway."

"Joc," the rider said with a twinge of concern.

"This doesn't concern you, Barrik," Joc snapped.

"You're not thinking right, Ella," Barrik said, removing the brismil scale from his skin to reveal his hidden identity.

Seeing his brown hair pulled back, the wide flare of his nostrils, his flat lips drawn tight, and his prominent brow scowling at her jogged her memory. Lark staggered and loosened her grip to keep her balance. He was so familiar. She recalled that he had influenced her when she was growing up, almost like family.

When will I break through this amnesia! The thought came with crippling frustration.

"Your memories, they have been displaced, hidden from you. But Joc and I can set them free. Let me show you who you are," Barrik offered.

"Not before the ceremony is complete," Joc argued.

"If she remembers, she'll know why we're doing this. I can help her clear the fog tainting her judgement," he said.

"We had a deal, Barrik. What will your King Greggor think if he knew you and I had gone behind his back and summoned forth the rimeshade?"

Rimeshade? Lark thought. *Those are the frost wielding shades that Sasja, Cheyanne, and I were opposing.*

"She has a right to know why," Barrik said.

"Break our deal and the sanctuary they offered is gone. Skol will have no longer be protected against the invasion brought on by the Flashover. The dragon, too, will be gone. You and your people will be back to the position of fighting against the rimeshade. Do you want Skol to end up like the others you've betrayed? Like what's been happening in Elderice and Fjern? Like what will happen to Wintermire and Lamar next?"

Barrik's shoulders sagged, then he clasped his brismil scale back into place, transforming in an instant to the armored figure Lark had faced in the firestorm.

"Bring forth the Hyalite," Joc said.

Sasja hesitated, her hands trembling as though she might drop the chest. A moment later, she lurched forward, her movements unnatural and not at all like her own. Watching her, Lark struggled against Venrick's grip but the power controlling him kept his grip firm.

Suddenly, Lark noticed that Nix had vanished. She'd disappeared from the room. The rider and the mage were too focused on the ceremony to notice.

Sasja presented the chest to Barrik, who ran his finger along the embossed markings. The lid opened and Joc wasted no time in placing open box holding the Hyalite in the center of the onyx binding stone.

What happens when they bind the Hyalite with the brismil set? Lark wondered.

"Now the dragon," Joc said to Barrik.

The rider stiffened and a moment later the black dragon with white eyes hopped down off the ledge. It sat on its haunches next to the stone.

Lark, Nix said through her thoughts.

Nix, why are you helping them do this?

I don't have much time. Joc can't see me in here and Barrik can't sense me when he is warging. Use your power. Destroy Joc and you end the curse he has on Venrick, Sasja, and the Morsythians.

How?

The necklace, Nix's said, her voice fading at the end.

Lark drew back on her instincts, feeling for the bond that tethered her to the flow of magic she'd used before. Ingamar's touch and energy were nowhere nearby. Lark's bond with her dragon, completely unknown to her now, also was absent. But something else resonated inside her.

Joc lifted his arms and the red lights in the amulets dwindled, flickering when he spoke in a foreign language. The light from the Hyalite glowed brighter as red tendrils of light crept through the air from the mage's fingertips. These red lights extended like little streaks of lightning, shocking in and out from his fingertips, ending a hand's width from the Hyalite, and finally arching around the blue orb. Joc snorted in frustration; green veins bulged from his temples and forehead as he spoke the chant again, louder this time.

The dragon beside the stone flinched, then reared away, his eyes turning back to gold for a second before Barrik let loose a force of energy. The dragon's eyes turned white again, and he relaxed. Something about the sight was surprisingly familiar to Lark.

"Binding the power of brismil with that of a Hyalite creates a third power. One that they are using to control others," Lark whispered, remembering now. She was momentarily taken back to the moment when Barrik first explained it to her. She blinked, to bring herself back to the dais and binding stone. "They're trying to create a new rider that they can control with this curse," she realized aloud.

"Lark," Venrick said under strain.

"Venrick?" Lark replied, hoping he'd broken the curse somehow. His strained expression, though, told her that he was only able to speak while Joc's attention remained consumed by the spell he was attempting that would combine the brismil with the Hyalite and force it into the dragon.

"Peel my fingers back. I think I can force myself to let go of you," he whispered through a frozen jaw.

Lark did, careful not to break his fingers as she wrenched.

"Break them if you must."

Lark heard three of his fingers pop, before his grip was weak enough for her to pull her arm free. Venrick's eyes watered in pain though the curse's control seemed to have lingered for the moment. Lark spun away from Venrick as his body acted against his will. Lacking a weapon, Venrick assaulted Lark with hand-to-hand combat. He kicked at her torso. She dodged. He spun, exposing his back. Lark pummeled his kidneys. The hits would've brought him to his knees had he not been controlled by Joc.

Venrick jerked himself in an unnatural motion, landing a punch to her cheek. Lark's head bounced back, a fresh split weeping blood under her eye. She hissed and kicked Venrick in the thigh as hard as she could. His face contorted as he crumpled to one knee, panting.

Lark shifted her focus to Joc.

A Morsythian with thick, widely spaced tusks, bulky muscles, and a heavy sword moved toward Lark. The amulet around his neck gave her pause. No spells came from the Morsythian wielder. While Joc's attention focused on the binding stone, he could not cast spells through these creatures. The curse alone forced them to attack.

Consequently, the Morsythian came in swinging. Lark ducked, spinning just in time to see Venrick's broken hand grabbing for her. She blocked it, kicked him again in the same spot on his thigh. She wanted to stop him from moving quickly without injuring him too badly. Venrick went down and struggled to get up. The Morsythian's blade came for her again. She bowed and it clipped fur from the borrowed cloak as it passed overhead.

Lark jumped, delivering a mighty kick to the back of the Morsythian's head. Without added power, though, Lark's hit did little damage. He reset his stance and struck again. This time the blade narrowly missed her chest as she backed away. A set of slender arms wrapped around her, long braids falling beside her head.

"Sasja?" Lark said, feeling the cold blade pressed up against the skin of her neck.

Lark flexed, pushing out against the impossible strength coming from Sasja. Screaming through the pain in her broken arm, Lark slowly pushed the blade away from her throat, her vision tunneling as a result of the pain and the effort. The Morsythian was coming at her again, his massive sword held aloft. Suddenly, Nix sparked, appearing before Lark as she buzzed around the Morsythian, flashing fire in his eyes. He swung wildly, missing them completely.

Venrick was on his feet, limping toward them on a swollen leg to join the fight. Lark forced herself to take hold of the dagger with her broken arm. She controlled Sasja's arm with the other as she rolled, tossing Sasja from her back and stealing her dagger. Venrick stumbled past, crashing into the frustrated Morsythian. Lark switched the dagger to her good hand. She pressed it against Sasja's throat, rage pounding through her.

If it wasn't for her, I would still have this Hyalite, Lark thought, preparing to do away with her one-time friend, enemy... *What was Sasja to me before?*

Joc shouted something, his voice crackling with red lightning. There was a flash. The light exploded, erupting in a violent outpouring of energy in all directions. Lark was sent flying. When she landed and the blast cleared, she saw the Hyalite.

Its blue light trickled out from the binding stone, where it had cracked along the surface. The light pulsed like lightning and joined tandem streams of red from the brismil. They twisted, coiling into tendrils of purple. One stream stretched out toward Joc's outstretched palm, the other two fed into the brismil from the Hyalite.

Joc burst into a maniacal laugh. He pointed a bony finger toward the dragon. "Your part comes next. The sacrifice of an unbonded life is all I need to become the ultimate dragonrider. I will become a god incarnate!"

Lark glanced down at the necklace around Sasja's neck. "The necklace," she wondered if this was a source of power she could draw from. She took hold of it and drew the chain tight.

"Lark, not that necklace," Nix cried out.

The dragon's eyes went golden again as Barrik emerged from his warging. He blinked and then turned to focus on Nix and Lark. His hand shot up. A hazy extension of his arm shot out across the room. He used this power to snatch Nix, his dusty haze catching her and snuffing out her fire.

"Lark, use the la—"

He squeezed the hazy cloud of debris around Nix. Her fire extinguished entirely; her body crumbled to charcoal as the ashes of her physical form fell to the ground. Barrik's extension vanished like dust drifting harmlessly on the wind.

The unbonded dragon, suddenly aware of his supposed fate, flapped his wings to escape. Joc pointed to the dragon while whispering his strange language. A stream of power arced from his arm to wrap around the dragon and hold him in place. Joc lowered his arm, and a trickle of the strange purple light continued to flow from Hyalite into the pinned dragon. All three streams passing from the Hyalite into the brismil and the dragon ebbed and ended. The Hyalite was now clear and empty.

Joc palmed the scale. An instant later a set of black armor formed around him. Between each link of the scale, the brismil glowed with a purple light. He took up Stormbreaker and stalked toward the dragon.

Lark sliced Sasja, wounding her but leaving her alive so she couldn't follow. She dodged Venrick, knocking his dazed body to the ground once again. Then she engaged with the Morsythian again.

"You promised this power would be bound to the Morsythian army. You were to create an ultimate soldier to help the rimeshade, not take it for yourself," Barrik accused Joc, summoning his brismil spear.

"This power can't be trusted to the Morsythians or the rimeshade. No, this energy, the power of a god, can only be wielded by someone strong enough to take it for themselves. With it, I will control all the kingdoms of Sataran, something not even the rimeshade have never been able to do. I alone will form an empire. Every time a storm of power produces a Hyalite, it will belong to me. Every time a shard of that power splinters into a Yogo Sapphire, it will belong to me. The gods will belong to me," Joc replied without a hint of guilt for having lied.

Barrik channeled his powers. A swirling vortex of dust

formed, twisting and shaping into a second version of himself made of stone. The mirage attacked Joc. He cut through the stone with his brismil, but the blow did nothing to slow the stone figure. It instantly stitched back together, crashing into Joc. Joc recovered quickly, sending a pulse of power into Barrik's chest. Barrik fell off the dais. The large black dragon flew in over the open room.

Lark danced around the Morsythian, cutting his hand and forcing him to drop his blade. She kicked his knee, forcing him to drop, then punched the hilt of the dagger against his temple. His eyes rolled and he toppled.

Barrik and Joc clashed, light exploding against the rock, sending rubble down into the throne room. The rock reformed into soldiers of stone to attack Joc. From the openings in the walls, Morsythians spilled into the room from all directions, swarming like sharks in bloody water.

Lark's necklace still tingled with warmth though Nix was gone. Lark's rage cleared enough now to remember her line of thinking. Every time she'd channeled magic through the bond, it had started with the sensation from the necklace. The necklace sent vibrations through her, driving her toward the firestorms, where the veil between realms thinned the most. Omirre, the eel, had told her to remember where the necklace had come from. That there were more ways than one to channel magic through the veil into this world.

"Use the lark necklace," she realized.

Nix hadn't been talking about the amulets. She was talking about Lark's necklace.

Suddenly, it came flooding back to her. The memories of how she'd traveled to the fae realm. How she had made a deal with the Night Court. How she'd bonded with a fire fae and returned with the ability to draw upon her magic through the veil using that necklace. The lark pendant was a direct line to a raw and wild magic from another world. It was the key to the source, and she was the conduit to release it.

Lark focused on the dais where Joc and Barrik continued their fight, fae magic swelling against the barrier she held around her neck. Joc was at the dragon's side, holding Barrik off with a cloud of purple light. He thrust Stormbreaker into the dragon's side. The dragon howled in pain, a breath of fire shooting up into the sky.

A white and purple light twisted out from the dragon, wrapping around the sword and onto Joc's arm. The magic siphoned continuously out of the dragon and into Joc.

Lark lifted her hands, reaching through her bond and opening the veil to the fae realm. Black energy crackled above, coalescing in a midnight fog that surrounded her. She sent the black fog forth, streaking across the gap at Joc.

A purple dome appeared, isolating Joc and the dragon from the rest of the dais. Lark's forces battered against the warding shield, but it held strong. She drew on the power tethering her to another world and funneled more onto the dome of light. The purple cracked, her forces filling the cracks but still not penetrating.

Come on, she urged them, calling on more power.

Hardin slumped onto the floor. Tears blurred his vision as he thought of the struggle his friends were going through.

"Help!" he cried again, his voice gone hoarse from screaming so often. He didn't know how long he'd been sealed in this room. A room that may have been warded, but that magic wasn't his downfall. The simple mechanics of a locked door had trapped him inside.

Muffled blasts sounded somewhere in the fortress. Hardin barely heard them. He tried the door again, but the handle wouldn't budge. He pounded on the door until his hands were numb.

Then, something small, something glowing sparked in the air in the room with him. Hardin's eyes instantly looked to it in the consuming darkness. More sparks appeared, shooting off in a spinning circle as a fire fae emerged. Her body was glowing with yellow and orange flame, her red dress and hair rippling with the otherworldly fire.

Hardin would not be intimidated by the fiery demon. He straightened himself, ready to fight for his life.

"Hardin," she said, her voice sweet but urgent.

"You're her, aren't you? You're Nix," he said. "How did you get in here?"

"We don't have time. I'm no longer in his control as he thinks he killed me when he destroyed my apparition."

"Who, the rider?"

"Barrik and Joc are going to get them all killed. You are the only one who can help Lark stop it."

"Why can't you help, too?" he asked.

"I need to wake up White Eye."

"What? Why?"

"No time to explain. You need to go to the throne room. It's a straight shot, just follow the noise,"

"How, I'm stuck in here."

Nix vanished.

"Nix!"

A second later the door handle turn from the outside. It twisted slowly, as if the effort to open it was coming at a great cost. Finally, it clicked. Hardin twisted the handle the rest of the way, pulling the door wide open.

Nix was there, panting from the effort. "I told Lark I could open some locks," she said with a smile and disappeared.

~

Lark strained under the effort it took to force open the shield of light encapsulating Joc and the juvenile unbonded dragon. She shook, the realization that she couldn't break through stabbing icy daggers of fear into her heart.

Hardin appeared through a break in the wall and ran toward Joc from behind. He sprinted across the throne room, approaching Joc fast, completely hidden from the mage's line of sight. Hardin had no dagger, no weapon on him, but he kept on as though he were wearing brismil himself. He passed through the purple shield, slowed to a silence stalk, moving in close to Joc's back. Hardin slipped his hand inside Joc's brismil suit to the place where the scale was held tight to his skin and wrenched the scale free.

Joc blinked, realizing his armor and half the conduit tapping into the dragon's magic were gone.

Hardin, now wearing the dark blue brismil armor, tossed Joc aside as the mage released a shrill, "No!" Hardin pulled the sword free, pushing his hand against the dragon's side to keep the light from escaping.

Lark channeled the fae magic down onto the dome of light, shattering it with a bolt of black lightning. The wards fell apart, and she struck again, this time aiming the force at Joc. Spikes of black lightning, darker than the night around them, pushed through the veil like spears. They lanced through Joc, pinning him to the dais floor. The five staves of darkness pushed through his chest, and then the power-hungry mage twitched, and went limp.

Lark now worked to tame the magic and force the torrent of power back through to the fae realm. She closed the veil. Heat sizzled against her chest from the necklace, a pain she welcomed as the cost of the mage's death.

All around them, Morsythians slowed, looking around as though they were waking from a dream. Venrick and Sasja also scanned their surroundings as though seeing where they were for the first time.

Lark slowly climbed onto the dais where the unbonded dragon lay on the ground, the light no longer flowing from his body. Hardin knelt at his side, the purple light dripped from within the brismil, then winked out.

"No, the Hyalite's power?" Barrik said, fear lacing his voice. "It wasn't meant to pass onto the dragon." He trained his brismil spear point to Hardin and shouted, "Do you realize what you've done?"

Hardin dopped Stormbreaker and the scale.

Barrik cocked his arm back, aiming to lance Hardin through the chest. Lark surged forward. She moved between Hardin and Barrik as he thrust the spear. She felt a sharp pain burn through her side. The brismil slid out of her, Barrik hesitating. In that moment Lark reached for her power.

38

REMEMBER

Lark ignored the fresh pain in her side and tugged on the line anchoring her to the fae realm. A rush of power flooded her whole being. It spread from her necklace, swelling out, and warming the rest of her body. Dark energy sped from her palms, slamming into a stone wall and breaking through. Barrik summoned stone slab after slab from the ground, using them as shields to block Lark's power.

"We've been through this before, Ella," Barrik said.

He muttered a quickly worded incantation. The ground under her feet began crumbling away. A dark abyss opened up, forcing Lark to scramble away. Pain flared through her arm as she ran to escape the earth falling away behind her. She called again on the fae bond and forced a bolt of black lightning down over Barrik.

Barrik shifted focus, quickly summoning a ward shield. The lightning struck, sending dark fissures across his energy shield. The shield held.

"Your powers from the dark fae aren't going to defeat me, Ella," he shouted. "I've been there, faced the rulers of the dark fae at the Night Court before. You would know this if you would just remember."

Lark escaped the chasm, nearing Hardin, Venrick and Sasja. "Lark," Hardin called. He had the brismil scabbard in his hand and threw it to Lark. She caught it with her good arm and forced herself to ignore the pain from her injuries. She drew Stormbreaker, power clearing her vision and giving her the energy to continue. Hardin fumbled with the scale, attempting to get it to Lark. Before he could, however, Barrik attacked.

He came in fast, angling his spear to deliver a blow. As he did, a hazy afterimage appeared, like a second spear, trailing past the first. The image doubled, multiplying as he arched the spear around to the apex of his wind-up.

Lark met his brismil spear with Stormbreaker. The initial exchange hit hard, sending vibrations into her hand. Her block was enough to dispel a single strike, but the afterimages collided one on top of the other, passing their energy into his swing. The added momentum of a hundred spear strikes carried through, slamming into Stormbreaker.

Lark cried out as the strike knocked the blade from her hand and sent her flying. She hit a stone wall that appeared out of nowhere, summoned into existence by Barrik's control over the earth. Her back crushed into the earthen wall. She slid to the ground in a daze.

She was seeing double as Barrik approached, his brismil spear pointed toward her. "Remember this, Ella? Remember why you gave up fighting? You could never defeat me."

Barrik whispered an incantation. Granite vines shot out of the ground, clasping around her legs and arms to pin her in place.

Venrick and Hardin streaked across the dais. Venrick slammed his sword into the back of Barrik's helmet. The blade shattered as he carried through with a war cry. Hardin pushed past Venrick, shouldering with the weight of the brismil armor into Barrik. Barrik stumbled, tossing Hardin down. Barrik summoned his power. Hardin rose and Venrick wrapped his arms around the rider's armor. Barrik spoke another quickly worded spell, summoning his power. Venrick and Hardin sank into the earth up to their knees. The ground hardened, trapping them.

Barrik walked unharmed away from Venrick, leaving him and Hardin struggling to break free. He held the spear tip level with Lark's chest, looking at her thoughtfully.

"You enslaved Nix," Lark growled, blood weeping from her side, her broken arm so swollen the skin felt like it was going to split. Despite the pain, she kept fighting, calling on her powers. "You killed her!" she shouted, forcing the dark energy to form around the granite vines that bound her. Tendrils of black seeped out of her to form around the bonds he'd created. Her power squeezed the stone, cracking it apart. Lark pushed through, forcing her limbs free.

"Think harder, Ella. I didn't enslave Nix, you did. You were the one who hauled her from the Night Court to our world kicking and screaming."

"No," Lark insisted, rising to her feet. Feeling the Night Court's magic channeling through her. "That's not true," she said, casting a line of energy like a black stave at him.

Barrik blocked the strike, letting it lodge into a stone shield. "You were the one who taught us how the dark fae can be used like tools. You showed us how to raise the rimeshade with the coming Flashover. These rimeshades are ancient beings capable of more magical agility than any magi, elf, orc, or dwarf. You showed us the rimeshade aren't just frost wielding shades. In numbers, they're capable of taking over this realm."

"Lies," she hissed.

"The motivations of their kind are not as evil as you've

been led to believe. Their strength is born of the fae. They're capable of go beyond the limits of what a dragon can bear, even with a rider to help them control their magic. If you need proof of what the dark fae's powers can do look no further than what you've done tonight without your dragon bond."

"Don't listen to him, Lark. You're stronger than he is," Venrick said.

"Venrick," Barrik tsked. "You're a pathetic replacement for Tel Roan. Now there was a Paragon who posed a real challenge. One who was truly of the old order and believed in what Lamar was fighting for, freedom from the oppressive Northern Kingdoms. His desire for Lamar to control the Everburning Forest was misguided, but pure."

Lark shot another spike at the rider. It glanced off his shields, digging into the ground near Venrick's feet. When the energy faded, Lark noticed the hole it left at Venrick's feet. Lark switched her focus, peppering the ground around Venrick.

"Ella!" Barrik shouted, sending one of his ghostly extensions out at her. The hand gripped around her throat, lifting her off the ground.

She punched at it. Her fist passed through, the earthy debris collecting, becoming more solid by the second.

Venrick tore his feet from the stone around him. He grabbed the Morsythian blade laying discarded on the dais nearby. As he did, Barrik slammed the butt end of his spear into Venrick's side. Venrick doubled over. He stabbed weakly, limping on his battered thigh to catch himself from falling. Barrik caught Venrick again in the ribs with the blunt end of his spear. Venrick dropped to all fours. Venrick struggled to rally another swing. Barrik planted his foot on his back, rolling him with an effortless kick. He pinned Venrick there, his armored boot resting on Venrick's chest.

Lark struggled, coughing to be able to breath. "Let him

go," she rasped. She struck at the arm with her fae power, tried to send tendrils of the energy around it as she had before, but each time they slipped off. Barrik now shielded them with newly formed wards.

The rider spun his spear, driving it down and stopping the tip of the brismil a hair before entering Venrick's neck. Barrik turned his helmet toward Lark and said, "Remember, Ella. Remember and I'll let him live."

"I can't remember anything," she shouted.

"Yes, you can. Focus on the bond with your dragon and remember."

"The bond with my dragon? He's not..." Her line of thought went to the other times when she had used magic. Each time ended with a different result. She had to speak to cast it, like Barrik did by wielding the earth. This fae power, however, required no verbal commands.

"Your dragon is alive. He has suffered greatly in the knowledge that you chose to use the bond you had with him to form a bond with another dragon. Riders were meant to share their powers with only one dragon. If I were to put Killaborden through that kind of misery, he would want me dead. He would kill me himself rather than let me share our bond with another dragon."

"I didn't know," Lark whispered.

"It's not your fault," Venrick shouted.

The rider pressed the blade down, cutting through his light armor with ease.

"No," Lark said, her throat closing. She struggled to focus. Struggled to search for a connection to that dragon bond. She was slowly suffocating. Barrik was going to kill Venrick if she didn't remember.

"Search yourself, Ella; find the truth, or you both die."

"Help me," she gasped.

"What was that?"

"Help me remember," she said.

"I thought you'd never ask," he said, lowering Lark down to her feet and loosening his grip on her neck.

"I'll let you uncover my lost memories, but not before you let my friends go free," Lark said.

"You were always prone to showing mercy. I thought I drove it out of you, yet you always seem to come back to it," he said.

Barrik lifted his spear, allowing Venrick to rise. Hardin removed the brismil armor and was struggling to squeeze his feet from the stone. Sasja helped him, the cut on her neck still trickling blood. Barrik spoke, manipulating his control over the stone and Hardin came free.

From outside the fortress, they could hear alarms ringing. It the sounded like fighting, again. Red Lodge was summoning a force to fight...

Cheyanne is here, she realized.

A bellowing roar sounded overhead and a moment later dragon fire splashed down around Barrik. Venrick, Hardin and Sasja backed away, toward Lark. Barrik's black dragon launched, colliding with Ingamar. They snapped and snarled, clawing at one another as they crashed down near the dais.

"Stop!" Lark cried.

Barrik's dragon pinned Ingamar to the ground, though he refrained from delivering a killing blow. Slowly, Killaborden released his jaw, backing away from Ingamar.

"Let them go," Lark said, clutching the stab wound in her side.

"For you, Ella, I will do this, but don't test me," Barrik said.

Ingamar bared his teeth as he moved in to stand next to Venrick. Hardin joined them, dropping the scale at Lark's feet before leaving.

"No," Barrik said. "Take the brismil scale and sword."

"What of the dragon?" Hardin asked.

"The one Joc killed?" Barrik replied.

"He is not dead," Hardin said.

Barrik gave a nod.

"Lark," Venrick said, his face contorted in pain. His body was broken and battered, and he was clearly unable to continue to fight. "Don't do this. We can beat him."

Lark shook her head. "I can't lose you. I won't let you, Hardin, or anyone else sacrifice themselves for me. All of you got what you came for. Now I need to get what I came for, answers."

"But," Venrick said.

Hardin and Sasja blocked Venrick. They forced him onto the dragon. He was too weak to stop the two of them. Ingamar walked with the three of them to where the wounded dragon lay. He stooped his head, dropping a tear from his eye on the dragon's side. The scale sealed. The dragon's chest rose with breath. He lifted himself up and they walked out of the throne room, the whole time Venrick continued to voice his frustration.

"Now," Barrik said, turning to Lark.

Lark opened the veil to the fae realm, pulled on the power and channeled it through her. Her vision blurred for a moment, her head felt light from the blood loss and energy drain before she was able to focus on her target. Black spines forced outward from her at Barrik.

"Bah," he growled as they peppered the stony shield wall he once again created around himself. Several of the spines lanced into the shield, becoming wedged there. "This was not what we agreed on, Ella," he scolded.

Barrik muttered his counter to Lark's silent attack. Stone debris scattered around the dais lifted, swirling around them so quickly it was all Lark could do to keep from being struck by flying rocks. She lost sight of him and moments later strong arms wrapped around her. Barrik held her firmly, pressing his gauntleted palm to her face. Through the cracks in his fingers, she saw Killaborden stomping over to her.

"Remember," he said as the dragon blew a sulphury gas over her.

Lark's vision blurred, the fog evaporating from her mind. The armored palm cupping her face lifted, Barrik's face appearing before her. Lark felt a needle driving into her mind. She tried to resist it, but the probe dug deeper. Lark struggled. Her body did not respond. She blinked, forcing her eyes closed in an attempt to focus on blocking his mental probe.

"Look at me!" he shouted, shaking her face. He peeled her eyes open to stare up at him. "I want you to remember everything from before. I want you to tell me why. Why did you betray me, Marcella?"

That name sizzled as the mental probe cleared the haze around it. *Ella. Marcella, she was the rider, known to the rest of the world as Marcel... No, that can't be!*

"That's it. Realize the truth. Own your memories as they come back," Barrik said.

The probe dug deeper. Images appeared, flashing in segments before forming into whole memories. They appeared to her as though they were happening right then.

In the memory, an older man waved her over. "Marcella, come here."

He was dressed in regal copper clothing and sat on a lavish throne. Nordraven banners hung on the walls of the grand room around them. A cast of Nobles and soldiers all bearing the Skol crest crowded the room.

She stepped up onto the dais to her grandfather's chair. She tripped over her feet on the way up the stairs. She wasn't used to the larger boots she had yet to grow into as a youth. She stood before the King as he held out an open chest holding a glowing Hyalite.

"For centuries the Kingdoms of our world have fought over the powers that allow us to bond with dragons. It wasn't until our forefathers formed the Northern Alliance, forging Nordraven into four united Kingdoms that we stood a chance of controlling the Everburning Forest," he said.

She absorbed the history her grandfather, the King of Skol, was recounting. At the time, she remembered truly believing that their people were the rightful owners of the region where firestorms produced gifts of power from the gods.

"Do you know what this is?" the King asked her.

She nodded slowly.

"It is your birthright," he said. The King snapped his fingers. A man in brismil armor led a small black dragon on a chain to the side of the throne. The dragon was no taller than she was. A hatchling.

Her memories suddenly flashed forward, speeding through the time she grew up with the unbonded hatchling, learning its behaviors, its personality. Then the ceremony where her grandfather, one of the four Kings of a unified Nordraven, cracked open the Hyalite. The power inside leached out into the dragon. She held her palm against him, and the dragon passed his power into her, forming their bond.

Time sped forward, through her training. How she discovered a pool beneath the forest that led into the fae realm. How she befriended a fire fae, supposedly a creature of evil and bad luck. Together, they formed their bond in secret, away from the influences of her elders. What she had to do to betray another Nordraven Paragon, making a deal with the rulers of the dark fae, the Night Court, to allow her fire fae to travel in and out of Sataran. But it was worth the cost to keep dark fae worse than the rimeshade trapped in their realm. Lark remembered what she and Nix would be forced to do in exchange at the next Flashover. Lark returned from the fae realm to her dragon changed, now responsible for sharing two bonds and having access to a whole new set of powers.

The memories ran on into her young adult years, extended beyond that of other humans. How her grandfather sent her to train with Barrik, the best dragonrider the North had ever seen, until she surpassed him.

Time flashed forward again. She was at her grandfather's side. This time, he looked ancient. Run down. So much weaker than he had been when she was a youth.

"Marcella," he said in a raspy voice.

"I've told you before, it's just Ella now."

"Ella isn't what they'll call you when you graduate and enter into your father's services."

"I thought I was meant for the Northern fight. To battle the rimeshade that are plaguing the northern reaches of our neighboring Kingdoms, Fjern and Elderice."

"No, the war against the rimeshade can be won in time. Their threat is not as pressing as Lamar's effort to drive us from collecting another Hyalite. You will serve your people better by becoming Skol's next Paragon."

"My skills will be wasted. I'll spend most of my time searching the firestorms when I could be put to better use with our armies."

"You are exactly what we need to ensure Nordraven continues to collect Hyalites."

"I could help bring an end to this war, for good, then turn our full might on the rimeshade. Why?"

"Lamar will continue to raise armies as long as they can continue to collect Hyalites. They will not commit their dragonriders to the war, instead securing their most coveted fortresses and using their most skilled fighters to collect more power from the forest. Your task is to become the most formidable dragonrider Lamar has ever faced. That is how we will win this war, by collecting more power than Lamar ever can."

"Is this order coming from my father, the Acting King of Skol, or my Grandfather who still sits on the throne?"

"We are both your elders. You will obey or be stripped of your dragon."

"Yes, Grandfather."

"By becoming Skol's Paragon, you'll allow your cousins time to develop the armies they need to crush Lamar and turn their sights on the rimeshade of the far North. You will no longer be known to the world as you are now."

He presented Lark with a matching onyx black brismil scale and sword set.

"With this brismil armor and sword, you will become death from above. The South will fear you, but they can't know you are Ella, my granddaughter. They must believe you are another rider. For the sake of our people, you will not go into battle unless you wear this. You will never take it off in front of anyone outside these halls. You will be known to the world as Marcel Heartfell."

"This is not what father wants for me," she said.

"While I live, your father has yet to truly become King. You will do as your kingdom commands. Become Marcel. Drive the fear of the gods into the Paragons of the South."

Again, time sped forward. She was fighting along the Southern border against Lamar. Facing troops sent by their King's Paragons. Holding their lands but never taking more when she could easily have flown east and wreaked havoc on Lamar's armies. Frustration in Nordraven grew as she focused their attacks at the Southern border while reports of rimeshade, frost wielding shades in the distant North, continued to fell Nordraven Paragons sent to squelch them.

Then her grandfather died. She felt the hope she had had for her future under her father's rule. She would be sent

North to find out why rimeshade were a plague that would not go away. Then her father's birthright to be King of Skol was challenged by her cousin, Greggor. He wanted to make a deal with the King of Lamar. A deal behind the back of the eastern kings of Fjern and Elderice, ensuring that the two western Kingdoms of Nordraven would split with Lamar all of the Hyalites the Everburning Forest produced. They fought in single combat, her cousin winning and killing her father. She was ordered to go back to the South, where the fight over Hyalites with Lamar's Paragons continued.

It wasn't until months later that she intercepted a damaging letter between her cousin, the King of Skol, and King Agadorn of Lamar. She brought it to Barrik, unsure what her cousin would do to her if she revealed that she knew.

"You must keep this information private. The eastern Kings would turn on ours if they knew," Barrik told her.

"Fjern and Elderice are the two kingdoms hit the hardest by this perpetual war with Lamar. How can your son go behind their back like this? Deciding which Paragon will win the Hyalite before the storm has even started? Is this a game for them?" Lark demanded.

"This is best for Skol. With Wintermire's help, we're collecting twice as many Hyalites and Yogos as ever."

"Because King Agadorn is letting us take them?"

"It's not like every time a Hyalite is produced we're deciding which Kingdom will have a chance at it. Only the ones where Skol, Wintermire and Lamar arrive at first," Barrik said.

"It does, though, you must see. You let Lamar take power away from us, then they purposefully let us win the next few storms? Where are all these Yogos and Hyalites going?"

"We're making a reserve for when the Flashover comes. We have it protected; it's safe," Barrik said.

"You're depriving half of our country the right to benefit

from Hyalites and Yogos. The half of Nordraven that is fighting Lamar on the ground."

"That is where the war must be fought, the Everburning Forest south of Skol and Wintermire burns too frequently and intensely. This is how it must be if we're going to make it through the Flashover and come out on top," Barrik stated flatly.

"I can't believe this. You and your son ignore the threat from the North. We could be using those powers to suppress the rimeshade before the Flashover has a chance to make things worse. Then we could use them to win this war against Lamar. Instead, you would have thousands of people die so that our Kingdom will have a better stockpile of wealth when the Night Court chooses to attack Sataran."

"It's how we as a Kingdom will survive," Barrik growled.

"I'll bring this to the other Kings," Lark said.

"And start a civil war, now? That will destroy Nordraven. The other kingdoms would fall. But if we do this, Skol will be able to protect them when the darkness comes."

"Your goal is to have Skol to be an empire over all others, isn't it? Is that what Greggor is trying to do, set us up to take over the North?"

"We must rule with an iron fist if we're going to survive the Flashover. The Night Court has had five hundred years to prepare for this. The rimeshade will welcome their cousins from the fae realm and, if we're not ready, we'll be taken out like the rest of the world," he insisted.

"Which is why we should be fighting the rimeshade now and not waiting," Lark said, trying to take the letter back from Barrik.

Barrik uttered a word, and the letter turned to stone. The writing vanished into a slate of smooth granite. "Don't be the catalyst to bring on the North's demise. Think of our people," Barrik said as Lark stormed off.

In the empty throne room, Lark's memories flashed by more rapidly now. Her reaction to this horrible truth became her violence when fighting in firestorms. She let herself go too far, killing any Paragon from either side of the conflict who challenged her. She couldn't control where every Hyalite or Yogo went, but those she won went to Fjern and Elderice. King Greggor's outrage drove Barrik to confront her time and again.

"Stop this rebellion you're playing at and put it behind you. Do this and your future will be secure. Greggor will not allow you to continue as a dragonrider if you don't back off. He'll make me put an end to it, and I will. You know I'm right," Barrik warned.

"You're right about one thing," she replied. "I never want to start a civil war in the North by letting the other Kings know. But I won't stop fighting anyone who comes near me in a firestorm. That is my arena and Greggor can't do anything to stop me there. Every time I go out into the Everburning Forest with White Eye, I'm showing the world that I'm not caged by a dictator. I'm representing the people of the North."

"This won't end well for you, Ella," Barrik warned.

Lark realized then that she'd become the very thing her grandfather wanted. She was death from above. But she was fine with this moniker as long as it meant that she was trying to put an end to the corruption that had infiltrated their politics. She needed to stop the pre-determined allocation of Hyalites before the greedy became the most powerful.

Her memories rolled forward to her first meeting with Cheyanne in a truly contested battle for a Hyalite. This elf Paragon from Gambria was not playing by the rules. She intrigued Lark when she spread the power of the Hyalites she won among those who followed her, rather than turning them over to Lamar's King. Those actions quickly forced Cheyanne out of the role of Paragon and into the role of instructor at a Paragon training Academy.

Time passed again and Lark's focus shifted to the growing threat of the rimeshade that the Kings of Skol and Wintermire continued to ignore. Morsythians were being displaced into regions of Skol they had agreed to leave centuries earlier. Whispers of a rebel force hiding in the Everburning Forest came to her attention. This group was trying to expose Lamar's and Skol's corruption, their plot to exclusively collect all of the Sapphires and Hyalites and keep the power for the elite few.

Then Lark began meeting with the Morsythians, the people most affected by the rimeshade attacks in northeastern Nordraven. Lark made a promise to help deliver Hyalites to them to create Morsythian dragonriders and give them the ability to defend themselves when the rest of Nordraven wouldn't.

Barrik's probe burned through, bringing up the memories of how she planned to rob her mentor. How she persuaded one of his servants to steal a most valuable object that had been trusted to his care. The astral lathe, a round object that forecasted firestorms. It was said to be from the original twelve dragons who came from the Light Court in the fae realm and settled here in Sataran. It foretold which storms would contain power and which god was producing that power.

The memories were painful, but Barrik's probe pushed on. Now she was plotting to betray her King, using the predictions offered by the astral lathe to steal a Hyalite. This was one of the most powerful Hyalites to have been produced since the last flashover nearly five hundred years earlier.

On the day of the firestorm, she went to meet with the elf leading the rebels, Cheyanne. But somehow Barrik had learned of their plan. He burned Cheyanne's home to the ground. Lark watched it burn, her rage building. The

Nordraven army had already been deceived and was too far off the mark to intervene. But Barrik. Barrik was coming for her.

She tried to throw him off, but he came prepared. He was dressed in the armor of a Paragon of the Vermillion Keep. Of course, Tel Roan was at the fire. His senses were keen when it came to the Hyalites. Lark tried to stop Barrik, but some chilling energy had prevented her. Tel's death was unavoidable, a result of Barrik's doing. Lark had to put her dragon and the Hyalite first. She couldn't save them all.

Then she and White Eye had slain Barrik's dragon. One that he'd been warging into while Killaborden, his bonded, hung back. Barrik knew she was stronger. But in the last moments of their battle, when she had broken the elven spells of Tel's chest to retrieve the Hyalite, she cast her spell at Barrik a moment too late. His hit first.

The probe slid out of her mind. Lark stumbled from the shock of so much information. "No," she said, horrified by the unfettered history of her past blending with everything that had happened to her following Barrik's spell.

"Yes," Barrik said.

She shook her head, struggling to sort out her emotions. "No. This can't be. This isn't right. I am not the enemy. You are," she said.

"You brainwashed yourself when you trusted that little pest of a boy in the forest village. Nix did nothing to help, which is why I needed to cage her and keep her from you," he said.

"I didn't know who I was," she said.

"You do now, don't you, Ella? You can see it all. You are Marcel. You are your own enemy. Stop this ridiculous crusade of yours and come home."

"I was never Marcel," she said.

"I trained you to become Marcel. You are what your

kingdom needs, a weapon. Come with me. Reunite with your dragon," he said.

She considered it now. She hated the King of Lamar. If he had it his way, he'd continue the war even if it didn't need to be fought, paying his Paragons to be actors in a grand show to the rest of the world. Her cousin, King Greggor of Skol, was no better. He used his armies and Paragons to fight to the death for his profit while others in the North suffered. And Barrik knew. Barrik didn't try to change or stop it as Lark had. Barrik was the corruption's greatest champion.

"What are you doing?" he asked.

"You said you wanted to know why I betrayed you," she replied.

"I saw why you betrayed me. You did it for the Morsythians. Do you know what they could do to us if they had that kind of power? That's why we needed to control them. We couldn't beat the Morsythian if they gained dragonriders, just like we can't beat the rimeshade and their corruptive influence," he said.

"You can't know that. Even if you did, what are you suggesting, that Skol either controls the world or join those who seek to dominate it?" Lark gawked.

"That's the Nordraven way. You see that now, don't you?"

"No. You're wrong, Barrik. You're wrong about everything. I didn't betray you for the Morsythians. You saw it through my memories and you're still wrong. You've been wrong since the day you failed my father and betrayed your King's wishes. The day you allowed that backstabbing fraud you call a son to take my father's throne." She was shouting now. Gaining more certainty on where she stood in this larger conflict.

"Enough!" he snapped, power coiling around him.

Lark felt a sense of calm washing over her. Whether it was the loss of blood, the blinding pain, or the crippling expenditure of energy she'd used, she felt euphoric. She started laughing and said, "Underneath it all, you're a coward, Barrik."

"Careful, Ella. Push me too far and I'll do to you what I did your precious fire fae," he said.

There was something familiar about the state of mind she'd passed into. Something that gave her strength and she realized something.

"You know, the thing about fire fae is, they're just like the phoenix. They always rise from the ashes," she said, drawing on a new sense of power.

Barrik backed away, Killaborden stooping his head alongside him. The dragon peered at her, his glossy white eyes like two clouded spheres of mystery. Lark saw the dragon anew with the foresight of her past, and she recognized him with shocking clarity.

It's you, she projected to him, though Barrik had ahold of his mind through warging.

Lark turned to Barrik, and said, "Nix may be regenerating in the fae realm and my powers are weakened without her, but so are yours. You've been warging into two dragons all evening. The unbonded was desperate to break free. I can only imagine the toll it has taken on your powers in your attempt to control a much stronger dragon, like White Eye."

Barrik's frustration flashed across his face. He twitched, and for a second, the dragon she'd assumed was Killaborden changed slightly. His eyes cleared for an instant, exposing the ring of gold around the white before Barrik took control again. As he did, Lark felt the confirmation she'd already known after seeing her dragon through her memories. Barrik hadn't flown Killaborden to Red Lodge.

"Keeping White Eye hidden from me for this long must be wearing you down. You're the strongest mage capable of warging in the North, but this time you've spread yourself too thin, Barrik. You can't control the will of two dragons."

Lark fully realized the sensation stirring in her bond. The familiar warmth of power vibrating through the part of her that had been missing for so long. A power thousands of times stronger than the thin line tying her to the fae realm. She opened the flow of magic, the power of a god pulsing through her.

"Anak Nye." She cast the spell with complete understanding. The power poured forth. Celestial light, bright white and pure, soared from her.

Barrik countered, funneling earth in to block it. Lark's power peeled apart the shields Barrik offered. Stone overlapped itself but she pushed harder. Barrik's shields fell faster than he could replace them. His legs shook from the effort to keep them coming.

"You can't defeat me," he said, dropping to a knee.

She pressed forward, her new sense of strength fading quickly. "You will never defeat me," she forced out, vision blurring.

Lark forced more of herself into the spell, drawing on more than just the dragon's power, but her connection to the fae realm. The starlight ripped through Barrik's shields, blasting his wards apart, and sending a ripple of bright light throughout the dais. The ray of light cut through the fortress walls, sheering them in two before dissipating into the night.

Lark staggered, willing her eyes to stay open, searching for Barrik. Downdrafts pounded the demolished throne room. Lark dropped to her knees, exhaustion taking over.

"Anaci," she whispered, ending the spell with a final whisper.

The flow of magic stopped. Lark's body gave out and she fell in a heap on her side. She lay there broken and bleeding,

Barrik was nowhere in sight. She rolled onto her back; the world spun around her as she struggled to cling to consciousness. She stared up at the vastness of the night sky, looking for the stars.

But a deep blackness blotted out the sky. For a moment Lark thought she'd already passed out. A large black dragon with white eyes rimmed in gold, descended. Lark smiled. She knew he was himself once again. White Eye's intentions came through as though they were her own thoughts. Their bond was whole, their wards strengthened, and he exuded an overwhelming need to protect her.

White Eye's wings closed in around her. She experienced a feeling of weightlessness as he picked her up, cradling her gently in his claws.

Lark was sure she'd died, but the cold northern air kept waking her, the pain of her injuries shouting that she was still in the land of the living. She let her head fall limp, hair blowing in the wind as she cracked her eyes open. Hundreds of feet below, a force of elves, humans, and dwarves were fighting Red Lodge's orc troops in the forest. Lark finally knew who she was and what she really stood for as she closed her eyes, falling asleep to the steady beating of her dragon's wings.

39

NOT ALONE

Venrick limped into the tent at Cheyanne's rebel base of operations in the Everburning Forest. The days of healing had somewhat mended his bruised and broken bones, but not his fear for where Lark had gone. He pulled the wooden chair out from the long table. To his left, Ezra gave him a tight-lipped nod as he joined the meeting with Cheyanne's rebel alliance. Cheyanne stood at the head of the table. A map of Sataran covered the wall behind her. The other leaders of the alliance: several humans, two orcs, a few more dwarves, and elves, were waiting patiently for her to begin.

Venrick shifted. In the days following the battle at the fortress in Red Lodge, he had been physically attended to by an elven healer, but his stiffness and pain lingered. Hardin and Sasja joined the group in the canvas tent, taking seats across from him.

"Now that we're all here, we need to debrief. We took a massive risk by exposing ourselves to the Nordraven troops in Red Lodge. I want us all to be on the same page before we discuss what to do moving forward in exposing the rimeshade corruption that is taking over the Kings and their trusted advisory and council members," Cheyanne started.

A muscular elf with long, light brown hair and sharp green eyes spoke up, "I want to know what happened to the dragonrider we fought to free. All of us know what happened outside the fortress in facing the orcs and helping the freed Morsythians escape. But where our communication is lacking in understanding is regarding what actually was transpiring inside the fortress. What happened to the Hyalite? Why did all the surviving Morsythians flee, abandoning the fortress, and agreeing to join us? Where did Barrik escape to? And what happened to this woman known as Lark?"

Venrick's chest tightened at the mention of her name. That was the person they had come to know her as. The revelation that she was the infamous Nordraven dragonrider known as Marcel Heartfell came as a shock. Venrick knew in his heart which person she really was. She wasn't Marcel, Ella, or any other alias for that matter. To him, she would always be Lark, no matter which side of the Everburning Forest she chose to fight for.

"We don't have any updates on where she has been taken," Cheyanne answered. "Our tracking charms have failed so far, meaning she either warded against them or she is no longer with us."

"Lark is still out there. They couldn't have traveled far given her condition," Venrick said with confidence.

"She was taken away by White Eye, her dragon. They could be anywhere by now." Cheyanne said.

"Not anywhere. They can't go back to Skol or Wintermire. Lamar is hunting for her. She has to be somewhere here in the forest," Venrick reasoned.

"Is it true, what the Morsythians are saying about her?" a dwarf asked.

"Lark sacrificed herself so that we could escape. She gave her life for us," Sasja answered.

"Does that mean she's not one of the most feared dragonriders in Nordraven history, Marcel Heartfell?" the dwarf asked.

"Word has spread that Marcel has returned. My sources in Skol say King Greggor announced Marcel's return," the mossy-toned orc replied. "It seems like too much of a coincidence that this mystery rider regains her memories, disappears, and days later the Northern Kings announce Marcel's return."

"Lark never acted anything like Marcel Heartfell," Venrick said earnestly.

"She could've been faking it the whole time. How do we know *Lark* isn't out there right now plotting to destroy everything this alliance has worked toward?" Cheyanne asked, looking him in the eye.

"We don't know that. We don't even know if Lark survived. The dragon that took her was the same one Barrik flew in on," Ezra interjected, trying to disrupt the stare down.

"Barrik was controlling both dragons, through warging. Hundreds of your soldiers said they saw the dragon's eyes when they left. They had the golden ring around them when they flew east over your forces. It was White Eye, not Killaborden," Venrick said.

"Lark is alive and she's not going to betray us. Even if she was Marcel, whatever happened to her, changed her. She may have been fierce, but Lark wasn't a ruthless assassin. Her intentions were not that different from those of this group, trying to root out corruption. She had strong morals, and that kind of thing isn't something you can fake," Hardin argued.

Cheyanne sighed, "This is a moot point since we don't know what happened to the rider we knew as Lark. Until we learn more, we will table this discussion."

"Maybe we should hear the whole story, from their points

of view," the orc suggested, pointing first at Hardin, then Ezra, Venrick and Sasja.

Venrick nodded in agreement, then helped fill in his parts of the story as Hardin, Ezra, and Sasja recapped the events leading up to their escape from Red Lodge with help from Cheyanne's forces.

"What happened to that Hyalite's powers?" an elf asked.

"They were taken up by the dragon and her chosen rider," Cheyanne answered.

"Her chosen rider? The dragon was stabbed while the Magus attempted to claim the magic of both a god and a dragon," Venrick said.

"But Lark killed this power-hungry Magus before he could complete the transfer. Hardin stopped the flow of energy out of the dragon and the dragon instinctively reversed it, drinking in the power. Hardin was the one the dragon chose in that moment to bond with. The dragon passed the powers to him," Cheyanne nodded toward Hardin.

"Him? The Ward Walker with no training is the one who bonded with the dragon?" an elf said.

"A dragon's choice to bond with a person, making them their rider, is based on more factors at the time than their training or background in magic," Cheyanne said.

"What powers does he have now?" an orc asked. "This Hyalite was said to be of rare quality."

"The powers haven't manifested," Hardin answered, looking a bit sheepish or confused.

"It can take time, sometime months to show which of the gods the Hyalite originated from," Cheyanne said. "Since the Hyalite split between the brismil and his dragon at the time of bonding, we don't know what to expect. No one has ever been bound to a Hyalite in the way this Doranian was."

"I thought you were stuck in a room, locked inside while the others faced the Magus?" the orc demanded.

"I broke through Joc's wards and provided the distraction Lark needed to destroy him and stop him from taking the Hyalite's power for himself," Hardin explained, lifting his shoulder and holding palms up over the table. "Lark's fire fae returned to the room to free me after Barrik thought he had killed her. She set me free before she went back to, in her words, *wake White Eye.*"

"Nix got you out of the room? Ironic, don't you think, given that you're a Ward Walker," Venrick asked with a smirk.

"I mentioned it, didn't I?" Hardin said, scratching his head. "Nix let me out and told me to find Lark."

"And you all stopped a rogue Magus from turning the wrath of the rimeshade on the rest of the continent," Cheyanne said matter-of-factly, preparing to change the subject. "Now, we need to prepare for the retaliation that's to come. For years we've amassed our numbers under the noses of Nordraven and Lamar. We've just exposed ourselves with this show of force in Red Lodge and effectively destroying one of their fortresses. Nordraven forces in Red Lodge, the local militia of orcs who rallied against us once the Morsythians were free of their curse, will know we now have two dragons. Barrik's knowledge about Hardin being bonded with the juvenile dragon will become widespread soon enough. Once Nordraven knows, Lamar will know, too. Our operatives recruiting and helping us with resupply aren't going to be safe in either kingdom. Our base of operations here in the forest is warded and I believe will remain hidden, but now both kingdoms will be sending their Paragons out to find us."

"We need to find Lark," Venrick said.

"I can't commit any resources to that; we're strapped as it is," Cheyanne said.

"I need to find her," Venrick clarified. "We know she went north. I'll start there."

"There's a more urgent task I had in mind for you,

Venrick. Ingamar can't be spared to go looking for Lark either," Cheyanne said.

"She's right, Ven. He would attract too much attention. If you were attacked, they could extract the location of Cheyanne's base from you. We can't stop you from leaving, but we need to keep this place and the forces here hidden from Nordraven and Lamar," Ezra said.

"I won't argue with you, Venrick. There is more at risk with protecting our organization than just your life. We have learned secrets about a dark force that is growing in the far north. If left unchecked, our world is going to have much larger problems by the end of the year when the Flashover comes," Cheyanne said.

"I will not rest until I find Lark," Venrick said, his determination unwavering despite the risks. He couldn't turn a blind eye to Lark, not after what they'd been through. He would be careful. He was going after her no matter what.

NEXT BOOK IN THIS SERIES
A DRAGONRIDER'S LAST HOPE

Coming Summer 2025

With her dragon finally at her side again, Lark should feel relief; but nothing is as it should be. Bone-weary from her brutal confrontation with Joc and Barrik in Red Lodge, she can barely maintain their connection as White Eye veers north, deeper into Nordraven territory against her wishes. His urgency drowns out her protests, his mind fixed on something far more vital than reuniting her with her companions.

As the frozen landscape unfolds beneath them, they stumble upon a hidden truth that shatters everything they know about the coming Flashover. The threat the rimeshade pose is far more pressing than Lamar and Nordraven ever knew. Magic itself stands on a precipice of transformation. Lark. exhausted, alone, and far from those she trusts, must decide whether to embrace or fight against the world that's taking shape around her.

For the latest book launch information and updates follow me on:

Amazon.com - Author A J Walker
Facebook - A J Walker Author
Instagram - @ajwalkerauthor

LEAVE A REVIEW

ENJOY THIS BOOK? YOU CAN MAKE A BIG DIFFERENCE BY LEAVING A REVIEW...

Reviews by readers like you are by far the most powerful tool in my cache when it comes down to receiving attention for my books. As an independent author, I don't have the same budget the New York publishers have and can't take out a full-page ad in the newspaper or have an entire poster display on the subway; not yet at least.

What I do have, that is far more powerful and effective than paid ads and something that those big-time publishers would kill to get their hands on. It's **a group of loyal and committed readers like you**.

Valued and honest reviews by my readers will help see my books into the hands of other readers who would enjoy discovering these stories.

If you've enjoyed this book, I would greatly appreciate it if you could spend just a few minutes of your time and leave a review (it can be as short as you want) on the book's Amazon page. Simply go to my amazon.com author page (A-J-Walker/Author), scroll to find the book you wish to review, then select: leave customer review.

Thank you very much.

ACKNOWLEDGMENTS

Words fail to express the depth of my gratitude to Susan, my editor extraordinaire, whose developmental insight and meticulous copy-editing transform this, and every manuscript she helps me with in ways I never could've imagined alone. The story you hold in your hands exists in its current form because of her unwavering dedication, brilliant mind, and willingness to push me beyond my comfort zone. Susan, you always see the potential in these pages when even I muddle them with typos, completely wondering on the timeline, and providing unfocused character descriptions. Thank you for believing in this world and these characters as much as I do.

To my family, who sometimes must deal with me being a 'space cadet' as I often find myself wandering the landscapes of my imagination and am often slow to return to the real world. Thank you for your patience and understanding. Your encouragement sustained me through the long days of writing and have been the brightest moments of inspiration. This journey would have been impossible without your unwavering faith in me.

To my friends who listened to my endless ramblings about plot points and character arcs, who read early drafts without complaint, and who celebrated each small victory alongside me; your support is the part of me that continues to always look on the sunny side of life.

My deepest appreciation goes to the artist, Mashfiq A. K. (@rare_art), whose vision brought the cover to life. He's managed to capture the essence of the 'Lost Dragonrider of Lamar' in ways words alone never could. Your artistry adds dimensions to this story that transcend the page.

And to the cartographer, Alec M (@alecmck), who meticulously crafted the map of this realm, Sataran, thank you for giving physical form to the landscapes that once existed only in my mind. Your influence has allowed readers to trace the journeys these characters embark on in their physical world.

Finally, to you, dear reader, for choosing to step into this world. Thank you for the greatest gift an author could ask for: your time and imagination. The story continues because you turn the page.

ABOUT THE AUTHOR

About the Author

A J Walker is the author of thirteen fantasy novels, including the Dragonriders of Lamar Series, Bond of a Dragon Series, Rulers of Tarmigan Series, and the Bonnie Glock Mystery Series. When not crafting tales of epic fantasy and dragonriders, he can be found floating the Yellowstone River or Backpacking in the Beartooth Mountains. A J (aka Andy) Walker lives in Columbus, Montana with his loving wife and dogs.

Connect with A J Walker
Email: ajwalkerauthor@gmail.com
Or Follow on Social Media:
Facebook, Instagram, Goodreads, Amazon.com

ALSO BY A J WALKER

FOR THE LATEST BOOK LAUNCH INFORMATION AND UPDATES FOLLOW ME ON AMAZON.COM

*Never miss a new book launch by following me on My Amazon Author Page, simply search A J Walker Author Page on Amazon and select +Follow button at the top.

New Books coming in 2025 – *The Dragonriders of Lamar Series.*

In the Bond of a Dragon Series – Prepare for an adrenaline-fueled dragonrider adventure with fierce dragons, powerful magic, and a hero fighting against all odds.

1 Zahara's Gift

2 Secrets of the Sapphire Soul

3 Fall of the Kings

4 Rise of the Dragonriders

In Rulers of Tarmigan Series – This one-of-a-kind fantasy world will push the limits of your imagination. Political tensions drive generals, emperors, and the rogue heroes of this epic saga to battle for control over an Empire torn apart with conflict. The return of dragons in the second installment shakes the foundation of their world. If you like lengthy, complex, high fantasy with unique worldbuilding, magic system, and political maneuvering, then you'll enjoy this series.

1 Emperor's Fate

2 Shepherds of Fire

3 Shattered Dragons

Bonnie Glock Mystery Series – Private Investigator Glock is a witch working as a consultant for the non-magical San Francisco Police Department. She and her partner Cy solve thrilling magical crimes in the non-magical world. Follow Bonnie as she protects the *Normals* from the underbelly of the wizarding world.

1 Into the Mixed

2 Finding Justice

3 Exiled and Forgotten

4 Dark Fae Rising

5 Soul Harvest

Printed in Dunstable, United Kingdom